DEEP SIX

BOOKS BY CLIVE CUSSLER

Mayday!
Night Probe!
Vixen 03
Iceberg
Raise the Titanic!
Pacific Vortex!

DEEP SIX

a novel by

CLIVE CUSSLER

BOOK CLUB ASSOCIATES
LONDON

This edition published 1984 by
Book Club Associates
By arrangement with Hamish Hamilton Ltd

Copyright © 1984 by Clive Cussler

Printed and bound in Great Britain by
Richard Clay (The Chaucer Press) Ltd, Bungay, Suffolk

THE SAN MARINO

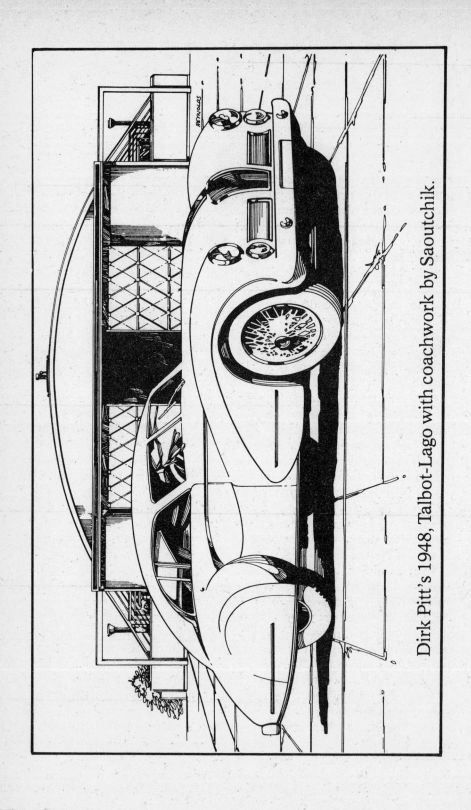

Dirk Pitt's 1948, Talbot-Lago with coachwork by Saoutchik.

The girl shaded the sun from her brown eyes with one hand and stared at a large petrel that glided above the ship's after cargo boom. She studied the bird's soaring grace for a few minutes, then growing bored, she rose to a sitting position, revealing evenly spaced red bars across her tanned back, etched there by the slats of an ancient steamer chair.

She looked around for signs of the deck crew, but as they were not to be seen, she shyly shifted her breasts to a more comfortable position inside the scoop-necked bra of her orange lycra bikini. Her body was hot and sweaty from the humid tropical air. She moved her hand across the firmness of her stomach and felt the wetness rising through her skin. She sagged against the back of the chair, soothed and relaxed, the throbbing beat of the old freighter's engines and the heavy warmth of the sun coaxing her into a state of drowsiness.

The fear that had churned inside her when she had come on board had eventually faded. She no longer lay awake feeling her heart pounding fast, no longer searched the crew's faces for expressions of suspicion, nor wondered when the captain would grimly inform her that she was under ship's arrest. She was slowly closing her mind to her criminal act and beginning to form a new course for the future. Guilt, indeed, was a fleeting emotion.

Out of the corner of her eye she caught the white jacket of the Oriental mess boy as he stepped from a companionway. He approached apprehensively, his eyes staring sheepishly down at the deck as if he was embarrassed to look upon her nearly nude figure.

'Excuse me, Miss Wallace,' he said awkwardly, 'but Captain Masters respectfully requests you please dine with him and his officers tonight if, that is, you are feeling better.'

Estelle Wallace was thankful the deepening tan covered her blush. She had feigned illness since embarking in San Francisco, and had taken all meals alone in her stateroom in an almost fanatical desire to avoid conversation with the ship's officers. She decided she could not remain a recluse forever. The time had come to practise living a lie.

'Tell Captain Masters I feel much improved and will be honoured to dine with him.'

'He'll be glad to hear that,' the mess boy said with a broad smile that revealed a large gap in the middle of his upper teeth. 'I'll see that the cook fixes you something real special.' He turned and shuffled away with a gait that seemed to Estelle a trifle too exaggerated, even for an Asian.

At ease with her decision, she idly stared up at the three-deck-high midship superstructure of the *San Marino*. The sky was remarkably blue above the black smoke curling from the single stack, contrasting starkly with the flaking white paint on the bulkheads.

A stout ship, the Captain boasted when leading her to a stateroom. He reassuringly ticked off the history and statistics as if Estelle was a frightened passenger on her first canoe ride down the rapids.

Built during 1943 to the standard Liberty Ship design, the *San Marino* carried military supplies across the Atlantic to England, making the roundtrip crossing sixteen times. On one occasion, when she had become separated from the convoy, she was struck by a torpedo but refused to sink, making it to Liverpool under her own power.

Since the war she had tramped the oceans of the world under the registry of Panama, one of thirty ships owned by the Manx Steamship Company of New York, plying in and out of backwater ports. Measuring 441 feet in length overall, raked stem, cruiser stern, she could only plod through the Pacific swells at eleven knots. With only a few more profitable years left in her, the *San Marino* would eventually end up ignobly cut into scrap.

Rust streaked her steel skin and she looked as sordid as a Bowery harlot, but in the eyes of Estelle Wallace she was virginal and beautiful.

Already Estelle's past was blurring. With each revolution of the bearing-worn engines the gap widened between a drab life of self-denial and an eagerly sought fantasy.

The first step of Arta Casilighio's metamorphosis into Estelle Wallace began when she discovered a lost passport wedged under the seat of a Wilshire Boulevard bus during the Los Angeles evening rush hour. Without really knowing why, Arta furtively slipped it into her purse and took it home.

Days later, she still could not fathom why she had not returned the document to the bus driver or mailed it to the rightful owner. She studied the official looking pages with their foreign stamps for hours at a time. She was intrigued by the face in the photo. Although more stylishly made-up, it bore a marked resemblance to her own: both women were about the same age, less than eight months separated their birthdays; the brown shade of their eyes matched, and, except for a difference in hair styles and a few shades of tint, they might have passed for sisters.

4

She began to make herself up to look like Estelle Wallace, an alter ego that could escape, mentally at least, to the exotic places of the world that were denied timid, mousy Arta Casilighio.

One evening, after closing hours at the bank where she worked, she found her eyes locked on the stacks of newly printed currency delivered that afternoon from the Federal Reserve Bank in downtown Los Angeles. She had become so used to handling large sums of money during her four-year tenure that she was immune to the mere sight; a lassitude that afflicts all tellers sooner or later. Yet inexplicably, this time the piles of green printed tender took on a new dimension.

Subconsciously she began to picture it as belonging to her.

Arta went home that weekend and locked herself in her apartment, fortifying her resolve and planning the crime she intended to commit, practising every gesture, every motion until they came smoothly without fumbling. All Sunday night she lay awake until the alarm went off, bathed in the cold sweat of nervous apprehension, but with her mind steeled to see the act through.

The cash shipment arrived every Monday by armoured car and usually totalled from six to eight hundred thousand dollars. It was then recounted and held until distribution on Wednesday to the bank's branch offices scattered throughout the Los Angeles basin. She figured the time to make her move was on Monday evening while she was putting her money drawer in the vault.

In the morning, after she had showered and put on her face, Arta donned a pair of tights. Then she wound a roll of two-sided sticky tape around her legs from mid-calf to the top of her thighs, leaving the protective outer layer of the tape in place. This odd bit of handiwork was covered with a long skirt that swirled almost to her ankles, hiding the tape with scant inches to spare. Next, she took neatly trimmed packets of bond paper and slipped them into a large pouch-style purse. Each displayed a crisp, new five dollar bill on the outer sides and was bound with genuine blue and white Federal Reserve Bank wrappers. To the casual and unsuspecting eye they appeared authentic.

Arta stood in front of a full-length mirror and repeated over and over: 'Arta Casilighio no longer exists. You are Estelle Wallace'. The deception seemed to work. She felt her muscles relax and her breathing became slower, shallower. Then she took a deep breath, threw back her shoulders and left for work.

In her anxiety to appear normal she inadvertently arrived at the bank ten minutes early, an astounding event to all who knew her well, but this was a Monday morning and no one took any notice. Once she settled behind her teller's counter every minute seemed an

5

hour, every hour a lifetime. It was as though time became mired in glue. She felt strangely detached from the familiar surroundings and yet any thought to forget the hazardous scheme was quickly ignored. Mercifully, fear and panic remained dormant.

When six o'clock finally rolled around, and one of the assistant vice presidents closed and locked the massive front doors, she quickly balanced her cash box and slipped quietly off to the ladies' room where, in the privacy of a stall, she unwound the tape's outer layer from her legs and flushed it down the toilet. She then took the bogus money packets and adhered them to the tape, stamping her feet to make certain none would drop off as she walked.

Satisfied everything was in readiness, she came out and dawdled in the lobby until the other tellers had placed their cash drawers in the vault and left. Two minutes alone inside that great steel cubicle was all she needed and two minutes alone was what she got.

Swiftly she pulled up the skirt and with precise movements exchanged the phoney packets for those containing genuine bills. When she stepped out of the vault and smiled a good evening to the assistant vice president as he nodded her out of a side door, she couldn't believe she'd actually got away with it.

Seconds after entering her apartment, she shed the skirt, stripped the money packets from her legs and counted them. The tally came to fifty-one thousand dollars.

Not nearly enough.

A searing wave of disappointment burned within her. She would need at least twice that amount to escape the country and live on a minimal level of comfort while increasing the lion's share through investments.

The ease of the operation had made her heady. Did she dare make another foray into the vault, she wondered? The Federal Reserve Bank money was already counted and wouldn't be distributed to the branch banks until Wednesday. Tomorrow was Tuesday. She still had another chance to strike again before the loss was discovered.

Why not?

The thought of ripping off the same bank twice in two days excited her. Perhaps Arta Casilighio lacked the guts for it, but Estelle Wallace required no coaxing, no coaxing at all.

That evening she bought a large, old fashioned suitcase at a second-hand store and made a false bottom in it. She packed the money along with her clothes and took a cab to the Los Angeles International Airport where she stored the suitcase overnight in a locker and purchased a ticket to San Francisco on an early evening Tuesday flight. Wrapping her unused Monday night ticket in a

6

newspaper, she dropped it in a wastebin. With nothing remaining to be done, she went home and slept like a rock.

The second robbery went as smoothly as the first. Three hours after leaving the Beverly-Wilshire Bank for the last time, she was re-counting the money in a San Francisco hotel. The combined total came to one hundred and twenty-eight thousand. Not a staggering prize by inflationary standards, she mused, but more than enough for her projected needs.

The next step was relatively simple. She checked through the newspapers for ship departures and found the *San Marino*, a cargo freighter bound for Auckland, New Zealand, at six-thirty the following morning.

An hour before sailing, she mounted the gangplank. The captain claimed he seldom took passengers but kindly consented to take her on board for a mutually agreed fare, which Estelle suspected went into his wallet instead of the steamship company coffers.

After a cool, invigorating bath, Estelle stepped across the threshold of the officer's dining saloon and paused uncertainly for a moment, soaking up the appraising stares of the six men sitting in the room.

Her coppery-tinted hair fell past her shoulders and nearly matched her tan. She wore a long, sleek, pink T-shirt dress that draped in all the right places. A bone white bracelet was her only accessory. To the seamen rising to their feet the simple elegance of her appearance created a knockout effect.

Captain Irwin Masters, a tall man with greying hair and merry blue eyes, came over and took her arm.

'Miss Wallace,' he said, smiling warmly. 'It's good to see you looking fit.'

'I think the worst is over,' she said, groping for words.

'I don't mind admitting, I was beginning to worry. Not venturing from your cabin for five days made me fear the worst. With no doctor on board, we would have been in a fix if your malady had required medical treatment.'

'Thank you,' she said softly.

He looked at her in mild surprise. 'Thank me, for what?'

'For your concern.' She gave his arm a gentle squeeze. 'It's been a long time since anyone worried about me.'

He nodded and winked. 'That's what ship captains are for.' Then he turned to the other officers. 'Gentlemen, may I present Miss Estelle Wallace, who is gracing us with her lovely presence until we dock in Auckland.'

The introductions were made, and she was amused by the fact that most of the men were numbered. The first officer, the second officer, even a fourth. They all shook her hand as if it were made of delicate china, all that is except the engineering officer, a short, ox-shouldered man with a Slavic accent. He stiffly bent over and kissed the tops of her fingers.

The first officer motioned at the mess boy who was standing behind a small mahogany bar. 'Miss Wallace, what will be your pleasure?'

'Would it be possible to have a Daiquiri? I'm in the mood for something sweet.'

'Absolutely,' the first officer replied. 'The *San Marino* may not be a luxurious cruise liner, but we do run the finest cocktail bar in this latitude of the Pacific.'

'Be honest,' the captain admonished goodnaturedly. 'You neglec-ted to mention we're probably the *only* ship in this latitude.'

'A mere detail,' the first officer shrugged. 'Lee, one of your famous Daiquiris for the young lady.'

Estelle watched with interest as the mess boy expertly squeezed the lime and poured the ingredients. Every movement came with a flourish. The frothy drink tasted good, and she had to fight a desire to down it all at once.

'Lee,' she said, 'you're a marvel.'

'He is that,' said Masters. 'We were lucky to sign him on.'

Estelle took another sip of her drink. 'You seem to have a number of Orientals in your crew.'

'Replacements,' Masters explained. 'Ten of the crew jumped ship after we docked in San Francisco. Fortunately, Lee and nine of his fellow Koreans arrived from the maritime hiring hall before sailing time.'

'All damned queer, if you ask me,' the second officer grunted.

Masters shrugged. 'Crew members jumping ship in port has been going on since Cro-Magnon man built the first raft. Nothing queer about it.'

The second officer shook his head doubtfully. 'One or two maybe, but not ten in one fell swoop. The *San Marino* is a tight ship, and the Captain here is a fair skipper. There was no reason for a mass exodus.'

'The way of the sea,' Masters sighed. 'The Koreans are clean, hard working seamen. I wouldn't trade them for half the cargo in our holds.'

'That's a pretty stiff price,' muttered the engineering officer.

'Is it improper,' Estelle ventured, 'to ask what cargo you're carrying?'

'Not at all,' the very young fourth officer offered eagerly. 'In San Francisco our holds were loaded with − '

8

'Titanium ingots,' Captain Masters cut in.

'Eight million dollars' worth,' added the first officer while eyeing the fourth sternly.

'Once again please,' Estelle said, handing her empty glass to the mess boy. She turned back to Masters. 'I've heard of titanium, but I have no idea what it's used for.'

'When properly processed in pure form, titanium becomes stronger and lighter than steel; an asset that puts it in great demand for builders of jet aircraft engines. It's also widely used in the manufacture of paints, rayon, plastics, and I suspect you have traces of it in your cosmetics.'

The cook, an anaemic-looking man with a sparkling white apron, leaned through a side door and nodded at Lee, who in turn tapped a glass with a mixing spoon.

'Dinner ready to be served,' he said in his heavily accented English, while flashing his split-toothed smile.

It was a fabulous meal, one Estelle promised herself never to forget. And to be surrounded by six handsomely uniformed and attentive men was all that her female vanity could endure in one evening.

After a demi-tasse, Captain Masters excused himself and headed for the bridge. One by one, the other officers drifted off to their duties and Estelle took a tour of the deck with the engineering officer. He entertained her with tales of sea superstitions, eerie monsters of the deep, and funny tidbits about the crew that made her laugh.

At last they reached the door of her stateroom, and he gallantly kissed her hand again. She accepted when he asked her to join him for breakfast in the morning.

Estelle entered the tiny cabin, clicked the lock on the door and switched on an overhead lamp. Then she tightly closed the curtain over the single porthole, pulled the suitcase from under the bed and opened it.

The top tray contained her cosmetics and carelessly jumbled underthings, which she removed. Next came several neatly folded blouses and skirts. These she also removed and set aside to steam out the wrinkles in the shower later. Gently inserting a nail file around the edges of the false bottom of the suitcase, she prised it up. Then she sat back and sighed with relief. The money was still there, stacked and bound in the Federal Reserve Bank wrappers. She had spent very little of it so far.

Estelle stood up, slipped her dress over her head – she daringly wore nothing beneath – and collapsed across the bed, hands behind her head. She closed her eyes and tried to picture the shocked expressions on her former employers' faces when they discovered the money and little, reliable Arta Casilighio missing at the same time. She had fooled them all, she thought smugly.

She felt a strange, almost sexual, thrill at knowing the FBI had posted her on their list of wanted criminals. The investigators would question all her friends and neighbours, search all her old haunts, check a thousand and one banks for sudden large deposits of consecutively numbered bills, but they would come up dry. Arta, alias Estelle, was not where they'd expect her to be.

She opened her eyes and stared at the now familiar walls of her stateroom. Oddly the room began to slip away from her. Objects were focusing and unfocusing into a dully coloured montage. Her bladder signalled a trip to the bathroom, but her body refused to obey any command to move – every muscle seemed frozen. And then the door opened and Lee, the mess boy, entered with another Oriental crewman.

Lee wasn't smiling.

This can't be happening, she told herself. The crew wouldn't dare intrude on her privacy while she was lying naked on the bed. It had to be a crazy dream brought on by the results of the lavish food and drink. A nightmare stoked by the fires of indigestion.

She felt detached from her body, as if she was watching the eerie scene from one corner of the stateroom. The two men gently lifted and carried her through the doorway, down the passageway and onto the deck.

Several of the Korean crewmen were there, their oval faces illuminated by bright overhead floodlights. They were hoisting large bundles and dropping them over the ship's railing. Abruptly, one of the bundles briefly stared at her. It was the ashen face of the young fourth officer, eyes wide in a mixture of disbelief and terror. Then he too disappeared over the side.

Lee was leaning over her, doing something to her feet. She could feel nothing, only a lethargic numbness. He appeared to be attaching a length of rusty chain to her ankles.

Why would he do that? she wondered vaguely. She watched indifferently as she was lifted into the air. Then she was released and floated through the darkness.

Something struck her a great blow, knocking the breath from her lungs. A cool, yielding force closed over her, and she felt as though she had regressed into her mother's womb. A relentless pressure enveloped her body and dragged her downward, squeezing her internal organs in a giant vice.

Her eardrums exploded, and in that instant of tearing pain, total

10

clarity flooded her mind and she knew it was no dream, and her mouth jerked open to emit a hysterical scream.

No sound came. The increasing water density soon crushed her chest cavity and her lifeless body drifted into the waiting arms of the abyss ten thousand feet below.

PART I
THE PILOTTOWN

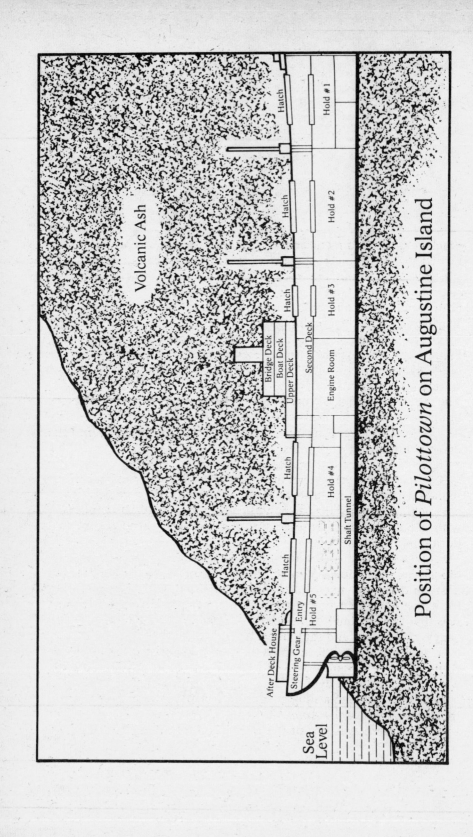

Position of *Pilottown* on Augustine Island

1

Black clouds rolled menacingly over the sea from Kodiak Island and turned the deep blue-green surface to lead. The orange glow of the sun was snuffed out like a candle flame. Unlike most storms that swept in from the Gulf of Alaska, creating fifty or a hundred mile an hour winds, this one bred a mild breeze. The rain began to fall, sparingly at first, then building to a deluge that beat the water white.

On the bridge wing of the Coast Guard cutter, *Catawaba*, Lieutenant Commander Amos Dover peered through a pair of binoculars, eyes straining to penetrate the downpour. It was like staring into a shimmering stage curtain. Visibility died at 400 metres. The rain felt cold against his face and colder yet as it trickled past the upturned collar of his foul-weather jacket and down his neck. Finally he spat a waterlogged cigarette over the railing and stepped into the dry warmth of the wheelhouse.

'Radar!' he called out gruffly.

'Contact 650 metres dead ahead and closing,' the radar operator replied without lifting his eyes from the tiny images on the scope.

Dover unbuttoned his jacket and wiped the moisture from his neck with a handkerchief. Trouble was the last thing he had expected during moderate weather.

Seldom did one of the fishing fleet or private pleasure craft go missing in midsummer. Winter was the season when the Gulf turned nasty and unforgiving: chilled Arctic air meeting warmer air rising from the Alaska current detonated incredible winds and towering seas that crushed hulls and iced deck structures until a boat grew top heavy, rolled over and sank like a brick.

A distress call had been received from a vessel calling herself the *Amie Marie*. One quick SOS followed by a Loran position and the words: '. . . think all dying'.

Repeated calls requesting further information were sent out, but the radio on board the *Amie Marie* remained silent.

An air search was out of the question until the weather cleared.

15

Every ship within a hundred miles changed course and steamed at full speed in response to the emergency signals. Because of her greater speed, Dover reckoned the *Catawaba* would be first to reach the stricken vessel. Her immense throbbing diesels had already pushed her past a coastal freighter and a halibut long-liner gulf boat, leaving them rocking in her wake.

Dover was a great bear of a man who had paid his dues in sea rescue. He'd spent twelve years in northern waters, stubbornly throwing his shoulder against every sadistic whim the Arctic had thrown him. He was tough and wind-worn, ambling in his physical movements but possessing a calculator-like mind that never failed to awe his crew. In less time than it had taken to programme the ship's computers, he had mentally figured the wind factor and current drift, arriving at a position where he knew the ship, wreckage or any survivors should be found, and he'd hit it right on the nose.

The hum of the engines below his feet seemed to take on a feverish pitch. Like an unleashed hound, the *Catawaba* seemed to pick up the scent of her quarry. Anticipation gripped all hands. Ignoring the rain, they lined the decks and bridge wings. It was a standing room only crowd. Every eye stared intently over the bows.

'Four hundred metres,' the radar operator sang out.

Then a seaman clutching the bow staff began pointing vigorously into the rain.

Dover leaned out of the wheelhouse door and shouted through a bullhorn. 'Is she afloat?'

'Buoyant as a rubber duck in a bathtub,' the seaman bellowed back through cupped hands.

Dover nodded to the lieutenant on watch. 'Slow engines.'

'Engines one third,' the watch lieutenant acknowledged as he moved a series of levers on the ship's automated console.

The *Amie Marie* slowly emerged through the precipitation. They expected to find her half awash in a sinking condition, but she sat proud in the water, drifting in the light swells without a hint of distress. There was a silence about her that seemed unnatural, almost ghostly. Her decks were deserted, and Dover's hail over the bullhorn went unanswered.

'A crabber by the look of her,' Dover muttered to no one in particular. 'Steel hull, about 110 feet. Probably out of a shipyard in New Orleans.'

The radio operator leaned out of the communications room and motioned to Dover. 'From the Board of Register, sir. The *Amie Marie*'s owner and skipper is Carl Keating. Home port is Kodiak.'

Again Dover hailed the strangely quiet crab boat, this time addressing Keating by name. Still no response. Everyone began to

16

feel as nervous as a boy on his first date wondering how it would turn out.

The *Catawaba* slowly circled and hove-to a hundred metres away, then stopped her engines and drifted alongside.

The steel-cage crab pots were neatly stacked on the deserted deck, and a wisp of exhaust smoke puffed from the funnel, suggesting that her diesel engines were idling in neutral. No human movement could be detected through the ports or the windows of the wheelhouse.

The boarding party consisted of two officers, Ensign Pat Murphy and Lieutenant Marty Lawrence. Without the usual small talk they donned their exposure suits which would protect them from the frigid waters if they accidentally fell into the sea. They had lost count of the times they conducted routine examinations of foreign fishing vessels that strayed inside the Alaskan 200-mile fishing limit, yet there was nothing routine about this investigation. No flesh and blood crew lined the rails to greet them. They climbed into a small rubber Zodiac, propelled by an outboard motor, and cast off.

Darkness was only a few hours away. The rain had eased to a drizzle but the wind increased, and the sea was rising. An eerie quiet gripped the *Catawaba*. No one spoke; it was as though they were afraid to, at least until the spell produced by the unknown was broken.

They watched as Murphy and Lawrence tied their tiny craft to the crab boat, hoisted themselves to the deck and disappeared through a doorway into the main cabin.

Several minutes dragged by. Occasionally one of the searchers would appear on the deck only to vanish again down a hatchway. The only sound in the *Catawaba*'s wheelhouse came from the static over the ship's open radio-phone loudspeaker, turned up to a high volume and tuned to an emergency frequency.

Suddenly, with unexpected abruptness that made even Dover twitch in surprise, Murphy's voice reverberated loudly inside the wheelhouse.

'*Catawaba*, this is *Amie Marie*.'

'Go ahead, *Amie Marie*,' Dover answered into a microphone.

'They're all dead.'

The words were so cold, so terse, nobody absorbed them at first.

'Repeat.'

'No sign of a pulse in any of them. Even a cat bought it.'

The boarding party had found a ship of the dead. Skipper Keating's body rested on the deck, his head leaning against a bulkhead beneath the radio. Scattered throughout the boat in the galley, the messroom and the sleeping quarters were the corpses of the *Amie Marie*'s crew: their facial expressions were frozen in twisted

17

agony and their limbs contorted in grotesque positions, as though they violently thrashed away their final moments of life; their skin had turned an odd black cast, and they had gushed blood from every orifice. The ship's mascot, a Siamese cat, lay beside a thick wool blanket it had shredded in its death throes.

Dover's face reflected puzzlement rather than shock at Murphy's description. 'Can you determine a cause?' he asked.

'Not even a good guess,' Murphy came back. 'No indication of struggle. No marks on the bodies, yet they bled like slaughtered pigs. Looks like whatever killed them struck everyone at the same time.'

'Stand by.'

Dover turned and surveyed the faces around him until he spotted the ship's surgeon, Lieutenant Commander Isaac Thayer.

Doc Thayer was the most popular man aboard the ship. An old timer in the Coast Guard service, he long ago gave up the plush offices and high income of shore medicine for the sometimes harsh but self-rewarding rigours of sea rescue.

'What do you make of it, Doc?' Dover put to him.

Thayer shrugged and smiled. 'Looks as though I'd better make a house call.'

Dover paced the bridge impatiently while Doc Thayer entered a second Zodiac and motored across the gap dividing the two vessels. Dover ordered the helmsman to position the *Catawaba* to take the crab boat in tow. He was concentrating on the manoeuvre and didn't notice the radio operator standing at his elbow.

'A signal just in, sir, from a bush pilot airlifting supplies to a team of scientists on Augustine Island.'

'Not now,' Dover said brusquely.

'It's urgent, Captain,' the radio operator persisted.

'Okay, read the guts of it.'

' "Scientific party all dead." Then something unintelligible and what sounds like ". . . save me".'

Dover stared at him blankly. 'That's all?'

'Yes, sir. I tried to raise him again, but there was no reply.'

Dover didn't have to study a chart to know Augustine was an uninhabited volcanic island only thirty miles slightly north-east of his present position. A sudden, sickening realisation coursed through his mind. He snatched the microphone and shouted into the mouthpiece.

'Murphy! You there?'

Nothing.

'Murphy . . . Lawrence . . . do you read me?'

Again no answer.

He looked through the bridge window and saw Doc Thayer climb over the rail of the *Amie Marie*. Dover could move fast for a man of his mountainous proportions. He snatched a bullhorn and ran outside.

'Doc! Come back, get off that boat!' his amplified voice boomed over the water.

He was too late. Thayer had already ducked into a hatchway and was gone.

The men on the bridge stared at their captain, incomprehension written in their eyes. His facial muscles tensed and there was a look of desperation about him as he rushed back into the wheelhouse and clutched the microphone.

'Doc, this is Dover, can you hear me?'

Two minutes passed, two endless minutes while Dover tried to raise his men on the *Amie Marie*. Even the earsplitting scream of the *Catawaba*'s siren failed to draw a response.

At last Thayer's voice came over the bridge speaker with a strange icy calm.

'I regret to report that Ensign Murphy and Lieutenant Lawrence are dead. I can find no lifesigns. Whatever the cause it will strike me before I can escape. You must quarantine this boat. Do you understand, Amos?'

Dover found it impossible to grasp that he was suddenly about to lose his old friend. 'Do not understand, but will comply.'

'Good. I'll describe the symptoms as they come. Beginning to feel lightheaded already. Pulse increasing to one fifty. May have contracted the cause by skin absorption. Pulse one seventy.'

Thayer paused. His next words came haltingly.

'Growing nausea. Legs . . . can no longer . . . support. Intense burning sensation . . . in sinus region. Internal organs feel like they're exploding.'

As one, everybody on the bridge of the *Catawaba* leaned closer to the speaker, unable to comprehend that a man they all knew and respected was dying a short distance away.

'Pulse . . . over two hundred. Pain . . . excruciating. Blackness closing vision.' There was an audible moan. 'Tell . . . tell my wife . . .'

The speaker went silent.

You could smell the shock, see it in the widened eyes of the crew standing in stricken horror.

Dover stared numbly at the tomb named the *Amie Marie*, his hands clenched in helplessness and despair.

'What's happening?' he murmured tonelessly. 'What in God's name is killing everyone?'

2

'I say hang the bastard!'

'Oscar, mind your language in front of the girls.'

'They've heard worse. It's insane. The scum murders four kids and some cretin of a judge throws the case out of court because the defendant was too stoned on drugs to understand his rights. God, can you believe it?'

Carolyn Lucas poured her husband's first cup of coffee of the day and whisked their two young daughters off to the school bus stop. He gestured menacingly at the TV as if it was the fault of the anchorman announcing the news that the killer roamed free.

Oscar Lucas had a way of talking with his hands that bore little resemblance to sign language for the deaf. He sat stooped-shouldered at the breakfast table, a position that camouflaged his lanky six foot frame. His head was as bald as an egg except for a few greying strands around the temples, and his bushy brows hovered over a pair of oak brown eyes. Never one to join the Washington DC blue pinstripe brigade, he was dressed in trousers and a sports jacket.

In his early forties, Lucas might have passed for a dentist or a bookkeeper instead of the Special Agent in Charge of the Presidential Protection Division of the Secret Service. During his twenty years as an agent he had fooled many people with his good neighbour-next-door appearance, from the presidents whose lives he safeguarded, to the potential assassins he'd stonewalled before they gained an opportunity to act. On the job he came across as aggressive and solemn, yet at home he was usually full of mischief and humour, except of course, when he was influenced by the eight a.m. news.

Lucas took a final sip of his coffee and rose from the table. He held open his coat – he was left handed – and adjusted the high-ride hip holster gripping a 357 magnum, model 19, Smith-Wesson revolver with a two and a half inch barrel. The standard issue gun was provided by the Service when training finished and he started out as a rookie agent in the Denver field office investigating counterfeiters and forgers. He had drawn it only twice in the line of duty – but he had yet to pull the trigger outside a firing range.

Carolyn was unloading the dishwasher when he came up behind her, pulled away a cascade of blonde hair and pecked her on the neck.

'I'm off.'

'Don't forget tonight is the pool party across the street at the Hardings'.'

'I should be home in time. The boss isn't scheduled to leave the White House today.'

She looked up at him and smiled devilishly. 'You see that he doesn't.'

'I'll inform the President first thing that my wife frowns on me working late.'

She laughed and leaned her head briefly on his shoulder. 'Six o'clock.'

'You win,' he said in mock weariness and stepped out of the back door.

Lucas backed his leased government car, a plush Buick sedan, into the street and headed downtown. Before reaching the end of the block, he called the Secret Service central command office over his car radio.

'Crown, this is Lucas. I'm en route to the White House.'

'Have a nice trip,' a metallic voice succinctly replied.

Already he began to sweat and turned on the air conditioner. The summer heat in the nation's capital never seemed to slacken. The humidity was in the nineties and the flags along embassy row on Massachusetts Avenue hung limp and lifeless in the muggy air.

He slowed and stopped at the checkpoint gate on West Executive Avenue and paused for a few moments while a uniformed guard of the Service nodded and passed him through. Lucas parked the car and entered the west executive entrance on the lower level of the White House.

At the SS command post, code named W-16, he stopped to chat with the men monitoring an array of electronic communication equipment. Then he took the stairs to his office on the second floor of the East Wing.

The first thing he did each morning after settling behind his desk was to check the President's schedule along with advance reports by the agents in change of planning security.

Lucas studied the folder containing future presidential 'movements' a second time, consternation growing across his face. There had been an unexpected addition, a big one. He flung down the folder in irritation, swung around in his swivel chair and stared at the wall.

Most presidents were creatures of habit, ran tight schedules and rigidly adhered to them. Clocks could be set by Nixon's coming and going. Reagan and Carter seldom deviated from fixed plans. But the new man in the oval office looked upon details as a nuisance, and worse, he was unpredictable as hell.

To Lucas and his deputy agents it became a twenty-four hour game, trying to keep one step ahead of 'the man', guessing where he might suddenly decide to go and when, and what visitors he might invite without providing enough time for proper security measures. It was a game Lucas too often lost.

In less than a minute he was down the stairs and in the West Wing confronting the second most powerful man in the Executive Branch, Chief of Staff, Daniel Fawcett.

'Good morning, Oscar,' Fawcett said, smiling benignly. 'I thought you'd come charging in about now.'

'There appears to be a new excursion in the schedule,' Lucas said, his tone businesslike.

'Sorry about that, but a big vote is coming up on aid to the Eastern Bloc Countries and the President wants to work his charms on Senator Larimer and Speaker of the House Moran to swing their support for his programme.'

'So he's taking them for a boat ride.'

'Why not? Every president since Herbert Hoover has used the presidential yacht for high level conferences.'

'I'm not arguing the reason,' Lucas replied firmly. 'I'm protesting the timing.'

Fawcett gave him an innocent look. 'What's wrong with Friday evening?'

'You know damn well what's wrong. That's only two days away.'

'So?'

'For a cruise down the Potomac with an overnight stopover at Mount Vernon my advance team needs five days to plan the security. A complete system of communications and alarms has to be installed on the grounds; the boat must be swept for explosives and listening devices; the shores checked out, and the Coast Guard requires leadtime to provide a cutter on the river as an escort. We can't do a decent job in two days!'

Fawcett was a fiesty, eager individual with a condor nose, square red face and intense eyes; he always looked like a demolition expert eyeing a deserted building.

'Don't you think you're making this into an overkill, Oscar? Assassinations take place on crowded streets or in theatres. Who ever heard of a head of state being attacked on a boat?'

'It can happen anywhere, any time,' Lucas said with an uncompromising look. 'Have you forgotten the guy we stopped who was attempting to hijack a plane he intended to crash into Air Force One? The fact is, most assassination operations take place when the President is away from his customary haunts.'

'The President is firm on the date,' Fawcett said matter of factly.

22

'As long as you work for the President you'll do as you're ordered, same as me. If he wants to row a dinghy alone to Miami, that's his choice.'

Fawcett struck the wrong nerve. Lucas's face turned rigid and he moved until he was standing toe to toe with the White House Chief of Staff.

'First off, by order of Congress, I don't work for the President but for the Treasury Department. So he can't tell me to bug off and go his own way. My duty is to provide him with the best security with the least inconvenience to his private life. When he takes the lift to his living quarters upstairs, my men and I remain below. But from the time he steps out on the first floor, until he goes up again, he belongs to the Secret Service.'

Fawcett was perceptive about the personalities of the men who worked around the President. He knew he'd stepped too far with Lucas and was wise enough to call off the war. They were men who were dedicated to their work and loyal beyond any standards to the man in the oval office. But there was no way they could be close friends; professional associates perhaps, reserved, watchful. And since they were not rivals for inner circle power, they would never be enemies.

Fawcett turned his lips up in a condescending smile. 'No need to get riled, Oscar. I stand reprimanded. I'll inform the President of your concern, but I doubt if he'll change his mind.'

Lucas sighed. 'We'll do our best with the time left. But he must be made to understand that it's imperative for him to cooperate with his security people.'

'What can I say? You know better than I, all politicians think they're immortal. To them power is more than an aphrodisiac; it's a drug high and alcoholic haze combined. Nothing excites or inflates their ego like a mob of people cheering and clamouring to shake their hand. That's why they're all vulnerable to a killer standing in the right place at the right time.'

'Tell me about it,' said Lucas. 'I've babysat four presidents.'

'And haven't lost a one,' Fawcett added.

'I came close; twice with Ford and once with Reagan.'

'You can't accurately predict behaviour patterns.'

'Maybe not, but after enough years in the protection racket you develop a gut reaction. That's why I feel uneasy about this boat cruise.'

Fawcett stiffened. 'You think someone is out to kill him?'

'Someone is always out to kill him. We investigate twenty possible crazies a day and carry an active caseload of 2000 persons we consider dangerous or capable of assassination.'

Fawcett put his hand on Lucas' shoulder. 'Don't worry, Oscar. Friday's excursion won't be given to the press until the last minute. I promise you that much.'

'I appreciate that, Dan.'

'Besides, what can happen out on the Potomac?'

'Maybe nothing, maybe the unexpected,' answered Lucas, a strange vacancy in his voice. 'It's the unexpected that gives me nightmares.'

Megan Blair, the President's secretary, caught Dan Fawcett standing in the doorway of her cubbyhole office out of the corner of one eye, and nodded over her typewriter.

'Hi, Dan. I didn't see you.'

'How's the Chief this morning?' he asked, his daily ritual of testing the water before entering the oval office.

'Tired,' she answered. 'The reception honouring the movie industry moguls ran past one a.m.'

Megan was a handsome, perky woman in her early forties. Possessed with bright small-town friendliness, she wore her black hair cropped short and was ten pounds on the skinny side. She was a dynamo who loved her job and her boss like nothing else in life. She arrived early, left late and worked weekends. Unmarried with but two casual affairs behind her, she relished her independent single life.

Fawcett was continually amazed that she could carry on a conversation and type at the same time.

He smiled. 'I'll tread lightly and keep his appointments to a minimum so he can take it easy.'

'You're too late. He's already in conference with Admiral Sandecker.'

'Who?'

'Admiral James Sandecker. Director of the National Underwater and Marine Agency.'

A look of annoyance crossed Fawcett's face. He tackled his role of presidential guardian of operations with fanatical piety and resented any intrusion on his territory. To him, any penetration of his protective ring was a threat to his power base. How in hell had Sandecker sneaked around him?

Megan read his mood. 'The President sent for the Admiral,' she explained. 'I think he's expecting you to sit in on the meeting.'

Pacified to a small degree, Fawcett nodded and walked into the oval office. The President was seated on a sofa studying several papers strewn on a large coffee table. A short, thin man with red hair and a matching Vandyke beard sat across from him.

The President looked up. 'Dan, I'm glad you're here . . . You know Admiral Sandecker?'

24

'Yes,' he said simply.

Sandecker rose and shook his hand. The Admiral's grip was firm and brief. He nodded wordlessly to Fawcett, curtly recognising his presence. It was not intended rudeness on Sandecker's part. He came across as a man who played straight ball, encasing himself in a cold, tensile shell, bowing to no one. He was hated and envied at the same time, but respected because he never chose sides and always delivered whatever was asked of him.

The President motioned to the sofa, patting a cushion next to him. 'Sit down, Dan. I've asked the Admiral to brief me on a crisis that's developed in the waters off Alaska.'

'I haven't heard of it.'

'I'm not surprised,' said the President. 'The report only came to my attention an hour ago.' He paused and pointed the tip of a pencil at an area circled in red on a large nautical chart. 'Here, 180 miles south-west of Anchorage in the Cook Inlet region, an undetermined poison is killing everything in the sea.'

Fawcett missed the main gist behind the President's ominous statement. 'Sounds like you're talking oil spill.'

'Far worse,' replied Sandecker, leaning back on the couch. 'What we have here is an unknown that causes death in both humans and sealife less than a minute after contact.'

'How is that possible?' asked Fawcett dumbly.

'Most poisonous compounds gain access to the body through ingestion or inhalation,' Sandecker explained. 'The stuff we're dealing with also kills by skin absorption.'

'Must be highly concentrated in a small area to be so potent.'

'If you call a thousand square miles of open water small.'

The President looked lost. 'I can't imagine a material with such awesome potency.'

Fawcett looked at the Admiral. 'What kind of death statistics are we facing?'

'A Coast Guard cutter found a Kodiak fishing boat drifting with the crew dead. Two investigators and a doctor were sent on board and died too. A team of geophysicists on an island thirty miles away were found dead by a bush pilot flying in supplies. He died while sending out a distress signal. A few hours later a Japanese fishing trawler reported seeing a school of nearly a hundred grey whales suddenly turn belly up. The trawler then disappeared. No trace was found. Crab beds, seal colonies, wiped out. That's only the opening chapter. There may be many more fatalities we don't have word on yet.'

'If the spread continues unchecked, what's the worst we can expect?'

25

'The virtual extinction of all marine life in the Alaskan Gulf. And if it enters the Japanese Current and is carried south it could poison every man, fish, animal and bird it touches along the west coast as far as Mexico. The human death toll could conceivably reach into the hundreds of thousands. Fishermen, swimmers, anyone who walked along a contaminated shoreline, anybody who ate contaminated fish; it's like a chain reaction. I don't even want to think what might happen if it evaporates into the atmosphere with moisture molecules and falls as rain over the inland states.'

Fawcett found it almost impossible to grasp the enormity of it. 'Christ, what in hell is it?'

'Too early to tell,' Sandecker replied. 'The Environmental Protective Agency has a computerised mass data storage and retrieval system that contains detailed information on 200 relevant characteristics of some 1100 chemical compounds. Within a few seconds they can determine the effects a hazardous substance can have when spilled, its trade name, formula, major producers, mode of transportation and threat to the environment. The Alaskan contamination doesn't fit any of the data in their computer files.'

'Surely they must have some idea?'

'No sir, they don't. There is one slim possibility, but without autopsy reports it's strictly conjecture.'

'I'd like to hear it,' the President probed.

Sandecker took a deep breath. 'The three worst poisonous substances known to man are Plutonium, Dioxine and a chemical warfare system. The first two don't fit the pattern. The third, at least in my mind, is a prime suspect.'

The President stared at Sandecker, realisation and shock on his face. 'Nerve Agent S?' he said slowly.

Sandecker nodded silently.

'That's why the EPA wouldn't have a handle on it,' said the President. 'The formula is ultra-secret.'

Fawcett turned to the President. 'I'm afraid I'm not familiar . . .'

'Nerve Agent S was an ungodly compound the scientists at the Rocky Mountain Arsenal developed about twenty years ago,' the President explained. 'I've read the report on the tests. It could kill within a few seconds of touching the skin. It seemed the ideal answer to an enemy wearing gas masks or protective gear. It clung to everything it touched. But its properties were too unstable, and it was as dangerous to the troops dispersing it as those on the receiving end. Finally the Army gave up and buried it in the Nevada desert.'

'I fail to see a connection between Nevada and Alaska,' said Fawcett.

'During the shipment by railroad from the arsenal outside of

26

Denver,' Sandecker enlightened him, 'a box-car containing nearly a thousand gallons of Nerve Agent S vanished. It is still missing and unaccounted for.'

'If the spill is indeed this nerve agent, once it's found, what is the process for eliminating it?'

Sandecker shrugged. 'Unfortunately, present state-of-the-art containment and cleanup technology, and the physical-chemical characteristics of Nerve Agent S are such that once it enters into the water, very little can be done to ameliorate the penetration. Our only hope is to cut off the source before it releases enough poison to turn the west coast into a cesspool devoid of all life.'

'Any lead on where it originates?' asked the President.

'In all probability a ship sunk between Kodiak Island and the Alaskan mainland,' replied Sandecker. 'Our next step is to back trace the currents and determine a search grid.'

The President leaned over the coffee table and studied the red circle on the chart for a few moments. Then he gave Sandecker an appraising stare. 'As director of NUMA, Admiral, you'll have the dirty job of neutralising this thing. You have my authority to tap any agency or department of the government with the necessary expertise; the National Science Board, the Army and Coast Guard, the EPA, whoever.' He paused thoughtfully, then asked, 'Exactly how potent is Nerve Agent S in seawater?'

Sandecker looked tired, his face drawn. 'One teaspoon will effectively kill every living organism in four million gallons of seawater.'

'Then we better find it,' said the President, a touch of desperation in his voice. 'And damned quick!'

3

Deep beneath the murky waters of the James River off the shoreline of Newport News, Virginia, a pair of divers struggled against the current as they burrowed their way through the muck that was packed against the rotting hull of a shipwreck.

There was no sense of direction in the black dimensionless liquid. Visibility was measured in inches as they grimly clutched the pipe of an airlift that sucked up the thick ooze and spat it onto a barge seventy feet above in the sunlight. They laboured almost by braille, their only illumination coming from the feeble glimmer of underwater lights mounted on the edge of the crater they'd slowly

27

excavated over the past several days. All they could see clearly were particles suspended in the water that drifted past their facemasks like windswept rain.

It was hard for them to believe there was a world above, sky and clouds and trees bending in a summer breeze. In the nightmare of swirling mud and perpetual darkness it didn't seem possible that five hundred yards away people and cars roamed the pavements and streets of the small city.

There are some who say you can't sweat underwater, but you can. The divers could feel the sweat forcing its way through the pores of their skin against the protective constriction of their drysuits. They were beginning to experience the creeping tendrils of weariness, yet they had only been on the bottom for eight minutes.

Inch by inch they worked their way into a gaping hole on the starboard bow of the hulk. The planking that framed the cavern-like opening was shattered and twisted as though a giant fist had rammed into the ship. They began to uncover artifacts; a shoe, the hinge from an old chest, brass calipers, tools, even a piece of cloth. It was an eerie sensation to touch objects that no one had looked upon in 120 years.

One of the men paused to check their air gauges. He calculated they could work another ten minutes and still have a safe supply of breathable air to reach the surface.

They turned off the valve on the airlift, stopping the suction, while they waited for the river current to carry away the cloud of disturbed silt. Except for the exhaust of their breathing regulators, it became very still. A little more of the wreck became visible. The deck timbers were crushed and broken inward. Coils of rope trailed into the murk like mud encrusted snakes. The interior of the hull seemed bleak and foreboding. They could almost sense the restless ghosts of the men who went down with the ship.

Suddenly they heard a strange humming, not the sound made by the outboard motor of a small boat, but heavier, like the distant drone of an aircraft engine. There was no way of telling its direction. They listened for a few moments as the sound grew louder, magnified by the density of the water. It was a surface sound and did not concern them, so they reactivated the airlift and turned back to their work.

No more than a minute later the end of the suction pipe struck something hard. Quickly they closed off the air valve again and excitedly brushed away the mud with their hands. Soon they realised they were touching, not wood, but an object harder, much harder, and covered with rust.

*

28

To the support crew on the barge over the wreck site time seemed to have reversed itself. They stood spellbound as an ancient PBY Catalina flying boat made a sweeping bank from the west, lined up on the river and kissed the water with the ungainly finesse of an inebriated goose. The sun glinted on the aquamarine colour scheme covering the aluminium hull, and the letters NUMA grew larger as the lumbering craft taxied towards the barge. The engines were shut down and the co-pilot emerged from a side hatch and threw a mooring rope to one of the men on the barge.

Then a woman appeared and jumped lightly onto the battered wooden deck. She was suavishly slim, her elegant frame covered by a narrow-falling tan shirt, long, loose, held low on the hip over tapering pants in green cotton. She wore moccasin-style boater shoes on her feet. In her mid-forties, about five-foot seven, her hair was the colour of aspen gold and her skin a copper tan. Her face was handsome with high cheek bones, the face of a woman who fits no mould but her own.

She picked her way around a maze of cables and salvage equipment and stopped when she found herself surrounded by a platoon of male stares registering speculation mixed with undisguised fascination. She raised her sunglasses and stared back through plum-brown eyes.

'Which one of you is Dirk Pitt?' she demanded without preamble.

A rugged individual shorter than she, but with shoulders twice the width of his waist stepped forward and pointed into the river.

'You'll find him down there.'

She turned and her eyes followed the protruding finger. A large orange buoy swayed in the rippling current, its cable angling into the dirty green depths. About thirty feet beyond, she could see the diver's bubbles boil to the surface.

'How soon before he comes up?'

'Another five minutes.'

'I see,' she said, pondering a moment. Then she asked, 'Is Albert Giordino with him?'

'He's standing here talking to you.'

Clad only in shabby sneakers, cut-off jeans and torn T-shirt, Giordino's tacky outfit was matched by his black, curly windblown hair and two-week beard. He definitely did not fit her picture of NUMA's Deputy Director of Special Projects.

She seemed more amused than taken back. 'My name is Julie Mendoza, Environmental Protection Agency. I have an urgent matter to discuss with the two of you, but perhaps I should wait until Mr Pitt surfaces.'

Giordino shrugged. 'Suit yourself.' He broke into a friendly smile.

29

'We don't stock much in the way of creature comforts but we do have cold beer.'

'Love one, thank you.'

Giordino pulled a can of Coors from an ice bucket and handed it to her. 'What's an EPA man . . . ah . . . woman doing flying around in a NUMA plane?'

'A suggestion of Admiral Sandecker.'

Mendoza didn't offer more so Giordino didn't press.

'What project is this?' Mendoza asked.

'The *Cumberland*.'

'A Civil War ship, wasn't she?'

'Yes, historically very significant. She was a Union frigate sunk in 1862 by the Confederate ironclad, *Merrimack*, or the *Virginia*, as she was known to the South.'

'As I recall, she went down before the *Merrimack* fought the *Monitor*, making her the first ship ever destroyed by one that was armoured.'

'You know your history,' said Giordino properly impressed.

'And NUMA is going to raise her?'

Giordino shook his head. 'Too costly. We're only after the ram.'

'Ram?'

'A hell of a battle,' Giordino explained. 'The crew of the *Cumberland* fought until the water came in their gun barrels, even though their cannon shot bounced the Confederate's casemate like golf balls off a Brink's truck. In the end the *Merrimack* rammed the *Cumberland*, sending her to the bottom, flag still flying. But in backing away the huge, wedge-shaped ram on the ironclad's bow embedded inside the frigate and broke off. We're searching for that ram.'

'What possible value could an old hunk of iron have?'

'Maybe it doesn't put dollar signs in the eyes of people like treasure from a Spanish galleon, but historically it's priceless, a piece of America's naval heritage.'

Mendoza was about to ask another question but her attention was diverted by two black, rubber helmeted heads that broke water beside the barge. The divers swam over, climbed a rusty ladder and shrugged off their heavy gear. Water streamed from their drysuits, gleaming in the sunlight.

The taller of the two pulled off his hood and ran his hands through a thick mane of ebony hair. His face was darkly tanned and the eyes were the most vivid green Mendoza had ever seen. He had the look of a man who smiled easily and often, who challenged life and accepted the wins and losses with equal indifference. When he stood at his full height he was three inches over six feet, and the

30

lean, hard body under the drysuit strained at the seams. Mendoza knew without asking that this was Dirk Pitt.

He waved at the barge crew's approach. 'We found it,' he said with a wide grin.

Giordino slapped him on the back delightedly. 'Nice going, pal.'

Everyone began asking the divers a barrage of questions, which was answered between swallows of beer. Finally Giordino remembered Mendoza and motioned her forward.

'This is Julie Mendoza of the EPA. She wants to have a chat with us.'

Dirk Pitt extended his hand, giving her an appraising stare. 'Julie.'

'Mr Pitt.'

'If you'll give me a minute to unsuit and dry off – '

'I'm afraid we're running late,' she interrupted. 'We can talk in the air. Admiral Sandecker thought the plane would be faster than a helicopter.'

'You've lost me.'

'I can't take the time to explain. We have to leave immediately. All I can say is that you've been ordered on a new project.'

There was a huskiness in her voice that intrigued Pitt, not masculine exactly, but a voice that would be at home in a Harold Robbins novel.

'Why the mad rush?'

'Not here or now,' she said glancing around at the salvage crew tuned into the conversation.

He turned to Giordino. 'What do you think, Al?'

Giordino faked a bemused look. 'Hard to say. The lady looks pretty determined. On the other hand, I've found a home here on the barge. I kind of hate to leave.'

Mendoza's face flushed in anger, realising the men were toying with her. 'Please, minutes count.'

'Mind telling us where we're going?'

'Langley Air Force Base where a military jet is waiting to take us to Kodiak, Alaska.'

She might as well have told them they were going to the moon. Pitt looked into her eyes, searching for something he wasn't sure he'd find. All he could read was dead seriousness.

'I think, to be on the safe side, I'd better contact the Admiral and confirm.'

'You can do that on the way to Langley,' she said, her tone unyielding. 'I've seen to your personal affairs. Your clothes and whatever else you might need for a two week operation have already been packed and loaded on board.' She paused and stared him squarely in the eye. 'So much for small talk, Mr Pitt. While we stand

31

here and you persist in your petty cross examination, people are dying. You couldn't know that. Take my word for it. If you're half the man you're reported to be, you'll stop screwing around and get on the plane, now!'

'You really go for the jugular, don't you lady?'

'If I have to.'

There was an icy silence. Pitt took a deep breath, then blew it out. He faced Giordino.

'I hear Alaska is beautiful this time of year.'

Giordino managed a faraway look. 'Some great saloons in Skagway we should check out.'

Pitt gestured to the other diver who was peeling off his drysuit. 'She's all yours, Charlie. Go ahead and bring up the *Merrimack*'s ram and get it over to the conservation lab.'

'I'll see to it.'

Pitt nodded and then, along with Giordino, walked towards the Catalina, talking between themselves as if Julie Mendoza no longer existed.

'I hope she packed my fishing pole,' said Giordino with a straight voice. 'The salmon should be running.'

'I've a mind to ride a caribou,' Pitt carried on. 'Heard tell they can outrun a dog sled.'

As Mendoza followed them, the words of Admiral Sandecker came back to haunt her.

'I don't envy you riding herd on those two devils, Pitt in particular. He could con a great white shark into becoming a vegetarian. So keep a sharp eye and your legs crossed.'

4

James Sandecker was considered a prime catch by the feminine circles of Washington society. A dedicated bachelor whose mistress was his work, he seldom entered into a relationship with the opposite sex that lasted more than a few weeks. Sentiment and romance, qualities women thrive on, were beyond him. In another life he might have been a hermit, or as some suggested, Ebenezer Scrooge.

In his late fifties and an exercise addict, he cut a trim figure. He was short and gimlet-eyed, and the red hair and beard had yet to show a tendency towards grey. He possessed an aloofness and coarse personality that appealed to women. Many cast out lures, but few ever put a hook in him.

Bonnie Cowan, an attorney for one of the city's respected law firms, considered herself fortunate indeed to have wangled a dinner date with him.

'You look pensive tonight, Jim,' she said.

He did not look directly at her. His gaze drifted over the diners seated amid the quiet decor of the Inkwell restaurant. 'I was wondering how many people would dine out if there were no seafood.'

She gave him a quizzical stare, and then laughed. 'After dealing with dull legal minds all day, it's like inhaling mountain air to sit with someone who wanders in aimless circles.'

His stare returned over the table's candle and into her eyes. Bonnie Cowan was not yet thirty-five years of age, and she was an unusually attractive and petite woman. She had learned long ago that feminine beauty was an asset in her chosen career, and she never tried to disguise it. Her hair was fine and silken and fell below her shoulders, her breasts were small but nicely proportioned as were the legs that were amply displayed under a short skirt. She was extremely intelligent and could hold her own in any courtroom or media interview. Sandecker felt remiss at his inattentiveness.

'That's a damned pretty dress,' he said, making a feeble attempt at looking attentive.

'Yes, I think the red material goes well with my blonde hair.'

'A nice match,' he came back vaguely.

'You're hopeless, Jim Sandecker,' she said, shaking her head. 'You'd say the same thing if I was sitting here in the nude.'

'Hmmmm?'

'For your information, the dress is brown and so is my hair.'

He shook his head as if to clear the cobwebs. 'I'm sorry, but I warned you I'd be poor company.'

'Your eyes are seeing something a thousand miles away.'

He reached across the table almost shyly and held her hand. 'For the rest of the evening, I'll focus my thoughts entirely on you. I promise.'

'Women are suckers for little boys who need mothering. And you are the most pathetic little boy I've ever seen.'

'Mind your language, woman. Admirals do not take kindly to being referred to as pathetic little boys.'

'All right, John Paul Jones, then how about a bite for a starving deckhand?'

'Anything to prevent a mutiny,' he said smiling for the first time that evening.

He recklessly ordered champagne and the most exotic seafood delicacies on the menu as though it might be his last opportunity.

He adroitly asked Bonnie about the cases she was involved with and masked his lack of interest as she relayed the latest gossip about the Supreme Court and legal manoeuvrings of Congress.

They finished the entree and were attacking the *peches cardinal* when a man with the build of a Denver Bronco linebacker entered the foyer, stared around and, recognising Sandecker, made his way over to the table.

He flashed a toothy smile at Bonnie. 'My apologies, ma'am, for the intrusion.' Then he spoke softly into Sandecker's ear.

The Admiral nodded and looked sadly across the table. 'Please forgive me, but I must go.'

'Government business?'

He nodded silently.

'Oh well,' she said resignedly. 'At least I had you all to myself until dessert.'

He came over and gave her a brotherly kiss on the cheek. 'We'll do it again.'

Then he paid the bill, asked the maître d' to call Bonnie a cab, and left the restaurant.

The Admiral's car rolled to a stop at the special tunnel entrance to the Kennedy Centre for the Performing Arts. The door was opened by a sober-faced man wearing a formal black suit.

'If you will please follow me, sir.'

'Secret Service?'

'Yes sir.'

Sandecker asked no more questions. He exited the car and trailed the agent down a carpeted corridor to a lift. When the doors parted, he was led along the tier level behind the box seats of the opera house to a small meeting room.

Daniel Fawcett, his expression the consistency of marble, simply waved an offhand greeting.

'Sorry to break up your date, Admiral.'

'The message emphasised, "urgent".'

'I've just received another report from Kodiak. The situation has worsened.'

'Does the President know?'

'Not yet,' answered Fawcett. 'Best to wait until the intermission. If he suddenly left his box during the second act of *Rigoletto*, it might fuel too many suspicious minds.'

A Kennedy Centre staff member entered the room carrying a tray of coffee. Sandecker helped himself while Fawcett idly paced the floor. The Admiral fought off an overwhelming desire to light a cigar.

After a wait of eight minutes, the President appeared. The audience applause for the end of the act was heard in the brief interval between the opening and closing of the door. He was dressed in black evening wear with a blue handkerchief nattily tucked in the breastpocket of his jacket.

'I wish I could say it was good seeing you again, Admiral, but every time we meet, we're up to our butts in a crisis.'

'Seems that way,' Sandecker answered.

The President turned to Fawcett. 'What's the bad news, Dan?'

'The captain of an auto ferry disregarded Coast Guard orders and took his ship on its normal run from Seward on the mainland of Kodiak. The ferry was found a few hours ago grounded on Marmot Island. All the passengers and crew were dead.'

'Christ!' the President blurted. 'What was the body count?'

'Three hundred and twelve.'

'That tears it,' said Sandecker. 'All hell will break loose when the news media gets the scent.'

'Nothing we can do,' Fawcett said helplessly. 'Word is already coming over the wire services.'

The President sank into a chair. He seemed a tall man on the TV screens. He carried himself like a tall man but he was only two inches taller than Sandecker. His hairline was recessed and greying, and his narrow face wore a set and solemn expression, a look rarely revealed to the public. He enjoyed tremendous popularity helped immensely by a warm personality and an infectious smile that could melt the most hostile audience. His successful negotiations to merge Canada and the United States into one nation, served to establish an image that was immune to partisan criticism.

'We can't delay another minute,' he said. 'The entire Alaskan gulf has got to be quarantined and everyone within twenty miles of the coast evacuated.'

'I must disagree,' Sandecker said quietly.

'I'd like to hear why.'

'As far as we know the contamination has kept to open waters. No trace has shown up on the mainland. Evacuation of the population would mean a time-consuming and massive operation. Alaskans are a tough breed, especially the fishermen who live in the region. I doubt if they'd willingly leave under any circumstances, least of all when ordered by the federal government.'

'A hardheaded lot.'

'Yes, but not stupid. The fisherman's associations have all agreed to restrict their vessels to port, and the canneries have begun burying all catches brought in during the past ten days.'

'They'll need economic assistance.'

35

'I expect so.'

'Then what do you recommend?'

'The Coast Guard lacks the men and ships to patrol the entire Gulf. The Navy will have to back them up.'

'That,' mused the President, 'presents a problem. Throwing more men and ships in there increases the threat of a higher death toll.'

'Not necessarily,' said Sandecker. 'The crew of the Coast Guard cutter that made the first discovery of the contamination, received no ill effects because the fishing boat had drifted out of the death area.'

'What about the boarding crew, the doctor? They died.'

'The contamination had already covered the decks, the railings, almost anything they touched on the exterior of the vessel. In the case of the ferry, its entire centre section is open to accommodate automobiles, the passengers and crew had no protection. Modern naval ships are constructed to be buttoned up in case of radioactivity from nuclear attack. They can patrol the contaminated currents with a very small, acceptable, degree of risk.'

The President nodded his consent. 'Okay, I'll order an assist from the Navy Department, but I'm not sold on dropping an evacuation plan. Stubborn Alaskans or not, there are still women and children to consider.'

'My other suggestion, Mr President, or request if you will, is a delay of forty-eight hours before you initiate the operation. That might give my response team time to find the source.'

The President fell silent. He stared at Sandecker with deepening interest. 'Who are the people orchestrating this mess?'

'The on-scene coordinator and chairman of the Regional Emergency Response Team is Dr Julie Mendoza, a senior biochemical engineer for the EPA.'

'I'm not familiar with the name.'

'She's recognised as the best in the country on assessment and control of hazardous contamination in water,' Sandecker said without hesitation. 'The underwater search for the shipwreck we believe contains the nerve agent will be headed by my Special Projects Director, Dirk Pitt.'

The President's eyes widened a millimetre. 'I know Mr Pitt. He proved most helpful on the Canadian affair a few months ago.'

You mean, saved your ass, Sandecker thought before he continued. 'We have nearly two hundred other pollution experts who have been called in to assist. Every expert in private industry has been tapped to provide the experience and technical data for a successful cleanup.'

The President glanced at his watch. 'I've got to cut this short,' he said. 'I suspect they won't start the third act without me. Anyway, you've got yourself forty-eight hours, Admiral. Then I order an evacuation and declare the area as a national disaster.'

Fawcett accompanied the President back to his box. He seated himself slightly to the rear but close enough so they could converse in low tones while feigning interest in the performance on stage.

'Do you wish to cancel the cruise with Moran and Larimer?'

The President imperceptibly shook his head. 'No, my economic recovery package for the Soviet satellite countries has top priority over any other business.'

'I strongly advise against it. You're waging a hopeless battle for a lost cause.'

'So you've informed me at least five times in the past week.' The President held a programme over his face to conceal a yawn. 'How do the votes stack up?'

'A wave of nonpartisan, conservative support is gaining ground against you. We'll need fifteen votes in the House and five, maybe six, to pass the measure in the Senate.'

'We've faced bigger odds.'

'Yes,' Fawcett muttered almost sadly. 'But if we're defeated this time, your administration may never see a second term.'

5

The dawn was creeping out of the east as a low, dark line on the horizon began to narrow and poke into the sky. Through the windows of the helicopter the black blur took on a symmetrical, cone-shaped feature and soon became a mountain peak rising from the sea. There was a three-quarter moon behind it, and the light altered from ivory to indigo blue and then to an orange radiance. The curved dome of the sun rose and the slopes could be seen mantled in snow.

Pitt glanced over at Giordino. He was asleep, a state he could slip in and out of like an old sweater. He had slept from the time they left Langley Field until they landed at Elmendorf Air Force Base outside of Anchorage. Five minutes after transferring to the helicopter, he promptly drifted off again.

Pitt turned to Mendoza. She sat perched there behind the pilot, the look on her face was that of a little girl eager to see a parade. Her gaze was fixed on the island. In the early light it seemed to Pitt her face had softened, her expression was not so businesslike and the lines of her mouth held a tenderness that was not there before.

'Augustine volcano,' she said, unaware that Pitt's attention was focused on her and not out of the window. 'Named by Captain Cook in 1778. You wouldn't know it to look at her but she's the most active volcano in Alaska, having erupted six times in the last century.'

Pitt regretfully turned away and stared below. The island seemed bare of any human habitation. Long swirling flows of lava rock spilled down the mountain's sides until they met the sea. A small cloud drifted about the summit.

'Very picturesque,' he said, yawning. 'Might have possibilities as a ski resort.'

'Don't bet on it,' she laughed. 'That cloud you see over the peak is steam. Augustine is a consistent performer. The last eruption in 1987 surpassed Mount St Helens in Washington. The fall of ash and pumice was measured as far away as Athens.'

Pitt had to ask, 'What's its status now?'

'Recent data confirms the heat around the summit is increasing, probably forecasting an impending explosion.'

'Naturally, you can't say when.'

'Naturally.' She shrugged. 'Volcanoes are unpredictable. Sometimes they get violent without the slightest warning, sometimes they take months to build up to a spectacular climax that never happens. They sputter, rumble a little and then go dormant. Those earth scientists I told you about who died from the nerve agent; they were on the island to study the impending activity.'

'Where are we setting down?'

'About ten miles off the shore,' she replied, 'on the Coast Guard cutter, *Catawaba*.'

'The *Catawaba*,' he repeated as if reminiscing.

'Yes, you know of her?'

'Set a 'copter on her flight pad myself a few years ago.'

'Where was that?'

'North Atlantic, near Iceland.' He was gazing beyond the island now. He sighed and massaged his temples. 'A good friend and I were hunting for a ship embedded in an iceberg.'

'Did you find it?'

He nodded. 'A burned out hulk. Barely beat the Russians to it. Later we crashed in the surf on the Icelandic coast. My friend was killed.'

She could see his mind was reliving the events. The expression on his face took on a faraway sadness. She changed the subject.

'We'll have to say goodbye – temporarily, I mean – when we land.'

38

He shook off the past and stared at her. 'You're leaving us?'

'You and Al will be staying on the *Catawaba* to search for the nerve agent's location. I'm going to the island where the local Response Team has set up a data base.'

'And part of my job is to send water samples from the ship to your lab.'

'Yes, by measuring trace levels of the contamination we can direct you towards the source.'

'Like following breadcrumbs.'

'One way of putting it.'

'After we find it, what then?'

'Once your salvage team brings up the drums containing the nerve agent, the Army will dispose of it by deep well injection on an island near the Arctic circle.'

'How deep is the well?'

'Four thousand feet.'

'All neat and tidy.'

The open-for-business look returned to her eyes. 'It happens to be the most efficient method open to us.'

'You're too optimistic.'

She looked at him questioningly. 'What do you mean?'

'The salvage. It could take months.'

'We can't afford weeks,' she came back almost vehemently.

'You're treading in my territory now,' Pitt said as if lecturing. 'Divers can't risk working in water where one drop on their skin will kill them. The only reasonably safe way is to use submersibles, a damned slow and tedious process. And submersibles require highly trained crews and specially constructed vessels to act as work platforms.'

'I've already explained,' she said impatiently, 'Presidential authority gives us carte blanche on any equipment we need.'

'The easy part,' Pitt continued. 'Despite your water sample directions, finding a shipwreck can be a frustrating venture. It's like looking for a coin in the middle of a football field in the dark with a candle. Then if we get lucky and make contact, we may find the hull broken in sections and the cargo scattered, or the drums too corroded to move. Murphy's law can hit us from every angle. No deep sea recovery operation is ever cut and dried.'

Mendoza's face reddened. 'I'd like to point out – '

'Don't bother,' Pitt cut her off. 'I'm the wrong guy for a gung ho speech. Besides, I've heard them all before. You won't get a chorus of the Notre Dame fight song from me. And save your breath for the "countless lives hang in the balance" routine. I'm aware of it, and don't have to be reminded every five minutes.'

39

She looked at him, annoyed with him for his arrogant charm, feeling that he was testing her somehow, for some purpose she could not comprehend.

'Have you ever seen someone who came in contact with Nerve Agent S?'

'No.'

'It's not a pretty sight. They literally drown in their own blood as their internal membranes burst. Every body orifice bleeds like a river. Then the corpse turns black.'

'You're very descriptive.'

'It's all a game to you,' she lashed out. 'It's not a game to me.'

He didn't reply, simply nodded downward at the *Catawaba* looming through the pilot's windscreen. 'We're landing . . .'

The pilot noted that the ship had turned bow-on to the wind from the fluttering ensign on the halyards. He eased the helicopter over the stern, hovered a few moments and set down on the pad. The rotor blades had hardly swung to a stop when two figures dressed from head to toe in astronaut-type suits approached while unfolding a circular plastic tube about five feet in diameter that looked like a huge umbilical cord. When they secured it around the exit door, they gave three knocks. Pitt undid the latches and swung the door inward. The men outside passed him cloth hoods with see-through lenses and gloves.

'Best put them on,' commanded a muffled voice.

Pitt prodded Giordino awake and handed him a hood and pair of gloves.

'What in hell are these?' Giordino mumbled, emerging from the cobwebs.

'Welcome gifts from the sanitation department.'

Two more crewmen appeared in the plastic tunnel and took their gear. Giordino, still half asleep, stumbled from the helicopter. Pitt hesitated and stared into Mendoza's eyes.

'What's my reward if I find your poison in forty-eight hours?'

'What do you want it to be?'

'Are you as hard as you pretend?'

'Harder, Mr Pitt, much harder.'

'Then you decide.'

He gave her a rakish smile and was gone.

6

The cars that made up the presidential motorcade were lined in a row beside the south portico of the White House. As soon as the Secret Service detail was in position, Oscar Lucas spoke into a tiny microphone whose wire looped around the watch on his wrist and ran up the sleeve of his coat.

'Tell the "Boss", we're ready.'

Three minutes later the President, accompanied by Fawcett, walked briskly down the steps and entered the presidential limousine. Lucas got in next to the driver, and the cars moved out through the south-west gate.

The President relaxed into the leather of the rear seat and idly stared out of the window at the passing buildings. Fawcett sat with an open attaché case on his lap and made a series of notations inside the top folder. After a few minutes of silence, he sighed, snapped the case shut and set it on the floor.

'There it is, arguments from both sides of the fence, statistics, CIA projections, and the latest reports from your economic council on Communist bloc debts. Everything you should need to sell Larimer and Moran to your way of thinking.'

'The American public doesn't think much of my plan, does it?' the President asked quietly.

'To be perfectly honest, no sir,' Lucas replied. 'The general feeling is to let the Reds stew in their own problems. Most Americans are cheering the fact that the Soviets and their satellites are facing starvation and financial ruin. They consider it proof positive that the Marxist system is a pathetic joke.'

'It won't be a joke if the Kremlin leaders, backs against an economic wall, strike out in desperation and march through Europe.'

'Your opposition in Congress feel the risk is offset by the very real threat of starvation, which will undermine Russia's capacity to maintain its military machine. And there are those who are banking on the eroding morale of the Russian people to crystallise in active resistance towards the ruling party.'

The President shook his head. 'The Kremlin is fanatical about their military build up. They'll never slacken off in spite of their economic dilemma. And the people will never rise up or stage mass demonstrations. The party's collar is too tight.'

41

'The bottom line,' said Fawcett, 'is that both Larimer and Moran are dead set against taking the burden off Moscow.'

The President's face twisted in disgust. 'Larimer is a drunk and Moran is tainted with corruption.'

'Still, there is no getting around the fact you have to sell them on your philosophy.'

'I can't deny their opinions,' the President admitted grudgingly. 'But I am convinced that if the United States saves the Eastern Bloc nations from almost total disintegration, they will turn away from the Soviet Union and join with the West.'

'There are many who see that as wishful thinking, Mr President.'

'The French and Germans see it my way.'

'Sure, and why not? They're playing both ends of the field, relying on our NATO forces for security while expanding economic ties with the east.'

'You're forgetting that the grassroots American voters are behind my aid plan too,' said the President, his chin thrust forward at his words. 'Even they realise its potential for defusing the threat of nuclear holocaust and pulling down the iron curtain for good.'

Fawcett knew it was senseless to sway the President when he was in a crusading mood and passionately convinced he was right. There was a kind of virtue in killing your enemies with kindness, a truly civilised tactic that might move the consciences of reasonable people, but Fawcett failed to see the reality of it.

Fawcett turned inward to his thoughts and remained silent as the limousine turned off M Street into the Washington Naval Yard and rolled to a stop on one of the long docks.

A dark skinned man with the stony facial features of an American Indian approached as Lucas stepped from the car.

'Evening George.'

'Hello Oscar, how's the golf game?'

'Sad shape,' answered Lucas. 'I haven't played in almost two weeks.'

As Lucas spoke he looked into the piercing dark eyes of George Blackowl, the acting supervisor and advance agent for the President's movement. Blackowl was about Lucas' height, five years younger and inclined to be about ten pounds of excess weight. A habitual gum chewer, his jaws worked constantly, he was half Sioux and was constantly kidded about his ancestors' role at the Little Big Horn.

'Safe to board?' asked Lucas.

'The boat has been swept for explosives and listening devices. The frogmen finished checking the hull about ten minutes ago, and the outboard chase boat is manned and ready to follow.'

42

Lucas nodded. 'A hundred and ten foot Coast Guard cutter will be standing by when you reach Mount Vernon.'

'Then I guess we're ready for "the Boss".'

Lucas paused for nearly a minute while he scanned the surrounding dock area. Detecting nothing suspicious he opened the door for the President. Then the agents formed a security diamond around him. Blackowl walked ahead of the point man who was directly in front of the President. Lucas, because he was left handed and required ease of movement in case he had to draw his gun, walked the left point and slightly to the rear. Fawcett trailed several yards behind and out of the way.

At the boarding ramp Lucas and Blackowl stood aside to let the others pass.

'Okay, George, he's all yours.'

'Lucky you,' Blackowl said smiling. 'You get the weekend off.'

'First time this month.'

'Heading home from here?'

'Not yet. I have to run by the office and clear off the desk first. There were a few hitches during the last trip to Los Angeles and I want to review the planning.'

They turned in unison as another government limousine pulled up to the dock. Senator Marcus Larimer climbed out and strode towards the presidential yacht followed by an aide who dutifully carried an overnight bag.

Larimer wore a brown suit with a vest – he always wore a brown suit with a vest. It was suggested by one of his fellow legislators that he was born in one. His hair was sandy coloured and styled in the 'dry' look. He was big and rough cut, with the look of a hod carrier trying to crash a celebrity benefit.

He simply nodded to Blackowl and threw Lucas the standard politician's greeting.

'Nice to see you, Oscar.'

'You're looking healthy, Senator.'

'Nothing a bottle of scotch won't cure,' Larimer replied with a booming laugh. Then he swept up the ramp and disappeared into the main salon.

'Have fun,' Lucas said sarcastically to Blackowl. 'I don't envy you this trip.'

A few minutes later, while driving through the naval yard gate onto M Street, Lucas passed a compact Chevrolet carrying Congressman Alan Moran going in the opposite direction. Lucas didn't like the Speaker of the House. Not nearly as flamboyant as his predecessor, Moran was an Horatio Alger kind of hero who had succeeded not so much from intelligence and perception, but by stowing away in the Congressional power circles and supplying more favours than he begged. Once accused of masterminding an oil leasing scheme on government lines, he had greased his way out of any scandal by calling in his political IOUs. He looked neither right nor left as he drove; his mind, Lucas deduced, grinding on ways to pick the President's influential pocket.

Not quite an hour later, as the crew of the presidential yacht were preparing to cast off, Vice President Vincent Margolin came aboard with a holdall in one hand. He hesitated a moment and then spied the President seated alone in a deckchair near the stern, watching the sun begin to set over the city. A steward appeared and relieved Margolin of the holdall.

The President looked up and stared as though not fully recognising him.

'Vince?'

'Sorry I'm late,' Margolin apologised. 'But one of my aides misplaced your invitation and I only discovered it an hour ago.'

'I wasn't sure you could make it,' the President murmured obscurely.

'Perfect timing. Beth is visiting our son at Stanford and won't be home until Tuesday, and I had nothing on my schedule that couldn't be shoved ahead.'

The President stood up, forcing a friendly smile. 'Senator Larimer and Congressman Moran are on board too.'

A friendly persuasion operation, Margolin mused. Strange the President wanted him along for backup. Though he supported the White House policies in public, Margolin never held back his objections to the Eastern Bloc aid programme in private conversations with his boss.

'They're in the dining salon,' the President continued. 'Why don't you say hello and rustle up a drink.'

'A drink I could use.'

Margolin bumped into Fawcett in the doorway and they exchanged a few words.

The President's face was a study in anger. As much as he and Margolin differed in style and appearance – the Vice President was tall, nicely proportioned, not a bit of fat with a handsome face and bright eyes and a warm, outgoing personality – so they differed in their politics.

The President achieved a high degree of personal popularity by his inspirational speeches. An idealist and a visionary, he was almost totally occupied with creating policies that would be of global benefit ten to fifty years in the future. Unfortunately, they were for the most

44

part policies that did not fit in with the selfish realities of existing politics.

Margolin, on the other hand, kept a low profile with the public and news media, aiming his energies more towards domestic issues. His stand on the President's communist aid programme was that the money would be better spent at home.

The Vice President was a born politician, he had the Constitution in his blood. He had come up the hard way; through the ranks, beginning with the state legislature, then governor and later the Congressional Senate.

Once entrenched in his office in the Russell Building, he surrounded himself with a powerhouse staff of advisers who possessed a flair for strategic compromise and innovative political concepts. While it was the President who created legislation, it was Margolin who orchestrated its passage through the maze of committees in action and policy, all too often making the White House staff appear as fumbling amateurs; a situation that did not sit well with the President and caused considerable internal backstabbing.

Margolin might have been the people's choice for the presidency, but he was not the party's. Here his integrity and image as a 'shaker and doer' worked against him. He too often refused to fall in line on partisan issues if he believed in a better path: a maverick who followed his own dictates.

As with others who came before him, he was tapped for Vice President to get him out of the way, and the spear carriers of the party were astonished when he accepted the invitation.

The President watched Margolin disappear into the main salon, irritation and jealousy burning within him. He could not help but recognise that Margolin was a better man than he for the job.

Fawcett came across the deck, his expression blank. 'What in hell is Vince doing here?' he asked nervously.

'Damned if I know,' snapped the President. 'He said he was invited.'

Fawcett looked stricken. 'Christ, somebody on the staff must have screwed up.'

'Too late now. I can't tell him he's not wanted and please to leave.'

Fawcett was still confused. 'I don't understand.'

'Neither do I, but we're stuck with him.'

'He could blow it.'

'I don't think so. Regardless of what we think about Vince, he's never made a statement that's tarnished my image. That's more than a lot of presidents could say about their VP.'

Fawcett resigned himself to the situation. 'There aren't enough staterooms to go around. I'll give up mine and stay on shore.'

45

'I appreciate that, Dan.'

'I can stay on the boat until tonight and then bunk at a nearby motel.'

'Perhaps, under the circumstances,' said the President slowly, 'it would be best if you remained behind. With Vince along I don't want our guests to think we're ganging up on them.'

'I'll leave the documents supporting your position in your stateroom.'

'Thank you. I'll study them before dinner.' Then the President paused. 'By the way, any word on the Alaskan situation?'

'Only that the search for the nerve agent is underway.'

The President's eyes reflected a disturbed look. He nodded and shook Fawcett's hand. 'See you tomorrow.'

Later, Fawcett stood on the dock among the irritated Secret Service agents of the Vice President's detail. As he watched the aging white yacht cut into the Anacostia River before turning south towards the Potomac, a knot began to tighten in the pit of his stomach.

He had personally invited Senator Larimer and Congressman Moran by phone. Margolin said his invitation had been misplaced.

But there were no written invitations.

None of it made any sense.

Lucas was putting on his coat, about to leave his office when the phone linked to the command post buzzed.

'Lucas.'

'This is "Love Boat",' replied George Blackowl's voice, giving the code name of the movement in progress.

The call was unexpected and like a father with a daughter on a date, Lucas immediately feared the worst. 'Go ahead,' he said tersely.

'We have a situation. This is no emergency, I repeat, no emergency. But something's come up that isn't in the movement.'

Lucas expelled a sigh of relief. 'I'm listening.'

' "Shakespeare" is on the boat,' said Blackowl giving the code name for the Vice President.

'He's where?' Lucas gasped, unbelievingly.

'Margolin showed up out of nowhere and came on board as we were casting off. Dan Fawcett gave him his stateroom and went ashore. When I queried the President about the last minute switch in passengers, he told me to let it ride. But I smell a screwup.'

'Where's Rhinemann?'

'Right here with me on the yacht.'

'Put him on.'

46

There was a pause and then Hank Rhinemann, the supervisor in charge of the Vice President's security detail came on. 'Oscar, we've got an unscheduled movement.'

'Understood. How did you lose him?'

'He came charging out of his office and said he had to attend an urgent meeting with the President on the yacht. He didn't tell me it was an overnight affair.'

'He kept it from you?'

'"Shakespeare" is tightmouthed as hell. I should have known when I saw the holdall. I'm sorry as hell, Oscar.'

A wave of frustration swept Lucas. God, he thought; the leaders of the world's leading superpowers were like kids when it came to their security.

'It's happened,' said Lucas sharply, 'so we'll make the best of it. Where is your detail?'

'Standing on the dock,' answered Rhinemann.

'Send them down to Mount Vernon and back up Blackowl's people. I want that yacht cordoned off tighter than a bass drum.'

'Will do.'

'At the slightest hint of trouble, call me. I'm spending the night at the command post.'

'You got a line on something?' Rhinemann asked.

'Nothing tangible,' Lucas replied, his voice so hollow it seemed to come from a distant source. 'But knowing the President and the next three men in line for his office are all in the same place at the same time scares the hell out of me.'

7

'We've turned against the current.' Pitt's voice was quiet, almost casual, and he stared at the colour video screen on the Klein Hydroscan sonar which read the sea floor. 'Increase speed about two knots.'

Bleached Levis, Irish knit turtleneck sweater and brown tennis shoes, his brushed hair laid back under a NUMA baseball cap – he looked cool and comfortable with a bored, indifferent air about him.

The wheel moved slowly under the helmsman's hands and the *Catawaba* lazily shoved aside the three foot swells as it swept the sea back and forth like a lawnmower. Trailing behind the stern like a tin can tied to the tail of a dog, the side scan sonar's sensor pinged the depths, sending a signal to the video display which translated it into a detailed image of the bottom.

They took up the search for the nerve agent source in the southern end of Cook Inlet and discovered that the residual traces rose as they worked westward into Kamishak Bay. Water samples were taken every half hour and ferried by helicopter to the chemical lab on Augustine Island. Amos Dover philosophically compared the project to a children's game of finding hidden candy with an unseen voice giving 'warmer or colder' clues.

As the day wore on, the nervous tension that had been building up on the *Catawaba* suddenly seemed so physical you could almost reach out and grasp it. To the crew, the unbearable part was not being able to go on deck for a breath of air. Only the EPA chemists were allowed outside the exterior bulkheads, and they were protected by airtight encapsulating suits. And yet everyone sensed they were groping within spitting range of their target.

'Anything yet?' Dover asked, peering over Pitt's shoulder at the high resolution screen.

'Nothing manmade,' Pitt answered. 'Bottom terrain is rugged, broken, mostly lava rock.'

'Good clear picture.'

Pitt nodded. 'Yes, the detail is quite sharp.'

'What's that dark smudge?'

'A school of fish, maybe a herd of seals.'

Dover turned and stared through the bridge windows at the volcanic peak on Augustine Island, now only a few miles away. 'Better make a strike soon. We're coming close to shore –'

'Lab to ship,' Mendoza's feminine voice broke over the bridge speaker.

Dover picked up the communications phone. 'Go ahead lab.'

'Steer zero-seven-zero degrees. Trace elements appear to be in higher concentrations in that direction.'

Dover gave the nearby island an apprehensive eye. 'If we hold that course for twenty minutes we'll park on your doorstep for supper.'

'Come in as far as you can and take samples,' Mendoza answered. 'My indications are that you're practically on top of it.'

Dover hung up without further discussion and called out, 'What's the depth?'

The watch officer tapped a dial on the instrument console. 'One hundred and forty feet and rising.'

'How far can you see on that thing?' Dover asked Pitt.

'We read the seabed six hundred metres on either side of our hull.'

'Then we're cutting a swath nearly two-thirds of a mile wide.'

'Close enough,' Pitt admitted.

48

'We should have detected the ship by now,' Dover said irritably. 'Maybe we missed it.'

'No need to get uptight,' Pitt said. He paused, leaned over the computer keyboard and fine tuned the image. 'Nothing in this world is more elusive than a shipwreck that isn't ready to be found. Deducing the murderer in an Agatha Christie novel is kindergarten stuff compared to finding a lost derelict under hundreds of square miles of water. Sometimes you get lucky early, most of the time you don't.'

'Very poetic,' Dover said drily.

Pitt stared at the overhead bulkhead for a long and considering moment. 'What's visibility under the water surface?'

'The water turns crystal fifty yards from shore. On the flood tide I've seen a hundred feet or better.'

'I'd like to borrow your 'copter and take aerial photos of this area.'

'Why bother?' Dover said curtly. '*Semper Paratus*, Always Ready, is not the Coast Guard's motto for laughs.' He motioned through a doorway. 'We have charts showing three thousand miles of Alaskan coastline in colour and incredible detail, courtesy of satellite reconnaissance.'

Pitt nodded for Giordino to take his place in front of the Hydroscan as he rose and followed the *Catawaba*'s skipper into a small compartment stacked with cabinets containing nautical charts. Dover checked the label inserts, pulled open a drawer, and rummaged inside. Finally, he extracted a large chart marked 'Satellite Survey Number 2430A, South Shore of Augustine Island'. Then he laid it on a table and spread it out.

'Is this what you have in mind?'

Pitt leaned over and studied the bird's eye view of the sea off the volcanic island's coast. 'Perfect. Got a magnifying glass?'

'In the shelf under the table.'

Pitt found the thick, square lens and peered through it at the tiny shadows on the photo survey. Dover left and returned shortly with two mugs of coffee.

'Your chances are nil,' he said, 'of spotting an anomaly in that geological nightmare on the seafloor. A ship could stay lost forever in there.'

'I'm not looking at the seafloor.'

Dover heard Pitt's words all right, but the meaning didn't register. Vague curiosity reflected in his eyes, but before he could ask the obvious question, the speaker above the doorway crackled.

'Skipper, we've got breakers ahead.' The watch officer's voice was tense. 'The fathometer reads thirty feet of water under the hull and rising damned fast.'

'All stop!' Dover ordered. A pause, then: 'No, reverse engines until speed is zero.'

'Tell him to have the sonar sensor pulled in before it drags bottom,' Pitt said offhandedly. 'Then I suggest we drop anchor.'

Dover gave Pitt a strange look indeed, and issued the command. The deck trembled beneath their feet as the twin screws reversed direction. After a few moments the vibration ceased.

'Speed zero,' the watch officer notified them from the bridge. 'Anchor away.'

Dover acknowledged, then sat on a stool, cupped his hands around the coffee mug and looked directly at Pitt.

'Okay, what do you see?'

'I have the ship we're looking for,' Pitt said, speaking slowly and distinctly. 'There are no other possibilities. You were mistaken in one respect, Dover, but correct in another. Mother nature seldom makes rock formations that run in a perfectly straight line for several hundred feet. Consequently, the outline of a ship *can* be detected against an irregular background. You were right though in saying our chances were nil of finding it on the seafloor.'

'Get to the point,' Dover said impatiently.

'The target is in shore.'

'You mean on shore, like grounded in the shallows.'

'I mean in shore as in high and dry.'

'You can't be serious?'

Pitt ignored the question and handed Dover the magnifying glass. 'See for yourself.' He took a pencil and circled a section of cliffs above the tideline.

Dover bent over and put his eye to the glass. 'All I see is rock.'

'Look closer. The projection from the lower part of the slope into the sea.'

Dover's expression turned incredulous. 'Oh, Jesus, it's the stern of a ship!'

'You can make out the fantail and the top half of the rudder.'

'Yes, yes, and a piece of the afterdeck house.' Dover's frustration was suddenly washed away by the mounting excitement of the discovery. 'Incredible that she lies buried bow-on into the shore as though covered by an avalanche. Judging from the cruiser shape of her stern and the balanced rudder, I'd say she's an old Liberty Ship.' He looked up, a deepening interest in his eyes. 'I wonder if she might be the *Pilottown*?'

'Sounds vaguely familiar.'

'One of the most stubborn mysteries of the Northern Seas. The *Pilottown* tramped back and forth between Tokyo and the West Coast until ten years ago when her crew reported her sinking in a storm. A search was launched and no trace of the ship was found. Two years later an Eskimo stumbled on the *Pilottown* caught in the ice about ninety miles above Nome. He went aboard but found the ship deserted, no sign of the crew or cargo. A month later, when he returned with his tribe to remove whatever they could find of value, it was gone again. Nearly two years passed, and then she was reported drifting below the Bering Strait. The Coast Guard was sent out but couldn't locate her. The restless *Pilottown* wasn't sighted again for eight months. She was boarded by the crew of a fishing trawler. They found her in reasonable good shape. Then she disappeared for the last time.'

'I seem to recall reading something . . .' Pitt's voice paused. 'Ah yes, the Magic Ship.'

'That's what the news media dubbed her,' acknowledged Dover. 'They described her disappearing act as a "now you see it, now you don't" routine.'

'They'll have a field day when it gets out that she was drifting around for years with a cargo of nerve agent.'

'No way of predicting the horror if the hull had been crushed in an ice pack or shattered on a rocky shore, creating an instant and massive spill,' Dover added.

'We've got to get in her cargo holds,' said Pitt. 'Contact Mendoza, give her the position of the wreck and tell her to airlift a team of chemists to the site. We'll do a survey from the water.'

Dover nodded. 'I'll see to the launch.'

'Throw in acetylene equipment in case we have to cut our way inside.'

Dover bent over the chart table and stared solemnly at the centre of the marked circle. 'I never thought for a minute I'd stand on the deck of the Magic Ship.'

'If you're right,' said Pitt, staring vacantly into his coffee mug. 'The *Pilottown* is about to make her last performance.'

8

The sea had been calm, but by the time the *Catawaba*'s launch was a quarter of a mile from the lonely, forbidding coast, a twenty knot wind kicked up the water. The spray, tainted by the nerve agent, struck the cabin windows with the fury of driven sand. Yet where the derelict lay beached, the water looked reasonably peaceful, protected as it was by jagged pinnacles of rock that rose up a hundred yards offshore like solitary chimneys from burned out houses.

Far above the turbulent waters Augustine Volcano seemed calm and serene in the later afternoon sun. It was one of the most beautifully sculptured mountains in the Pacific, rivalling the classic contour of Mount Fuji in Japan.

The powerful launch surfed for an instant on a whitecapped swell before driving over the crest. Pitt braced his feet and gripped a railing with both hands while his eyes studied the shore.

The wreck was heeled over at a twenty degree angle and her stern section blanketed in brown rust. The rudder was canted in the full starboard position and two barnacle encrusted blades of the propeller protruded from the black sand. The letters of her name and home port were too obscured to read.

Pitt and Giordino, Dover, the two EPA scientists, and one of the *Catawaba*'s junior officers were all garbed in white encapsulating suits to protect them from the plumes of deadly spray. They communicated by tiny transmitters inside their protective head gear. Attached to their waist belts were intricate filter systems designed to refine clean, breathable air.

The sea around them was carpeted with dead fish of every species. A pair of whales rolled lifelessly back and forth with the tide, united in rotting decay with porpoise, sea lions and spotted seals. Birds by the thousand floated amid the morbid debris. Nothing that had lived in the area escaped.

Dover expertly threaded the launch between the threatening offshore barrier of projecting rock, the remnants of an ancient coastline. He slowed, waiting for a momentary lull in the surf, biding his time while carefully eyeing the depth. Then as a wave slammed onto the shore and its backwash spilled against the next one coming in, he aimed the bow at the small spit of sand formed around the base of the wreck and pushed the throttle forward. Like a horse bracing for the next hurdle at the Grand National, the launch rose up on the wave crest and rode it through the swirling foam until the keel dropped and scraped onto the spit.

'A neat bit of handiwork,' Pitt complimented him.

'All in the timing,' Dover said, a grin visible behind his helmet's facemask. 'Of course, it helps if you land at low tide.'

They tilted back their heads and stared up at the wreck towering above them like a colossus. The faded name on the stern could be deciphered now.

It read *Pilottown*.

'Almost a pity,' Dover said reverently, 'to write *finish* to an enigma.'

'The sooner the better,' Pitt said, his tone grim as he contemplated the mass death inside.

Within five minutes the equipment was unloaded, the launch securely moored to the *Pilottown*'s rudder, and the men laboriously climbing the steep slope on the port side of the stern. Pitt took the lead, followed by Giordino and the rest as Dover brought up the rear.

The incline was not made up of solid rock but rather a combination of cinder ash and mud with the consistency of loose gravel. Their boots struggled to find a foothold, but mostly they slid back two steps for every three they gained. The dust from the ash rose and clung to their suits, coating them a dark grey. Soon the sweat was seeping through their pores and the increasingly heavy rasp of their breathing became more audible over the earphones inside their helmets.

Pitt called a halt on a narrow ledge, not four feet wide and just long enough to hold all six men. Wearily Giordino sank to a sitting position and readjusted the straps that held the acetylene tank to his back. When he could finally pant a coherent sentence, he said, 'How in hell did this old rust bucket jam herself in here?'

'She probably drifted into what was a shelving inlet before 1987,' replied Pitt. 'According to Mendoza, that was the year the volcano last erupted. The explosion gases must have melted the ice around the mantle, forming millions of gallons of water. The mudflow, along with the cloud of ash, poured down the mountain until it met the sea and buried the ship.'

'Funny the stern wasn't spotted before now.'

'Not remarkable,' Pitt answered. 'So little is showing it was next to impossible to detect from the air, and beyond a mile from shore it blends into the rugged shoreline until nearly invisible. Erosion caused by recent storms are the reason she's been uncovered.'

Dover stood up, pressing his weight against the steep embankment to maintain his balance. He unravelled a thin, knotted nylon rope from his waist and unfolded a small grappling hook tied to the end.

He looked down at Pitt. 'If you'll support my legs, I think I can heave the hook over the ship's railing.'

Pitt grasped his left leg as Giordino edged over and held the right. The burly Coast Guardsman leaned back over the lip of the ledge, swung the hook in a widening arc and let it fly.

It sailed over the stern rails and caught.

The rest of the ascent took only a few minutes. Pulling themselves upward hand over hand, they soon climbed onto the deck. Heavy layers of rust mingled with ash flaked away beneath their feet. What little they could see of the *Pilottown* looked a dirty, ugly mess.

'No sign of Mendoza,' said Dover.

'Nearest flat ground to land a 'copter is a thousand yards away,' Pitt replied. 'She and her team will have to hike in.'

Giordino walked over to the railing beside the corroded shaft of the jackstaff and stared at the water below. 'The poison must be seeping through the hull during high tide.'

'Must be stored in the afterhold,' said Dover.

'The cargo hatches are buried under tons of this lava crap,' Giordino said disgustedly. 'We'll need a fleet of bulldozers to get through.'

'You familiar with Liberty Ships?' Pitt asked Dover.

'Should be. I've inspected enough of them over the years, looking for illegal cargo.' He knelt down and began tracing a ship's outline in the rust. 'Inside the aft deck house we should find a hatch to an escape trunk that leads to the tunnel holding the screw shaft. At the bottom is a small recess, we might be able to cut our way into the hold from there.'

They all stood silent when Dover finished. They should have all felt a sense of accomplishment at having found the source of the nerve agent. But instead they experienced apprehension. A reaction, Pitt supposed, that stemmed from a let down after the excitement of the search. Then also, there was a hidden dread of what they might actually find behind the steel bulkheads of the *Pilottown*.

'Maybe . . . maybe we better wait for the lab people?' one of the chemists stammered.

'They can catch up,' Pitt said pleasantly, but with cold eyes.

Giordino silently took a racking bar from the toolpack strapped on Pitt's back and attacked the steel door to the afterdeck house. To his surprise it creaked and moved. He put his muscle to it, the protesting hinges surrendered and the door sprung open. The interior was completely empty, no fittings, no gear, not even a scrap of trash.

'Looks as though the movers have been here,' observed Pitt.

'Odd it was never in use,' Dover mused.

'The escape trunk?' Pitt prompted.

'This way.'

Dover led them through another compartment that was also barren. He stopped at a round hatch in the centre of the deck. Giordino moved forward, prised open the cover and stepped back. Dover aimed a flashlight down the yawning tunnel; the beam stabbing the darkness.

'So much for that idea,' he said dejectedly. 'The tunnel recess is blocked with debris.'

'What's on the next deck below?'

'The steering gear compartment.' Dover paused, his mind working. Then he thought aloud. 'Just forward of the steering gear there's an after steering room. A holdover from the war years. It's possible, barely possible, it might have an access hatch to the hold.'

They went aft then and returned to the first compartment. It felt strange to walk the decks of a ghost ship, wondering what had happened to the crew that abandoned her. They found the hatchway and climbed down the ladder to the steering gear compartment and made their way around the old, still oily machinery to the forward bulkhead. Dover scanned the steel plates with his flashlight. Suddenly the wavering beam stopped.

'Son of a bitch!' he grunted. 'The hatch is here, but it's been welded shut.'

'You're certain we're in the right spot?' Pitt asked.

'Absolutely,' Dover answered. He rapped his gloved fist against the bulkhead. 'On the other side lies cargo hold number five, the most likely storage of the poison.'

'What about the other holds?' asked one of the EPA men.

'Too far forward to leak into the sea.'

'Okay, then let's do it,' Pitt said impatiently.

Quickly they assembled the cutting torch and connected the oxygen-acetylene bottles. The flame from the tip of the torch hissed as Giordino adjusted the gas mixture. Blue flame shot out and assaulted the steel plate, turning it red, then a bright orange white. A narrow gap appeared and lengthened, crackling and melting under the intense heat.

As Giordino was cutting an opening large enough to crawl through, Julie Mendoza and her lab people appeared, packing nearly five hundred pounds of chemical analysis instruments.

'You found it,' she stated, obviously.

'We can't be sure yet,' Pitt cautioned.

'But our test samples show the water around this area reeks with Nerve Agent S,' she protested.

'Disappointment comes easy,' said Pitt. 'I never count my chickens till the cheque clears the bank.'

Further conversation broke off as Giordino stood back and extinguished the cutting torch. He handed it to Dover and picked up his trusty racking bar.

'Stand back,' he ordered. 'This thing is red hot and it's damned heavy.'

He hooked one end of the bar into the jagged, glowing seam and shoved. Grudgingly, the steel plate twisted away from the bulkhead and crashed to the deck with a heavy clang and spray of molten metal.

A hush fell over the dark compartment as Pitt took a flashlight and leaned carefully through the opening, staying clear of the superheated edges. He probed the beam into the bowels of the darkened cargo hold, sweeping it around in an 180 degree arc.

It seemed a long time before he straightened and faced the bizarrely clad, faceless figures pressing against him.

'Well?' Mendoza demanded anxiously.

Pitt answered with one word.

'Eureka!'

9

Four thousand miles and five hours ahead in a different time zone, the Soviet representative to the World Health Assembly worked late at his desk. There was nothing elaborate about his office in the Secretariat Building of the United Nations, the furnishings were cheap and spartan. Instead of the usual hanging photographs of Russian leaders living and dead, the only piece of wall decor was a small, amateurish watercolour of a house in the country.

The light blinked and a soft chime emitted from his private phone line. He stared at it suspiciously for a long moment before picking up the receiver.

'This is Lugovoy.'

'Who?'

'Aleksei Lugovoy.'

'Is Willie dere?' asked a voice, heavy with the New York City accent that always grated on Lugovoy's ears.

'There is no Willie here,' Lugovoy said brusquely. 'You must have the wrong number.' Then he abruptly hung up.

Lugovoy's face was expressionless, but a faint pallor was there that had been missing before. He flexed his fists, inhaled deeply and eyed the phone, waiting.

The light blinked and chimed again.

'Lugovoy.'

'Youse sure Willie ain't dere?'

'Willie ain't here!' he replied, mimicking the caller's accent. He slammed the receiver onto the cradle.

Lugovoy sat stock-still for almost thirty seconds, hands tightly clasped together on the desk, head lowered, eyes staring into space. Nervously, he rubbed a hand over his bald head and adjusted his hornrimmed glasses on a squat Slavic nose. Still lost in thought, he rose, dutifully turned out the lights and walked from the office.

He exited from the lift into the main lobby and strode past the stained glass panel by Marc Chagall, symbolising man's struggle for peace. He ignored it as he always had.

There were no cabs at the stand in front of the building so he hailed one on First Avenue. He gave the driver his destination and sat stiffly in the back seat, too tense to relax.

Lugovoy was not worried that he might be followed. He was a respected psychologist, admired for his work in mental health among the underdeveloped countries. His papers on thought processes and mind response were widely studied. During his six months in New York with the United Nations he had kept his nose clean. He indulged in no espionage work and held no direct ties with the undercover people of the KGB. He was discreetly told by a friend with the Embassy in Washington that the FBI had given him a low priority, and only performed an occasional, almost perfunctory, observation.

Lugovoy was not in the United States to steal secrets. His purpose went way beyond anything the American counterspy investigators ever dreamed. The phone call meant the plan conceived seven years ago had been put into motion.

The cab pulled to a stop at West and Liberty Streets in front of the Vista International Hotel. Lugovoy paid the driver and walked through the ornate lobby into the concourse outside. He paused and stared up at the awesome dimensions of the World Trade Centre. The two enormous towers seemed to drop from the sky, their sheer grandeur was overwhelming.

Lugovoy often wondered what he was doing here in this land of glass buildings, uncountable automobiles, people always rushing, restaurants and grocery stores in every block. It was not his kind of world.

He showed his identification to a guard standing by a private express lift and took it to the one hundredth floor. The doors parted and he entered the open lobby of the Bougainville Maritime Lines, Inc., whose offices covered the entire floor. His shoes sank into a thick white carpet. The walls were panelled in a gleaming hand-rubbed rosewood, and the room was richly decorated in oriental antiques. Curio cases containing exquisite ceramic horses stood in the corners while rare examples of what looked to Lugovoy like Japanese designed textiles hung from the ceiling.

An attractive woman with large, dark eyes, a delicate oval Asian face and amber smooth skin smiled as he approached. 'May I help you, sir?'

'My name is Lugovoy.'

'Yes, Mr Lugovoy,' she said, pronouncing his name correctly. 'Madame Bougainville is expecting you.'

57

She spoke softly into an intercom and a tall, raven-haired woman with Eurasion features appeared in a high arched doorway.

'If you will please follow me, Mr Lugovoy.'

Lugovoy was impressed. Like many Russians naïve in Western business methods, he wrongly assumed the office employees remained late for his benefit. He trailed the woman down a long corridor hung with paintings of cargo ships flying the Bougainville Maritime flag, their bows surging through turquoise seas. The guide knocked lightly on an arched door, opened it and stepped aside.

Lugovoy crossed the threshold and stiffened in astonishment. The room was vast with a mosaic floor in blue and gold floral patterns, and a massive conference table supported by ten carved dragons that seemed to stretch into infinity. But it was the lifesize terra-cotta warriors in armour and prancing horses standing in silent splendour under soft spotlights in alcoves that held him in awe. He instantly recognised them as the tomb guardians of China's first emperor, Ch'in Shih Huang Ti. The effect was dazzling. He marvelled that they had somehow slipped through the Chinese government's fingers into private hands.

'Please come forward and sit down, Mr Lugovoy.'

He was so taken back by the magnificence of the room that he'd failed to notice a frail, oriental woman sitting in a wheelchair. In front of her was an ebony chair with gold silk cushions, and a small table with a teapot and cups.

'Madame Bougainville,' he said, 'we meet at last.'

The little old matriarch of the Bougainville shipping dynasty was eighty-nine years old and weighed about the same number of pounds. Her glistening grey hair was pulled back from her temples in a bun. Her face was strangely unlined, yet her body looked ancient and frail. Her intense blue eyes absorbed Lugovoy and blazed with a ferocity that made him uncomfortable.

'You are prompt,' she said simply. Her voice was soft and clear without the usual hesitation of advanced age.

'I came as soon as I received the coded telephone call.'

'Are you prepared to conduct your brainwashing project?'

'Brainwashing is an ugly term. I prefer mind intervention.'

'Academic terminology is irrelevant,' she said indifferently.

'My staff has been assembled for months. With the proper facilities we can begin in two days.'

'You'll begin tomorrow morning.'

Lugovoy forced a calm expression. 'So soon?'

'I've been informed by my grandson that ideal conditions have turned in our favour. The transfer will take place tonight.'

Lugovoy instinctively looked at his watch. 'You don't give me much time.'

'The opportunity has to be snatched when it arrives,' she said firmly. 'I made a bargain with your government, and I am about to fulfil the first half of it. Everything depends on speed. You and your staff have ten days to finish your part of the project – '

'Ten days!' he gasped.

'Ten days,' she repeated. 'That is your deadline. Beyond then I will cast you adrift.'

A shiver ran up Lugovoy's spine. He didn't need a detailed picture. It was plain that if something went wrong, he and his people would conveniently vanish . . . probably in the ocean.

A quiet muffled the huge boardroom. Then Madame Bougainville leaned forward in the wheelchair.

'Would you like some tea?'

Lugovoy hated tea, but he nodded. 'Yes, thank you.'

'The finest blend of Chinese herbs. Costs over a hundred dollars a pound on the retail market.'

He took the offered cup and made a polite sip before he set it on the table. 'You've been informed, I assume, that my work is still in the research stage. My experiments have only proven successful eleven times out of fifteen. I cannot guarantee perfect results within a set time limit.'

'Smarter minds than yours have calculated how long White House advisers can be stalled.'

Lugovoy's eyebrows rose. 'My understanding was my subject is to be a minor American Congressman whose temporary disappearance would go unnoticed.'

'You were misled,' she explained matter-of-factly. 'Your General Secretary and President thought it best you did not know your subject's identity before we were ready.'

'If I was given time to study his personality traits, I could have been better prepared.'

'I shouldn't have to lecture on security requirements to a Russian,' she said, her eyes burning into him. 'Why do you think we've had no contact between us until tonight?'

Unsure of what to answer, Lugovoy took a long swallow of the tea. To his peasant taste it was like drinking watered down perfume.

'I must know who my subject is,' he said finally, mustering his courage and returning her stare.

Her answer literally burst like a bomb in the cavernous room, reverberated in Lugovoy's brain and left him stunned. He felt as though he'd been thrown into a depthless pit with no hope of escape.

10

After years of buffeting by storms at sea, the drums containing the nerve agent had broken the chains holding them to wooden cradles and now they lay scattered about the deck of the cargo hold. The one ton, standard shipping containers, as approved by the Department of Transportation, measured exactly 81½ inches in length by 30½ inches in diameter, concave ends, silver in colour. Neatly stencilled on the sides in green paint were the Army code letters GS.

'I make the count twenty drums,' said Pitt.

'That tallies with the inventory of the missing shipment,' Mendoza said, the relief audible in her voice.

They stood in the hold's depths, now brightly lit by floodlights connected to a portable generator from the *Catawaba*. Nearly a foot of water flooded the deck, and the sloshing sounds as they waded between the deadly containers echoed off the rusting sides of the hold.

An EPA chemist made a violent pointing motion with his gloved hand. 'Here's the drum responsible for the leak!' he said excitedly. 'The valve is broken from its threads.'

'Satisfied, Mendoza?' Pitt asked her.

'You bet your sweet ass,' she exclaimed happily. Pitt moved toward her until their faceplates were almost touching. 'Have you given any thought to my reward?'

'Reward?'

'Our bargain,' he said, trying to sound earnest. 'I found your nerve agent thirty-six hours ahead of schedule.'

'You're not going to hold me to a silly proposition?'

'I'd be foolish not to.'

She was glad he couldn't see her face redden under the helmet. They were on an open radio frequency and every man in the room could hear what they were saying.

'You pick strange places to make a date.'

'What I thought,' Pitt continued, 'was dinner in Anchorage, cocktails chilled by glacial ice, smoked salmon, elk remington, baked Alaska. After that – '

'That's enough,' she said, her embarrassment growing.

'Are you a party girl?'

'Only when the occasion demands,' she replied, coming back on even keel. 'And this is definitely not the occasion.'

He threw up his arms and then let them drop dejectedly. 'A sad day for Pitt, a lucky day for NUMA.'

'Why NUMA?'

'The contamination is on dry land. No need for an underwater salvage job. My crew and I can pack up and head for home.'

Her helmet nodded imperceptibly. 'A neat sidestep, Mr Pitt, dropping the problem straight into the Army's lap.'

'Do they know?' he asked seriously.

'Alaskan Command was alerted seconds after you reported discovering the *Pilottown*. A chemical warfare disposal team is on their way from the mainland to remove the agent.'

'The world applauds efficiency.'

'It's not important to you, is it?'

'Of course, it's important,' said Pitt. 'But for me it's finished, and until there's another spill and more dead bodies, who the hell cares? Tomorrow this stuff will be at the bottom of a deep pit and the sea will mend itself within a month.

'Talk about a hardnosed cynic.'

'Say yes.'

Thrust, parry, then lunge. He caught her on an exposed flank. She felt trapped, impaled, and was annoyed with herself for enjoying it. She answered before she could form a negative thought.

'Yes.'

The men in the hold stopped their work amid enough death to murder half the earth's population and clapped muted gloves together, cheering and whistling into their transmitters. She suddenly realised that her stock shot up on the Dow Jones. Men admired a woman who could ramrod a dirty job and not be a bitch.

It was as simple as that. Abruptly, her embarrassment fled.

Later, Dover found Pitt thoughtfully studying a small open hatchway, shining his flashlight inside. The glow diminished into the darkness beyond, reflecting in dull sparkles on the oil-slicked water rippling from the cargo hold.

'Got something in mind?' Dover asked.

'Thought I'd do a little exploring,' Pitt answered.

'You won't get far in there.'

'Where does it lead?'

'Into the shaft tunnel, but it's flooded nearly to the roof. You'd need air tanks to get through.'

Pitt swung his light up the forward bulkhead until it spotlighted a small hatch at the top of a ladder. 'How about that one?'

'Should open into cargo hold four.'

Pitt merely nodded and began scaling the rusty rungs of the ladder, closely followed by Dover. He muscled the dog latches securing the hatch, swung it open and they clambered down into the next hold. A quick traverse of their lights told them it was bone empty.

'The ship must have been travelling in ballast,' Pitt speculated out loud.

'It would appear so,' said Dover.

'Now where?'

'Up one more ladder to the alleyway that runs between the fresh water tanks into the ship's storerooms.'

Slowly they made their way through the bowels of the *Pilottown*, feeling like gravediggers probing a cemetery at midnight. Around every corner they half expected to find the skeletal bones of a ghostly crew. But there were no bones. The crew's living quarters should have looked like an anniversary sale at Macy's. Clothes, personal belongings, everything that should have been strewn about by a crew hastily abandoning a ship. Instead, the pitch black interior of the *Pilottown* looked like the tunnels and chambers of a desert cavern. All that was missing were the bats.

The food lockers were bare. No dishes or cups lined the shelves of the crew mess. Even the toilets lacked paper. Fire extinguishers, door latches, furnishings, anything that could be unbolted or was of the slightest value was gone.

'Mighty peculiar,' muttered Dover.

'My thoughts too,' said Pitt. 'She's been systematically stripped.'

'Scavengers must have boarded and carried away everything during the years she was adrift.'

'Scavengers leave a mess,' Pitt disagreed. 'Whoever was behind this fleece job had a fetish for neatness.'

It was an eerie trip. Their shadows flitted on the dark walls of the alleyways, and on the silent and deserted machinery. Pitt felt a longing to see the sky again.

'Incredible,' mumbled Dover, still awed by what they found, or rather not found. 'They even removed all the valves and gauges.'

'If I was a gambling man,' said Pitt thoughtfully, 'I'd bet we've stumbled on an insurance scam.'

'Wouldn't be the first ship that was posted missing for a Lloyds of London payday,' Dover said consideringly.

'You told me the crew claimed they abandoned the *Pilottown* in a storm. They abandoned her all right, but they left nothing but a barren, worthless shell.'

'Easy enough to check out,' said Dover. 'Two ways to scuttle a ship at sea. Open the seacocks and let her flood, or blow out the bottom with explosive charges.'

'How would you do it?'

'Flooding through the seacocks could take twenty-four hours or more. Time enough for a passing ship to appear and investigate. I opt for the charges. Quick and dirty; put her on the seafloor in a matter of minutes.'

'Something must have prevented the explosives from detonating.'

'It's only a theory.'

'Next question,' Pitt persisted. 'Where would you lay them?'

'Cargo holds, engine room, most any place against the hull plates so long as it was below the waterline.'

'No sign of charges in the after holds,' said Pitt. 'That leaves the engine room and the forward cargo holds.'

'We've come this far,' Dover said woodenly. 'We might as well finish the job.'

'Faster if we split up. I'll search the engine room. You know your way around the ship better than I do . . .'

'The forward cargo holds it is,' Dover said, anticipating him.

The big Coast Guardsman started up a companionway, whistling the Notre Dame fight song under his breath. His bear-like gait and hulking build silhouetted by the wavering flashlight in his hand grew smaller and finally faded. A few moments later the steel bulkheads cut out his radio transmission and his whistling died too.

Pitt began probing around the maze of steam pipes leading from the old, obsolete steam reciprocating engines and boilers. The walkway gratings over the machinery were nearly eaten through with rust, and he trod lightly. The engine room seemed to come alive in his imagination – creaks and moans, murmurings drifting out of the ventilators, whispering sounds.

He found a pair of seacocks. Their handwheels were frozen in the closed position.

So much for the seacock theory, he thought.

An icy chill crept up the back of Pitt's neck and spread throughout his body, and he realised the batteries operating the heater in his suit were nearly drained. He switched off the light for a moment. The pure blackness nearly smothered him. He flicked it on again and quickly swept the beam around as if expecting to see a spectre of the crew reaching out for him. Only there were no spectres, there was nothing except the dank resignation of metal walls, the tired and worn machinery. He could have sworn he felt the grating shudder as if the engines, looming above him in shadowy bulkiness were starting up again.

Pitt shook his head to clear his imagination of primitive fears, and methodically began searching the sides of the hull, crawling between pumps and asbestos covered pipes that led into the darkness and nowhere. He fell down a ladder into six feet of greasy water. He

63

struggled back up, out of the seeming clutches of the dead and evil and ugly bilge, his suit now black with oil. Out of breath, he hung there a minute, making a conscious effort to relax.

It was then he noticed an object dimly outlined in the farthest reach of the light beam. A corroded aluminium cannister about the size of a five gallon petron can was wired to a beam welded on the inner hull plates. Pitt had set explosives on marine salvage projects and he quickly recognised the detonator unit attached to the bottom of the cannister. An electrical wire trailed upward through the grating to the deck above.

Sweat was pouring from his body but he was shivering from the cold. He left the explosive charge where he found it and climbed back up the ladder, then he began inspecting the engines and boilers. There were no markings anywhere, no manufacturers' names, no inspectors' stamped dates. Wherever there had been a metal ID tag, it was removed. Wherever there had been letters or numbers stamped into the metal, they were filed away. After probing endless nooks and crannies around the machinery, he got lucky when he felt a small protrusion through his gloved hand. It was a small metal plate partially hidden by grease under one of the boilers. He rubbed away the grime and aimed the light on the indented surface. It read:

Pressure   220 psi.
Temperature   450°F.
Heating Surface   5,017 sq. ft.
Manufactured by the
Alhambra Iron and Boiler Company
Charleston, South Carolina
Ser. No. 38874

Pitt memorised the serial number and then made his way back to where he started. He wearily sank to the deck and tried to rest while suffering from the cold.

Dover returned in a little under an hour carrying an explosive cannister under one arm as indifferently as if it was a jumbo can of peaches. Cursing fluently and often as he slipped on the oily deck, he stopped and sat down heavily next to Pitt.

'There's four more between here and the fore peak,' Dover said tiredly.

'I found another one about forty feet aft,' Pitt replied.

'Wonder why they didn't go off.'

'The timer must have screwed up.'

'Timer?'

'The crew needed time to jump ship before the bottom was blown out. Trace the wires leading from the cannisters and you'll find they all meet at a timing device hidden somewhere on the deck above. When the crew realised something was wrong, it must have been too late to reboard the ship.'

'Or they were too scared it would go up in their faces.'

'There's that,' Pitt agreed.

'So the old *Pilottown* began her legendary drift. A deserted ship in an empty sea.'

'How is a ship officially identified?'

'What's on your mind?'

'Just curious.'

Dover accepted that and stared up at the shadows of the engines. 'Well . . . ID can be found most anywhere. Lifejackets, lifeboats, the name on the stern. On the bows the name is often bead welded, outlining the painted letters. Then you have the builder's plates, one on the exterior of the superstructure, one in the engine room. And, oh yeah, the ship's official number is burned into a beam around the outer base of the hatch covers.'

'I'll wager a month's pay that if you could dig the ship from under the mountain you'd find the hatch number burned off and the builder's plate gone.'

'That leaves one in the engine room.'

'Missing too, I checked, along with all the manufacturer's markings.'

'Sounds devious,' said Dover quietly.

'You're damn right,' Pitt replied abruptly. 'There's more to the *Pilottown* than a marine insurance ripoff.'

'I'm in no mood to solve mysteries,' said Dover, rising awkwardly to his feet. 'I'm freezing, half starved and tired as hell. I vote we head back.'

Pitt looked and saw Dover was still clutching the cannister of explosives. 'Bringing that along?'

'Evidence.'

'Don't drop it,' Pitt said with a sarcastic edge in his voice.

They climbed from the engine room and hurried through the ship's storerooms, anxious to escape the damp blackness and touch daylight again. Suddenly Pitt stopped in his tracks. Dover, walking head down, bumped into him.

'Why'd you stop?'

'You feel it?'

Before Dover could answer, the deck beneath their feet trembled and the bulkheads creaked ominously. What sounded like the muffled roar of a distant explosion rumbled closer and closer, quickly followed by a tremendous shock wave. The *Pilottown* shuddered under the impact and her welded seams screeched as they split under enormous pressure. The shock flung the two men violently against the steel walls. Pitt managed to remain on his feet, but Dover, unbalanced by his heavy burden, crashed like a tree to the deck, embracing the cannister with his arms and cushioning its fall with his body. A grunt of pain passed his lips as he dislocated his shoulder and wrenched a knee. He dazedly struggled to a sitting position and looked up at Pitt.

'What in God's name was that?' he gasped.

'Augustine Volcano,' Pitt said, almost clinically. 'It must have erupted.'

'Jesus, what next?'

Pitt helped the big man to his feet. He could feel Dover's arm tense through the heavy suit. 'You hurt?'

'A little bent, but I don't think anything's broken.'

'Can you make a run for it?'

'I'm all right,' Dover lied through clenched teeth. 'What about the evidence?'

'Forget it,' Pitt said urgently, 'Let's get the hell out of here.'

Without another word they took off through the storerooms and into the narrow alleyways between the fresh water tanks. Pitt slung his arm around Dover's waist and half dragged, half carried him through the darkness.

Pitt thought the alleyway would never end. His breath began to come in gasps and his heart pounded against his ribs. He struggled to stay on his feet as the old *Pilottown* shook and swayed from the earth's tremors. They reached cargo hold number four and scrambled down the ladder. He lost his grip and Dover fell to the deck. The precious seconds lost manhandling Dover over to the opposite ladder seemed like hours.

Pitt had barely set foot on the scaly rungs when there was a crack like thunder and something fell past him and struck the deck. He threw the light beam up. At that instant the hatch cover disintegrated and tons of rock and debris cascaded into the hold.

'Climb, damn it, climb!' he yelled at Dover. His chest heaved and the blood roared in his ears. With an inner strength he thrust Dover's two hundred and twenty pounds up the ladder.

Suddenly a voice shouted. The light showed a figure leaning through the upper hatch, his hands grabbing Dover and pulling him through into the aft hold. Pitt instinctively knew it was Giordino. The burly little Italian had a keen sense of arriving at the right place at the right moment.

Then Pitt was at the top and crawling into the hold containing the nerve agent containers. The hatch cover was still intact because the sloping ground above was not as dense near the stern section. When he reached the bottom of the ladder, willing hands were helping Dover towards the afterdeck house and temporary safety. Giordino gripped Pitt's arm.

'We took casualities during the 'quake,' he said grimly.

'How bad?' asked Pitt.

'Four injured, mostly broken bones and one dead.'

Giordino hesitated and Pitt knew.

'Mendoza?'

'One of the drums crushed her legs,' Giordino explained, his voice more solemn than Pitt had ever known it. 'She suffered a compound fracture. A bone splinter pierced her suit . . .' His words died.

'The nerve agent leaked onto her skin,' Pitt finished, a sense of helplessness and shock flooding through him.

Giordino nodded. 'We carried her outside.'

Pitt found Julie Mendoza lying on the *Pilottown*'s stern deck. Overhead a great cloud of volcanic ash rose into a blue sky and fortuitously drifted to the north, away from the ship.

Mendoza lay along and off to one side. The uninjured EPA people were attending to the living. Only the young officer from the *Catawaba* stood beside her, and his entire body was arching convulsively as he was violently sick into his air filter.

Someone had removed her helmet. Her hair flared out on the rusty deck and glinted orange under the setting sun. Pitt would never forget afterwards how her face looked. He would carry the memory with him to the grave. Her eyes were open and staring into nothingness, the jaw jutting and rigid in what must have been indescribable agony. The blood was hardening as it dried in sun tinted copper rivers that had gushed from her gaping mouth, nose and ears. It had even seeped from around the edges of her eyes. What little facial skin still showed was already turning a bluish black.

Pitt's only emotion was cold rage. It swelled up inside him as he knelt down beside her and struck the deck repeatedly with his fist.

'It won't end here,' he snarled bitterly. 'I won't let it end here.'

11

Oscar Lucas stared moodily at his desk top. Everything depressed him: the acid tasting coffee in a cold cup, his cheaply furnished government office, the long hours on his job. For the first time since he became Special Agent in Charge of the Presidential Detail, he found himself longing for retirement, crosscountry skiing in Colorado, building a mountain retreat with his own hands.

He shook his head to clear the fantasies, sipped at a diet soft drink and studied the plans of the Presidential yacht for perhaps the tenth time.

Built in 1919 for a wealthy Philadelphia businessman, the *Eagle* was purchased by the Department of Commerce in 1921 for presidential use. From that point in time thirteen presidents had paced her decks. Herbert Hoover tossed medicine balls while on board, Roosevelt mixed martinis and discussed war strategy with Winston Churchill, Harry Truman played poker and the piano, John Kennedy celebrated his birthdays, Lyndon Johnson entertained the Royal Family, and Richard Nixon hosted Leonid Brezhnev.

Designed with old straight up and down bows, the mahogany-trimmed yacht displaced 100 tons and measured 110 feet in length with a beam of twenty feet. Her draft was five feet and she could slice the water at fourteen knots.

The *Eagle* was originally constructed with five master staterooms, four baths and a large glass-enclosed deck house, used as a combination dining and living room. A crew of thirteen Coast Guardsmen manned the yacht during a cruise, their quarters and galley located forward.

Lucas went through the files on the crew, rechecking their personal backgrounds, family history, personality traits, the results of psychological interviews. He could find nothing that merited any suspicion.

He sat back and yawned. His watch read 9:20 p.m. The *Eagle* had tied up at Mount Vernon three hours ago. The President was a night owl and a late riser. He would keep his guests, Lucas was certain, sitting around the deckhouse, thrashing out government affairs with little thought given to sleep.

He twisted sideways and looked out the window. A falling mist was a welcome sight. The reduced visibility eliminated the chances of a sniper, the greatest danger to a president's life. Lucas persuaded himself that he was chasing ghosts. Every detail that could be covered was covered.

If there was a threat, its source and method eluded him.

The mist had not yet reached Mount Vernon. The summer night still sparkled clear and the lights from nearby streets and farms danced on the water. The river at this stretch widened to slightly over a mile, with trees and shrubs lining its sweeping banks. A hundred yards from the shoreline, a Coast Guard cutter stood at anchor, her bow pointing upriver, radar antenna in constant rotation.

The President was sitting in a lounge chair on the foredeck, earnestly promoting his Eastern Europe aid programme to Marcus Larimer and Alan Moran. Suddenly, he came to his feet and stepped to the railing, his head tilted, listening. A small herd of cows were mooing in a nearby pasture. He became momentarily absorbed, the problems of the nation vanished and a country boy surfaced. After several seconds, he turned and sat down again.

'Sorry for the interruption,' he said with a broad smile. 'For a minute there, I was tempted to find a bucket and squeeze us some fresh milk for breakfast.'

'The news media would have a field day with a picture of you milking a cow in the dead of night,' Larimer laughed.

'Better yet,' said Moran sarcastically, 'you could sell the milk to the Russians for a fat profit.'

'Not as farfetched as it sounds,' said Margolin, who was sitting off to one side. 'Milk and butter have all but disappeared from Moscow state food stores.'

'It's a fact, Mr President,' said Larimer seriously. 'The average Russian is only two hundred calories a day from a starvation diet. The Poles and Hungarians are even worse off. Why hell, our pigs eat better than they do.'

'Exactly my point,' said the President in a fervent voice. 'We cannot turn our backs on starving women and children simply because they live under Communist domination. Their plight makes my aid plan all the more important to echo the humanitarian generosity of the American people. Think of the benefits such a policy will bring in good will from the Third World countries. Think of how such an act could inspire future generations. The potential rewards are incalculable.'

'I beg to differ,' said Moran, coldly, brushing off the President's words. 'In my mind what you propose is foolish, a sucker play. The billions of dollars they spend annually propping up their satellite countries have nearly wiped out their financial resources. I'll take bets the money they save by your proposed bail-out plan would go directly into their military budget.'

'Perhaps, but if their troubles continue unchecked the Soviets will become more dangerous to the US,' the President argued. 'Historically, nations with deep economic problems have lashed out in foreign adventures.'

'Like grabbing control of the Persian Gulf oil?' said Larimer.

'A Gulf takeover is the threat they constantly dangle. But they know damned well the Western nations would intervene with force to keep the life blood of their economies flowing. No, Marcus, their sights are set on a far easier target. One that would open up their complete dominance of the Mediterranean.'

Larimer's eyebrows rose. 'Turkey?'

'Precisely,' the President answered bluntly.

'But Turkey is a member of NATO,' Moran protested.

'Yes, but would France go to war over Turkey? Would England or West Germany? Better yet, ask yourselves if we would send American boys to die there any more than we would in Afghanistan? The truth is Turkey has few natural resources worth fighting over. Soviet armour could sweep across the country to the Bosporus in a few weeks, and the West would only protest with words.'

'You're talking remote possibilities,' said Moran, 'not high probabilities.'

'I agree,' said Larimer. 'In my opinion further Soviet expansion on the face of their faltering system is extremely remote.'

The President raised a hand to protest. 'But this is far different, Marcus. Any internal upheaval in Russia is certain to spill over her borders, particularly into Western Europe.'

'I'm not an isolationist, Mr President. God knows my record in the Senate shows otherwise. But I for one am getting damned sick and tired of the United States being constantly twisted in the wind by the whims of the Europeans. We've left more than our share of dead in their soil from two wars. I say if the Russians want to eat the rest of Europe, then let them choke on it, and good riddance.'

Larimer sat back satisfied. He had got the words off his chest that he didn't dare utter in public. Though the President fervently disagreed, he couldn't help wondering how many grass roots Americans shared the same thoughts.

'Let's be realistic,' he said quietly. 'You know and I know we cannot desert our allies.'

'Then what about our constituents?' Moran jumped back in. 'What do you call it when you take their tax dollars from a budget overburdened with deficit spending and use it to feed and support our enemies?'

'I call it the humane thing to do,' the President replied wearily. He realised he was fighting a no-win war.

'Sorry, Mr President,' Larimer said, rising to his feet. 'But I cannot, with a clear conscience, support your Eastern Bloc aid plan. Now if you'll excuse me, I think I'll hit the sack.'

'Me too,' Moran said yawning. 'I can hardly keep my eyes open.'

'Are you settled in all right?' asked the President.

'Yes, thank you,' replied Moran.

'If I haven't been seasick by now,' said Larimer with a half grin, 'I should keep my supper till morning.'

They bid their goodnights and disappeared together down the

stairs to their staterooms. As soon as they were out of earshot, the President turned to Margolin.

'What do you think, Vince?'

'To be perfectly honest, sir, I think you're pissing up a rope.'

'You're saying it's hopeless?'

'Let's look at another side to this,' Margolin began. 'Your plan calls for buying surplus grain and other agricultural products to give to the Communist world for prices less than our farmers could receive on the export market. Yet thanks to poor weather conditions, during the last two years and the inflationary spiral in diesel fuel costs, farms are going bankrupt at the highest rate since 1934. If you persist in handing out aid money, I respectfully suggest you do it here . . . not Russia.'

'Charity begins at home. Is that it?'

'What better place? Also, you must consider the fact that you're rapidly losing party support while getting murdered in the polls.'

The President shook his head. 'I can't remain mute while millions of men, women and children die of starvation.'

'A noble stand, but hardly practical.'

The President's features became shrouded with sadness. 'Don't you see,' he said staring out over the dark waters of the river, 'by proving that Marxism has failed no guerilla movement anywhere in the world will be justified in using it as a battlecry for revolution.'

'Which brings us to the final argument,' said Margolin. 'The Russians don't want our help. As you know, I've met with Foreign Minister Gromyko. He told me in no uncertain terms that if Congress should pass your aid programme, any food shipments will be stopped at the borders.'

'Still, we must try.'

Margolin sighed softly to himself. Any argument was a waste of time. The President could not be moved.

'If you're tired,' said the President, 'please don't hesitate to go to bed. You don't have to stay awake just to keep me company.'

'I'm not really in the mood for sleep.'

'How about another brandy then?'

'Sounds good.'

The President pressed a call button beside his chair and a figure in the white coat of a steward appeared on deck.

'Yes, Mr President? What is your pleasure?'

'Please bring the Vice President and myself another brandy.'

'Yes, sir.'

The steward turned to bring the order, but the President held up his hand.

'One moment.'

71

'Sir?'

'You're not Jack Klosner, the regular steward.'

'No, Mr President. I'm Seaman First Class Tong. Seaman Klosner was relieved at ten o'clock. I'm on duty until tomorrow morning.'

The President was one of the few politicians whose ego was attuned to people. He spoke as graciously to an eight year old boy as he did to an eighty year old woman. He genuinely enjoyed drawing strangers out, calling them by their Christian names as if he'd known them for years.

'Your family Chinese, Tong?'

'No sir, Korean. They immigrated to America in nineteen fifty-two.'

'Why did you join the Coast Guard?'

'A love of the sea, I guess.'

'Do you enjoy catering to old bureaucrats like me?'

Seaman Tong hesitated, obviously uneasy. 'Well . . . if I had my choice, I'd rather be serving on an icebreaker.'

'I'm not sure I like coming in second to an icebreaker,' the President laughed good-naturedly. 'Remind me in the morning to put in a word to Commandant Collins for a transfer. We're old friends.'

'Thank you, Mr President,' Seaman Tong mumbled excitedly. 'I'll get your brandies right away.'

Just before Tong turned away he flashed a wide smile that revealed a large gap in the middle of his upper teeth.

12

A heavy fog crept over the *Eagle*, smothering her hull in damp, eerie stillness. Gradually the red warning lights of a radio antenna on the opposite shore blurred and disappeared. Somewhere overhead a gull shrieked, but it was a muted, ghostly sound; impossible to tell where it came from. The teak decks soon bled moisture and took on a dull sheen under the mist-veiled floodlights standing above the pilings of the old creaking pier anchored to the bank.

A small army of Secret Service agents, stationed at strategic posts around the landscaped slope that gently rose towards George Washington's elegant, colonial home, guarded the nearly invisible yacht. Voice contact was kept by shortwave, miniature radios. So that both hands were free at all times, they wore earpiece receivers, battery units on their belts and tiny microphones on their wrists.

Every hour the agents changed posts, moving on to their next prescheduled security area while their shift leader wandered the grounds, checking the efficiency of the surveillance network.

In a motorhome parked in the drive beside the old manor house, agent Blackowl sat scanning a row of television monitors. Another agent manned the communications equipment, while a third eye-balled a series of warning lights wired to an intricate system of alarms spaced around the yacht.

'You'd think the National Weather Service could give an accurate report ten miles from its forecast office,' Blackowl groused as he sipped his fourth coffee of the night. 'They said "light mist". If this is light mist, I'd like to know what in hell they call fog so thick you can dish it with a spoon.'

The agent in charge of radio communications turned and lifted the earphones on his headset. 'The chase boat says they can't see beyond their bow. They request permission to tie up and come ashore.'

'Can't say as I blame them,' said Blackowl. 'Tell them affirmative.' He stood up and massaged the back of his neck. Then he patted the communications agent on the shoulder. 'I'll take over the radio. You get some sleep.'

'As advance agent you should be bedded down yourself.'

'I'm not tired. Besides, I can't see crap on the monitors anyway.'

The agent looked up at a large digital clock on the wall. 'O-one fifty hours. Ten minutes till the next post change.'

Blackowl nodded and slid into the vacated chair. He had no sooner settled the earphones on his head when a call came from the Coast Guard cutter anchored near the yacht.

'Control, this is River Watch.'

'This is Control,' Blackowl replied, recognising the voice of the cutter's commander.

'We're experiencing a problem with our scanning equipment.'

'What kind of problem?'

'A high energy signal on the same frequency as our radar is fouling reception.'

A look of concern crossed Blackowl's face. 'Could someone be jamming you?'

'I don't think so. It looks like crosstraffic. The signal comes and goes as if messages are being transmitted. I suspect that some neighbourhood radio freak has plugged onto our frequency by accident.'

'Do you read any contacts?'

'Boat traffic this time of night is nil,' answered the commander. 'The only blip we've seen on the oscilloscope in the last two hours was from a city sanitation tug pushing trash barges out to sea.'

'What time did it go by?'

73

'Didn't. The blip merged with the riverbank a few hundred yards upstream. The tug's skipper probably tied up to wait out the fog.'

'Okay, River Watch, keep me assessed of your radar problem.'

'Will do, Control. River Watch out.'

Blackowl sat back and mentally calculated the potential hazards. With river traffic at a standstill, there was little danger of another ship colliding with the *Eagle*. The Coast Guard cutter's radar, though operating intermittently, *was* operating. And any assault from the river side was ruled out because the absence of visibility made it next to impossible to home in on the yacht. The fog, it seemed was a blessing in disguise.

Blackowl glanced up at the clock. It read one minute before the post change. He quickly reread the security plan that listed the names of the agents, the areas they were scheduled to patrol and the times. He noted that agent Lyle Brock was due to stand post number seven, the yacht itself, while agent Karl Polaski was slated for post number six, which was the pier.

He pressed the transmit button and spoke into the tiny microphone attached to his headset. 'Attention all stations. Time, O-two hundred hours. Move to your next post. Repeat, move to the next post on your schedule.' Then he changed frequencies and uttered the codename of the shift leader. 'Cutty Sark, this is Control.'

A veteran of fifteen years in the service, agent Ed McGrath answered almost immediately. 'Cutty Sark here.'

'Tell posts numbers six and seven to keep a sharp watch on the river.'

'They won't see much in this slop.'

'How bad is it around the dock area?'

'Let's just say you should have issued us white canes with red tips.'

'Do the best you can,' said Blackowl.

'Where have I heard that line before?' McGrath said in a droll tone.

A light blinked and Blackowl cut transmission to McGrath and answered the incoming call.

'Control.'

'This is River Watch, Control. Whoever is screwing up our radar signals seems to be transmitting continuously now.'

'You read nothing?' asked Blackowl.

'The geographic display on the oscilloscope is forty percent blanked out. Instead of blips we receive a large wedge shape.'

'Okay, River Watch, let me pass the word to the Special Agent in Charge. Maybe he can track the interference and stop any further transmission.'

Before he appraised Oscar Lucas at the White House of the radar problem, Blackowl turned and gazed curiously at the television monitors. They reflected no discernible image, only vague shadows wavering in wraith-like undulation.

Agent Karl Polaski refixed the moulded earplug of his Motorola HT–220 radio receiver and wiped the dampness from a Bismarck moustache. Forty minutes into his watch on the pier, he felt damp and downright miserable. He wiped the moisture from his face and thought it odd that it felt oily.

His eyes wandered to the overhead floodlights. They gave out a dim yellowish halo, but the edges had a prismatic effect and displayed the colours of the rainbow. From where he stood, about mid-point on the thirty foot dock, the *Eagle* was completely hidden by the oppressive mist. Not even her deck or mast lights were visible.

Polaski walked over the weatherworn boards, occasionally stopping and listening. But all he heard was the gentle lapping of the water around the pilings and the soft hum of the yacht's generators. He was only a few steps from the end of the pier when the *Eagle* finally materialised from the grey tentacles of the fog.

He called softly to agent Lyle Brock, who was manning post seven on board the boat. 'Hey, Lyle. Can you hear me?'

A voice replied slightly above a whisper. 'What do you want?'

'How about a cup of coffee from the galley?'

'The next post change is in twenty minutes. You can get a cup when you come on board and take my place.'

'I can't wait twenty minutes,' Polaski protested mildly. 'I'm already soaked to the bones.'

'Tough, you'll have to suffer.'

Polaski knew that Brock couldn't leave the decks under any circumstances, but he goaded the other agent good-naturedly. 'Wait till you want a favour from me.'

'Speaking of favours, I forgot where I go from here.'

Polaski gave a quizzical look to the figure in the shadows on the *Eagle*'s deck. 'Look at your diagram, numb brain.'

'It got soggy and I can't read it.'

'Post eight is fifty yards down the bank.'

'Thanks.'

'If you want to know where post nine is it'll cost you a cup of coffee,' Polaski said grinning.

'Screw you. I remember that one.'

Later, during the next post exchange, the agents merely waved as they passed each other, two indistinct forms in the mist.

*

Ed McGrath could never recall seeing fog this thick. He sniffed the air trying to identify the strange aroma that hung everywhere, and finally wrote it off as a common oily smell. Somewhere in the mist he heard a dog bark. He paused, cocking one ear. It was not the baying of a hound in chase or the frightened yelps of a mutt, but the sharp yap of a dog alert to an unfamiliar presence. Not too far away, judging by the volume. Seventy-five, maybe a hundred yards beyond the security perimeter, McGrath estimated.

A potential assassin would have to be sick or brain damaged or both, he thought, to stumble blindly around a strange countryside in weather such as this. Already, McGrath had tripped and fallen down, walked into an unseen branch and scratched his cheek, found himself lost three times, and almost got himself shot when he accidentally walked onto a guard post before he could radio his approach.

The barking stopped abruptly, and McGrath figured a cat or some wild animal had set the dog off. He reached a familiar bench beside a fork in a gravelled path and made his way towards the riverbank below the yacht. He spoke into his lapel microphone.

'Post eight, coming up on you.'

There was no reply.

McGrath stopped in his tracks. 'Brock, this is McGrath, coming up on you.'

Still nothing.

'Brock, do you read me?'

Post number eight was oddly quiet and McGrath began to feel uneasy. Moving very slowly, one step at a time, he cautiously closed on the guard area. He called faintly through the mist, his voice weirdly magnified by the heavy dampness. Silence was his only reply.

'Control, this is Cutty Sark.'

'Go ahead, Cutty Sark,' came back Blackowl's tired voice.

'We're missing a man on post eight.'

Blackowl's tone sharpened considerably. 'No sign of him?'

'None.'

'Check the boat,' Blackowl said without hesitation. 'I'll meet you there after I inform headquarters.'

McGrath signed off and hurried along the bank to the dock. 'Post six, coming up on you.'

'Aiken, post six, come ahead.'

He groped his way onto the dock and found agent John Aiken's hulking shape under a floodlight. 'Have you seen Brock?'

'You kidding?' answered Aiken. 'I haven't seen shit since the fog hit.'

McGrath dogtrotted along the dock, repeating the call-warning

76

process. By the time he reached the *Eagle*, Polaski had come around from the opposite deck to meet him.

'I'm missing Brock,' he said tersely.

Polaski shrugged. 'Last I saw of him was about half an hour ago when we changed posts.'

'Okay, stay here by the dockside. I'm going to take a look below decks. And keep an eye peeled for Blackowl. He's on his way down from control.'

When Blackowl lurched out into the damp morning, the fog was thinning and he could see the faint glimmer of stars through the fading overcast above. He steered his way from post to post, breaking into a run along the pathway to the pier as the visibility improved. Fear smouldered in his stomach, a dread that something was terribly wrong. Agents did not desert their posts without warning, without reason.

When at last he leaped aboard the yacht, the fog had disappeared as if by magic. The ruby lights of the radio antenna across the river sparkled in the newly cleared air. He brushed by Polaski and found McGrath sitting alone in the deck house, staring trance-like into nothingness.

Blackowl froze.

McGrath's face was as pale as a white plaster death mask. He stared with such horror in his eyes that Blackowl immediately feared the worst.

'The President?' he demanded.

McGrath looked at him dully, his mouth moving but no words coming out.

'For Christ's sake, is the President safe?'

'Gone,' McGrath finally muttered.

'What are you talking about?'

'The President, the Vice President, the crew, everybody, they're all gone.'

'You're talking crazy!' Blackowl snapped.

'True . . . it's true,' McGrath said lifelessly. 'See for yourself.'

Blackowl tore down the steps of the nearest companionway and ran to the President's stateroom. He threw open the door without knocking. It was deserted. The bed was still neatly made and there were no clothes in the closet, no toilet articles in the bathroom. His heart felt as if it was being squeezed between two blocks of ice.

As though in a nightmare he rushed from stateroom to stateroom. Everywhere it was the same, even the crew's quarters lay in undisturbed emptiness.

The horror was real.

Everyone on the yacht had vanished as though they had never been born.

77

PART II

THE EAGLE

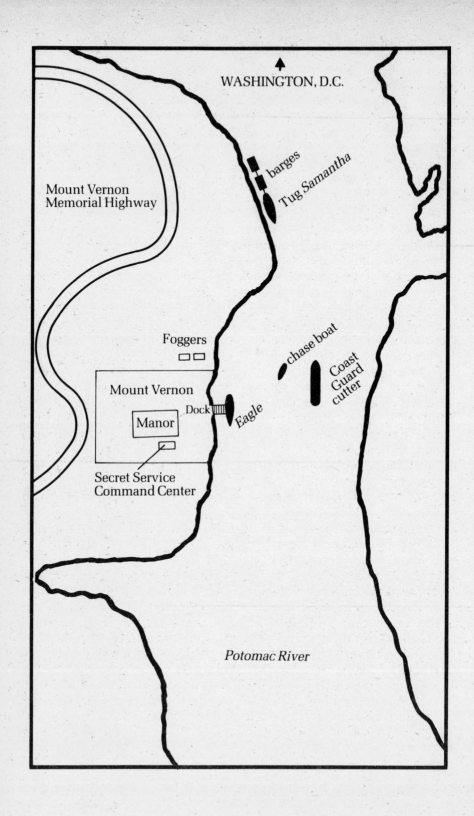

13

Unlike actors in motion pictures who take forever to wake up and answer a ringing telephone in bed, Ben Greenwald, Director of the Secret Service, came instantly alert and snatched the receiver before the second ring.

'Greenwald.'

'Greetings,' said the familiar voice of Oscar Lucas. 'Sorry to wake you, but I knew you were anxious to hear the score of the soccer game.'

Greenwald tensed. Any Secret Service communication opening with the word 'greetings' meant the beginning of an urgent, top secret report on a critical or grave situation. The sentence that followed was meaningless; a caution in case the telephone line might not be secure. A real possibility since the Kissinger State Department had allowed the Russians to build their new embassy on a rise overlooking the city, vastly increasing their telephone eavesdropping capacity.

'Okay,' said Greenwald, trying to sound conversational. 'Who won?'

'You lost your bet.'

'Bet' was another key word indicating that the next statement was coming in coded doubletalk.

'Jasper College, one,' Lucas continued, 'Drinkwater Tech, nothing. Three of the Jasper players were sidelined for injuries.'

The dire news exploded in Greenwald's ears. Jasper College was the code for a presidental abduction. The reference to the sidelined players meant the next three men in succession were taken too. It was a code that in Greenwald's wildest dreams he never thought he would hear.

'There's no mistake?' he asked, dreading the answer.

'None,' replied Lucas, his tone like the thin edge of broken glass.

'Who else in the office pool knows the score?'

'Only Blackowl, McGrath and myself.'

'Keep it that way.'

'To be on the safe side,' said Lucas, 'I initiated an immediate assessment of the second string players and future rookies.'

Greenwald instantly picked up on Lucas's drift. The wives and children of the missing parties were being located and protected, along with the men next in line for the Presidency.

He took a deep breath and quickly arranged his thoughts. Speed was essential. Even now, if the Soviets were behind the President's kidnapping to gain an edge for a pre-emptive nuclear strike, it was too late. On the other hand, with the top four men in American government effectively removed, it hinted of a plot to overthrow the government.

There was no time left to be shackled by security. 'Amen,' said Greenwald, signalling Lucas that he was dropping the doubletalk.

'Understood.'

A sudden terrifying thought swept Greenwald's mind. 'The bag man?' he asked nervously.

'Gone with the rest.'

Oh dear God, Greenwald agonised to himself silently. Disaster was piling on top of disaster. Bag man was the irreverent nickname for the field-grade officer, at the President's side day and night, who carried the briefcase containing codes called release messages that could unleash the nation's 10,000 strategic nuclear warheads on preselected targets inside Soviet Russia. The consequences of the ultra secret codes falling into alien hands were beyond conceivable horror.

'Alert the Chairman of the Joint Chiefs of Staff,' he ordered. 'Then send a detail to pick up the Secretaries of State and Defence, also the National Security Adviser, and rush them to the White House situation room.'

'Anyone on the Presidential staff?'

'Okay, bring in Dan Fawcett. But for now let's keep it a closed club. The fewer that know "the man" is missing until we can sort things out, the better.'

'In that case, it might be wise to hold the meeting someplace besides the situation room,' said Lucas. 'The press constantly monitors the White House. They'd be on us like locusts if the heads of state suddenly converged there at this time of morning.'

'Sound thinking,' replied Greenwald. He paused a moment, then said, 'Make it the observatory.'

'The Vice President's residence?'

'Press cars are almost never in evidence there.'

'I'll have everyone on the premises as soon as possible.'

'Oscar?'

'Yes.'

'Very briefly, what happened?'

There was a slight hesitation and then Lucas said, 'They all vanished from the Presidential yacht.'

'I see,' said Greenwald heavily, but it was clear he didn't.

Greenwald wasted no more time on talk. He hung up and hurriedly dressed On the drive to the Observatory his stomach twisted into knots, a delayed reaction to the catastrophic news. His vision blurred and he fought off an overwhelming urge to vomit.

He drove in a mental haze through the deserted streets of the capital. Except for an occasional delivery truck, traffic was nearly nonexistent and most of the traffic signals were simply blinking on a cautious 'yellow'.

Too late, he saw a city streetsweeper make a sudden U-turn from the righthand gutter. The windscreen was abruptly filled with the bulky white painted vehicle. In the cab the driver jumped sideways at the protesting scream of tyres, his eyes wide in the glare of Greenwald's headlights.

There was a metal tearing crunch and the splash of flying glass. The hood bent double, flew up and the steering wheel rammed into Greenwald's chest, crushing his rib cage.

Greenwald sat pinned to the seat as the water from the mangled radiator hissed and steamed over the car's engine. His eyes were open as though staring in vague indifference at the abstract cracks on the shattered windscreen.

Oscar Lucas stood in front of the corner fireplace in the living-room of the Vice President's mansion and described the presidential kidnapping. Every few seconds he glanced nervously at his watch, wondering what was keeping Greenwald. The five men seated around the room listened to him in undisguised astonishment.

Secretary of Defence, Jesse Simmons, clamped his teeth on the stem of an unlit meerschaum pipe. He was dressed casually in a summer jacket and trousers, as was Dan Fawcett and National Security Adviser, Alan Mercier. Army General Clayton Metcalf was in uniform while Douglas Oates, the Secretary of State sat fastidiously groomed in a dark suit and necktie.

Lucas came to the end of his briefing and waited for the barrage of questions he was certain would be fired. Instead, there was a prolonged hush. They just sat there numb and immobile. Oates was the first to break the stunned silence.

'Good Lord!' he gasped. 'How could such a thing happen? How could everyone on the yacht simply evaporate into thin air?'

'We don't know,' Lucas answered helplessly. 'I haven't ordered an investigating team to the site yet for obvious security reasons. Ben Greenwald slammed a lid on the affair until you gentlemen could be informed. Outside this room, only three Secret Service personnel, including Greenwald, are privy to the facts.'

'There has to be a logical explanation,' said Mercier. The President's adviser on National Security rose to his feet and paced the room. 'Twenty people were not whisked away by supernatural sources or aliens from space. If, and I make that a questionable *if*, the President and the others are indeed missing from the *Eagle*, it has to be a highly organised conspiracy.'

'I assure you, sir,' said Lucas staring directly into Mercier's eyes, 'my deputy agent found the boat totally deserted.'

'You say the fog was thick,' Mercier continued.

'That's how Agent Blackowl described it.'

'Could they have somehow penetrated your security network and driven away?'

Lucas shook his head. 'Even if they managed to elude my security detail in the fog, their movement would have been detected by the sensitive alarm systems we installed around the estate.'

'That leaves the river,' observed Jesse Simmons. The Secretary of Defence was a taciturn man, given to telegram-like statements. A leathery tan face was evidence of his weekends as an avid waterskier. 'Suppose the *Eagle* was boarded from the water? Suppose they were forcibly removed to another boat?'

Oates gave Simmons a dubious stare. 'You make it sound like Blackbeard the pirate was responsible.'

'Agents were patrolling the dock and riverbank,' explained Lucas. 'No way passengers and crew could be subdued and carried off without a sound.'

'Maybe they were drugged,' suggested Dan Fawcett.

'A possibility,' admitted Lucas.

'Let's look at this head on,' said Oates. 'Rather than speculate on how the abduction occurred, I think we must concentrate on the reason and the force responsible before we can plan a response.'

'I agree,' said Simmons. He turned to Metcalf. 'General, any evidence the Russians are behind this as a time cushion to launch a first strike?'

'If that was the case,' answered Metcalf, 'their Strategic Rocket Forces would have taken us out an hour ago.'

'They still might.'

Metcalf gave a slight negative tilt to his head. 'Nothing indicates they're in a state of readiness. Our Kremlin intelligence sources report no signs of increased activity in or around the eighty underground command posts in Moscow, and our satellite surveillance shows no troop build-up along the Eastern Bloc border. Also, President Antonov is on a state visit to Paris.'

'So much for World War Three,' voiced Mercier with a look of relief.

'We're not out of shallow water yet,' said Fawcett. 'The officer carrying the codes designating nuclear strike sites is also gone.'

'Not to worry on that score,' said Metcalf, smiling for the first time. 'As soon as Lucas here alerted me to the situation, I ordered the alphabetical code words changed.'

'What's to stop whoever has them from using the old code words to break the new ones?'

'For what purpose?'

'Blackmail, or maybe an insane attempt to hit the Russians first.'

'Can't be done,' Metcalf replied simply. 'There are too many built-in safeguards. Why hell, even the President, while in a fit of madness, couldn't launch our nuclear arsenal on his own. The order to start a war has to be transmitted through Secretary of Defence Simmons and the Joint Chiefs. If any of us knew for certain the order was invalid, we could countermand it.'

'All right,' said Simmons, 'we temporarily shelve a Soviet conspiracy or an act of war. What are we left with?'

'Damned little,' grunted Mercier.

Metcalf looked squarely at Oates. 'As things stand, Mr Secretary, you are the constitutionally designated successor to the President.'

'He's right,' said Simmons. 'Until the President, Margolin, Larimer or Moran are found alive, you're the leader of the band.'

For several seconds there was no sound in the library. Oates' flamboyant and forceful facial exterior cracked ever so slightly, and he seemed suddenly to age five years. Then, just as suddenly, he regained control and his eyes took on a cold, visceral expression.

'The first thing we must do,' he said in a level tone, 'is act as though nothing has happened.'

Mercier tilted back and gazed unseeing at the high ceiling. 'Granted we can't hold a press conference and announce to the world we've misplaced the nation's four ranking leaders. I don't care to think about the repercussions when the word leaks out. But we can't hide the facts from the press for more than a few hours.'

'And we have to consider the likelihood the people responsible for the kidnapping will give us an ultimatum or make a ransom demand through the news media,' added Simmons.

Metcalf looked doubtful. 'My guess is that when contact is made, it will come without a trumpet blast to Secretary Oates and any demand will be for something besides money.'

'I can't fault your thinking, General,' said Oates. 'But our top priority is still to conceal the facts and stall for as long as it takes to find the President.'

Mercier had the look of an atheist buttonholed by a Hare Krishna at an airport. 'Lincoln said it, "you can't fool all the people all the time". It won't be easy keeping the President and Vice President out of the public eye for more than a day at most. And you can't simply erase Larimer and Moran; they're too highly visible around Washington. Then there is the *Eagle*'s crew to consider. What do you tell their families?'

'Jack Sutton!' Fawcett blurted as though he was having a revelation.

'Who?' demanded Simmons.

'The actor, the spitting image of the President who plays him in TV commercials and on comedy shows.'

Oates sat up. 'I think I see your point. The resemblance is remarkable, but we'd never get away with it, not on a face-to-face basis. Sutton's voice is far from a perfect imitation, and anyone who is in close daily contact with the President would see through the deception.'

'Yes, but from thirty feet his own wife couldn't tell the difference.'

'Where is this leading?' Metcalf asked Fawcett.

The White House Chief of Staff took his cue. 'Press Secretary Thompson can hand out a press release saying the President is taking a working vacation on his New Mexico farm to study Congressional reaction to his Eastern Aid Programme. The élite White House Press Corps will be kept on the sidelines, a situation not uncommon when the President isn't in the mood to answer questions. All they'd see from a roped off distance would be him – in this case, Sutton the actor – entering the helicopter for the flight to Andrews Force Base for departure in Air Force One. They could follow on a later plane, of course, but be denied entry onto the farm itself.'

'Why not have a phoney vice president go with Sutton?' suggested Mercier.

'Both men can't fly on the same plane,' Lucas reminded him.

'Okay, send him on a plane leaving at night,' Mercier pressed on. 'Little news coverage is devoted to Margolin's movements. No one would notice a stand-in.'

'Or care,' added Oates, alluding to the apathy paid to vice presidents.

'I can handle the details from the White House end,' offered Fawcett.

'Two down,' said Simmons. 'Now what about Larimer and Moran?'

'This is an odd numbered year,' said Mercier, warming up to the scheme. 'Congress recesses for the entire month of August, only a day away. Our one slice of luck. Why not invent a mutual fishing trip or junket to some out-of-the-way third world country?'

Simmons shook his head. 'Scratch the fishing trip.'

'Why?'

Simmons gave a tight smile. 'Because it's known all over Capitol Hill Moran and Larimer relate like syrup and vinegar.'

'No matter, a fishing hole conference to discuss foreign relations sounds logical,' said Oates. 'I'll write up the memorandum from the State Department end.'

'What do you tell their office staffs?'

'This is Saturday, we've got two days' grace to iron out the bugs.'

Simmons began making notes on a pad. 'Four down. That leaves the *Eagle*'s crew.'

'I think I can come up with a convenient cover,' offered Metcalf. 'I'll work through the Coast Guard Commandant. The crew's families can be told the yacht was ordered on an unscheduled cruise for a top secret military meeting. No further details need be given.'

Oates stared around the room at his companions. 'If there are no further questions – ?'

'Who else do we let in on the hoax?' queried Fawcett.

'A poor choice of words, Dan,' said Oates. 'Let's call it a "distraction".'

'It goes without saying,' said Metcalf, 'Emmett of the FBI will have to handle the domestic end of the investigation. And, of course, Brogan of CIA must be called in to check out the international conspiracy angle.'

'You've just touched on an ungodly thought, General,' said Simmons.

'Sir?'

'What if the President and the rest have already been spirited out of the country?'

Simmons's speculation brought no immediate response. It was a grim possibility none of them dared to consider. With the President beyond reach of their vast internal resources, their investigative effectiveness would be cut by eighty percent.

'They could also be dead,' Oates said in a controlled voice. 'But we'll operate on the premise they're alive and held somewhere in the United States.'

'Lucas and I will brief Emmett and Brogan,' Fawcett volunteered.

There was a knock on the door. A Secret Service agent entered, walked over to Lucas and spoke softly in his ear. Lucas' eyebrows arched upward and he paled slightly. Then the agent retreated from the room, closing the door behind him.

Oates stared at Lucas questioningly. 'A new development, Oscar?'

'Ben Greenwald,' Lucas answered vacantly. 'He was killed thirty minutes ago. His car struck a city maintenance vehicle.'

Oates wasted no words of sympathy. 'With the powers temporarily invested in me, I name you as the new Director of the Secret Service.'

Lucas visibly recoiled. 'No, please, I don't think I can . . .'

'Doesn't make sense to select somebody else,' Oates interrupted him. 'Like it or not, Oscar, you're the only man who can be named for the job.'

'Somehow it doesn't seem right to be promoted for losing the men I'm sworn to protect,' said Lucas dejectedly.

'Blame me,' said Fawcett. 'I forced the yacht cruise on you before your people were fully prepared.'

'There's no time for self-recrimination,' said Oates sharply. 'We each have our jobs cut out for us. I suggest we get to work.'

'When should we meet again?' asked Simmons.

Oates looked at his watch. 'Four hours from now,' he replied. 'The White House situation room.'

'We're flirting with exposure if everyone shows up at the same time,' said Fawcett. 'That's why Oscar came up with the suggestion for meeting here.'

'There's an underground utility tunnel running from the basement of the Treasury Building beneath the street to the White House,' Lucas explained. 'Perhaps some of you gentlemen could enter unseen from that direction.'

'Good idea,' Metcalf agreed. 'We can arrive at the Treasury Building in unmarked government cars, cross under the street through the tunnel and take the elevator to the situation room.'

'That settles it then,' Oates said, rising from his chair. 'If any of you ever dreamed of going on the stage, this is your big chance. And I don't have to tell you, if the show's a flop, we just may bring down the whole country along with the curtain.'

14

After the brisk air of Alaska, the hot, humid atmosphere of South Carolina felt like the inside of a sauna. Pitt made a phone call and then rented a car at Charleston Airport. He drove south on highway 52 towards the city and took the turn off for the sprawling Naval Base. About a mile after turning right on Spruill Avenue, he came to a large, red brick building with an ancient, rusting sign perched on the roof, advertising the Alhambra Iron and Boiler Company.

He parked the car and walked under a high iron archway with the date 1861 suspended on a panel. The reception area took him by surprise. The furnishings were ultra modern. Chrome was everywhere. He felt as though he'd walked onto a photo layout of *Architectural Digest*.

A sweet young thing looked up, pursed an ever so small smile and said, 'Can ah help you, sir?'

Pitt stared into the mossy green, magnolia eyes and imagined her as a former homecoming queen. 'I called from the airport and set an appointment with Mr Oaks. My name is Pitt.'

The recognition was automatic and the smile didn't alter so much as a millimetre. 'Yes, he's expecting you. Please come this way.'

She lived in a body any woman would be proud to own. Pitt was fascinated. He had never seen anyone walk so straight. Her hips maintained a vertical rigidity that defied any tendency to swing and sway.

She led him into an office decorated entirely in brown tones. Pitt was suddenly overwhelmed with the sensation of drowning in oatmeal. A rotund, smiling, unedged little man rose from behind an enormous kidney-shaped desk and extended his hand.

'Mr Pitt. I'm Charlie Oaks.'

'Mr Oaks,' said Pitt, shaking hands. 'Thank you for seeing me.'

'Not at all. Your phone call tickled my curiosity. You're the first person to ask about our boiler making capacity in, golly, must be almost forty years.'

'You're out of the business?'

'Heavens, yes. Gave it up during the summer of '51. End of an era, you might say. My great granddaddy rolled armour plate for the Confederate ironclad fleet. After World War Two, my daddy figured the time had come for a change. He retooled the plant and started fabricating metal furniture. As things turned out it was a shrewd decision.'

'Did you, by chance, save any of your old production records?' Pitt asked.

'Unlike you Yankees, who throw out everything,' said Oaks in a gentle Mason-Dixon accent and a sly smile, 'we Southern boys hold onto everything, including our women.'

Pitt laughed politely and didn't bother asking how his own California upbringing qualified him as a Yankee.

'After your call,' Oaks continued, 'I ran a search in our file storage room. You didn't give me a date, but since we only supplied forty water-tube boilers with the specifications you mentioned for Liberty

Ships, I found the invoice listing the serial number in question in fifteen minutes. Unfortunately, I can't tell you what you don't already know.'

'Was the boiler shipped to the company that supplied the engines or direct to the shipyard for installation?'

Oaks picked up the yellowing paper from his desk and studied it for a moment. 'It says here we shipped to the Georgia Shipbuilding Corporation in Savannah on June fourteenth, nineteen forty-three.' Oaks picked up another piece of paper. 'Here's a report from one of our men who inspected the boilers after they were installed in the ship and connected to the engines. All that is mentioned of any interest is the name of the ship.'

'Yes, I have that,' said Pitt. 'It was the *Pilottown*.'

A strange expression of puzzlement crossed Oaks' face as he restudied the inspector's report. 'We must be talking 'bout two different ships.'

Pitt looked at him. 'Could there be a mistake?'

'Not unless you wrote down the wrong serial number.'

'I was careful,' Pitt replied firmly.

'Then I don't know what to tell you,' said Oaks passing the paper across the desk, 'but according to the inspection report, boiler number three-eight-eight-seven-four, went into a Liberty Ship called the *San Marino*.'

15

Congresswoman Loren Smith was waiting on the concourse when Pitt's flight from Charleston arrived at Washington's National Airport. She waved to get his attention, and he smiled. The gesture was unnecessary. She was an easy woman to spot.

Loren stood tall, slightly over five foot eight. Her cinnamon hair was long but cut at vertical angles around the face which accented her prominent cheekbones and deep violet eyes. She was dressed in a pink cotton knitted tunic style dress with scoop neck and long sleeves that were rolled up. For an elegant touch, she wore a glittery Chinese patterned sash around her waist. Her feet were casually strapped into calf-leather sandals.

She possessed an aura of breezy sophistication, yet underneath one could sense a tomboyish daring. A representative elected from the State of Colorado, Loren was serving her second term. She loved her job, it was her life. Feminine and softspoken, she could be an unleashed tiger on the floor of Congress when she tackled an issue. Her colleague respected her for her shrewdness as well as her beauty. She was a private woman, shunning the parties and dinners unless they were of political necessity. Her only outside activity was an 'on again, off again' affair with Pitt. She approached him and kissed him lightly on the mouth. 'Welcome home voyager.'

He put his arm around her and they set off toward the baggage claim. 'Thank you for meeting me.'

'I borrowed one of your cars. I hope you don't mind.'

'Depends,' he said. 'Which one?'

'My favourite, the blue Talbot-Lago.'

'Yes, the coupé with the Saoutchik coachwork. You have expensive tastes. That's a two hundred thousand dollar car.'

'Oh dear, I hope it doesn't get dented in the parking lot.'

Pitt gave her a solemn look. 'If it does, the sovereign state of Colorado will have a vacant seat in Congress.'

She clutched his arm and laughed. 'You think more of your cars than you do of your women.'

'Cars never nag and complain.'

'I can think of a few other things they never do,' she said with a girlish smile.

They threaded their way through the crowded terminal and waited at the baggage claim. Finally the conveyor belt hummed into motion and Pitt retrieved his two suitcases. They passed outside into a grey, sticky morning and found the blue 1948 Talbot-Lago sitting peacefully under the watchful eye of an airport security guard. Pitt relaxed in the passenger's seat as Loren slipped behind the wheel. The rakish car was a righthand drive, and it always struck Pitt as odd to sit and stare out the left side of the windscreen at the approaching traffic with nothing to do.

'Did you call Perlmutter?' he asked.

'About an hour before you landed,' she answered. 'He was quite agreeable for someone who was jolted out of a sound sleep. He said he'd dig through his library for data on the ships you asked about.'

'If anyone knows ships, it's St Julien Perlmutter.'

'He sounds like a character over the phone.'

'An understatement. Wait till you meet him.'

Pitt watched the passing scenery for a few moments without speaking. He stared at the Potomac River as Loren drove north along the George Washington Memorial Parkway and cut over the Francis Scott Key Bridge to Georgetown.

Pitt was not fond of Georgetown, phoneyville he called it. The drab brick townhouses looked as if they had all been popped from the same biscuit mould. Loren steered the Talbot onto N Street.

91

Parked cars jammed the kerbs, rubbish lay in the gutters, little of the sidewalk shrubbery was trimmed, and yet it was perhaps four blocks of the most overpriced accommodation in the country. Tiny houses, Pitt mused, filled with gigantic egos generously coated with mega doses of forged veneer.

Loren squeezed into a vacant parking space and turned off the ignition. They locked the car and walked between two vine encrusted homes to a carriage house in the rear. Before Pitt could lift a bronze knocker shaped like a ship's anchor, the door was thrown open by a great monster of a man who mashed the scales at nearly four hundred pounds. His sky blue eyes twinkled and his crimson face lay mostly hidden under a thick forest of grey hair and beard. Except for a small tulip nose he looked like Santa Claus gone to seed.

'Dirk,' he fairly boomed. 'Where've you been hiding?'

St Julien Perlmutter was dressed in purple silk pyjamas under a red and gold paisley robe. He encompassed Pitt with his chunky arms and lifted him off the doorstep in a bearhug without a hint of strain. Loren's eyes widened in astonishment. She'd never met Perlmutter in person and wasn't prepared.

'You kiss me, Julien,' said Pitt sternly, 'and I'll kick you in the crotch.'

Perlmutter gave a bellylaugh and released Pitt's hundred and eighty pounds. 'Come in, come in. I've made breakfast. You must be starved after your travels.'

Pitt introduced Loren. Perlmutter kissed her hand with a continental flourish, and then led them into a huge combination living-room, bedroom and study. Shelves supporting the weight of thousands of books sagged from floor to ceiling on every wall. There were books on tables, books on chairs. They were even stacked on a kingsize waterbed that rippled in an alcove.

Perlmutter possessed what was acknowledged by experts as the finest collection of historical ship literature ever assembled. At least twenty marine museums were constantly angling to have it donated to their libraries after a lifetime of excess calories sent him to a mortuary.

He motioned Pitt and Loren to sit at a hatchcover table laid with an elegant silver and china service bearing the emblem of a French Transatlantic Steamship Line.

'It's all so lovely,' said Loren admiringly.

'From the famous French liner, *Normandy*,' explained Perlmutter. 'Found it all in a warehouse where it had been packed away since the ship burned and rolled over in New York Harbour.'

He served them a German breakfast beginning with Schnapps. Then came Westphalian ham thin-sliced, garnished with pickles and

92

accompanied by pumpernickel bread. For a side dish he'd whipped up potato dumplings with a prune-butter filling.

'Tastes marvellous,' said Loren. 'I love eating something besides eggs and bacon for a change.'

'I'm addicted to German cooking,' Perlmutter laughed, patting his ample stomach. 'Lots more substance than that candy-ass French fare which is nothing but an exotic way to prepare garbage.'

'Did you find any information on the *San Marino* and the *Pilottown*?' asked Pitt, turning the conversation to the subject on his mind.

'Yes, as a matter of fact, I did.' Perlmutter hefted his bulk from the table and soon returned with a large, dusty volume on Liberty Ships. He donned a pair of reading glasses and turned to a marked page.

'Here we are. The *San Marino*, launched by the Georgia Shipbuilding Corp, July of 1943. Hull number 2356, classed as a cargo carrier. Sailed Atlantic convoys until the end of the war. Damaged by submarine torpedo from the U-573. Reached Liverpool under her own power and was repaired. Sold after the war to the Bristol Steamship Company of Bristol, England. Sold 1956 to the Manx Steamship Company of New York, Panamanian registry. Vanished with all hands, North Pacific, 1966.'

'So that was the end of her.'

'Maybe, maybe not,' said Perlmutter. 'There's a postscript. I found a report in another reference source. About three years after the ship was posted missing, a Mr Rodney Dewhurst who was a marine insurance underwriter for the Lloyds' office in Singapore, noticed a ship moored in the harbour that struck him as vaguely familiar. There was an unusual design to the cargo booms he'd seen on only one other Liberty class ship. He managed to talk his way on board and after a brief search smelled a rat. Unfortunately, it was a holiday and it took him several hours to round up the harbour authorities and persuade them to arrest the ship in port and hold it for an investigation. By the time they reached the dock, the vessel was long gone, steaming somewhere out to sea. A check of custom records showed her to be the *Belle Chasse*, Korean registry, owned by the Sosan Trading Company of Inchon, Korea. Her next destination was Seattle. Dewhurst cabled an alert to the Seattle Harbour Police, but the *Belle Chasse* never arrived.'

'Why was Dewhurst suspicious of her?' Pitt asked.

'He had inspected the *San Marino* before underwriting the insurance on her and was dead certain she and the *Belle Chasse* were one and the same ship.'

'Surely the *Belle Chasse* turned up in another port?' Loren asked.

Perlmutter shook his head. 'She faded from the records until two years later when she was reported scrapped in Pusan, Korea.' He paused and looked across the table. 'Does any of this help you?'

Pitt took another swallow of the Schnapps. 'That's the problem. I don't know.' He went on to briefly relate the discovery of the *Pilottown*, but omitted any mention of the nerve gas cargo. He described finding the serial number on the ship's boiler and running a check on it in Charleston.

'So the old *Pilottown*'s been tracked down at last,' sighed Perlmutter wistfully. 'She wanders the sea no more.'

'But her discovery opened a new can of worms,' said Pitt. 'Why was she carrying a boiler that was recorded by the manufacturer as installed in the *San Marino*? It doesn't add up. Both ships were probably constructed on adjoining slipways and launched about the same time. The on-site inspector must have been confused. He simply wrote up the boiler as placed in the wrong hull.'

'I hate to spoil your black mood,' said Perlmutter, 'but you may be wrong.'

'Isn't there a connection between the two ships?'

Perlmutter gave Pitt a scholarly gaze over the tops of his glasses. 'Yes, but not what you think.' He turned to the book again and began reading aloud. 'The Liberty Ship, *Bart Pulver*, later the *Rosthena* and *Pilottown*, launched by Astoria Iron & Steel Company, Portland, Oregon in November of 1942 – '

'She was built on the West Coast?' Pitt interrupted in surprise.

'About twenty-five hundred miles from Savannah as the crow flies,' Perlmutter replied indirectly, 'and nine months earlier than the *San Marino*.' He turned to Loren. 'Would you like some coffee, dear lady?'

Loren stood up. 'You two keep talking. I'll get it.'

'It's expresso.'

'I know how to operate the machine.'

Perlmutter looked at Pitt and gave a jolly wink. 'She's a winner.'

Pitt nodded and continued. 'It's not logical a Charleston boiler-maker would ship across the country to Oregon with a Savannah shipyard only ninety miles away.'

'Not logical at all,' Perlmutter agreed.

'What else do you have on the *Pilottown*?'

Perlmutter read on. 'Hull number 793, also classed as a cargo carrier. Sold after the war to the Kassandra Phosphate Company Limited of Athens. Greek registry. Ran aground with a cargo of phosphates off Jamaica, June of 1954. Refloated four months later. Sold 1962 to the Sosan Trading Company – '

'Inchon, Korea,' Pitt finished. 'Our first connection.'

Loren returned with a tray of small cups and passed the expresso coffee around the table.

94

'This is indeed a treat,' said Perlmutter gallantly. 'I've never been waited on by a member of Congress before.'

'I hope I didn't make it too strong,' said Loren, testing the brew and making a face.

'A little mud on the bottom sharpens a woolly mind,' Perlmutter reassured her philosophically.

'Getting back to the *Pilottown*,' Pitt said. 'What happened to her after 1962?'

'No other entry is shown until 1979, when she's listed as sunk during a storm in the Northern Pacific with all hands. After that she became something of a cause célèbre by reappearing on a number of occasions along the Alaskan Coast.'

'Then she went missing in the same area of the sea as the *San Marino*,' said Pitt thoughtfully. 'Another possible tie-in.'

'You're grabbing at bubbles,' said Loren. 'I can't see where any of this is taking you.'

'I'm with her,' Perlmutter nodded. 'There's no concrete pattern.'

'I think there is,' Pitt said confidently. 'What began as a cheap insurance fraud is unravelling into a cover-up of far greater proportions.'

'What's your interest in this?' Perlmutter asked, staring Pitt in the eyes.

Pitt's gaze was distant. 'I can't tell you.'

'A classified government investigation maybe?'

'I'm on my own in this one, but it's related to a "most secret" project.'

Perlmutter gave in good-naturedly. 'Okay, old friend, no more prying questions.' He helped himself to another dumpling. 'If you suspect the ship buried under the volcano is the *San Marino* and not the *Pilottown*, where do you go from here?'

'Inchon, Korea. The Sosan Trading Company might hold the key.'

'Don't waste your time. The trading company is most certainly a false front, a name on a registry certificate. As is the case with most shipping companies, all trace of ownership ends at an obscure post office box. If I were you I'd give it up as a lost cause.'

'You'd never make a football coach,' Pitt said, with a laugh. 'Your halftime, locker room speech would discourage your team into throwing away a twenty point lead.'

'Another glass of Schnapps, if you please,' said Perlmutter in a grumbling tone, holding out his glass as Pitt poured. 'Tell you what I'll do. Two of my corresponding friends on nautical research are Koreans. I'll have them check out Sosan Trading for you.'

'And the Pusan shipyards for any records covering the scrapping of the *Belle Chasse*.'

'All right, I'll throw that in too.'

'I'm grateful for your help.'

'No guarantees.'

'I don't expect any.'

'What's your next move?'

'Send out press releases.'

Loren looked up, puzzled. 'Send what?'

'Press releases,' Pitt answered casually, 'to announce the discovery of both the *San Marino* and the *Pilottown* and describe NUMA's plans for inspecting the wrecks.'

'When did you dream up that foolish stunt?' Loren asked.

'About ten seconds ago.'

Perlmutter gave Pitt the stare of a psychiatrist about to commit a hopeless mental case. 'I fail to see the purpose.'

'No one in the world is immune from curiosity,' Pitt exclaimed with a devious glint in his green eyes. 'Somebody from the parent company that owned those ships will step from behind the shroud of corporate anonymity to check the story. And when they do, I'll have their ass.'

16

When Oates entered the White House situation room, the men seated around the conference table instinctively came to their feet. It was a sign of respect for the man who now bore the vast problems of the nation's uncertain future. The responsibility for the far-reaching decisions of the next few days, and perhaps longer, would be his alone. There were some in the room who had mistrusted his cold aloofness, his cultivated holy image. They now cast off personal dislike and rallied to his side.

He automatically took the chair at the head of the table. He motioned them to sit and turned to Sam Emmett, the gruff-spoken chief of the FBI, and Martin Brogan, the urbane intellectual director of the CIA.

'Have you gentlemen been fully briefed?'

Emmett nodded towards Fawcett seated at the table's lower end. 'Dan has described the situation.'

'Either of you got anything on this?'

Brogan shook his head slowly. 'Off the top of my head I can't recall hearing any indications or rumours from our intelligence sources pointing to an operation of this magnitude. But that doesn't mean we don't have something that was misinterpreted.'

'I'm in pretty much the same boat as Martin,' said Emmett. 'It's beyond comprehension that a presidential abduction could slip through the Bureau's fingers without even a vague clue.'

Oates' next question was put to Brogan. 'Do we have any intelligence that might lead us to suspect the Russians?'

'Soviet President Antonov doesn't consider our President half the threat he did Reagan. He'd be risking a massive confrontation if it ever leaked to the American public his government was involved. You could compare it to striking a hornet's nest with a stick. I can't see what, if any, gains the Russians would net.'

'What's your gut reaction, Sam?' Oates asked Emmett. 'Could this be terrorist inspired?'

'Too elaborate. This operation took an immense amount of planning and money. The ingenuity is incredible. It goes far beyond the capabilities of any terrorist organisation.'

'Any theories?' asked Oates, addressing the table.

'I can think of at least four Arab leaders who might have a motive for blackmailing the US,' said General Metcalf. 'And Gaddafi of Libya heads the list.'

'They certainly have the financial resources,' said Defence Secretary Simmons.

'But hardly the sophistication,' added Brogan.

Alan Mercier, the NS adviser motioned with his hand to speak. 'In my estimation the conspiracy is of domestic origin rather than foreign.'

'What's your reasoning?' asked Oates.

'Our land and space listening systems monitor every telephone and radio transmission around the world, and it's no secret to everyone present that our new tenth generation computers can break any code the Russians or our Allies devise. It stands to reason that an intricate operation of this size would require a flow of international message traffic leading up the act and a report of success afterwards.' Mercier paused to make his point. 'Our analysts have not intercepted a foreign communication that suggests the slightest connection with the disappearance.'

Simmons sucked noisily on his pipe. 'I think Alan makes a good case.'

'Okay,' said Oates, 'foreign blackmail rates a low score. So what are we looking at from the domestic angle?'

Dan Fawcett who had been silent until now, spoke up. 'It may sound a bit far-fetched, but we can't eliminate a corporate plot to overthrow the government.'

Oates leaned back and straightened his shoulders. 'Maybe not as far-fetched as we think. The President went after the oil companies and the multi-national conglomerates with a vengeance. His tax programme took a hell of a bite out of their profits. They're pumping money into the opposition party's campaign coffers faster than their banks can print the cheques.'

'I warned him about slinging the old political hack line of supporting the poor by taxing the rich,' Fawcett said. 'But he refused to listen. He alienated the nation's businessmen, as well as the working middle-class. Politicians can't seem to get it in their heads that a vast number of American families with a working wife are in a fifty percent tax bracket.'

'The President had powerful enemies,' Mercier conceded, 'however it's inconceivable to me, that any corporate empire could steal away the President and Congressional leaders without it leaking to a law enforcement agency.'

'That'd be my idea,' Emmett said. 'Too many people had to be in on it. Somebody would have got cold feet and spilled the plan.'

'I think we'd better call a halt to speculation,' said Oates. 'Let's get back on the track. The first step is to launch a massive investigation while keeping up a "business-as-usual" front. Use whatever cover story you feel is plausible. If at all possible, don't even let your key people in on this.'

'What about a central command post during the investigation?' asked Emmett.

'We'll continue to gather here every eight hours to assess incoming evidence and coordinate efforts between your respective investigative agencies.'

Simmons pushed forward in his chair. 'I have a problem. I'm scheduled to fly to Cairo this afternoon to confer with Egypt's minister of defence.'

'By all means go,' replied Oates. 'Keep up normal appearances. General Metcalf can cover for you at the Pentagon.'

Emmett shifted in his chair. 'I'm supposed to speak before a law class at Princeton tomorrow morning.'

Oates pondered a moment. 'Claim you have the flu and can't make it.' He turned to Lucas. 'Oscar, if you forgive me for saying so, you're the most expendable. Substitute for Sam. Certainly no one would suspect a presidential kidnapping if the new Director of the Secret Service can take time out to give a speech.'

Lucas nodded. 'I'll be there.'

'Good.' Oates looked around the table. 'Everybody plan on being back here at two o'clock. Maybe we'll know something by then.'

'I've already sent a crack lab team over to the yacht,' volunteered Emmett. 'Hopefully they'll turn up some solid leads.'

'Let's pray they do.' Oates' shoulders sagged and he appeared to stare through the table top. 'My God,' he muttered quietly. 'Is this any way to run a government?'

17

Blackowl stood on the dock and watched as a team of FBI agents swarmed over the *Eagle*. They were an efficient lot, he observed. Each man was a specialist in his particular field of scientific detection. They went about their job of scrutinising the yacht from bilge to radio mast with a minimum of conversation.

A constant parade of them crossed the dock to vans parked along the shore, removing furniture, carpeting, anything that wasn't screwed down and a considerable amount that was. Each item was carefully wrapped in a plastic covering and inventoried.

More agents arrived, expanding the search for a mile around the first President's estate, examining every square inch of ground, the trees and shrubbery. In the water beside the yacht, divers scoured the muddy bottom.

The agent in charge noticed Blackowl rubbernecking beside the loading ramp and came over. 'You got permission to be in the area?' he asked.

Blackowl showed his ID without answering.

'What brings the Secret Service to Mount Vernon on a weekend?'

'Practice mission,' Blackowl replied conversationally. 'How about the FBI?'

'Same thing. The Director must have thought we were getting lazy, so he dreamed up a top priority exercise.'

'Looking for anything in particular?' Blackowl asked, feigning indifferent interest.

'Whatever we can determine about the last people who were on board, identification through fingerprints, where they came from. You know.'

Before Blackowl could reply, Ed McGrath stepped onto the dock from the gravel path. His forehead was glistening with sweat and his face was flushed. Blackowl guessed he had been running.

'Excuse me George,' he panted between intakes of breath. 'You got a minute?'

'Sure.' Blackowl waved to the FBI agent. 'Nice talking with you.'

'Same to you.'

As soon as they were out of earshot, Blackowl asked softly, 'What's going down, Ed?'

'The FBI guys found something you should see.'

'Where?'

'About a hundred and fifty yards upriver, hidden away in trees. I'll show you.'

McGrath led him along a path that bordered the river. When it curved towards the outer estate buildings, they stayed in a straight line across a manicured lawn. Then they climbed a wooden rail fence into the unkept undergrowth on the other side. Working their way into a dense thicket, they suddenly came upon two FBI investigators who were kneeling down studying two large tanks connected to what looked like electrical generators.

'What in hell are these things?' demanded Blackowl without a greeting.

One of the men looked up. 'They're foggers.'

Blackowl stared, puzzled. Then his eyes widened. 'Foggers!' he blurted out. 'Machines that make fog!'

'Yeah, that's right. Fog generators. The Navy used to mount them on destroyers during World War Two for making smokescreens.'

'Christ!' Blackowl gasped. 'So that's how it was done!'

18

Official Washington turns into a ghost town over the weekends. The government power structure grinds to a halt at five o'clock Friday evening and hibernates until Monday morning, when it fires to life again with the obstinacy of a cold engine. The huge buildings are as dead as mausoleums. The cleaning crews have come and gone and, what is most surprising, the phone systems are shut down.

Only the tourists are out in force, crawling over the mall and the Capitol, throwing frisbees on the grass, climbing the endless staircases and staring slackjawed at the underside of the dome.

Some were peering through the iron fence around the White House around noontime when the President came out, quick stepped across the lawn and gave a jaunty wave before entering a helicopter. He was followed by a small entourage of aides and Secret Service agents. Few of the élite press corps were present. Most were home watching baseball on TV or roaming a golf course.

Fawcett and Lucas stood on the portico and watched until the ungainly craft lifted over E Street and dissolved to a speck as it beat its way towards Andrews Air Force Base.

'That was fast work,' said Fawcett quietly. 'You made the switch in less than five hours.'

'My Los Angeles office tracked down Sutton and crammed him into the cockpit of a Navy F-20 fighter forty minutes after they were alerted.'

'What about Margolin?'

'One of my agents is a reasonable facsimile. He'll be on board an executive jet for New Mexico as soon as it's dusk.'

'Can your people be trusted not to leak this charade?'

Lucas shot Fawcett a sharp look. 'They're trained to keep quiet. If there's a leak it will come from the Presidential Staff.'

Fawcett smiled faintly. He was on shaky footing, and he knew it. The looseness of the White House staff was open territory for the press corps. 'They can't spill what they didn't know. Only now will they be waking up to the fact that the man in the helicopter with them isn't the President.'

'They'll be well guarded at the farm,' said Lucas. 'Once they arrive no one gets off the property, and I've seen to it that all communications are monitored.'

'If a correspondent figures the game, Watergate will seem as tame as an Easter egg hunt.'

'How are the wives taking it?'

'Cooperating a hundred percent,' answered Fawcett. 'The First Lady and Mrs Margolin have volunteered to stay shut up in their bedrooms, claiming to have a virus.'

'What now?' asked Lucas. 'What else can we do?'

'We wait,' Lucas replied, his voice wooden. 'We stick it out until we find the President.'

'Looks to me like you're overloading the circuits,' said Don Miller, Emmett's Deputy Director of the FBI.

Emmett didn't look up at Miller's negative remark. Within minutes after he had returned to the Bureau's headquarters at Pennsylvania Avenue and Tenth Street he set into motion an 'All Bureau Alert', followed by a standby for 'Emergency Action of the Highest Priority' to every office in the fifty states and all agents on assignments overseas. Next came orders to pull files, records and descriptions on every criminal or terrorist who specialised in abduction.

His cover story to the Bureau's six thousand agents was that the Secret Service had come on evidence of a planned abduction attempt on Secretary of State Oates and other as yet unnamed officials on high government levels.

'It may be a heavy conspiracy,' said Emmett finally, his tone vague. 'We can't take the chance the Secret Service is wrong.'

101

'They've been wrong before,' Miller said.

'Not on this one.'

Miller gave Emmett a curious look. 'You've given out damned little information to work with. Why the great secrecy?'

Emmett didn't answer so Miller dropped the subject. He passed three file folders across the desk. 'Here's the latest data on PLO kidnapping operations, the Mexican Zapata Brigade's hostage activities, and one I'm in the dark about.'

Emmett gave him a cold stare. 'Can you be more explicit?'

'I doubt if there's a connection, but since they acted strange – '

'Who are you talking about?' Emmett demanded, picking up the file and opening the cover.

'A Soviet representative to the United Nations, name of Aleksei Lugovoy . . .'

'A prominent psychologist,' Emmett noted aloud as he read.

'Yes, he and several of his staff members on the World Health Assembly have gone missing.'

Emmett looked up. 'We've lost them?'

Miller nodded. 'Our United Nations surveillance agents report that the Russians left the building Friday night – '

'This is Saturday morning,' Emmett interrupted. 'You're talking of a few hours. What's suspicious about that?'

'They went to great lengths to shake our shadows. The Special Agent in Charge of the New York Bureau checked it out and discovered none of the Russians returned to their apartments or hotels. Collectively they dropped from sight.'

'Anything on Lugovoy?'

'All indications are he's straight. He appears to steer clear of the Soviet Mission's KGB agents.'

'And his staff?'

'None of them have been observed engaged in espionage activities either.'

Emmett looked thoughtful for several moments. Ordinarily he might have brushed the report aside or at most ordered a routine followup. But he had a nagging doubt. The disappearance of the President and Lugovoy on the same night could be a mere coincidence.

At last he said, 'I'd like your opinion, Don.'

'Hard to second guess this one,' replied Miller. 'They may all show up at the United Nations on Monday as though nothing happened. On the other hand, I'd have to suggest that the squeaky clean image Lugovoy and his staff have projected may be a screen.'

'For what purpose?'

Miller shrugged. 'I haven't a clue.'

Emmett closed the file. 'Have the New York Bureau stay on this. I want "priority one" updates whenever they're available.'

'The more I think about it,' said Miller, 'the more it intrigues me.'

'How so?'

'What vital secrets could a bunch of Soviet psychologists want to steal?'

19

Successful shipping line magnates navigate through the glittering waters of the international jet set in grand fashion. From exotic yachts to personalised airliners, from magnificent villas to resplendent hotel suites, they roam the world in an unending crusade for the accumulation of power and wealth.

Min Koryo Bougainville cared nothing for a freewheeling lifestyle. She spent her waking hours in her office and nights in small but elegant quarters on the floor above. She was frugal in most matters, her only weakness was a fondness for Chinese antiques.

When she was twelve, her father sold her to a Frenchman who operated a small shipping line consisting of three tramp steamers that plied the coastal ports between Pusan and Hong Kong. The line prospered and Min Koryo bore Rene Bougainville three sons. Then the war came and the Japanese overran China and Korea. Rene was killed in a bombing raid and the three sons were lost somewhere in the South Pacific after being forced into the Imperial Japanese Army. Only Min Koryo and one grandson, Lee Tong, survived.

After Japan surrendered, she raised and salvaged one of her husband's ships which had been sunk in Pusan Harbour. Slowly she built up the Bougainville fleet, buying old surplus cargo ships, never paying more than their scrap value. Profits were few and far between, but she hung on until Lee Tong finished his master's degree at the University of Pennsylvania Wharton school of business and began running the day to day operation. Then, almost magically, the Bougainville Shipping Line grew like a fertilised weed, and Lee Tong moved the principal offices to New York. In a ritual going back thirty years, he sat dutifully near her bedside in the evening discussing the current dealings of their far-flung financial empire.

Lee Tong wore the misleading look of a jolly oriental peasant. His round, brown face split in a perpetual smile that seemed chiselled in ivory. If the Justice Department and half the Federal law enforcement agencies wanted to close the book on a backlog of unsolved maritime crimes, they would have hung him from the nearest street light, but oddly, none had ever heard of him. He skirted in the shadow of his grandmother; he was not even listed as a director or an employee of Bougainville Shipping. Yet it was he, the anonymous member of the family, who handled the dirty tricks department and built the base of the company.

Too systematic to place his faith in hired hands, he preferred to direct the highly profitable illicit operations from the front rank. His act often ran on blood. Lee Tong was not above murder to achieve a profit. He was equally at home during a business luncheon at the '21' Club as he was at a waterfront throat cutting.

He sat a respectful distance from Min Koryo's bedside, a long, silver cigarette holder planted between his uneven teeth. She disliked his smoking habit, but he clung to it, not so much as a pleasure but as a small measure of independence.

'By tomorrow the FBI will know how the President disappeared,' said Min Koryo.

'I doubt it,' Lee Tong said confidently. 'Their chemical analysis people are good, but not that good. I say, closer to three days. And then a week to find the ship.'

'Enough time so no loose threads can be traced to us?'

'Time enough, *aumuni*,' said Lee Tong, addressing her in the Korean term for mother. 'Rest assured, all threads lead to the grave.'

Min Koryo nodded. The inference was crystal: the handpicked team of seven men who aided Lee Tong in the abduction were murdered by his own hand.

'Still no news from Washington?' she asked.

'Not a word. The White House is acting as though nothing happened. In fact, they're using a double for the President.'

She looked at him. 'How did you learn that?'

'The six o'clock news. The TV cameras showed the President boarding Air Force One for a flight to his farm in New Mexico.'

'And the others?'

'They appear to have stand-ins too.'

Min Koryo sipped at a cup of tea. 'Seems odd that we must depend on Secretary of State Oates and the President's cabinet to provide a successful masquerade until Lugovoy is ready.'

'The only road open to them,' said Lee Tong. 'They won't dare make any kind of announcement until they know what happened to the President.'

Min Koryo stared at the tea leaves in the bottom of her cup. 'Still, I must believe we may have taken too large a bite.'

Lee Tong nodded at her meaning. 'I understand, *aumuni*. The Congressmen just happened to be fish in the same net.'

'But not Margolin. It was your scheme to misguide him onto the yacht.'

'True, but Aleksei Lugovoy has stated his experiments have proven successful eleven out of fifteen times. Not exactly a perfect ratio. If he fails with the President, he has an extra guinea pig to produce the required result.'

'You mean *three* guinea pigs.'

'If you include Larimer and Moran in the rank of succession, yes.'

'And if Lugovoy succeeds in each case?' asked Min Koryo.

'So much the better,' answered Lee Tong. 'Our influence would reach further than we originally dared hope. But I sometimes wonder, *aumuni*, if the financial rewards are worth risking imprisonment and the loss of our business.'

'Do not forget, grandson, the Americans killed my husband, your father and his two brothers during the war.'

'Revenge makes a poor gambling game.'

'All the more reason we must protect our interests and guard against double-dealing by the Russians. President Antonov will do everything in his power to keep from paying our fee.'

'Should they be stupid enough to betray us at this crucial stage, they'd lose the whole project.'

'They don't think that way,' said Min Koryo gravely. 'The Communist mind thrives on mistrust. Integrity is beyond their comprehension. They're driven to take the devious path. And that, my grandson, is their achilles heel.'

'What are you thinking?'

'We continue to play the role of their honest, but gullible partner . . .' She paused, thinking.

'And when Lugovoy's project is finished?' Lee Tong prompted her.

She looked up and a crafty smile cut across her aging face. Her eyes gleamed with a cunning look.

'Then we'll pull the rug from under them.'

20

All identification and wristwatches were taken from the Russians when Bougainville's men transferred them from the Staten Island ferry in midchannel. They were blindfolded and padded radio receivers placed over their ears that emitted soothing chamber music. Minutes later they were airborne, lifted from the dark harbour waters by a jet engined seaplane.

The flight seemed long and wearisome, terminating at last on what Lugovoy judged was a lake by the smooth landing. After a short drive of twenty minutes, the disoriented Russians were led across a metal walkway and into a lift. Only when they stepped out and were led across a carpeted surface to individual bedrooms were the blindfolds and the earphones removed.

Lugovoy was profoundly impressed by the facilities provided by the Bougainvilles. The electronics and laboratory equipment went far beyond any he'd seen in the Soviet Union. Every piece of the several hundred items he had requested was present and installed. Nor had any creature comforts been overlooked for his staff. They were assigned sleeping quarters with private bathrooms, while at the end of the central corridor stretched an elegant dining-room that was serviced by an excellent Korean chef and two waiters.

Furnishings, including kitchen freezers and ovens, office fixtures and the data control room were tastefully colour coordinated with walls and carpeting in cool blue and greens. The design and execution of every detail was as exotic as it was complex.

And yet, the self-contained habitat also served as a luxurious prison. Lugovoy's staff was not permitted to come and go. The elevator doors were sealed at all times and there were no outer controls. He made a compartment to compartment search but detected no windows or visible crack of an exterior exit. No sounds filtered in from the outside.

An inspection tour was cut short by the arrival of his subjects. They were semi-conscious from the effects of sedation and oblivious to their surroundings. Each was prepared and laid inside separate cubicles called cocoons. The padded insides were seamless with rounded corners, giving no reference point for the eye to dwell on. Dim illumination came by reflection from an indirect light source, tinting the cocoon monochrome grey. Specially constructed walls shielded all sound and electrical current that could interfere with or enhance brain activity.

Lugovoy sat at a console with two of his assistants and studied the row of colour video monitors that revealed the subjects lying in their cocoons. Most remained in a trancelike state of limbo. One, however, was raised to a near level of consciousness, vulnerable to suggestion and mentally disoriented. Drugs were injected that numbed his muscle control, effectively paralysing any body movement. His head was covered by a plastic skull cap.

Lugovoy still found it difficult to grasp the power he held. He trembled inwardly at knowing he was embarking on one of the great experiments of the century. What he did in the next ten days could dramatically affect the world as radically as the development of atomic energy.

106

'Dr Lugovoy?'

Lugovoy's concentration was interrupted by the strange voice, and he turned, surprised to see a stocky man with rugged Slavic features and shaggy black hair, who seemingly stepped out of a wall.

'Who are you?' he blurted.

The stranger spoke very softly as though he didn't wish to be overheard. 'Suvorov, Yuri Suvorov, foreign security.'

Lugovoy paled. 'My God, you're KGB! How did you get here?'

'Pure luck,' Suvorov muttered sarcastically. 'You were assigned to my security section for observation from the day you set foot in New York. After your suspicious visit to the Bougainville Shipping offices, I took over your surveillance myself. I was present on the ferryboat when you were contacted by the men who brought you here. Due to the darkness it was easy to mingle with your staff and be included for the trip to wherever it is we are. Since arrival I've kept to my room.'

'Do you have any idea what you've stuck your nose into?' Lugovoy said, his face flushing with anger.

'Not yet,' Suvorov said unperturbed. 'But it is my duty to find out.'

'This operation originates from the highest level. It is of no concern to the KGB.'

'I'll be the judge – '

'You'll be crap in Siberian frost,' Lugovoy hissed, 'if you interfere with my work here.'

Suvorov appeared mildly amused at Lugovoy's irritated tone. It slowly began to dawn on him that he might have overstepped his authority. 'Perhaps I could be of help to you.'

'How?'

'You may have need of my special skills.'

'I don't require the services of an assassin.'

'I was thinking more of escape.'

'There is no reason to escape.'

Suvorov was becoming increasingly annoyed. 'You must try to understand my position.'

Lugovoy was in command now. 'There are more important problems to occupy my mind than your bureaucratic interference.'

'Like what?' Suvorov swept his hand around the room. 'Just what is going on here?'

Lugovoy stared at him consideringly for a long moment before he answered. 'A mind intervention project.'

Suvorov's eyebrows rose. 'Mind intervention?'

'Brain control if you prefer.'

Suvorov faced the video monitor and nodded at the image. 'Is that the reason behind the small helmet?'

'On the subject's head?'

107

'The same.'

'A microelectronic integrated circuit module containing a hundred and ten probes, measuring internal body functions ranging from common pulse to hormone secretions. It also intercepts data flowing through the subject's brain and transmits it to the computers here in this room. The brain's talk, so to speak, is then translated into a comprehensible language.'

'I see no electrode terminals.'

'From a bygone era,' answered Lugovoy. 'Everything we wish to record can be telemetered through the atmosphere. We no longer rely on the unneccessary bulk of wires and terminals.'

'You can actually understand what he's thinking?' asked Suvorov incredulously.

Lugovoy nodded. 'The brain speaks a language of its own, and what it says reveals the inner thoughts of its landlord. Night and day, the brain speaks, incessantly, providing us with a vivid look into the working mind, how a man thinks and why. The impressions are subliminal, so lightning quick that only a computer designed to operate in picoseconds can memorise and decipher them.'

'I had no idea brain science had advanced to such a high level.'

'After we establish and chart his brain rhythms,' Lugovoy continued, 'we can forecast his intentions and physical movements. We can tell when he is about to say or do something in error. And most important, we can intervene in time to stop him. In less than the blink of an eye the computer can erase his mistaken intent and rephrase his thought.'

Suvorov was awed. 'A religious capitalist would accuse you of breaching man's soul.'

'Like you, I am a loyal member of the Communist Party, Comrade Suvorov. I do not believe in the salvation of souls. However, in this case we can't tolerate a drastic conversion. There'll be no disruption of his fundamental thought processes. No change in speech patterns or mannerisms.'

'A form of controlled brainwashing.'

'This is not a crude brainwashing,' Lugovoy replied indignantly. 'Our sophistication goes far beyond anything the Chinese invented. They still believe in destructing a subject's ego in order to re-educate him. Their experiments in drugs and hypnosis have met with little success. Hypnosis is too vague, too slippery to have lasting value. And drugs have proved dangerous by accidentally producing a sudden shift in personality and behaviour. When I finish with the subject, he will re-enter reality and return to his personal lifestyle as though he had never left it. All I intend to do is alter his political perspective.'

'Who is the subject?'

'Don't you know? Don't you recognise him?'

Suvorov studied the video display. Gradually his eyes widened and he moved two steps closer to the screen, his face taut, his mouth working mechanically.

'The President . . . ?' His voice was an unbelieving whisper. 'Is that really the President of the United States?'

'In the flesh.'

'How . . . where . . . ?'

'A gift from our hosts,' Lugovoy explained vaguely.

'He'll suffer no side-effects?' Suvorov asked in a haze.

'None.'

'Will he remember any of this?'

'He will only recall going to bed when he wakes up ten days from now.'

'You can do this thing, really do it?' Suvorov questioned with a security man's persistence.

'Yes,' Lugovoy said with a confident gleam behind his eyes. 'And much more.'

21

A mad flapping of wings broke the early morning stillness as two pheasants broke towards the sky. Soviet President Georgi Antonov snapped the over-and-under Purdey shotgun to his shoulder and pulled the two triggers in quick succession. The twin blasts echoed through the mist dampened forest. One of the birds suddenly ceased its flight and tumbled to the ground.

Vladimir Polevoi, head of the Committe for State Security, waited an instant until he was sure Antonov had missed the second pheasant before he brought it down with one shot.

Antonov fixed his KGB director with a hard-eyed stare. 'Showing up your boss again, Vladimir?'

Polevoi read Antonov's mock anger correctly. 'Your shot was difficult, Comrade President. Mine was quite easy.'

'You should have joined the Foreign Ministry instead of the Secret Police,' Antonov said laughing. 'Your diplomacy ranks with Gromyko's.' He paused and looked around the forest. 'Where is our French host?'

'President L'Estrange is seventy metres to our left.' Polevoi's statement was punctuated by a volley of gunshots somewhere out of sight beyond the undergrowth.

'Good,' grunted Antonov. 'We can have a few minutes of conversation.' He held out the Purdey to Polevoi, who replaced the empty shells and clicked the safety switch.

Polevoi moved in close and spoke in a low tone. 'I would caution about speaking too freely. French intelligence has listening probes everywhere.'

'Secrets seldom last long these days,' Antonov said with a sigh.

Polevoi cracked a knowing smile. 'Yes, our operatives recorded the meeting between L'Estrange and his finance minister last night.'

'Any revelations I should know about?'

'Nothing of value. Most of their conversation centred around persuading you to accept the American President's financial assistance programme.'

'If they're stupid enough to believe I would not take advantage of the President's naïve generosity, they're also stupid enough to think I agreed to fly here to discuss it.'

'Rest assured, the French are completely unaware of the true nature behind your visit.'

'Any late word from New York?'

'Only that Huckleberry Finn exceeded our projections.' Polevoi's Russian tongue pronounced Huckleberry as Gulkleberry.

'And all goes well?'

'The trip is underway.'

'So the old bitch accomplished what we thought was impossible.'

'The mystery is how she managed it.'

Antonov stared at him. 'We don't know?'

'No sir. She refused to take us into her confidence. Her son shielded her operation like the Kremlin wall. So far we haven't been able to penetrate her security.'

'The Chinese whore,' Antonov snarled. 'Who does she think she's dealing with, emptyheaded schoolboys?'

'I believe her ancestry is Korean,' said Polevoi.

'No difference.' Antonov stopped and sat down heavily on a fallen log. 'Where is the experiment taking place?'

Polevoi shook his head. 'We don't know that either.'

'Have you no communication with Comrade Lugovoy?'

'He and his staff departed Lower Manhattan Island on the Staten Island ferry late Friday night. They never stepped ashore at the landing. We lost all contact.'

'I want to know where they are,' Antonov said evenly. 'I want to know the exact location of the experiment.'

'I have our best agents working on it.'

110

'We can't allow her to keep us wandering in the dark, especially when there is one billion American dollars' worth of our gold reserves at stake.'

Polevoi gave the Communist Party Chairman a crafty look. 'Do you intend to pay her fee?'

'Does the Volga melt in January?' Antonov replied with a broad grin.

'She won't be an easy prey to outfox.'

The sound of feet tramping through the underbrush could be heard. Antonov's eyes flickered to the approaching groundskeepers, who were coming with the downed pheasants, and then back to Polevoi.

'Just find Lugovoy,' he said softly, 'and the rest will take care of itself.'

Four miles away, in a sound truck two men sat in front of a sophisticated microwave receiving set. Beside them two reel-to-reel tape decks were recording Antonov and Polevoi's conversation in the woods.

The men were electronic surveillance specialists with the SDECE, France's intelligence service. Both could interpret six languages, including Russian. In unison they lifted their earphones and exchanged curious looks.

'What in hell do you suppose that was all about?' said one.

The second man gave a Gallic shrug. 'Who can say? Probably some kind of Russian doubletalk.'

'I wonder if an analyst can make anything important out of it?'

'Important or not, we'll never know.'

The first man paused, held an earphone to his ear for a few moments and then set it down again. 'They're talking with President L'Estrange now. That's all we're going to get.'

'Okay, let's close down shop and get the recordings to Paris. I've got a date at six o'clock.'

22

The sun was two hours above the eastern edge of the city when Sandecker drove through a back gate of the Washington National Airport. He stopped the car beside a seemingly deserted hangar standing in a weed covered part of the field far beyond the airline's maintenance area. He walked to a side door whose weathered wood had long since shed its paint and pressed a small button opposite a large rusting padlock. After a few seconds the door silently swung open.

The cavernous interior was painted a gloss white which brightly reflected the sun's rays through huge skylights in the curved roof. It looked like a transportation museum. The polished concrete floor held four long orderly rows of antique and classic automobiles. Most gleamed as elegantly as the day their coachmakers added the finishing touch. A few were in various stages of restoration. Sandecker lingered by a majestic 1921 Rolls-Royce Silver Ghost with coachwork by Park-Ward and a massive red 1925 Isotta-Fraschini with a torpedo body by Sala.

The two centrepieces were an old Ford trimotor aircraft known to aviation enthusiasts as the 'tin goose' and an early 20th century railroad Pullman car with the words MANHATTAN LIMITED painted in gilded letters on its steel side.

Sandecker made his way up a circular iron stairway to a glass enclosed apartment that spanned the upper level across one end of the hangar. The living room was decorated in marine antiques. One wall was lined with shelves supporting delicately crafted shipmodels in glass cases.

He found Pitt standing in front of a stove studying a strange looking mixture in a frying pan. Pitt wore a pair of khaki hiking shorts, tattered tennis shoes and a T-shirt with the words, '*Raise the Lusitania*' across the front.

'You're just in time to eat, Admiral.'

'What have you got there?' asked Sandecker, eyeing the mixture with suspicion.

'Nothing fancy. A spicy Mexican omelette.'

'I'll settle for a cup of coffee and half a grapefruit.'

Pitt served as they sat down at a kitchen table and poured the coffee. Sandecker frowned and waved a newspaper in the air. 'You made page two.'

'I hope I do as well in other papers.'

'What do you expect to prove?' Sandecker demanded. 'Holding a press conference and claiming you found the *San Marino*, which you didn't, and the *Pilottown*, which is supposed to be top secret. Have you lost your grey matter?'

Pitt paused between bites of the omelette. 'I made no mention of the nerve agent.'

'Fortunately, the Army quietly buried it yesterday.'

'No harm done. Now that the *Pilottown* is empty, she's just another rusting shipwreck.'

'The President won't see it that way. If he wasn't in New Mexico,

112

we'd both be picking our asses out of a White House carpet by now – '

Sandecker was interrupted by a buzzing noise. Pitt rose from the table and pushed a switch on a small panel.

'Somebody at the door?' inquired Sandecker.

Pitt nodded.

'This is a Florida grapefruit,' Sandecker grumbled, spitting out a rind.

'So?'

'I prefer Texas.'

'I'll make a note,' said Pitt with a grin.

'Getting back to your cockamamy story,' Sandecker said, squeezing out the final juice drops in a spoon. 'I'd like to know your reasoning.'

Pitt told him.

'Why not let the Justice Department handle it?' asked Sandecker. 'That's what they're paid for.'

Pitt's eyes hardened and he pointed his fork menacingly. 'Because the Justice people will never be called in to investigate. The government isn't about to admit over three hundred deaths were caused by a stolen nerve agent that isn't suppose to exist. Lawsuits and damaging publicity would go on for years. They want to whitewash the whole mess into oblivion. The Augustine Volcano eruption was timely. Later today, the President's Press Secretary will hand out a bogus cover-up blaming sulphuric gas clouds for the deaths.'

Sandecker looked at him sternly for a moment. Then he asked, 'Who told you that?'

'I did,' came a feminine voice from the doorway.

Loren's face was wrapped in a disarming smile. She had been out jogging and was dressed in brief, red satin shorts with a matching tank top and headband. The Virginia humidity had brought out the sweat and she was still a little breathless. She dried her face with a small towel that was tucked in her waistband.

Pitt made the introductions. 'Admiral James Sandecker, Congresswoman Loren Smith.'

'We've sat across from each other during maritime committee meetings,' said Loren extending her hand.

Sandecker didn't require the powers of a psychic to read Pitt and Loren's relationship. 'Now I see why you've always looked kindly on my NUMA budget proposals.'

If Loren felt any embarrassment at his indirect insinuation, she didn't show it. 'Dirk is a very persuasive lobbyist,' she said sweetly.

'Like some coffee?' asked Pitt.

'No thanks, I'm too thirsty for coffee.' She went over to the refrigerator and poured herself a glass of buttermilk.

'You know the subject of Press Secretary Thompson's news release?' Sandecker prodded her.

Loren nodded. 'My press aide and his wife are chummy with the Sonny Thompsons. They all had dinner together last night. Thompson mentioned that the White House was laying the Alaskan tragedy to rest, but that was all. He didn't slip the details.'

Sandecker turned to Pitt. 'If you persist in this vendetta, you'll be stepping on a lot of toes.'

'I won't give it up,' Pitt said gravely.

Sandecker looked at Loren. 'And you, Congresswoman Smith?'

'Loren.'

'Loren,' he obliged. 'May ask what your interest is in this?'

She hesitated for a fraction of a second and then said, 'Let's just say Congressional curiosity about a possible government scandal.'

'You haven't told her the true purpose behind your Alaskan fishing expedition?' Sandecker asked Pitt.

'No.'

'I think you should tell her.'

'Do I have your official permission?'

The Admiral nodded. 'A friend in Congress will come in handy before your hunt is over.'

'And you, Admiral, where do you stand?' Pitt asked him.

Sandecker stared hard across the table at Pitt, examining every feature of the craggy face as though he were seeing it for the first time, wondering what manner of man would step far beyond normal bounds for no personal gain. He read only a fierce determination. It was an expression he had seen many times in the years he'd known Pitt.

'I'll back you until the President orders your ass shot,' he said at last. 'Then you're on your own.'

Pitt held back an audible sigh of relief. It was going to be all right. Better than all right.

Min Koryo looked down at the newspaper on her desk. 'What do you make of this?'

Lee Tong leaned over her shoulder and read the opening sentences of the article aloud. ' "It was announced yesterday by Dirk Pitt, Special Projects Director for NUMA, that two ships missing for over twenty years have been found. The *San Marino* and the *Pilottown*, both Liberty class vessels built during World War Two, were discovered on the seafloor in the North Pacific off Alaska." '

'A bluff!' Min Koryo suddenly snapped. 'Someone in Washington, probably from the Justice Department, had nothing better to do so they opened the coffin on a dead event. They're on a fishing trip, nothing more.'

'I think you're only half right, *aumuni*,' said Lee Tong thoughtfully. 'I suspect that while NUMA was searching for the source behind the deaths in Alaskan waters, they stumbled on the ship containing the nerve agent.'

'And this press release is a scheme to ferret out the true owners of that ship,' Min Koryo added.

Lee Tong nodded. 'The government is gambling we will make an inquiry that can be traced.'

Min Koryo sighed. 'A pity the ship wasn't sunk as planned.'

Lee Tong came around and sank into a chair in front of the desk. 'Bad luck,' he said, thinking back. 'After I realised the explosives didn't detonate, the storm hit and I was unable to reboard the ship.'

'You can't be faulted for nature's whims,' Min Koryo said impassively. 'The true blame lies with the Russians. If they hadn't backed out of their bargain to buy Nerve Agent S, there would have been no need to scuttle the ship.'

'They were afraid the agent was too unstable to transport across Siberia to their chemical warfare arsenal in the Urals.'

'What's puzzling is how did NUMA tie the two ships together?'

'I can't say, *aumuni*. We were careful to strip every piece of identification.'

'No matter,' Min Koryo said. 'The fact remains, the article in the newspaper is a ploy. We must remain silent and do nothing to jeopardise our anonymity.'

'What about the man who made the announcement?' Lee Tong asked. 'This Dirk Pitt?'

A long, cold brooding look came over Min Koryo's narrow face. 'Investigate his motives and observe his movements. See where he fits in the picture. If he appears to be a danger to us, arrange his funeral.'

The grey of evening softened the harsh outlines of Los Angeles, and the lights came on, pimpling the sides of the buildings. The crippling noise of the street traffic rose and seeped through the old-fashioned sash window. The tracks were warped and jammed under a dozen coats of paint. It hadn't been opened in thirty years. Outside, an air conditioner rattled in its brackets.

The man sat in an aging, wooden, swivel chair and stared unseeing through the grime filming the glass. He stared through eyes that had seen the worst the city had to give. They were hard, stark eyes, still clear and undimmed after sixty years. He sat in shirtsleeves, the well-worn leather of a holster slung over his left shoulder, the butt of a 45 automatic protruding like a cancerous growth. He was wide and stocky, the muscles had softened over the years, but he could still lift a two hundred pound man off the sidewalk and embed him in a brick wall.

The chair creaked as he swung around and leaned over a desk that was battlescarred with uncounted cigarette burns. He picked up a folded newspaper and read the article on the ship discoveries for perhaps the tenth time. Pulling open a drawer, he searched out a dogeared folder and stared at the cover for a long while. Long ago he had memorised every word on the papers inside. Along with the newspaper he slipped it inside a worn leather briefcase.

He rose and stepped over to a washbowl hung in one corner of the room and rinsed his face with cold water. Then he donned a coat and a battered fedora, turned off the light and left the office.

As he stood in the hallway waiting for the lift, he was surrounded by the smells of the aging building. The mould and rot seemed stronger with each passing day. Thirty-five years at the same stand was a long time, he mused, too long.

His thoughts were interrupted by the clatter of the lift door. An operator who looked to be in his seventies gave him a yellow toothed grin.

'Callin' quits for the night?' he asked.

'No, I'm taking the redeye flight to Washington.'

'New case?'

'An old one.'

There were no more questions and they rode the rest of the way in silence. As he stepped into the lobby he nodded at the operator. 'See you in a couple of days, Joe.'

Then he passed through the main door and melted into the night.

23

To most, his name was Hiram Yaeger. To a select few, he was known as Pinocchio because he could stick his nose into a vast number of computer networks and sift over their software. His playground was the tenth floor communications and information network of NUMA.

Sandecker hired him to collect and store every scrap of data ever written on the oceans, scientific or historical, fact and theory. Yaeger tackled the job with a fierce dedication, and within five years had accumulated a huge computer library of knowledge about the sea.

Yaeger worked erratic hours, sometimes coming in with the

116

morning sun and working straight through until the following dawn. He seldom showed up for departmental meetings, but Sandecker left him alone because there were none better, and because Yaeger had an uncanny ability to pry out secret access codes to a huge number of worldwide computer networks.

Always dressed in Levi jacket and pants, he wore his long blonde hair in a bun. A scraggly beard mixed with his probing eyes gave him the appearance of a desert prospector peering over the next hill for Eldorado.

He sat at a computer terminal stuck away in a far corner of NUMA's electronic maze. Pitt stood off to one side, watching with interest the green block letters on a display screen.

'That's all we're going to comb from the Maritime Administration's mass storage system.'

'Nothing new there,' Pitt agreed.

'What now?'

'Can you tap the Coast Guard headquarters documents?'

Yaeger gave a wolfish grin. 'Can Aunt Jemima make pancakes?'

He consulted a thick black notebook for a minute, found the insertion he was looking for, and punched the number into a push-botton telephone connected to a modem link. The Coast Guard computer system answered and accepted Yaeger's access code, and the green block letters swept across the display.

PLEASE STATE YOUR REQUEST

Yaeger gave Pitt a questioning look.

'Ask for an abstract of title on the *Pilottown*,' Pitt ordered.

Yaeger nodded and sent the request into the terminal. The answer flashed back and Pitt studied it closely, noting all the transactions of the vessel from the time she was built, who owned it as long as it was a documented vessel flying the United States flag, and the mortgages against it. The probe was redundant. The *Pilottown* had been removed from documentation when it was sold to an alien, in this case the Kassandra Phosphate Company of Athens, Greece.

'Anything promising?' Yaeger inquired.

'Another dry hole,' Pitt grunted.

'How about Lloyds of London? They'll have it in their register.'

'Okay, give it a shot.'

Yaeger logged out of the Coast Guard system, checked his book again, and routed the terminal to the computer bank of the great maritime insurance company. The data printed out at 400 characters a second. This time the history of the *Pilottown* was revealed in greater detail. And yet, little of it appeared useful. Then an item at the bottom of the display screen caught Pitt's attention.

'I think we might have something.'

'Looks pretty much like the same stuff to me,' said Yaeger.

'The line after Sosan Trading Company.'

'Where they're listed as operators? So what? That showed up before.'

'As owners, not operators. There's a difference.'

'What does it prove?'

Pitt straightened and his eyes took on a reflective look. 'The reason owners register their vessel with what is called a "country of convenience" is to save costly licences, taxes and restrictive operating regulations. Another reason is they become lost to any kind of investigation. So they set up a dummy front and carry the company headquarters' address as a post office box, in this case, Inchon, Korea. Now, if they contract with an operator to arrange cargoes and crew for the ship, the transfer of money from one to the other must take place. Banking facilities must be used, and banks keep records.'

'All right, but say I'm a parent outfit. Why let my shady shipping line be run by some sleazy second party if we leave traceable banking links? I fail to see the advantage.'

'An insurance scam,' Pitt answered. 'The operator does the dirty work while the owners collect. For example, take the case of a Greek tanker several years ago. A tramp called the *Trikeri*. It departed Surabaja, Indonesia with its oil tanks filled to the brim. After reaching Capetown, South Africa, it slipped onto an offshore pipeline and removed all but a few thousand gallons. A week later it mysteriously sank off West Africa. An insurance claim was filed on the ship and a full cargo of oil. Investigators were dead certain the sinking was intentional, but they couldn't prove it. The *Trikeri*'s operator took the heat and quietly went out of business. The registered owners collected the insurance payoff and then siphoned it off through a corporate maze to the power at the top.'

'This happen often?'

'More than anyone knows,' Pitt replied.

'You want to dig into the Sosan Trading Company's bank account?'

Pitt knew better than to ask Yaeger if he could do it. He simply said, 'Yes.'

Yaeger logged out of the Lloyd's computer network and walked over to a file cabinet. He returned with a large bookkeeping ledger.

'Bank security codes,' he said without elaboration.

Yaeger set to work and homed in on Sosan Trading's bank in two minutes. 'Got it!' he exclaimed. 'An obscure Inchon branch of a big bank headquartered in Seoul. Account was closed six years ago.'

'Are the statements still on file?'

Without answering, Yaeger stabbed the terminal's keys and then sat back, arms folded, and eyed the printout. The data blinked on with the account number and a request for the monthly statements desired. He looked up at Pitt expectantly.

'March through September, 1976,' Pitt directed.

The bank's computer system in Korea obliged.

'Most curious,' said Yaeger digesting the data. 'Only twelve transactions over a span of seven years. Sosan Trading must have cleared their overheads and payroll with cash.'

'Where did the deposits originate?' Pitt asked.

'Appears to be a bank in Bern, Switzerland.'

'One step closer.'

'Yes, but here it gets tricky,' said Yaeger. 'Swiss bank security codes are more complex. And if this shipping outfit is as cagey as they appear, they probably juggle bank accounts like a vaudeville act.'

'I'll get the coffee while you start digging.'

Yaeger looked pensively at Pitt for a moment. 'You never give up, do you?'

'No.'

Yaeger was surprised at the sudden coldness in Pitt's tone. He shrugged. 'Okay, pal, but this isn't going to be a walkover. It may take all night, and turn up zilch. I'll have to keep sending different number combinations until I strike the right codes.'

'You got something better to do?'

'No, but while you're getting the coffee, I'd appreciate it if you scare up some doughnuts.'

The bank in Bern, Switzerland, proved discouraging. Any trail to Sosan Trading's parent company ended there. They spot checked six other banks in the tiny alpine country, hoping they might get lucky like a treasure hunter who finds the shipwreck chart he's searching for hidden away in the wrong drawer of an archive. But they turned up nothing of value. Groping through the account records of every banking house in Europe presented a staggering problem. There were over six thousand of them.

'Looks pretty dismal,' said Yaeger after five hours of staring at the display screen.

'I agree,' said Pitt.

'Shall I keep punching away?'

'If you don't mind.'

Yaeger raised his arms and stretched. 'This is how I get my kicks. You look like you've had it though. Why don't you shove off and get some sleep. If I stumble on anything, I'll give you a call.'

*

Pitt gratefully left Yaeger at NUMA headquarters and drove across the river to the airport. Stopping the Talbot-Lago in front of his hangar door, he slipped a small transmitter from his coat pocket and pressed a pre-set code. In sequence the security alarm systems closed down and the massive door lifted to a height of seven feet. He parked the car inside and reversed the process. Then, wearily, he climbed the stairway, entered the living-room and turned on the lights.

A man was sitting in Pitt's favourite reading chair, his hands folded on a briefcase that rested on his lap. There was a patient look about him, almost deadly, with only the tiniest hint of an indifferent smile. He wore an old fashioned fedora hat and his custom tailored coat, specially cut to conceal a lethal bulge, was unbuttoned just enough to reveal the butt of a 45 automatic.

For a moment they stared at each other, neither speaking, like fighters sizing up their opponent. At last Pitt broke the silence.

'I guess the appropriate thing to say is: "Who the hell are you?"'

The thin smile broadened into a set grin. 'I'm a private investigator, Mr Pitt. My name is Casio, Sal Casio.'

24

'You have any problem entering?'

'Your security system is good, not great, but capable enough to discourage most burglars and juvenile vandals.'

'That mean I flunked the test?'

'Not entirely. I'd grade you a C plus.'

Pitt moved very slowly to an antique oak icebox he rebuilt into a liquor cabinet and eased open the door. 'Would you like a drink, Mr Casio?'

'A shot of Jack Daniels on ice, thanks.'

'A lucky guess. I happen to have a bottle.'

'I peeked,' said Casio. 'Oh, and by the way, I took the liberty of removing the clip from the gun.'

'Gun?' Pitt asked innocently.

'The 32 calibre Mauser automatic, serial number nine-two-two-three-seven-four, cleverly taped behind the half gallon bottle of gin.'

Pitt gave Casio a long look indeed. 'How long did it take?'

'To make a search?'

Pitt nodded silently as he opened the refrigerator door for the ice.

'About forty-five minutes.'

'And you found the other two guns I squirrelled away?'

'Three actually.'

'You're very thorough.'

'Nothing that is hidden in a house can't be found. And some of us are more talented at probing than others. It's simply a matter of technique.' There was nothing boastful in Casio's tone. He spoke as though merely stating an accepted truth.

Pitt poured the drink and brought it into the living-room on a tray. Casio took the glass with his right hand. Then suddenly, Pitt dropped the tray, exposing a small, vest pocket 25 calibre automatic aimed at Casio's forehead.

Casio's only reaction was a thin smile. 'Very good,' he said approvingly. 'So there were a total of five.'

'Inside an empty milk carton,' Pitt explained.

'Nicely done, Mr Pitt. A clever touch, waiting until my gun hand was holding a glass. That shows you were thinking. I'll have to mark you up to a B minus.'

Pitt clicked on the safety and lowered the gun. 'If you came here to kill me, Mr Casio, you could have blown me away when I stepped through the door. What's on your mind?'

Casio nodded down at his briefcase. 'May I?'

'Go ahead.'

He set the drink down, opened the case and pulled out a bulging cardboard folder that was held together with rubber bands. 'A case I've worked on since 1966.'

'A long time. You must be a stubborn man.'

'I hate to let loose of it,' Casio admitted. 'It's like walking away from a jigsaw before it's completed, or putting down a good book. Sooner or later every investigator gets on a case that has him staring at the ceiling nights, the case he can never solve. This one has a personal tie, Mr Pitt. It began twenty-three years ago when a girl, a bank teller by the name of Arta Casilighio, stole a hundred and twenty-eight thousand dollars from a bank in Los Angeles.'

'How can that concern me?'

'She was last seen boarding a ship called the *San Marino*.'

'Okay, so you read the press story about the shipwreck discovery.'

'Yes.'

'And you think this girl disappeared with the *San Marino*?'

'I'm certain of it.'

'Then your case is solved. The thief is dead and money gone forever.'

'Not that simple,' said Casio, staring into his glass. 'There's no doubt Arta Casilighio is dead, but the money is not *gone forever*. Arta took freshly printed currency from the Federal Reserve Bank. All serial numbers were recorded so it was an easy matter to account

121

for the missing bills.' Casio paused to look over his glass into Pitt's eyes. 'Two years ago the missing money finally turned up.'

Sudden interest flared in Pitt's eyes. He sat down in a chair facing Casio. 'All of it?' he asked cautiously.

Casio nodded. 'It appeared in dribbles and spurts. Five thousand in Frankfurt, a thousand in Cairo, all in foreign banks. None came to light in the United States, except one, one hundred dollar bill.'

'Then Arta didn't die on the *San Marino*.'

'She vanished with the ship all right. The FBI connected her to a stolen passport belonging to an Estelle Wallace. With that lead they were able to follow her as far as San Francisco. Then they lost her. I kept digging and finally ran down a drifter who sometimes drove a cab when he needed booze money. He remembered hauling her to the boarding ramp of the *San Marino*.'

'Can you trust the memory of a lush?'

Casio smiled confidently. 'Arta gave him a crisp new hundred dollar bill for the fare. He couldn't make change so she told him to keep it. Believe me, it took little effort for him to recall the event.'

'If stolen Federal Reserve currency is in FBI jurisdiction, where do you fit in the picture? Why the dogged pursuit of a criminal whose trail is ice cold?'

'Before I shortened my name for business reasons, it was Casilighio. Arta was my daughter.'

There was an uncomfortable silence. From outside the windows overlooking the river came the rumble of a jetliner taking off. Pitt stood up and went into the kitchen where he poured a cup of coffee from a cold pot and placed it in a microwave oven. 'Care for another drink, Mr Casio?'

Casio shook his head.

'So the bottom line is that you think there's something queer about your daughter's disappearance?'

'She and the ship never made port, but the money she stole turns up in a manner that suggests it's being laundered a little at a time. Doesn't that suggest a queer circumstance to you, Mr Pitt?'

'I can't deny you make a good case.' The microwave beeped and Pitt retrieved a steaming cup. 'But I'm not sure what you want from me.'

'I have some questions.'

Pitt sat down, his interest going beyond mere curiosity. 'Don't expect detailed answers.'

'I understand.'

'Fire away.'

'Where did you find the *San Marino*? I mean in what part of the Pacific Ocean?'

122

'Near the Southern Coast of Alaska,' Pitt replied vaguely.

'A bit far off the track for a ship, steaming from San Francisco to New Zealand, wouldn't you say?'

'Way off the track,' Pitt agreed.

'As far as two thousand miles?'

'And then some.' Pitt took a swallow of coffee and made a face. It was strong enough to use as brick mortar. He looked up. 'Before we continue it's going to cost you.'

Casio gave him a reappraising eye. 'Somehow you never struck me as the type who'd extend a greasy palm.'

'I'd like to have the names of the banks in Europe that passed the stolen money.'

'Any particular reason?' Casio asked, not bothering to conceal his puzzlement.

'None I can tell you about.'

'You're not very cooperative.'

Pitt started to reply, but the phone on an end table rang loudly.

'Hello.'

'Dirk, this is Yaeger. You still awake?'

'Thank you for calling. How is Sally? Is she out of intensive care yet?'

'Can't talk huh?'

'Not too well.'

'But you can listen.'

'No problem.'

'Bad news. I'm not getting anywhere. I'd stand a better chance of throwing a deck of cards in the air and catching a straight flush.'

'Maybe I can knock down the odds. Hold on a minute.' Pitt turned to Casio. 'About that list of banks.'

Casio slowly rose, poured himself another shot of Jack Daniels, stood with his back to Pitt.

'A trade off, Mr Pitt. The bank list for what you know about the *San Marino*.'

'Most of my information is government classified.'

'I don't give a damn if it's stencilled on the inside of the President's jockey shorts. Either we deal or I pack up and hike.'

'How do you know I won't lie?'

'My list could be phoney.'

'Then we'll just have to trust each other,' said Pitt with a loose grin.

'The hell we will,' grunted Casio. 'But neither of us has any choice.'

He took a sheet of paper from the folder and handed it to Pitt who in turn read off the names over the phone to Yaeger.

'Now what?' Casio demanded.

'Now I tell you what happened to the *San Marino*. And by breakfast I may also be able to tell you who killed your daughter.'

25

Fifteen minutes after sunrise, the photo electric controllers in each of Washington's streetlights closed off their circuits. One by one, separated by no more than a few seconds, the yellow and red rays of the high pressure sodium lamps faded and died, waiting through the daylight hours until fifteen minutes before sunset, when their light sensitive controllers boosted them to life again.

Beneath the dimming glow of the streetlights, Sam Emmett could hear the vibration from the early morning traffic as he walked hurriedly through the utility tunnel. There was no Marine Corp or Secret Service escort. He came alone, as did the others. The only person he met since leaving his car under the Treasury Department was the White House guard who was stationed at the basement door. At the head of the hallway leading to the situation room, Emmett was greeted by Alan Mercier.

'You're the last,' Mercier informed him.

Emmett checked his watch and noted he was five minutes early, 'Everyone?' he questioned.

'Except for Simmons in Egypt and Lucas, who's giving your speech at Princeton, they're all present.'

As he entered Oates motioned him to a chair beside his, while Dan Fawcett, General Metcalf, CIA chief, Martin Brogan and Mercier gathered around the conference table.

'I'm sorry for moving the scheduled meeting up by four hours,' Oates began, 'but Sam informed me that his investigators have determined how the kidnapping took place.' Without further explanation he nodded to the FBI Director.

Emmett passed out folders to each of the men at the table, and then rose, moved to a blackboard and took a piece of chalk. Quickly and to precise scale, he drew in the river, the grounds of Mount Vernon and the presidential yacht tied to the dock. Then he filled in the detail and labelled specific areas. The completed drawing had a realism about it that suggested a talent towards architectural draughtsmanship.

Satisfied, finally, that each piece of the drama was in its correct place, he turned and refaced his audience. 'We'll walk through the event chronologically,' he explained. 'I'll briefly summarise while you gentlemen study the details shown in the report. Some of what I'm about to describe is based on fact and hard evidence. Some is conjecture. We have to fill in the blanks as best we can.'

Emmett wrote in a time on the upper left corner of the blackboard.

'18:25: The *Eagle* arrives at Mount Vernon where the Secret Service has installed its security network and the surveillance begins.

'20:15: The President and his guests sit down to dinner. In the same hour, officers and the crew began their meal in the messroom. The only men on duty were the chef, one assistant and the dining-room steward. This fact is important because we feel that it was during dinner when the President, his party and ship's crew were drugged.'

'Drugged or poisoned?' Oates said, looking up.

'Nothing so drastic as poison,' answered Emmett. 'A mild drug that induced a gradual state of drowsiness was probably administered into their food by either the chef or the steward who served the table.'

'Sounds practical,' said Brogan. 'It wouldn't do to have bodies dropping all over the decks.'

Emmett paused to gather his thoughts. 'The Secret Service agent, whose post was on board the yacht the hour before midnight, reported the President and Vice President Margolin were the last to retire. Time: 23:10.'

'That's early for the President,' said Dan Fawcett. 'I've seldom known him to be in bed before two in the morning.'

'00:25: A light mist drifts in from the north-east. Followed at 01:35 by a heavy fog caused by two navy surplus fogging generators concealed in the trees one hundred and sixty yards upriver from the *Eagle*.'

'They could blanket the entire area?' asked Oates.

'Under the right atmospheric conditions – in this case, no wind – the units left on site by the kidnappers can cover two square acres.'

Fawcett looked lost. 'My God, this operation must have taken an army.'

Emmett shook his head. 'Our projections figure it took as few as seven and certainly no more than ten men.'

'Surely the Secret Service scouted the woods surrounding Mount Vernon before the President's arrival,' said Fawcett. 'How did they miss the foggers?'

'The units weren't in place prior to 17:00, the night of the abduction,' replied Emmett.

'How could the equipment operators see what they were doing in the dark?' Fawcett pressed. 'Why weren't their movements or the sound of the generators overheard?'

125

'Infra red night visual gear would answer your first question. And the noise made by the equipment was muffled by the mooing of cows.'

Brogan gave a thoughtful twist of his head. 'Who would have ever thought of that?'

'Somebody did,' said Emmett. 'They left the tape recorder and an amplifier behind with the foggers.'

'It says here the only thing the security people noticed was an oily aroma to the fog.'

Emmett nodded. 'The fogger heats a deodorised kerosene type of fuel to a high pressure and blows it out a nozzle in very fine droplets, producing the fog.'

'Let's move on to the next event,' said Oates.

'01:50: The small chase boat moors to the dock because of limited visibility. Three minutes later the Coast Guard cutter notifies agent George Blackowl at the Secret Service command post that a high intensity signal was jamming their radar reception. They also appraised agent Blackowl that before their equipment went blind the only contact on their oscilloscope was a city sanitation tugboat and its trash barges that tied up to the bank to wait out the fog.'

Metcalf looked up. 'Tied up how far away?'

'Two hundred yards up river.'

'Then the tug was above the artificial fog.'

'A crucial point,' Emmett acknowledged, 'which we'll come to later.'

He turned to the blackboard and wrote in another time sequence. The room fell quiet. The men seated around the long table sat in rock-like stillness, waiting for Emmett to reveal the final solution to the presidential abduction.

'02:00: The agents moved to their new guard posts. Agent Lyle Brock took up station on board the *Eagle* while agent Karl Polaski relieved him on the pier. For the next forty minutes Polaski remained close to the pier entrance. What is most important is that during this time the *Eagle* was hidden from his sight. He later walked to the boarding steps of the yacht and talked to who he thought was Brock. Brock by now was either unconscious or dead. Polaski did not note anything suspicious except that Brock appeared to have forgotten his next post.'

'Polaski couldn't tell he was talking with a stranger?' questioned Oates.

'They conversed at least ten feet away from each other in low tones so they wouldn't disturb anyone on the yacht. When the 03:00 post change came around, Brock simply melted into the fog. Agent Polaski states that he was never able to see more than a vague figure.

It wasn't until 03:48 that agent Edward McGrath discovered that Brock was not at his scheduled post. McGrath then notified Blackowl who met him on the *Eagle* four minutes later. The yacht was searched and found empty, except for Polaski who had moved on board to replace Brock.' Emmett placed the chalk back in the tray and wiped his hands together. 'The rest is cut and dried. Who was alerted and when . . . the results of a fruitless search on the river and around the grounds of Mount Vernon . . . the roadblocks that failed to produce the missing men . . . and so on.'

'What was the disposition of the tug boat and trash barges after the alert?' questioned Metcalf cannily.

'The barges were found moored to the river bank,' Emmett answered him. 'The tug was gone.'

'So much for facts,' said Oates. 'The prize question is, how were almost twenty men spirited off the yacht under the noses of an army of Secret Service agents and passed undetected through the most advanced security alarm systems that money can buy?'

'Your answer is, Mr Secretary, they weren't.'

Oates' eyebrows rose. 'How was it done?'

Emmett noticed a smug expression on Metcalf's face. 'I think the General has figured it out.'

'I wish someone would tell me,' said Fawcett.

Emmett took a deep breath before he spoke. 'The yacht that agents Blackowl and McGrath found deserted is not the same yacht that carried the President and his party to Mount Vernon.'

'Son of a bitch!' gasped Mercier.

'That's hard to swallow,' said Oates sceptically.

Emmett picked up the chalk again and began diagramming. 'About fifteen minutes after the fogging generators began laying a dense cloud over the river and Mount Vernon, the abduction team transmitted on the Coast Guard's radar frequency and knocked it out of commission. Up river the sanitation tug boat – except in this instance it was not a river tug but a yacht identical in every detail to the *Eagle* – cast off from the barges, which we found to be empty, and slowly cruised downstream. Its radar, of course, was working on a different frequency than the Coast Guards.'

Emmett drew in the path of the approaching yacht. 'When it was fifty yards from the Mount Vernon pier and the stern of the *Eagle*, it shut down its engines and drifted with the current, which was running about one knot. The abductors on the yacht – '

'What I'd like to know, is how they got on board in the first place,' Mercier interrupted.

Emmett made a shrugging gesture with his hands. 'We don't know. Our best guess at the moment is they killed the galley crew earlier in

127

the day and took their place, using counterfeit Coast Guard identification and orders.'

'Please continue your findings,' Oates persisted.

'The abductors on the yacht,' Emmett repeated, 'untied the mooring lines, allowing the *Eagle* to drift silently from the pier to make room for its double. Polaski heard nothing from his post near the bank because any strange sounds were covered by the hum of the engine room generators. Then, once the bogus yacht was in place, its crew, probably no more than two men, rowed a small dinghy to the *Eagle* and escaped with the others downriver. One remained, however, to impersonate agent Brock. By the time Polaski conversed with Brock's impersonator, the switch had already been made. At the next post change, the man calling himself Brock slipped off and joined the men operating the foggers. Together they drove off and swung on the highway towards Alexandria. We know that much by foot prints and tyre tracks.'

Everyone but Emmett focused their attention on the blackboard as if trying to visualise the scene in their minds. The incredible timing, the ease in which Presidential security was penetrated, the smoothness of the entire operation, staggered them.

'I can't help but admire the execution,' General Metcalf said. 'They must have taken a long time to plan this thing.'

'Our estimate is three years,' said Emmett.

'Where could they have possibly found an identical boat?' Fawcett muttered to no one in particular.

'My investigating team considered that. They traced the old boating records and found that the original builder constructed the *Eagle* and a sister ship, named the *Samantha* at the same time. The last registered owner was a stockbroker in Baltimore. He sold it about three years ago to a guy named Dunn. That's all he could tell us. It was an under-the-table cash transaction to beat a profit tax. He never saw Dunn or the yacht again. The *Samantha* was never registered or licensed under the new owner. They both dropped from sight.'

'Was it identical in every respect to the *Eagle*?' Brogan asked.

'A creative job of deception. Every stick of furniture, bulkhead decor, paint, and equipment is a perfect match.'

Fawcett nervously tapped a pencil on the table. 'How did you catch on?'

'Every time you enter and exit a room, you leave particles of your presence behind. Hair, dandruff, lint, fingerprints, they can all be detected. My lab people couldn't find one tiny hint that the President or the others had ever been on board.'

Oates straightened in his chair. 'The Bureau has done a magnificent job, Sam. We're all grateful.'

Emmett gave a curt nod and sat down.

'The yacht transfer brings up a new angle,' Oates continued, 'as gruesome as it sounds, we have to consider the possibility they were all assassinated.'

'We've got to find the yacht,' Mercier said grimly.

Emmett looked at him. 'I've already ordered a surface and air search.'

'You won't find it that way,' Metcalf interjected. 'We're dealing with damned smart people. They're not about to leave it lying around where it can be found.'

Fawcett poised his pencil in midair. 'Are you saying the yacht was destroyed?'

'That may well be the case,' Metcalf said, apprehension forming in his eyes. 'If so, we have to be prepared to find corpses.'

Oates leaned on his elbows and rubbed his face with his hands and wished he was any place but in that room at that moment. 'We're going to have to spread our trust,' he said finally. 'The best man I can think of for an underwater search is Jim Sandecker over at NUMA.'

'I concur,' said Fawcett. 'His special projects team has just wrapped up a ticklish job off Alaska where they found the ship responsible for widespread contamination.'

'Will you brief him, Sam?' Oates put to Emmett.

'I'll go directly from here to his office.'

'Well, I guess that's it for now,' said Oates, exhaustion creeping into his voice. 'Good or bad, we have a lead. Only God knows what we'll have after we find the *Eagle*.' He hesitated, staring up at the blackboard. Then he said, 'I don't envy the first man who steps inside.'

26

Every morning, including Saturdays and Sundays, Admiral Sandecker jogged the six miles from his Watergate apartment to the NUMA headquarters building. He had just stepped out of the bathroom shower adjoining his office when his secretary's voice came over a speaker above the sink.

'Admiral, Mr Emmett is here to see you.'

Sandecker was vigorously towelling his hair and he was not sure he heard the name right. 'Sam Emmett, as in FBI?'

'Yes sir. He asked to see you immediately. He says it's extremely urgent.'

Sandecker saw his face turn incredulous in the mirror. The esteemed Director of the FBI did not make office calls at eight o'clock in the morning. The Washington bureaucratic game had rules. Everyone from the President on down abided by them. Emmett's unannounced visit could only mean a dire emergency.

'Send him right in.'

He barely had time to throw on a terrycloth robe, his skin still dripping, when Emmett strode through the door.

'Jim, we've got a hell of a problem.' Emmett didn't bother with a preliminary handshake. He quickly laid his briefcase on Sandecker's desk, opened it and handed the admiral a folder. 'Sit down and look this over, and then we'll discuss it.'

Sandecker was not a man to be shoved and ordered around, but he could read the tension in Emmett's eyes, and he did as he was asked without comment.

Sandecker studied the contents of the folder for nearly ten minutes without speaking. Emmett sat on the other side of the desk and looked for an expression of shock or anger. There was none. Sandecker remained enigmatic. At last he closed the folder and said simply, 'How can I help?'

'Find the *Eagle*.'

'You think they sank her?'

'An air and surface search has turned up nothing.'

'All right, I'll get my best people on it.' Sandecker made a movement towards his intercom. Emmett raised his hand in a negative gesture.

'I don't have to describe the chaos if this leaks out.'

'I've never lied to my staff before.'

'You'll have to keep them in the dark on this one.'

Sandecker gave a curt nod and spoke into the intercom. 'Sylvia, please get Pitt on the phone.'

'Pitt?' Emmett inquired in an official tone.

'My Special Projects Director. He'll head up the search.'

'You'll tell him only what's necessary?' It was more an order than a request.

A yellow caution light glimmered in Sandecker's eyes. 'That will be at my discretion.'

Emmett started to say something but was interrupted by the intercom.

'Admiral?'

'Yes, Sylvia.'

'Mr Pitt's line is busy.'

'Keep trying until he answers,' Sandecker said gruffly. 'Better yet, call the operator and cut in on his line. Tell her this is a government priority.'

'Will you be able to mount a full scale search operation by evening?' asked Emmett.

Sandecker's lips parted in an all-devouring grin. 'If I know Pitt, he'll have a crew scanning the depths of the Potomac River before lunch.'

Pitt was speaking to Hiram Yaeger when the operator broke in. He cut the conversation short and then dialled the admiral's private line. After listening without doing any of the talking for several moments, he replaced the receiver in its cradle.

'Well,' asked Casio expectantly.

'The money was exchanged, never deposited,' Pitt said, looking miserably down at the floor. 'That's all. That's all there is. No thread left to pick up.'

There was only a flicker of disappointment in Casio's face. He'd been there before. He let out a long sigh and slowly read his watch. He struck Pitt as a man drained of emotional display.

'I appreciate your help,' he said quietly. He snapped his briefcase shut and stood up. 'I'd better go now. If I don't lag, I can catch the next flight back to LA.'

'I'm sorry I couldn't have provided an answer . . .'

Casio shook Pitt's hand in a tight grip. 'Nobody scores one hundred percent every time. Those responsible for the death of my daughter and your friend have made a mistake. Somewhere, sometime, they overlooked a detail. I'm glad to have you on my side, Mr Pitt. It's been a lonely job until now.'

Pitt was genuinely moved. 'I'll keep digging from my end.'

'I couldn't ask for more.' Casio nodded and then walked down the stairs. Pitt watched him shuffle across the hangar floor, a proud, hardened old man, battling his own private windmill.

27

The President sat upright in a black leather cushioned, chrome chair, his body held firmly in place by nylon belts. His eyes stared off in the distance, unfocused and vacant. Wireless sensor scans were taped onto his chest and forehead, transmitting the physical signatures of eight different life functions to a computer network.

The operating room was small, no more than a hundred square feet, and crammed with electronic monitoring equipment. Lugovoy and four members of his surgical team were quietly and efficiently

131

preparing for the delicate operation. Yuri Suvorov stood in the only empty corner, looking uncomfortable in a green sterile gown. He watched as one of Lugovoy's technicians, a woman, pressed a small needle into one side of the President's neck and then the other.

'Odd place for an anaesthetic,' Suvorov remarked.

'For the actual penetration we'll use a local,' Lugovoy replied while staring at an image-intensified X-ray on a video display. 'However, a tiny dose of Amytal into the carotid arteries puts the left and right hemispheres of the brain in a drowsy state. This procedure is to eliminate any conscious memory of the operation.'

'Shouldn't you shave his head?' Suvorov asked gesturing to the President's hair that protruded through an opening of a metal helmet encasing his skull.

'We must ignore normal surgical procedures,' Lugovoy patiently answered. 'For obvious reasons, we cannot alter his appearance in any form.'

'Who will direct the operation?'

'Who do you think?'

'I'm asking you, comrade.'

'I will.'

Suvorov looked puzzled. 'I've studied your file and the file of every member of your staff. I can almost repeat their contents by heart. Your field is psychology, most of the others are electronic technicians, and one is a biochemist. None of you have surgical qualifications.'

'Because we don't require them.' He dismissed Suvorov and scrutinised the TV display again. Then he nodded. 'We can begin now. Set the laser in place.'

A technician pressed his face against the rubber eyepiece of a microscope attached to an argon laser. The machine tied into a computer and displayed a set of coordinates in orange numbers across the bottom of the microscope's position fixer. When the numbers read only zeros the placement was exact.

The man at the laser nodded. 'Position set.'

'Commence,' Lugovoy directed.

A wisp of smoke, so tiny that only the laser operator could see it in the microscope, signalled the contact of the imperceptibly thin blue-green beam on the President's skull.

It was a strange scene. Everyone stood with their back to the patient, watching the monitors. The images were magnified until the beam could be seen as a weblike filament strand. With a precision far above human dexterity, the computer guided the laser in cutting a minute hole one thirtieth of a millimetre in the bone, penetrating only to the membrane covering the brain and its fluid. Suvorov moved closer in rapt fascination.

132

'What happens next?' he asked hoarsely.

Lugovoy motioned him over to an electron microscope. 'See for yourself.'

Suvorov peered through the twin lenses. 'All I make out is a dark speck.'

'Adjust the focus to your eyes.'

Suvorov did so and the speck became a chip – an integrated circuit.

'A microminiaturised implant that can transmit and receive brain signals. We're going to place it in his cerebral cortex where the brain's thought process originates from.'

'What does the implant use for an energy source?'

'The brain itself produces ten watts of electricity,' Lugovoy explained. 'The President's brain waves can be telemetered to a control unit thousands of miles away, translated and any required commands returned. You might say it's like changing TV channels with a remote control box.'

Suvorov stepped back from the microscope and stared at Lugovoy. 'The possibilities are even more overwhelming than I thought,' he murmured. 'We'll be able to learn every secret of the United States government.'

'We'll also be able to manipulate his days and nights for as long as he lives,' Lugovoy continued. 'And through the computer, direct his personality so that neither he nor anyone close to him will notice.'

A technician stepped behind him. 'We're ready to position the implant.'

He nodded. 'Proceed.'

A robot-like machine was moved in place of the laser. The incredibly diminutive implant was taken from under the microscope and exactingly fitted into the end of a single slim wire protruding from a mechanical arm. It was then aligned with the opening in the President's skull.

'Beginning penetration ... now,' droned the voice of the man seated at a console.

As with the viewer on the laser, he studied a series of numbers on a display screen. The entire procedure was preprogrammed. No human hand was lifted. Led by the computer, the robot delicately eased the wire through the protective membrane into the soft folds of the brain. After six minutes the display screen flashed, 'MARK.'

Lugovoy's eyes never left the colour X-ray monitor. 'Release and withdraw the probe.'

'Released and withdrawing,' a voice echoed.

After the wire was removed it was replaced with a miniature tube-like instrument containing a small plug with three hairs and their roots, removed from one of the Russian staff whose head growth

133

closely resembled the President's. The plug was then inserted into the tiny hole neatly cut by the laser beam. When the robot unit was pulled back, Lugovoy approached and studied the results with a large magnifying glass.

'What little scabbing that transpires should flake away in a few days,' he remarked. Satisfied, he straightened and viewed the computer directed screens.

'The implant is operational,' announced his female assistant.

Lugovoy massaged his hands in a pleased gesture. 'Good, we can begin the second penetration.'

'You're going to place another implant?' Suvorov asked.

'No, inject a small amount of RNA into the hippocampus.'

'Could you enlighten me in layman terms?'

Lugovoy reached over the shoulder of the man sitting at the computer console and twisted a knob. The image of the President's brain enlarged until it covered the entire screen of the X-ray monitor.

'There,' he said, tapping the glass screen, 'the seahorse-shaped ridge running under the horns of the lateral ventricles, a vital section of the brain's limbic system. It's called the hippocampus. It's here where new memories are received and dispersed. By injecting RNA – ribonucleic acid which transmits genetic instructions – from another subject, one who's been programmed with certain thoughts, we can accomplish what we term a "memory transfer".'

Suvorov had been furiously storing what he saw and heard in his mind, but he was falling behind. He could not absorb it all. Now he stared down at the President, eyes uncertain.

'You can actually inject the memory of one man into another's brain?'

'Exactly,' Lugovoy said nonchalantly. 'What do you think happens in the mental hospitals where the KGB sends enemies of the state? Not all are re-educated to become good party lovers. Many are used for important psychological experiments. For example, the RNA we are about to administer into the President's hippocampus comes from an artist who insisted on creating illustrations depicting our leaders in awkward and uncomplimentary poses – I can't recall his name.'

'Belkaya?'

'Yes, Oskar Belkaya. A sociological misfit. His paintings were either masterpieces of modern art or nightmarish abstractions, depending upon your tastes. After your fellow state security agents arrested him at his studio, he was secretly taken to a remote sanatorium outside of Kiev. There he was placed in a cocoon like the ones we have here for two years. With new memory storage techniques, discovered through biochemistry, his memory was erased and indoctrinated with political concepts we wish the President to implement within his government.'

'But can't you accomplish the same thing with the control implant?'

'The implant and its computerised network is extremely complex and liable to break down. The memory transfer acts as a backup system. Also, our experiments have shown that the control process operates more efficiently when the subject creates the thought himself, and the implant then commands a positive or negative response.'

'Very impressive,' Suvorov said earnestly. 'And that's the end of it?'

'Not entirely. As an added safety margin, one of my staff, a highly skilled hypnotist, will put the President in a trance and wipe out any subconscious sensations he might have absorbed while under our care. He'll also be primed with a story of where he's been for ten days, in vivid detail.'

'As the Americans are fond of saying, you have all the bases covered.'

Lugovoy shook his head. 'The human brain is a magical universe we will never fully understand. We may think we've finally harnessed its three and a half pounds of greyish-pink jelly, but its capricious nature is as unpredictable as the weather.'

'What you're saying is that the President might not react the way you want him to.'

'It's possible,' Lugovoy said seriously. 'It's also possible for his brain to break the bonds of reality, and in spite of our control, command him to do something that has terrible consequences for us all.'

28

Sandecker stopped his car in the car park of a small yacht marina forty miles below Washington. He climbed from under the wheel and stood looking out over the Potomac River. The sky sparkled in a clear blue as the dull green water rolled eastward towards Chesapeake Bay. He walked down a sagging stairway to a floating dock. Tied up at the end was a tired old clamming boat, its rusting tongs hanging from a deck boom like the claws of some freakish animal.

The hull was worn from years of hard use and most of the paint was gone. Her diesel engine chugged out little puffs of exhaust that leaped from the tip of the stack and dissolved into a soft breeze. The name that was barely discernible over the stern transom read, *Hoki Jamoki.*

Sandecker glanced at his watch. It showed twenty minutes to noon. He nodded in approval. Only three hours after he'd briefed Pitt, the search for the *Eagle* was ready to go. He jumped on deck and greeted the two engineers who were connecting the sonar sensor to the recorder cable, then entered the wheelhouse. He found Pitt eyeballing a large satellite photograph through a magnifying glass.

'Is this the best you can do?' Sandecker asked.

Pitt looked up and grinned humorously. 'You mean the boat?'

'I do.'

'Not up to your spit and polish naval standards, but she'll serve nicely.'

'None of our research vessels were available?'

'They were, but I chose this old tub for two reasons. One, she's a damn good little work boat; and two, if somebody really snatched a government boat with a party of VIP's on board and deep sixed her, they'll expect a major search effort and will be watching for it. This way, we'll be in and out before they're wise.'

Sandecker had only told him a boat belonging to the Naval yard had been stolen from the pier at Mount Vernon and presumed sunk. Little else. 'Who said anything about VIP's being on board?'

'Army and Navy helicopters are as thick as locusts overhead, and you can walk across the river on the Coast Guard ships crowding the water. There's more to this search project that you've let on, Admiral. A hell of a lot more.'

Sandecker didn't reply. He could only admit to himself that Pitt was thinking four jumps ahead. His silence, he knew, only heightened Pitt's suspicions.

Sidestepping the issue, he asked. 'You see something that caused you to begin looking this far below Mount Vernon?'

'Enough to save us four days and twenty-five miles,' Pitt answered. 'I figured the boat would be spotted by one of our space cameras, but which one? Military spy satellites don't orbit over Washington, and space weather pictures won't enhance to pinpoint small detail.'

'Where did you get that one?' Sandecker asked, motioning towards the photograph.

'From a friend at the Department of Interior. One of their geological survey satellites flew 590 miles overhead and shot an infra-red portrait of Chesapeake Bay and the adjoining rivers. Time: 4:40 the morning of the boat's disappearance. If you look through the glass at the blow-up of this section of the Potomac, the only boat that can be seen downriver from Mount Vernon is cruising a mile below this dock.'

136

Sandecker peered at the tiny white dot on the photograph. The enhancement was incredibly sharp. He could detect every piece of gear on the decks and the figures of two people. He stared into Pitt's eyes.

'No way of proving that's the boat we're after,' he said flatly.

'I didn't fall off a pumpkin truck, Admiral. That's the presidential yacht, *Eagle*.'

'I won't run you around the Horn,' Sandecker spoke quietly, 'but I can't tell you any more than I already have.'

Pitt gave a noncommittal shrug and said nothing.

'So where do you think it is?'

Pitt's green eyes deepened. he gave Sandecker a sly stare and picked up a pair of dividers. 'I looked up the *Eagle*'s specifications. Her top speed was 14 knots. Now, the space photo was taken at 4:40. Daylight was an hour and a half away. The crew who pirated the yacht couldn't risk being seen, so they put her on the bottom under cover of darkness. Taking all that into consideration, she could have only travelled twenty-one miles before sun-up.'

'That still takes in a lot of water.'

'I think we can slice it some.'

'By staying in the channel?'

'Yes, sir, deep water. If I was running the show, I'd sink her deep to prevent accidental discovery.'

'What's the average depth of your search grid?'

'Thirty to forty feet.'

'Not enough.'

'True, but according to the depth soundings on the navigation charts, there are several holes that drop over a hundred.'

Sandecker paused and gazed out of the wheelhouse windows as Al Giordino marched along the dock carrying a pair of air tanks on his beefy shoulders. He turned back to Pitt and observed him thoughtfully.

'If you dive on it,' he said coldly, 'you're not to enter. Our job is strictly to discover and identify, nothing else.'

'What's down there that we can't see?'

'Don't ask.'

Pitt smiled wryly. 'Humour me, I'm fickle.'

'The hell you are,' grunted Sandecker. 'What do you think is in the yacht?'

'Make that *who*.'

'Does it matter?' Sandecker asked guardedly. 'It's probably empty.'

'You're jerking me around, Admiral. I'm sure of it. After we find the yacht, what then?'

'The FBI takes over.'

'So we do our little act and step aside.'

'That's what the orders say.'

'I say screw them.'

'Them?'

'The powers who play petty secret games.'

'Believe me, this project isn't petty.'

A hard look crossed Pitt's face. 'We'll make that judgement when we find the yacht, won't we?'

'Take my word for it,' said Sandecker, 'you don't want to see what might be inside the wreck.'

Almost as the words came out, Sandecker knew he'd waved a flag in front of a bull elephant. Once Pitt dropped beneath the river's surface, the thin leash of command was broken.

29

Six hours later and twelve miles downriver, target number seventeen crept across the recording screen of the Klein High Resolution Sonar. It lay in 109 feet of water between Persimmon and Mathias Points directly opposite Popes Creek and two miles above the Potomac River Bridge.

'Dimensions?' asked Pitt of the sonar operator.

'Approximately thirty-six metres long by seven metres wide.'

'What kind of size are we looking for?' asked Giordino.

'The *Eagle* has an overall length of a hundred and ten feet with a twenty foot beam,' Pitt replied.

'That matches,' Giordino said, mentally juggling metres to feet.

'I think we've got her,' Pitt said as he examined the configurations revealed by the sidescan sonar. 'Let's make another pass – this time about twenty metres to starboard – and throw out a buoy.'

Sandecker, who was standing outside on the after deck, keeping an eye on the sensor cable, leaned in the wheelhouse. 'Got something?'

Pitt nodded. 'A prime contact.'

'Going to check it out?'

'After we drop a buoy, Al and I'll go down for a look.'

Sandecker stared at the weathered deck and said nothing. Then he turned and walked back to the stern where he helped Giordino hoist a fifty pound lead weight, attached to a bright orange buoy, onto the *Hoki Jamoki*'s bulwark.

Pitt took the helm and brought the boat about. When the target began to rise on the depth sounder, he shouted: 'Now!'

The buoy was thrown overboard as the boat slowed. One of the engineers moved to the bow and lowered the anchor. The *Hoki Jamoki* drifted to a stop with her stern pointed downstream.

'Too bad you didn't include an underwater TV camera,' said Sandecker as he helped Pitt into his dive gear. 'You could have saved yourself a trip.'

'A wasted effort,' Pitt said. 'Visibility is measured in inches down there.'

'The current is running about two knots,' Sandecker judged.

'When we begin our ascent to the surface, it will carry us astern. Better throw out a hundred yard lifeline on a floating buoy to pull us aboard.'

Giordino tightened his weight belt and flashed a jaunty grin. 'Ready when you are.'

Sandecker gripped Pitt on the shoulder. 'Mind what I said about entering the wreck.'

'I'll try not to look too hard,' Pitt said flatly.

Before the Admiral could reply, Pitt adjusted his facemask over his eyes and dropped backwards into the river.

The water closed over him and the sun diffused into a greenish orange blur. The current pulled at his body and he had to swim on a diagonal course against it until he found the buoy. He reached out and clutched the line and stared downward. Less than three feet away the white nylon braid faded into the opaque murk.

Using the line as a guide and a support, Pitt slipped into the depths of the Potomac. Tiny filaments of vegetation and fine particles of sediment swept past his facemask. He switched on his dive light, but the dim beam only added a few inches to his sight. He paused to work his jaws and equalise the growing pressure within his ear canals.

The density increased as he dived deeper. Then suddenly, as if he'd passed through a door, the water temperature dropped by ten degrees and visibility stretched to almost ten feet. The colder layer acted as a cushion pushing against the warm current above. The bottom appeared and Pitt discerned the shadowy outline of a boat off to his right. He turned and gestured to Giordino who gave an affirmative nod of his head.

As though growing out of a fog, the superstructure of the *Eagle* slowly took on shape. It lay like a lifeless animal, alone in haunted silence and watery gloom.

Pitt swam around one side of the hull while Giordino kicked around the other. The yacht was sitting perfectly upright with no

139

indication of list. Except for a thin coating of algae that was forming on her white paint, she looked as pristine as when she robe the surface.

They met at the stern and Pitt wrote on his message board. 'ANY DAMAGE?'

Giordino wrote back, 'NONE'.

Then they slowly worked their way over the decks, past the darkened windows of the staterooms and up to the bridge. There was nothing to suggest death or tragedy. They probed their lights through the bridge windows into the black interior, but all they saw was eerie desolation. Pitt noted the engine room telegraph read, 'ALL STOP'.

He hesitated for a brief moment and wrote a new message on his board, 'I'M GOING IN'.

Giordino's eyes glistened under the facemask lens and he scrawled back, 'I'M WITH YOU'.

Out of habit they checked their air gauges. There was enough time left for another twelve minutes of diving. Pitt tried the door to the wheelhouse. His heart squeezed within his chest. Even with Giordino at his side, the apprehension was oppressive. The latch turned and he pushed the door open. Taking a deep breath, Pitt swam inside.

The brass still gave off a dull gleam under the dive lights. Pitt was curious at the barren look about the room. Nothing was out of place. The floor was clean of any spilled debris. It reminded him of the *Pilottown*.

Seeing nothing of interest they threaded their way down a stairway into the lounge area of the deckhouse. In the fluid darkness the large enclosure seemed to yawn into infinity. Everywhere was the same strange neatness. Giordino aimed his light upward. The overhead beams and mahogany panelling had a stark, naked appearance. Then Pitt realised what was wrong. The ceiling should have been littered with objects that float. Everything that should have drifted to the surface and washed ashore must have been removed.

Accompanied by the gurgle of their escaping air bubbles, they glided through the hallway separating the staterooms. The same neat look was everywhere, even the beds and mattresses had been stripped. Their lights darted amid the furniture securely bolted to the carpeted deck. Pitt checked the bathrooms as Giordino probed the closets. By the time they reached the crew's quarters, they only had seven minutes of air left. Communicating briefly with hand signals, they divided up; Giordino searching the galley and store rooms while Pitt took the engine room.

He found the hatch cover over the engine room locked and bolted. Without a second of lost motion, he quickly removed his dive knife from its leg sheath and prised out the pins in the hinges. The hatch cover, released from its mountings and thrust upward by its buoyancy, sailed past him.

And so did a bloated corpse that burst through the open hatch like a jack-in-the-box.

30

Pitt reeled backwards into a bulkhead and watched numbly as an unearthly assortment of floating debris and bodies erupted from the engine room. They drifted up to the ceiling where they hung in grotesque postures like trapped balloons. Though the internal gases had begun to expand, the flesh had not yet started to decompose. Sightless eyes bulged beneath strands of hair that wavered from the disturbance in the water.

Pitt struggled to fight off the grip of shock and revulsion, hardening his mind for the repugnant job he could not leave undone. With creeping nausea merged with cold fear he snaked through the hatch into the engine room.

His eyes met a charnel house of death. Bedding, clothing from half-open suitcases, pillows and cushions, anything buoyant enough to float, mingled between a crush of bodies. The scene was a nightmare that could never be imagined or remotely duplicated by a Hollywood horror film.

Most of the corpses wore white Coast Guard uniforms, adding to their ghostly appearance. Several had on ordinary work clothes. None showed signs of injury or wounds.

He spent two minutes, no more, in there, cringing when a lifeless hand brushed across his arm or a white, expressionless face drifted inches in front of his face mask. He could have sworn they were all staring at him, begging for something that was not his to give. One was dressed differently from the others, in a knitted sweater, covered by a stylish raincoat. Pitt swiftly rifled through the dead man's pockets.

Pitt had seen enough to be permanently etched in his mind for a lifetime. He hurriedly kicked up the ladder and out of the engine room. Once free of the morbid scene below, he hesitated to read his air gauge. The needle indicated a hundred pounds, an ample supply to reach the sun again if he didn't linger. He found Giordino rummaging through a cavernous food locker and made an upward gesture with his thumbs. Giordino nodded and led the way through a passageway to the outside deck.

141

A great wave of relief swept over Pitt as the yacht receded into the murk. There wasn't time to search for the buoy line so they ascended with the bubbles that flowed from their air regulator's exhaust valve. The water slowly transformed from an almost brown-black to a leaden green. At last they broke the surface and found themselves fifty yards downstream from the *Hoki Jamoki*.

Sandecker and the boat's crew of engineers spotted them immediately and quickly began hauling on the lifeline. Sandecker cupped his hands to his mouth and shouted.

'Hang on, we'll pull you in.'

Pitt waved, thankful he could lie back and relax. He felt too drained to do anything but lazily float against the current and watch the trees lining the banks slip past. A few minutes later he and Giordino were lifted onto the deck of the old fishing boat.

'Is it the *Eagle*?' Sandecker asked, unable to mask his curiosity.

Pitt hesitated in answering until he removed his air tank. 'Yes,' he said finally, 'it's the *Eagle*.'

Sandecker could not bring himself to ask the question that was gripping his mind. He sidestepped it.

'Find anything you want to talk about?'

'The outside is undamaged. She's sitting upright, her keel resting in about two feet of silt.'

'No sign of life?'

'Not from the exterior.'

It was obvious that Pitt wasn't going to volunteer any information unless asked. His healthy tan seemed strangely paled.

'Could you see inside?' Sandecker demanded.

'Too dark to make out anything.'

'All right, dammit, let's have it straight.'

'Now that you've so pleasantly asked,' said Pitt stonily, staring Sandecker in the eye, 'there's more dead bodies in the yacht than a cemetery. They were stacked in the engine room from deck to overhead. I counted twenty-one of them.'

'Christ!' Sandecker rasped, suddenly taken back. 'Could you recognise any of them?'

'Thirteen were crewmen. The rest looked to be civilians.'

'Eight civilians?' Sandecker seemed stunned.

'As near as I could judge by their clothing. They weren't in any condition to interrogate.'

'Eight.' Sandecker repeated. 'And none of them looked remotely familiar to you?'

'I'm not sure their own mothers could identify them,' said Pitt. 'Why? Was I supposed to know somebody?'

Sandecker shook his head. 'I can't say.'

142

Pitt couldn't recall seeing the Admiral so distraught. The iron armour had fallen away. The penetrating, intelligent eyes seemed stricken. Pitt watched for a reaction as he spoke.

'If I had to venture an opinion, I'd say someone snuffed the candle on half the Chinese Embassy.'

'Chinese?' The eyes suddenly turned as sharp as ice picks. 'What are you saying?'

'Seven of the eight civilians were from eastern Asia.'

'Could you be in error?' Sandecker asked, regaining a foothold. 'With little or no visibility . . .'

'Visibility was ten feet. And, I'm well aware of the difference between the eye folds of a Caucasian and an Oriental.'

'Thank God,' Sandecker said, exhaling a deep breath.

'I'd be much obliged if you would inform me what in hell you expected Al and me to find down there.'

Sandecker's eyes softened. 'I owe you an explanation,' he said, 'But I can't give you one because there are events occurring around us that we have no need to know.'

'I have my own project,' said Pitt, his voice turning cold. 'I'm not interested in this one.'

'Yes, Julie Mendoza. I understand.'

Pitt pulled something from under the sleeve of his wetsuit. 'Here, I almost forgot. I took this from one of the bodies.'

'What is it?'

Pitt held up a soggy leather billfold. On the inside was a waterproof ID card with a man's photograph. Opposite, was a badge in the shape of a shield. 'A Secret Service agent's identification,' Pitt answered. 'His name was Brock, Lyle Brock.'

Sandecker took the billfold without comment. He glanced at his watch. 'I've got to contact Sam Emmett at FBI. This is his problem now.'

'You can't drop it that easily, Admiral. We both know NUMA will be called on to raise the *Eagle*.'

'You're right, of course,' Sandecker said wearily. 'You're relieved of that project. You do what you have to do. I'll have Giordino handle the salvage.' He turned then and stepped into the wheelhouse to use the ship-to-shore phone.

Pitt stood looking for a long time at the dark forbidding water of the river, reliving the terrible scene below. A line from an old seaman's poem ran through his head.

'A ghostly ship with a ghostly crew with no place to go.'

Then as though closing a curtain, he turned his thoughts back to the *Pilottown*.

*

143

On the east bank of the river, concealed in a thicket of ash trees, a man dressed in Vietnam leaf camouflage fatigues pressed his eye to the viewfinder of a video camera. The warm sun and the heavy humidity caused sweat to trickle down his face. He ignored the discomfort and kept taping, zooming in the telephoto lens until Pitt's upper body filled the miniature viewing screen. Then he panned along the entire length of the fishing boat, holding for a few seconds on each member of the crew.

Half an hour after the divers climbed out of the water, a small fleet of Coast Guard boats descended around the *Hoki Jamoki*. A derrick on one of the vessels lifted a large red banded buoy with a flashing light over the side and dropped it beside the wreck of the *Eagle*.

When the battery of his recording unit died, the hidden cameraman neatly packed away his equipment and slipped into the approaching dusk.

31

Pitt was contemplating a menu when the mâitre d' of the Le Bagatelle restaurant on K Street steered Loren to his table.

Her head was held high and proud on the long, slender stem of her neck and the hair was stylishly swirled to one side. Her eyes were as blue-purple as the mountains at dusk and took in the world with a sensual, enigmatic gaze. She moved with an athletic grace, nodding and exchanging a few words with the Capitol crowd eating lunch amid the restaurant's garden decor.

Women studied her with a tinge of envy while she left men with a feeling of uncertainty, never knowing whether they made an impression on her or whether she simply looked down upon them as would an elementary school teacher on boys who brought her apples.

She wore a soft textured corduroy cardigan jacket with a single button at the throat, matching skirt and a silky, long-sleeved blouse. In one hand she carried her trademark, a slim attaché case whose exterior matched her current outfit.

Pitt looked up and their eyes met. She returned his frank, appraising stare with an even smile. He slowly lowered his eyes, gauging her every curve and dimension down to her toes and back up again. Then he rose and pulled back her chair.

'Damn, you look ugly today,' he said.

She laughed. 'You continue to mystify me.'

'How so?'

'One minute you're a gentleman, and the next, a slob.'

'I was told women crave variety.'

Her eyes, clear and soft, were amused. 'I do give you credit though. You're the only man I know who doesn't kiss my fanny.'

Pitt's face broke into his infectious grin. 'That's because I don't need any political favours.'

She made a face and opened a menu. 'I don't have time to be made fun of. I have to get back to my office and respond to a ton of constituents' mail. What looks good?'

'I thought I'd try the venison.'

'My scale said I was up a pound this morning. I think I'll have a salad.'

The waiter approached.

'A drink?' Pitt asked.

'You order.'

'Two sazerac cocktails, and please ask the bartender to pour rye instead of bourbon.'

'Very good, sir,' the waiter acknowledged.

Loren laid her napkin in her lap. 'I've phoned for two days. Where've you been?'

'The Admiral sent me on an emergency salvage job.'

'Was she pretty?' she asked, playing the age old game.

'A coroner might think so. But drowned bodies never turned me on.'

'Sorry,' she said and went sober and quiet until the drinks were brought. They stirred the ice around the glasses and then sipped the reddish contents.

'One of my aides ran across something that might help you,' she said finally.

'What is it?'

She pulled several stapled sheets of typewritten paper from her attaché case and passed them to Pitt. Then she began explaining in a soft undertone: 'Not much meat, I'm afraid, but an interesting report on the CIA's phantom navy.'

'Didn't know they had one,' Pitt said, scanning the pages.

'Since 1963 they have accumulated a small fleet of ships that few people inside the government know about. And the few who are aware of the fleet won't admit it exists. Besides surveillance, its primary function is to carry out clandestine operations involving the transporting of men and supplies for the infiltration of agents or guerillas into unfriendly countries. Originally it was put together to harass Castro after his takeover of Cuba. Several years later, when it became apparent that Castro was too strong to topple, their activities were curtailed, partly because the Cubans threatened to retaliate against American fishing vessels. From that time on the CIA Navy expanded their sphere of operations from Central America to the fighting in Vietnam to Africa and the Middle East. Do you follow?'

'I'm with you, but I have no idea where it's leading.'

'Just be patient,' she said. 'Several years ago an attack cargo transport called the *Hobson* was a part of the Navy's reserve mothball fleet at Philadelphia. She was decommissioned and sold to a commercial shipping company, a cover for the CIA. They spared no expense in rebuilding her to outwardly resemble a common cargo carrier, while her interior was filled with concealed armaments, including a new missile system, highly sophisticated communications and listening gear, and a facility for launching fast patrol and landing boats through swinging bow doors.

'She was manned and ready on station during Iran's disastrous invasion of Kuwait and Saudi Arabia in 1985. Flying the maritime flag of Panama, she secretly sank two Soviet spy ships in the Persian Gulf. The Russians could never prove who did it because none of our Navy ships were within range. They still think the missiles that destroyed their ships came from the Saudi shore.'

'And you found out about all this?'

'I have my sources,' she informed him.

'Does the *Hobson* have anything to do with the *Pilottown*?'

'Indirectly,' Loren answered.

'Go on.'

'Three years ago, the *Hobson* vanished with all hands off the Pacific coast of Mexico.'

'So?'

'So three months later the CIA found her again.'

'Sounds familiar,' Pitt mused.

'My thoughts too,' Loren nodded. 'A replay of the *San Marino* and the *Belle Chasse*.'

'Where was the *Hobson* discovered?'

Before Loren could answer, the waiter set their plates on the table. The venison looked sensational, but Pitt's appetite was waning. As soon as the waiter walked out of earshot he nodded to her.

'Go on.'

'I don't know how the CIA tracked the ship down, but they came on her sitting in a drydock in Sydney, Australia where she was undergoing a major facelift.'

'They find who she was registered to?'

'She flew the Philippine flag under the registry of Samar Exporters. A bogus firm that was incorporated only a few weeks earlier in Manila. Her new name was *Buras*.'

146

'*Buras*,' Pitt echoed. 'Must be the name of a person. How's your salad?'

'The dressing is very tasty. Your venison?'

'Tender, and the sauce is exceptional,' he answered. 'An act of sheer stupidity on the part of the pirates to steal a ship belonging to the CIA.'

'A case of a mugger rolling a drunk and finding out it was an undercover detective.'

'What happened next in Sydney?'

'Nothing. The CIA, working with the Australian branch of the British Secret Service, tried to apprehend the owners of the *Buras* but were never able to find them.'

'No leads, no witnesses?'

'The small Korean crew living on board were recruited in Singapore. They knew little and could only give a description of the captain who had vanished.'

Pitt took a swallow of water and examined a page of the report. 'Not much of an ID. Korean, medium height, one hundred and sixty five pounds, black hair, gap in front teeth. That narrows it down to about five or ten million men,' he said sarcastically. 'Well, at least now I don't feel so bad. If the CIA can't pin a make on whoever is sailing around the world hijacking ships, I sure as hell can't.'

'Has St Julien Perlmutter called you?'

Pitt shook his head. 'Haven't heard a word. Probably lost heart and deserted the cause.'

'I have to desert the cause too,' Loren said gently. 'But only for a little while.'

Pitt looked at her sternly a moment, then relaxed and laughed. 'How did a nice girl like you ever become a politician?'

She wrinkled her nose. 'Chauvinist.'

'Seriously, where will you be?'

'A short fact-finding junket on a Russian cruise ship sailing the Caribbean.'

'Of course,' said Pitt. 'I'd forgotten you chair the committee for Merchant Marine Transport.'

Loren nodded and patted her mouth with her napkin. 'The last cruise ship to fly the stars and stripes was taken out of service in 1984. To many people this is a national disgrace. The President feels strongly that we should be represented in ocean commerce as well as naval defence. He's asking Congress for a budget outlay of ninety dollars to restore the *SS United States*, which has been laid up at Norfolk for twenty years, and put her back in service to compete with the foreign cruise lines.'

'And you're going to study the Russian method of lavishing their passengers with vodka and caviar.'

'That,' she said looking suddenly official, 'and the economics of their government operated cruise ship.'

'When do you sail?'

'Day after tomorrow. I fly to Miami and board the *Leonid Andreyev*. I'll be back in five days. What will you do?'

'The Admiral has given me time off to pursue the *Pilottown* investigation.'

'Does any of this information help you?'

'Every bit helps,' he said, straining to focus on a thought that was a distant shadow on the horizon. Then he looked at her. 'Have you heard anything through the Congressional grapevine?'

'You mean gossip. Like who's screwing who?'

'Something heavier. Rumours of a missing party high in government or a foreign diplomat.'

Loren shook her head. 'No, nothing quite so sinister. The Capitol scene is pretty dull while Congress is in recess. Why? You know of a scandal brewing I don't?'

'Just asking,' Pitt said noncommittally.

Her hand crept across the table and clasped his. 'I have no idea where all this is taking you, but please be careful. Fu Manchu might get wise you're on his scent and lie in ambush.'

Pitt turned and laughed. 'I haven't read Sax Rohmer since I was a kid. Fu Manchu, the yellow peril. What made you think of him?'

She gave a little shrug. 'I don't really know. A mental association with an old Peter Sellers movie, the Sosan Trading Corporation and the Korean crew of the *Buras*, I guess.'

A faraway look came over Pitt's eyes and then they widened. The thought on the horizon crystallised. He hailed the waiter and paid the bill with a credit card.

'I've got to make a couple of phone calls,' he explained briefly.

He kissed her lightly on the lips and hurried onto the crowded sidewalk.

32

Pitt quickly drove to the NUMA building and closed himself in his office. He assembled his priorities for several moments and dialled Los Angeles on his private phone line. On the fifth ring a girl answered who couldn't pronounce her r's.

'Casio and Associates Investigatahs.'

'I'd like to speak to Mr Casio, please.'

'Who shall I say is calling?'

'My name is Pitt.'

'He's with a client. Can you call back?'

'No!' Pitt growled menacingly. 'I'm calling from Washington and it's urgent.'

Suitably intimidated, the receptionist replied, 'One moment.'

Casio came on the line almost immediately. 'Mr Pitt. Good to hear from you.'

'Sorry to interrupt your meeting,' said Pitt, 'but I need a few answers.'

'I'll do my best.'

'What do you know about the crew of the *San Marino*?'

'Not much. I ran a make on the officers, but nothing unusual turned up. They were all professional merchant mariners. The Captain, as I recall, had a very respectable record.'

'No ties to any kind of organised crime?'

'Nothing that came to light in the computers of the National Crime Information Centre.'

'How about the rest of the crew?'

'Not much there. Only a few had maritime union records.'

'Nationality?' Pitt asked.

'Nationality?' Casio repeated, thought a moment, then said: 'A mixture. A few Greek, a few Americans, several Koreans.'

'Koreans?' Pitt came back, suddenly alert. 'There were Koreans on board?'

'Yeah, that's right. Now that you mention it, as I remember, a group of about ten signed on just before the *San Marino* sailed.'

'Would it be possible to trace the ships and companies they served prior to the *San Marino*?'

'You're going back a long time, but the files should still be available.'

'Could you throw in the history of the *Pilottown*'s crew as well?'

'Don't see why not.'

'I'd appreciate it.'

'What are you after exactly?' Casio asked.

'Should be obvious to you.'

'A link between the crew and our unknown parent company, is that it?'

'Close enough.'

'You're going back before the ships disappeared,' said Casio thoughtfully.

'The most practical way to take over a ship is by the crew.'

'I thought mutiny went out with the *Bounty*.'

'The modern term is hijacking.'

149

'You've got a good hunch going,' said Casio. 'I'll see what I can do.'

'Thank you, Mr Casio.'

'We've danced enough to know each other. Call me Sal.'

'Okay Sal, and make it Dirk.'

'I'll do that,' Casio said seriously. 'Goodbye.'

After he hung up, Pitt leaned back and put his feet on the desk. He felt good, optimistic that a vague instinct was about to pay off. Now he was about to try another long shot, one that was so crazy he almost felt foolish for pursuing it. He wrote down a number out of the National University Directory and called it.

'University of Pennsylvania, Department of Anthropology?'

'May I speak to Dr Grace Perth.'

'Just a sec.'

'Thank you.'

Pitt waited for nearly two minutes before a motherly voice said, 'Hello.'

'Dr Perth?'

'Speaking.'

'My name is Dirk Pitt and I'm with the National Underwater and Marine Agency. Have you got a moment to answer a couple of academic questions for me?'

'What do you wish to know, Mr Pitt?' Dr Perth asked sweetly.

Pitt tried to picture her in his mind. His initial image was that of a prim, white haired lady in a tweed suit. He erased it as a stereotype and pushed it aside.

'If we take a male, between the ages of thirty and forty, of medium height and weight, who was a native of Peking, China, and another male of the same description from Seoul, South Korea, how could we tell them apart?'

'You're not doing a number on me, are you Mr Pitt?'

Pitt laughed. 'No, Doctor, I'm quite serious,' he assured her.

'Hmmm, Chinese versus Korean,' she muttered while thinking. 'By and large, people of Korean ancestry tend to be more classic or extreme Mongoloid. Chinese features, on the other hand, lean more generally Asian. But I wouldn't want to make my living guessing which was which because the overlap is so great. It would be far simpler to judge them by their clothes or behaviour, or the way they cut their hair, in short, their cultural characteristics.'

'I thought they might have certain facial features that could separate them, such as you find between Chinese and Japanese.'

'Well now, here the genetic spread is more obvious. If your Oriental male has a fairly dense beard growth, you'd have a rather strong indication that he's Japanese. But in the case of China and

150

Korea, you're dealing with two racial groups that have intermixed for centuries, so much so that individual variation would tend to blur any distinction.'

'You make it sound hopeless.'

'Awfully difficult, maybe, but not hopeless,' Dr Perth said. 'A series of laboratory tests could raise your probability factor.'

'My interest is strictly from a visual view.'

'Are your subjects living?'

'No, drowning victims.'

'A pity. With a living individual there are little traits of facial expressions that are culturally acquired and can be detected by someone who has had a lot of experience with both races. A pretty good guess may be made on that basis alone.'

'No such luck.'

'Perhaps if you could define their facial characteristics to me.'

Pitt dreaded the thought, but he closed his eyes and began describing the lifeless heads he saw on the *Eagle*. At first the vision was vague, but soon it focused with clarity and he found himself dissecting each detail with the callous routine of a surgeon narrating a heart transplant into a tape recorder. At one point he suddenly broke off.

'Yes, Mr Pitt, please go on,' said Dr Perth.

'I just remembered something that escaped me,' Pitt said. 'Two of the bodies did in fact have thick facial hair. One had a moustache while another sprouted a goatee.'

'Interesting.'

'So they weren't Korean or Chinese?'

'Not necessarily.'

'What else could they be but Japanese?'

'You're leaping before you look, Mr Pitt,' she said as if lecturing a student. 'The features you've described to me suggest a heavy tendency toward the classic Mongoloid.'

'But the facial hair?'

'You must consider history. The Japanese have been invading and marauding Korea since the sixteenth century. And for thirty-five years, from 1910 until 1945, Korea was a colony of Japan, so there was a great blending of their particular genetic variations.'

Pitt hesitated before he put the next question to Dr Perth. Then he chose his words carefully. 'If you were to stick your neck out and give an opinion on the race of the men I've described, what would you say?'

Grace Perth came back with all flags flying. 'Looking at it from a percentage factor, I'd say your test group's ancestry was ten percent Japanese, thirty percent Chinese and sixty percent Korean.'

151

'Sounds like you've constructed the genetic makeup of your average Korean.'

'You read it any way you wish to see it, Mr Pitt. I've gone as far as I can go.'

'Thank you, Dr Perth,' Pitt said suddenly exultant. 'Thank you very much.'

33

'So that's Dirk Pitt,' Min Koryo said. She sat in her wheelchair, peering over a breakfast tray at a large TV screen in her office wall.

Lee Tong sat beside her watching the video tape of the *Hoki Jamoki* anchored over the presidential yacht. 'What puzzles me,' he said quietly, 'is how he discovered the wreck so quickly. It's as though he knew exactly where to search.'

Min Koryo set her chin in frail hands and bowed her greying head, eyes locked on the screen, the thin blue veins in her temples pulsing in concentration. Her face slowly tightened in anger.

She looked like an ancient Egyptian mummy whose skin had somehow bleached white and remained smooth.

'Pitt and NUMA,' she hissed in exasperation. 'What are those wily bastards up to? First the *San Marino* and *Pilottown* publicity hoax, and now this.'

'It can only be coincidence,' Lee Tong suggested. 'There is no direct link between the freighters and the yacht.'

'Better an informer,' her voice cut like a whip. 'We've been sold out.'

'Not a valid conclusion, *aumuni*,' said Lee Tong, amused at her sudden outburst. 'Only you and I know the facts. Everyone else is dead.'

'Nothing is ever immune to failure. Only fools think they're perfect.'

Lee Tong was in no mood for his mother's Oriental philosophy. 'Do not concern yourself unnecessarily,' he said acidly. 'A government investigating team would have eventually stumbled onto the yacht anyway. We could not make the President's transfer in broad daylight without running the danger of being seen and stopped. And since the yacht wasn't reported after sunrise, simple mathematics suggested that it was still somewhere on or below the river between Washington and Chesapeake Bay.'

'A conclusion Mr Pitt apparently had no trouble arriving at.'

'It changes nothing,' said Lee Tong. 'Time is still on our side. Once Lugovoy is satisfied at his results, all that remains for us is to oversee the gold shipment. After that, Chairman Antonov can have the President. But we keep Margolin, Latimer and Moran for insurance and future bargaining power. Trust me, *aumuni*, the tricky part is past. The Bougainville corporate fortress is secure.'

'Maybe so, but the hounds are getting too close.'

'We're matching ourselves against highly trained and intelligent people who possess the finest technology in the world. They may come within reach, but they'll never fully grasp our involvement.'

Mollified somewhat, Min Koryo sighed and sipped at her ever present teacup. 'Have you talked to Lugovoy in the past eight hours?'

'Yes. He claims he's encountered no setbacks and can complete the project in five more days.'

'Five days,' she said pensively. 'I think it is time we put the final machinery into motion and firm our arrangement with Antonov for payment. Has our ship arrived?'

'The *Venice* docked at the Black Sea port of Odessa two days ago.'

'Who is ship's master?'

'Captain James Mangyai, a trusted employee of the company,' Lee Tong answered.

Min Koryo nodded approvingly. 'And a good seaman. He's worked for me almost twenty years.'

'He has his orders to cast off and set sail the minute the last crate of gold is loaded aboard.'

'Good. Now we'll see what kind of stalling tactics Antonov will try. To begin with, he'll no doubt demand to hold up payment until Lugovoy's experiment is a proven success. This we will not do. In the meantime, he'll have an army of KGB agents combing the American countryside, looking for the President and our laboratory facilities.'

'No Russian nor American will figure out where we have Lugovoy and his staff hidden,' Lee Tong said firmly.

'They found the yacht,' Min Koryo reminded him.

Before Lee Tong could retort, the video screen turned to snow as the tape played out. He set the control for 'rewind'. 'Do you wish to view it again?' he asked.

'Yes, I want to examine the diving crew more closely.'

When the recorder automatically switched off, Lee Tong pressed the 'play' button and the picture returned to life.

Min Koryo watched it impassively for a minute and then said, 'What is the latest status report on the wreck site?'

'A NUMA salvage crew is bringing up the bodies and preparing to raise the yacht.'

'Who is the man with the red beard talking with Pitt?'

153

Lee Tong enlarged the scene until both men filled the screen. 'That's Admiral James Sandecker, Director of NUMA.'

'Your man was not seen filming Pitt's movements?'

'No, he's one of the best in the business. An ex-FBI agent. He was contracted for the job through one of our subsidiary corporations and was told Pitt is suspected of selling NUMA equipment to outside sources.'

'What do we know about Pitt?'

'I have a complete dossier flying in from Washington. It should be here within the hour.'

Min Koryo's mouth tightened as she moved closer to the TV. 'How could he know so much? NUMA is an oceanographic agency. They don't emply secret agents. Why is he coming after us?'

'It'll pay us to find out.'

'Move in closer,' she ordered.

Lee Tong again enlarged the image, moving past Sandecker's shoulder until it seemed as though Pitt was talking to the camera. Then he froze the picture.

Min Koryo placed a pair of square-lensed glasses over her narrow nose and stared at the weathered but handsome face that stared back. Her dark eyes flashed briefly.

'Goodbye, Mr Pitt.'

Then she reached over and pushed the 'off' switch and the screen went black.

The smoke from Suvorov's cigarette hung heavily in the air of the dining-room as he and Lugovoy shared a bottle of 1966 Croft Vintage Port. Suvorov looked at the red liquid in his glass and scowled.

'All these Mongolians ever serve us is beer and wine. What I wouldn't give for a bottle of good vodka.'

Lugovoy selected a cigar out of a box that was held by one of the Korean waiters. 'You have no culture, Suvorov. This happens to be a very excellent port.'

'American decadence has not rubbed off on me,' Suvorov said arrogantly.

'Call it what you will, but you rarely see Americans defecting to Russia because of *our* disciplined lifestyle,' Lugovoy retorted sarcastically.

'You're beginning to talk like them, drink like them; next you'll want to murder and rape in the streets like them. At least I know where my loyalties lie.'

Lugovoy studied the cigar thoughtfully. 'So do I. What I accomplish here will have grave effects on our nation's policy towards the

United States. It is of far greater importance than your petty theft of industrial secrets.'

Suvorov appeared too mellowed by the wine to respond angrily to the psychologist's remarks. 'Your actions will be reported to our superiors.'

'I've told you endlessly. This project is underwritten by President Antonov himself.'

'I don't believe you.'

Lugovoy lit the cigar and blew a puff of smoke towards the ceiling. 'Your opinion is irrelevant.'

'We must find a means to contact the outside,' Suvorov's voice rose.

'You're crazy,' Lugovoy said seriously. 'I'm telling you, no! I'm ordering you not to interfere. Can't you use your eyes, your brain? Look around you. All this was in preparation for years. Every detail has been carefully planned to carry out this operation. Without Madame Bougainville's organisation, none of this would have been possible.'

'We are her prisoners,' Suvorov protested.

'What's the difference as long as our government benefits.'

'We should be masters of the situation,' Suvorov insisted. 'We must get the President out of here and into the hands of our own people so he can be interrogated. The secrets you can pry from his mind are beyond comprehension.'

Lugovoy shook his head in exasperation. He did not know what else to say. Trying to reason with a mind scored by patriotic fervour was like teaching calculus to a drunk. He knew that when it was all over Suvorov would write up a report depicting him as unreliable and a potential threat to Soviet security. Yet he laughed inwardly. If the experiment succeeded, President Antonov might be of a mood to name him Hero of the Soviet Union.

He stood up, stretched and yawned. 'I think I'll catch a few hours' sleep. We'll begin programming the President's responses first thing in the morning.'

'What time is it now?' Suvorov inquired dully. 'I've lost all track of day and night in this tomb.'

'Five minutes to midnight.'

Suvorov yawned and sprawled on a couch. 'You go ahead to bed. I'm going to have another drink. A good Russian never leaves the room before the bottle is empty.'

'Goodnight,' said Lugovoy. He turned and entered the hallway.

Suvorov waved half-heartedly and pretended he was on the verge of dozing off. But he studied the second hand of his watch for three minutes. Then he rose swiftly, crossed the room and noiselessly made

155

his way down the hallway to where it made a ninety degree turn towards the sealed lift. He stopped and pressed his body to the wall and glanced around the edge of the corner.

Lugovoy was standing there patiently smoking his cigar. In less than forty seconds the lift door silently opened and Lugovoy stepped inside. The time was exactly twelve o'clock. Every twelve hours, Suvorov noted, the project's psychologist escaped the laboratory, returning twenty to thirty minutes later.

He left and walked past the monitoring room. Two of the staff members were intently examining the President's brain rhythms and life signs. One of them looked up at Suvorov and nodded, smiling slightly.

'Going smoothly?' Suvorov asked, making conversation.

'Like a prima ballerina's debut,' answered the technician.

Suvorov entered and looked up at the TV monitors. 'What's happening with the others?' he inquired, nodding toward the images of Margolin, Larimer and Moran in their sealed cocoons.

'Sedated and fed heavy liquid concentrations of protein and carbohydrates intravenously.'

'Until it's their turn for programming?' Suvorov asked.

'Can't say. You'll have to ask Dr Lugovoy that question.'

Suvorov watched one of the screens as an attendant in a laboratory coat lifted a panel on Senator Larimer's cocoon and inserted a hypodermic needle into one arm.

'What's he doing?' Suvorov asked, pointing.

The technician looked up. 'We have to administer a sedative every eight hours or the subject will regain consciousness.'

'I see,' said Suvorov quietly. It all became clear in his mind suddenly as the details of his escape plan fell into place. He felt good, better than he had in days. To celebrate, he returned to the dining-room and opened another bottle of port. Then he took a small notebook from his pocket and furiously scribbled on its pages.

34

Oscar Lucas parked his car in a VIP slot at the Walter Reed Army Medical Centre and hurried through a side entrance. He jogged around a maze of corridors, finally stopping at a double door guarded by a Marine sergeant whose face had a Mount Rushmore solemnity about it. The sergeant carefully screened his identification and directed him into the hospital wing where sensitive and highly secret autopsies were held. Lucas quickly found the door marked LABORATORY – AUTHORISED PERSONNEL ONLY and entered.

'I hope I haven't kept you waiting,' he said.

'No, Oscar,' said Alan Mercier. 'I only walked in a minute ago myself.'

Lucas nodded and looked around the glass enclosed room. There were five men besides himself; General Metcalf, Sam Emmett, Martin Brogan, Mercier, and a short, chesty man with rimless glasses introduced as Colonel Thomas Thornburg, who carried the heavy title of Director of Comparative Forensics and Clinical Pathology.

'Now that everyone is here,' said Colonel Thornburg in a strange alto voice. 'I can show you gentlemen our results.'

He went over to a large window and peered at a huge circular machine on the other side of the glass. It looked like a finned turbine attached by a shaft to a generator. Half of the turbine disappeared into the concrete floor. Inside its inner diameter was a cylindrical opening, while just outside lay a corpse on a translucent tray.

'A Spatial Analyser Probe, or SAP as it's affectionately called by my staff of researchers who developed it. What it does essentially is explore the body electronically through enhanced X-rays while revealing precise moving pictures of every millimetre of tissue and bone.'

'A kind of CAT scanner,' ventured Brogan.

'Their basic function is the same, yes,' answered Thornburg. 'But that's like comparing a propeller aircraft to a supersonic jet. The CAT scanner takes several seconds to display a single cross section of the body. The SAP will deliver twenty-five thousand in less time. The findings are then automatically fed into a computer which offers its mechanical opinion on the cause of death. I've over simplified the process, of course, but that's a nuts and bolts description.'

'I assume your data banks hold nutritional and metabolic disorders associated with all known poisons and infectious diseases,' said Emmett. 'The same information as our computer records at the Bureau.'

Thornburg nodded. 'Yes. Except our data are more extensive because we occasionally deal with living tissue.'

'In a pathology lab?' asked Lucas.

'We also examine the living. Quite often we receive field agents from our intelligence services – and from our allies too – who have been injected by a poisonous material or artificially infected by a contagious disease and are still alive. With SAP we can analyse the cause and come up with an antidote. We've saved a few, but most arrive too late.'

'You can do an entire analysis and determine a cause in a few seconds?' General Metcalf asked incredulously.

157

'Actually in micro-seconds,' Thornburg corrected him. 'Instead of gutting the corpse and going through an extensive series of tests, we can now do it in the wink of an eye with one elaborate piece of equipment, which I might add, cost the taxpayer somewhere in the neighbourhood of thirty million dollars.'

'What did you find on the bodies from the river? Mercier asked.

As if cued, Thornburg smiled and patted the shoulder of a technician who was sitting at a massive panel of lights and buttons. 'I'll show you.'

All eyes instinctively turned to the naked body lying on the tray. Slowly it began moving towards the turbine and disappeared into the centre cylinder. Then the turbine began to revolve at sixty revolutions a minute. The X-ray guns encircling the corpse fired in sequence as a battery of cameras received the images from a fluorescent screen, enhanced them and fed the results into the computer bank. Before any of the men in the lab control room turned around, the cause of the corpse's demise flashed out in green letters across the centre of a display screen. Most of the wording was in anatomical terminology, giving a description of the internal organs, the amount of toxicity present and its chemical code. At the bottom were the words, 'Conium maculatum'.

'What in hell is Conium maculatum?' wondered Lucas out loud.

'A member of the parsley family,' said Thornburg, 'more commonly known as hemlock.'

'Rather an old fashioned means of execution,' remarked Metcalf.

'Yes, hemlock was very popular during classical times. Best remembered as the drink given the philosopher Socrates. Seldom used these days, but still easy to come by and quite lethal. A large enough dose will paralyse the respiratory organs.'

'How was it administered?' inquired Sam Emmett.

'According to SAP, the poison was ingested by this particular victim along with peppermint ice cream.'

'Death for dessert,' Mercier muttered philosophically.

'Of the Coast Guard crewmen we identified,' Thornburg continued, 'eight took the hemlock with the ice cream, four with coffee, and one with a diet soft drink.'

'SAP could tell all that from bodies immersed in water for five days?' asked Lucas.

'Decay starts immediately at death,' explained Thornburg, 'and travels outward from the intestines and other organs containing body bacteria. The process develops rapidly in the presence of air. But when the body is under water, where the oxygen content is low, decay proceeds very slowly. The preservation factor that worked in our favour was the confinement of the bodies. A drowning victim, for example, will float to the surface after a few days as the decomposing gases begin to expand, thereby hastening decay from air exposure. The bodies you brought in, however, had been totally submerged until an hour before we began the autopsies.'

'The chef was a busy man,' noted Metcalf.

Lucas shook his head. 'Not the chef, but the dining-room steward. He's the only crewman unaccounted for.'

'An imposter,' said Brogan. 'The real steward was probably murdered and his corpse hidden.'

'What about the others?' queried Emmett.

'The Asians?'

'Were they poisoned too?'

'Yes, but in a different manner. They were all shot.'

'Shot, poisoned, which is it?'

'They were killed by fragmenting darts loaded with a highly lethal venom that comes from the dorsal spines of the Stonefish.'

'No amateurs, these guys,' commented Emmett.

Thornburg nodded in agreement. 'The method was most professional, especially the means of penetration. I removed a similar dart two years ago from a Soviet agent brought in by Mr Brogan's people. As I recall, the poison was injected by a Bio-Inoculator.'

'I'm not familiar with it,' said Lucas.

'An electrically operated handgun,' said Brogan, giving Thornburg an icy stare. 'Totally silent, used on occasion by our resident agents.'

'A little loose with your arsenal, aren't you, Martin,' Mercier goaded him good-naturedly.

'The unit in question was most likely smuggled from the manufacturer,' Brogan said defensively.

'Has an ID been made on any of the bodies?' Lucas asked.

'They have no records in FBI files,' admitted Emmett.

'Nor with the CIA and Interpol,' Brogan added. 'None of the intelligence services of friendly Asian countries have anything on them either.'

Mercier stared idly at the corpse moving out from the interior of the Spatial Analyser Probe. 'It appears, gentlemen, that every time we open a door we walk into an empty room.'

35

'What kind of monsters are we dealing with?' Douglas Oates growled after listening to General Metcalf's report on the autopsies. His face wore a chalky pallor and his voice was cold with fury. 'Twenty-one murders. And for what purpose? Where is the motive? Is the President dead or alive? If this is a grand extortion scheme? Why haven't we received a ransom demand?'

Metcalf, Dan Fawcett and Secretary of Defence Jesse Simmons sat silently in front of Oates' desk and did not reply.

'We can't sit on this thing much longer,' he went on. 'Any minute now the news media will become suspicious and stampede into an investigation. Already they're grousing because no presidential interviews have been granted. Press Secretary Thompson has run out of excuses.'

'Why not have the President face the press?' suggested Fawcett.

Oates looked dubious. 'That actor . . . what's his name . . . Sutton? He would never get away with it.'

'Not up close on a podium under a battery of lights, but in a setting under shadows at a distance of a hundred feet . . . well, it might work.'

'You got something in mind?' asked Oates.

'We stage a photo opportunity to enhance the President's image. It's done all the time.'

'Like Carter playing softball and Reagan chopping wood,' said Oates thoughtfully. 'I think I see a down-home scene on the President's farm.'

'Complete with crowing roosters and bleating sheep,' allowed Fawcett.

'And Vice President Margolin? Our double for him can't be faked in shadows at a hundred feet.'

'A few references by Sutton and a friendly wave by the double at a distance should suffice,' Fawcett answered, becoming more enthused with his brainstorm.

Simmons gazed steadily at Fawcett. 'How soon can you have everyone ready?'

'First thing in the morning. Dawn, as a matter of fact. Reporters are night owls. They hang around waiting for late news to break. They're not at their best before sun-up.'

Oates looked at Metcalf and Simmons. 'Well, what do you think?'

160

'We've got to throw the reporters a bone before they become bored and start snooping,' answered Simmons. 'I vote yes.'

Metcalf nodded. 'The only stalling tactic we've got.'

Fawcett came to his feet and peered at his watch. 'If I leave for Andrews Air Force Base now, I should arrive at the farm in four hours. Plenty of time to arrange the details with Thompson and make an announcement to the press corps.'

Fawcett's hand froze on the doorknob as Oates' voice cut across the room like a bayonet.

'Don't bungle it, Dan. For God's sake, don't bungle it.'

36

Vladimir Polevoi caught up with Antonov as the Soviet leader strolled beneath the outer Kremlin wall with his bodyguards. They were moving past the burial area where heroes of the Soviet Union were interred. The weather was unusually warm and Antonov carried his coat over one arm.

'Taking advantage of the fine summer day?' Polevoi asked conversationally as he approached.

Antonov turned. He was young for a Russian head of state, sixty-two, and he walked with a brisk step. 'Too pleasant to waste behind a desk,' he said with a curt nod.

They walked for a while in silence as Polevoi waited for a sign or a word that Antonov was ready to talk business. Antonov paused before the small sculpture marking Stalin's grave site.

'You know him?' he asked.

Polevoi shook his head. 'I was too far down the party ladder for him to notice me.'

Antonov's expression became stern and he muttered tensely. 'You were damned fortunate.' Then he stepped on, dabbing a handkerchief at the perspiration forming on the back of his neck.

Polevoi could see his chief was in no mood for small talk so he came to the point. 'We may have a break on the Huckleberry Finn Project.'

'We could use one,' Antonov said grudgingly.

'One of our agents in New York who is in charge of security for our United Nations workers has turned up missing.'

'How does that concern Huckleberry Finn?'

'He disappeared while following Dr Lugovoy.'

'Any possibility he defected?'

161

'I don't think so.'

Antonov stopped in midstep and gave Polevoi a hard stare. 'We'd have a disaster in the making if he went over to the Americans.'

'I personally vouch for Suvorov,' said Polevoi firmly. 'I'd stake my reputation on his loyalty.'

'The name is familiar.'

'He is the son of Viktor Suvorov, the Agriculture Specialist.'

Antonov seemed appeased. 'Viktor is a dedicated party member.'

'So is Suvorov,' said Polevoi. 'If anything, he's over-zealous.'

'What do you think happened to him?'

'I suspect he somehow passed himself off as one of Lugovoy's staff of psychologists and was taken along with them by Madame Bougainville's men.'

'Then we have a security man on the inside?'

'An assumption. We have no proof.'

'This Suvorov. Did he know anything?'

'He was aware of nothing,' Polevoi said unequivocally. 'His involvement is purely coincidental.'

'A mistake to have Dr Lugovoy watched.'

Polevoi took a deep breath. 'The FBI keeps a tight collar on our United Nations delegates. If we had allowed Dr Lugovoy and his team of psychologists to roam freely about New York without our security agents observing their actions, the Americans would have become suspicious.'

'So they watch us while we watch ours.'

'In the last seven months, three of our people have asked for political asylum. We can't be too careful.'

Antonov threw up his hand in a vague gesture. 'I accept your argument.'

'If Suvorov is indeed with Lugovoy, he will no doubt attempt to make contact and disclose the location of the laboratory facility.'

'Yes, but if Suvorov, in his ignorance, makes a stupid move, there is no predicting how that old bitch Bougainville will react.'

'She might raise the ante.'

'Or worse, sell the President and the others to the highest bidder.'

'I can't see that,' said Polevoi thoughtfully. 'Without Dr Lugovoy, the project isn't possible.'

Antonov made a thin smile. 'Excuse my cautious nature, Comrade Polevoi, but I tend to look on the dark side. That way I'm seldom taken by surprise.'

'The completion of Lugovoy's experiment is only three days away. We should be thinking of how to handle the payment.'

'What are your proposals?'

'Not to pay her, of course.'

162

'How?'

'There are any number of ways. Switching the gold bars after her representative has examined them. Substituting lead that is painted gold or bars of lesser purity.'

'And the old bitch would smell out every one of them.'

'Still, we must try.'

'How will it be transferred?' Antonov asked.

'One of Madame Bougainville's ships is already docked at Odessa, waiting to load the gold on board.'

'Then we'll do what she least expects.'

'Which is?' Polevoi asked expectantly.

'We hold up our end of the bargain,' said Antonov slowly.

'You mean pay?' Polevoi asked incredulously.

'Down to the last troy ounce.'

Polevoi was stunned. 'I'm sorry, Comrade President, but it was my understanding . . .'

'I've changed my mind,' Antonov said sharply. 'I have a better solution.'

Polevoi waited several moments in silence, but it was apparent Antonov wasn't going to confide in him. He slowly dropped back, finally coming to a halt.

Surrounded by his entourage, Antonov kept walking, his mind rapidly altering course and dwelling on other matters of state concern.

Suvorov pressed the switch to his night light and checked the time on his watch. It read 4:04. Not too bad, he thought. He had programmed his mind to awaken at four in the morning and he'd only missed by four minutes.

Unable to suppress a yawn, he quickly pulled on a shirt and pair of trousers, not bothering with socks or shoes. Stepping into the bathroom, he splashed his face with cold water, then moved across the small bedroom and opened the door a crack.

The brightly lit corridor was empty. Except for two psychologists monitoring the subjects, everyone else was asleep. As he walked the carpet in his bare feet, he began measuring the interior dimensions of the facilities and jotting them down in his notebook. Between the four outer walls he arrived at 168 feet in length by thirty-three feet in width. The ceiling was nearly ten feet high.

He came to the door of the medical supply room and gently eased open the door. It was never locked because Lugovoy saw no reason for anyone to steal anything. He stepped inside, closed the door and turned on the light. Moving swiftly, Suvorov found the small bottles containing sedative solutions. He set them in a row on the sink and sucked out their contents with a syringe, emptying the fluid down the drain. Then he refilled the bottles with water and neatly rearranged them on the shelf.

He returned unseen to his sleeping quarters and slipped into bed once again and stared at the ceiling.

He was pleased with himself. His moves were undetected and with no sign of the slightest suspicion. Now all he had to do was wait for the right moment.

37

It was a shadowy dream. The kind he could never remember when he woke up. He was searching for someone in the bowels of a deserted ship. Dust and gloom obscured his vision. Like the dive on the *Eagle*: green river algae and russet silt.

His quarry drifted in front of him, blurred, always beyond reach. He hesitated and tried to focus through the gloom but the form taunted him, beckoning him closer.

Then a high-pitched ringing sound went off in his ear and he floated out of the dream and groped for the telephone.

'Dirk?' came a cheery voice from a throat he wanted to throttle.

'Yes.'

'Got some news for you.'

'Huh?'

'You asleep? This is St Julien.'

'Perlmutter?'

'Wake up. I found something.'

Then Pitt switched on the bed light and sat up. 'Okay, I'm listening.'

'I've received a written report from my friends in Korea. They went through Korean shipyard records. Guess what, the *Belle Chasse* was never scrapped.'

Pitt threw back the covers and dropped his feet on the floor. 'Go on.'

'Sorry I took so long getting back to you, but this is the most incredible maritime puzzle I've ever seen. For thirty years somebody has been playing musical chairs with ships like you wouldn't believe.'

'Try me.'

'First, let me ask you a question,' said Perlmutter. 'The name on the stern of the ship you found in Alaska?'

'The *Pilottown*?'

164

'Were the painted letters framed by welded beading?'

Pitt thought back. 'As I recall it was faded paint. The raised edges must have been ground away.'

Perlmutter uttered a heavy sigh of relief over the phone. 'I was hoping you'd say that.'

'Why?'

'Your suspicions are confirmed. The *San Marino*, the *Belle Chasse* and the *Pilottown* are indeed one and the same ship.'

'Damn!' Pitt said suddenly excited. 'How'd you make the link?'

'By discovering what happened to the genuine *Pilottown*,' said Perlmutter with a dramatic inflection. 'My sources found no record of a *Belle Chasse* being scrapped in the shipyards of Pusan. So I played a hunch and asked them to check out any other yards along the coast. They turned up a lead in the port of Inchon. Shipyard foremen are interesting guys. They never forget a ship, especially one they've junked. They act hard nosed about it, but deep down they're sad to see a tired old vessel pulled into their dock for the last time. Anyway, one old retired foreman talked for hours about the good old days. A real gold mine of ship lore.'

'What did he say?' Pitt asked impatiently.

'He recalled in great detail when he was in charge of the crew who converted the *San Marino* from a cargo transport into an ore carrier renamed the *Belle Chasse*.'

'But the shipyard records?'

'Obviously falsified by the shipyard owners, who, by the way, happened to be our old friends the Sosan Trading Company. The foreman also remembered breaking up the original *Pilottown*. It looks like Sosan Trading, or the shady outfit behind it, hijacked the *San Marino* and its cargo and killed the crew. Then they modified the cargo holds to carry ore, documented it under a different name and sent it tramping around the seas.'

'Where does the *Pilottown* come in?' asked Pitt.

'She was a legitimate purchase by Sosan Trading. You may be interested to know the International Maritime Crime Centre has her listed with ten suspected custom violations. A hell of a high number. It's thought she smuggled everything from plutonium to Libya, rebel arms to Argentina, secret American technology to Russia, you name it. She sailed under a smart bunch of operators. The violations were never proven. On five occasions she was known to leave port with clandestine cargo but was never caught unloading it. When her hull and engines finally wore out, she was conveniently scrapped and all records destroyed.'

'But why claim her as sunk if it was really the *San Marino* alias the *Belle Chasse* they scuttled?'

165

'Because questions might be raised regarding the *Belle Chasse*'s pedigree. The *Pilottown* had solid documentation so they claimed it was she that sank in 1979, along with a nonexistent cargo, and demanded a fat settlement from the insurance companies.'

Pitt glanced down at his toes and wiggled them. 'Did the old foreman talk about other ship conversions for Sosan Trading?'

'He mentioned two, a tanker and a container ship,' Perlmutter answered. 'But they were both refits and not conversions. Their new names were the *Boothville* and the *Venice*.'

'What were their former names?'

'According to my friend's report, the foreman claimed all previous identification had been removed.'

'Looks like somebody built themselves a fleet out of hijacked ships.'

'A cheap and dirty way of doing business.'

'Anything new on the parent company?' Pitt asked.

'Still a closed door,' Perlmutter replied. 'The foreman did say, however, that some bigshot used to show up to inspect the ships when they were completed and ready to sail.'

Pitt stood up. 'What else?'

'That's about it.'

'There has to be something, a physical description, a name, something.'

'Wait a minute while I check through the report again.'

Pitt could hear the rustle of paper and Perlmutter mumbling to himself. 'Okay, here it is. "The VIP always arrived in a big black limousine." No make mentioned. "He was tall for a Korean . . ."'

'Korean?'

'That's what it says,' replied Perlmutter. ' "And he spoke Korean with an American accent." '

The shadowed figure in Pitt's dream moved a step closer. 'St Julien, you do good work.'

'Sorry I couldn't take it all the way.'

'You bought us a first down.'

'Nail the bastard, Dirk.'

'I intend to.'

'If you need me, I'm more than willing.'

'Thank you St Julien.'

Pitt walked to the closet, threw on a brief kimono and knotted the sash. Then he padded into the kitchen, treated himself to a glass of guava juice laced with dark rum and dialled a number on the phone.

After several rings an indifferent voice answered.

'Yeah?'

'Hiram, crank up your computer. I've got a new problem for you.'

38

The tension was like a twisting knot in the pit of Suvorov's stomach. For most of the evening he had sat in the monitoring room, making small talk with the two psychologists who manned the telemetry equipment, telling jokes and bringing them coffee from the kitchen. They failed to notice that Suvorov's eyes seldom strayed from the digital clock on one wall.

Lugovoy entered the room at 11:20 and made his routine examination of the analogous data on the President. At 11:38 he turned to Suvorov.

'Join me in a glass of port?'

'Not tonight,' Suvorov said, making a pained face. 'I have a heavy case of indigestion. I'll settle for a glass of milk later.'

'As you wish,' Lugovoy said agreeably. 'See you at breakfast.'

Ten minutes after Lugovoy left, Suvorov noticed a small movement on one of the TV monitors. It was almost imperceptible at first, but then it was caught by one of the psychologists.

'What in hell!' he gasped.

'Something wrong?' asked the other.

'Senator Larimer . . . he's waking up.'

'Can't be.'

'I don't see anything,' said Suvorov moving closer.

'His Alpha activity is a clear nine to ten cycle per second set of waves that shouldn't be there if he was in his programmed sleep stage.'

'Vice President Margolin's waves are increasing too.'

'We'd better call Dr Lugovoy . . .'

The words hardly escaped his mouth when Suvorov cut him down with a savage judo chop to the base of the skull. In almost the same gesture, Suvorov swung a crosscut with the palm of his other hand into the throat of the second psychologist, crushing the man's windpipe.

Even before his victims hit the floor, Suvorov gazed coldly at the clock. The blinking red numbers displayed 11:49. Eleven minutes before Lugovoy was scheduled to exit the laboratory in the lift. Suvorov had practised his movements many times, allowing no more than two minutes for unpredictable delays.

He stepped over the lifeless bodies and ran from the monitor room into the chamber containing the subjects in their sound proofed

167

cocoons. He unlatched the top of the third one, threw back the cover and peered inside.

Senator Marcus Larimer stared back at him.

'What is this place? Who the hell are you?' the Senator mumbled.

'A friend,' answered Suvorov, lifting Larimer out of the cocoon and half carrying, half dragging him to a chair.

'What's going on?'

'Be quiet and trust me.'

Suvorov took a syringe from his pocket and injected Larimer with a stimulant. He repeated the process with Vice President Margolin, who looked around dazedly and offered no resistance. They were naked and Suvorov brusquely threw them blankets.

'Wrap yourselves in these,' he ordered.

Congressman Alan Moran had not yet awakened. Suvorov lifted him out of the cocoon and laid him on the floor. Then he turned and walked over to the unit enclosing the President. The American leader was still unconscious. The latch mechanism was different from the other cocoons, and Suvorov wasted precious seconds trying to prise open the cover. His fingers seemed to lose all feeling and he fought to control them. He began to sense the first prickle of fear.

His watch read 11:57. He was beyond his timetable; his two minute reserve evaporated. Panic was replacing fear. He reached down and snatched a Colt Woodsman twenty-two calibre automatic from a holster strapped to his right calf. He screwed on a four-inch suppressor and for a brief instant he was not himself, a man outside himself, a man whose only code of duty and unleashed emotion blinded his perception. He aimed the gun at the President's forehead on the other side of the transparent cover.

Despite his drug-misted mind, Margolin recognised what Suvorov was about to do. He staggered across the cocoon chamber and lurched into the Russian agent, grabbing for the gun. Suvorov just side-stepped and pushed him against the wall. Somehow Margolin remained on his feet. His vision was blurred and distorted, and a wave of sudden nausea threatened to gag him. He flung himself forward in another feeble effort to save the President's life.

Suvorov smashed the barrel of the gun against Margolin's temple and the Vice President dropped limply in a heap, blood streaming down the side of his face. For a moment Suvorov stood rooted. His well rehearsed plan was cracking and crumbling apart. Time had run out.

His last fleeting hope lay in salvaging the pieces. He forgot the President, kicked Margolin out of the way and shoved Larimer through the door. Heaving the still unconscious Moran over his shoulder, he herded the uncomprehending Senator down the corridor to the lift. They stumbled around the final corner just as the concealed doors parted and Lugovoy was about to step inside.

'Stop right where you are, Doctor.'

Lugovoy whirled and stared dumbly. The Colt Woodsman was held rock-steady in Suvorov's hand. The eyes of the KGB agent blazed with a contemptuous disdain.

'You fool!' Lugovoy blurted as the full realisation of what was happening struck him. 'You bloody fool!'

'Shut up!' Suvorov snapped. 'And step back out of the way.'

'You don't know what you're doing.'

'I know exactly what I'm doing,' said Suvorov, roughly elbowing Lugovoy aside and shoving the unprotesting Americans into the lift.

'You're ruining years of planning. President Antonov will have you shot.'

'I have no time to argue.'

A wave of despair swept Lugovoy. 'Please, you can't do this,' he pleaded.

Suvorov did not reply. He turned and glared malevolently as the lift doors closed and blocked him from view.

39

As the lift rose, Suvorov reversed the gun and smashed out the overhead light with the butt. Moran moaned and went through the motions of coming to, rubbing his eyes and shaking his head to clear the fog. Larimer became sick and vomited in a corner, his breath coming in great croaking heaves.

The lift eased to a smooth stop and the doors automatically opened to a smothering rush of warm air. The only light came from three dim yellow bulbs that hung suspended on a wire like ailing glow-worms. The sudden rush of air was dank and heavy and smelled of diesel oil and rotting vegetation.

Two men stood about ten feet away, engaged in conversation, waiting for Lugovoy to make his scheduled progress report. They turned and peered questioningly into the darkened lift. One of them held an attaché case. The only other detail Suvorov noted before he shot them each twice in the chest was the Oriental fold of their eyes.

He slung his free arm under Moran's waist and hauled him across what seemed like a rusting iron floor. He kicked Larimer ahead of him as he would a remorseful dog that had run away from home. The Senator reeled like a drunk, too sick to speak, too stunned to resist.

Suvorov pushed the gun inside his belt and took Larimer's arm, guiding him. The skin under his hand felt goosefleshed and clammy. Suvorov hoped the old legislator's heart wasn't about to give out.

Suvorov cursed as he stumbled over a large chain. Then he stopped and peered down an enclosed ramp that stretched into the dark. He felt as if he was inside a sauna; his clothes were turning damp with sweat and his hair was plastered down his forehead and temples. He tripped and almost fell, regaining his balance just before he was about to sprawl on the cross-slats of the ramp.

Moran's dead weight was becoming increasingly burdensome, and Suvorov realised his strength was ebbing. He doubted whether he could lug the Congressman another fifty yards.

At last they exited the tunnel-like ramp and staggered out into the night. He looked up and was vastly relieved to see a diamond-clear sky carpeted with stars. Beneath his feet the ground felt like a gravelled road and there were no lights to be seen anywhere. In the shadows off to his left he dimly recognised the outline of a car. Pulling Larimer into a ditch beside the road, he gratefully dropped Moran like a bag of sand and cautiously circled around, approaching the car from the rear.

He froze into immobility, rigid against the shadowless landscape and listened. The engine was running and music was playing on the radio. The windows were tightly rolled up and Suvorov rightly assumed the air conditioner was on.

Silent as a cat, he crouched and moved in closer, keeping low and out of any reflection in the side view mirror on the door. The inside was too dark to make out more than one vague form behind the wheel. If there were others, Suvorov's only ally was the element of surprise.

The car was a stretch-bodied limousine, and to Suvorov it seemed to lengthen into infinity. From the raised letters on the rear of the trunk, he identified it as a Cadillac. He'd never driven one and hoped he would have no trouble finding the right switches and controls.

His groping fingers found the door handle. He took a deep breath and tore open the door. The interior light flicked on and the man in the front seat twisted his head around, his mouth opening to shout. Suvorov shot him twice, the silver-tip hollow point bullets tearing through the rib cage under the armpit.

Almost before the blood began to spurt, Suvorov jerked the driver's body out of the car and rolled it away from the wheels. Then he roughly crowded Larimer and Moran into the back seat. Both men had lost their blankets and were nude, but they were too deeply gripped by shock to even notice or care. No longer the power brokers of Capitol Hill, they were waxen effigies of themselves, as helpless as children lost in the forest.

Suvorov found the ignition key and prodded the big engine to life.

170

Dropping the shift lever into 'drive', he jammed the accelerator to the floor mat so fiercely the rear tyres spun and sprayed gravel before finally gaining traction nearly fifty yards down the road. Only then did Suvorov's fumbling hand find the light switch and pull it on. He sagged in relief at discovering the big car was hurtling down the precise middle of the rutted country road.

As he threw the heavy, softly sprung limousine over three miles of choppy, washboard road, he began to take stock of his surroundings. Cypress trees bordering the road had great tentacles of moss hanging from their limbs. This, and the heavy atmosphere, suggested they were somewhere in the southern United States. He spotted a narrow paved crossroad ahead and slid to a stop in a swirling cloud of dust. On one corner stood a deserted building, more of a shack actually, with a decrepit sign illuminated by the headlights. GLOVER CULPEPPER – Gas & Groceries. Apparently Glover had packed up and moved on many years before.

The intersection held no marker so he mentally flipped a coin and turned left. The cypress gave way to groves of pine and soon he began passing an occasional farmhouse. Traffic was scarce at this hour of the morning. Only one car and a pickup truck passed him going in the opposite direction. He came to a wider road and spotted a bent sign on a leaning post designating it as State Highway 700. The number meant nothing to him so he made another left turn and continued on.

Throughout the drive, Suvorov's mind remained cold and rigidly alert. Larimer and Moran sat silently, watchful, blindly putting their faith in the man at the wheel.

Suvorov relaxed and eased his foot from the accelerator. No following headlights showed in the driving mirror, and as long as he maintained the posted speed limit, his chances of being stopped by a local sheriff were remote. He wondered what state he was in. Georgia, Tennessee, Louisiana? It could be any one of a dozen. He watched for some clue as the roadside became more heavily populated; darkened buildings and houses squatted under increasing numbers of overhead floodlights.

After another half an hour he encountered a bridge spanning a waterway called the Stono River. He'd never heard of it. At the highpoint of the bridge, the lights of a large city blinked in the distance. Off to his right side the lights suddenly halted and the entire horizon went pure black. A seaport, he swiftly calculated. Then the headlights fell on a large black and white directional sign. The top line read, CHARLESTON 5 miles.

'Charleston!' Suvorov said aloud in a sudden burst of jubilation, sifting through his knowledge of American geography. 'I'm in Charleston, South Carolina.'

171

Two miles further he found an all night chemist with a public telephone. Keeping a wary eye on Larimer and Moran, he dialled the long-distance operator and made a collect call.

40

A lone cloud was drifting overhead, scattering a few drops of moisture when Pitt slipped the Talbot beside the passenger departure doors of Washington's International Airport. The morning sun roasted the capital city, and the rain steamed and evaporated almost as soon as it struck the ground. He lifted Loren's suitcase out of the car and passed it to a waiting porter.

Loren unwound her long legs from the cramped sports car, demurely keeping her knees locked together, and climbed out. She was wearing a summery short-sleeved blouse and a gathered print skirt with tight waistband. She had impishly tied her hair in an old fashioned pony tail.

The porter stapled the luggage claim to the flight ticket and Pitt handed it to her.

'I'll park the car and babysit you until boarding time.'

'No need,' she said, standing close. 'I've some pending legislation to scan. You head back to the office.'

He nodded at the briefcase clamped in her left hand. 'Your crutch. You'd be lost without it.'

'I've noticed you never carry one.'

'Not the type.'

'Afraid you might be taken for a business executive.'

'This is Washington, you must mean bureaucrat.'

'You are one, you know. The government pays your salary same as mine.'

Pitt laughed. 'We all carry a curse.'

She set the briefcase on the ground and pressed her hands against his chest. 'I'll miss you.'

He circled his arms around her waist and gave a gentle squeeze. 'Beware of dashing Russian officers, bugged staterooms, and vodka hangovers.'

'I will,' she said smiling at his off hand humour. 'You'll be there when I return?'

'Your flight and arrival time is duly memorised.'

She tilted her head up and kissed him. He seemed to want to say something more, but finally he released her and stood back. She

172

slowly entered the terminal through the automatic sliding glass doors. A few steps into the lobby she turned to wave but the blue Talbot was pulling away.

On the President's farm, thirty miles south of Raton, New Mexico, members of the White House Press Corps were spaced along a barbed wire fence, their cameras trained on an adjoining field of alfalfa. It was seven in the morning, Mountain Standard Time, and they were soaking their stomachs in black coffee and complaining about the early hour, the high-plains heat, the watery scrambled eggs and burned bacon catered by a highway truck stop, and any other discontent, real or imagined.

Presidential Press Secretary Jacob (Sunny) Thompson walked brightly through the dusty press camp, prepping the bleary-eyed correspondents like a high school cheerleader and assuring them of great homespun, unrehearsed pictures of the President working the soil.

The charm was artfully contrived. Bright white teeth capped with precision, long sleek black hair, tinted grey at the temples, dark eyes with the tightened look of cosmetic surgery. No second chin. No visible sign of a potbelly. He moved and gestured with a bouncy enthusiasm that didn't sit well with journalists whose major physical activities consisted of pounding typewriters, word processors, and lifting cigarettes.

The clothes didn't hurt the image either; the tailored seersucker suit with the blue silk shirt and matching tie; black Gucci moccasins coated lightly with New Mexico dust. A classy, breezy guy who was no dummy. He never showed anger; never let the correspondent's vocal needles slip under his fingernails. Bob Finkel of the *Baltimore Sun* slyly suggested that an undercover investigation revealed that Thompson had graduated with honours from the Joseph Goebbels School of Propaganda.

He stopped at the CNB television motorhome. Curtis Mayo, the White House Correspondent network newscaster, sagged in a director's chair looking generally miserable.

'Got your crew set up, Curt?' asked Thompson jovially.

Mayo leaned back, pushed a baseball cap to the rear of a head forested with billowy silver hair and gazed up through orange-tinted glasses.

'I don't see anything worth capturing for posterity.'

Sarcasm ran off Thompson like oil from a cylinder wall. 'In five minutes the President is going to step from his house, walk to the barn, and start up a tractor.'

'Bravo,' grunted Mayo. 'What does he do for an encore?'

Mayo's voice had a resonance to it that made a symphonic kettle drum sound like a bongo; deep, booming, with every word enunciated with the sharpness of a bayonet.

'He is going to drive back and forth across the field with a mower and cut the grass.'

'That's alfalfa, city slicker.'

'Whatever,' Thompson acknowledged with a good-natured shrug. 'Anyway, I thought it would be a good chance to roll tape on him in the rural environment he loves best.'

Mayo levelled his gaze into Thompson's eyes, searching for a flicker of deception. 'What's going down, sonny?'

'Sorry?'

'Why the hide and seek? The President hasn't put in an appearance for over a week.'

Thompson stared back, his nut-brown eyes unreadable. 'He's been extremely busy, catching up on his homework away from the pressures of Washington.'

Mayo wasn't satisfied. 'I've never known a President to go this long without facing the cameras.'

'Nothing devious about it,' said Thompson. 'At the moment, he has nothing of national interest to say.'

'Has he been sick or something?'

'Far from it. He's as fit as one of his champion bulls. You'll see.'

Thompson saw through the verbal ambush and moved on along the fence, priming the other news people, slapping backs and shaking hands. Mayo watched him with interest for a few moments before he reluctantly rose out of the chair and assembled his crew.

Norm Mitchell, a loose, ambling scarecrow character, set up his video camera on a tripod, aiming it towards the back porch of the President's farm house, while the beefy sound man, whose name was Rocky Montrose, connected the recording equipment on a small folding table. Mayo stood with one booted foot on a strand of barbed wire, holding a microphone.

'How do you want to stand for your commentary?' asked Mitchell.

'I'll stay off camera,' answered Mayo. 'How far do you make it to the house and barn?'

Mitchell sighted through a pocket rangefinder. 'About a hundred and ten yards from here to the house. Maybe ninety to the barn.'

'How close can you bring him in?'

Mitchell leaned over the camera's eyepiece and lengthened the zoom lens, using the rear screen door for a reference. 'I can frame him with a couple of feet to spare.'

'I want a tight close-up.'

174

'That means a 2X converter to double the range.'

'Put it on.'

Mitchell gave him a questioning look. 'I can't promise you sharp detail. At that distance, we'll be giving up resolution and depth of field.'

'No problem,' said Mayo. 'We're not going for air time.'

Montrose looked up from his audio gear. 'Then you don't need me.'

'Roll sound anyway and record my comments.'

Suddenly the battalion of news correspondents came alive as someone shouted, 'Here he comes!'

Fifty cameras went into action as the screen door swung open and the President stepped into the porch. He was dressed in cowboy boots and a cotton shirt tucked into a pair of faded Levis. Vice President Margolin followed him over the threshold, a large Stetson pulled low over his forehead. They paused for a minute in conversation, the President gesturing animatedly while Margolin appeared to listen thoughtfully.

'Go tight on the Vice President,' Mayo ordered.

'Have him,' Mitchell responded.

The sun was climbing towards the middle of the sky and the heat waves were rising over the reddish earth. The President's farm swept away in all directions, mostly fields of hay and alfalfa, with a few pastures for his small herd of breeding cattle. The crops were a contrasting green to the barren areas watered by huge circular sprinkling systems. Except for a string of cottonwoods bordering an irrigation ditch, the land unfolded in flat solitude.

How could a man who spent most of his life in such desolation drive himself to influence billions of people, Mayo wondered. The more he saw of the strange egomania of politicians, the more he came to despise them. He turned and spat at a colony of red ants, missing their tunnel entrance by only a few inches. Then he cleared his throat and began describing the scene into the microphone.

Margolin turned and went back into the house. The President, acting as though the press corps was still back in Washington, hiked to the barn without turning in their direction. The exhaust of a diesel engine was soon heard and he reappeared seated on a green John Deere tractor, Model 2640, that was hooked to a hay mower. There was no canopy and the President sat out in the open, a small transistor radio clipped to his belt and earphones clamped to his head. The correspondents began yelling questions at him, but it was obvious he couldn't hear them above the rap of the exhaust and music from the local FM station.

He wrapped a red handkerchief over the lower part of his face, bandit style, to keep from breathing dust and exhaust fumes. Then he

175

swung down the mower's sliding blades and started cutting the field, driving back and forth in long rows, working away from the people crowding the fence.

After about twenty minutes, the correspondents slowly packed away their equipment and returned to the air conditioned comfort of their trailers and motorhomes.

'That's it,' announced Mitchell. 'No more tape, unless you want me to reload.'

'Forget it.' Mayo wrapped the cord around the microphone and handed it to Montrose. 'Let's get out of this heat and see what we've got.'

They tramped into the cool of the motorhome. Mitchell removed the cassette, holding the three-quarter inch video tape from the camera, inserted it into the playback recorder and rewound it. When he was ready to roll from the beginning, Mayo pulled up a chair and parked himself less than two feet away from the monitor.

'What are we looking for?' asked Montrose.

Mayo's concentration didn't waver from the images moving before his eyes. 'Would you say that's the Vice President?'

'Of course,' said Mitchell. 'Who else could it be?'

'You're taking what you see for granted. Look closer.'

Mitchell leaned in. 'The cowboy hat is covering the eyes, but the mouth and chin match. The build fits too. Looks like him to me.'

'Anything odd about his mannerisms?'

'The guy is standing there with his hands in his pockets,' said Montrose dumbly. 'What are we supposed to read in that?'

'Nothing unusual about him at all?' Mayo persisted.

'Don't notice a thing,' said Mitchell.

'All right, forget him,' said Mayo as Margolin turned and went back into the house. 'Now eyeball the President.'

'If that ain't him,' muttered Montrose acidly, 'then he's got an identical twin brother.'

Mayo brushed off the remark and sat there quietly as the camera followed the President across the barnyard, revealing the slow, recognisable gait known to millions of television viewers. He disappeared into the dark of the barn, and two minutes later, emerged on the tractor.

Mayo snapped erect. 'Stop the tape!' he shouted.

Startled, Mitchell pressed a button on the recorder and the image froze.

'The hands!' Mayo said excitedly. 'The hands on the steering wheel!'

'So he's got ten fingers,' mumbled Mitchell, his expression sour. 'So what?'

'The President only wears a wedding band. Look again. No ring on the middle finger of the left hand, but on the index finger you see a good sized sparkler. And the pinkie on the right . . .'

'I see what you mean,' Montrose interrupted. 'A flat blue stone in a silver setting, probably an amethyst.'

'Doesn't the President usually sport a Timex watch with an Indian silver band inlaid with turquoise?,' observed Mitchell, becoming swept along.

'I think you're right,' Mayo recalled.

'The detail is fuzzy, but I'd say that's one of those big Rolex chronometers on his wrist.'

Mayo pounded a fist on his knee. 'That clinches it. The President is known never to buy or wear anything of foreign manufacture.'

'Hold on,' Montrose said slowly. 'This is crazy. We're talking about the President of the United States as though he wasn't real.'

'Oh he's flesh and bone all right,' said Mayo, 'but the body sitting on that tractor belongs to someone else.'

'If you're right, you've got a live bomb in your hands,' said Montrose.

Mitchell's enthusiasm began to dim. 'We may be digging for clams in Kansas. Seems to me the evidence is damned shaky. You can't go on the air, Curt, and claim some clown is impersonating the President unless you have documented proof.'

'Nobody knows that better than me,' Mayo admitted. 'But I'm not about to let this story slip through my hands.'

'You're launching a quiet investigation then?'

'I'd turn in my press card if I didn't have the guts to see it through.' He looked at his watch. 'If I leave now, I should be in Washington by noon.'

Montrose crouched in front of the TV screen. His face had the look of a child who still found his tooth in a glass of water the next morning.

'It makes you wonder,' he said in a hurt tone, 'how many times one of our presidents used a double to fool the public.'

41

Vladimir Polevoi glanced up from his desk as his chief deputy and number two man of the world's largest intelligence gathering oranisation, Sergei Iranov, walked purposefully into the room. 'You look as if you've got a hot stake up your ass this morning, Sergei.'

'He's escaped,' Iranov said tersely.

'Who are you talking about?'

'Paul Suvorov, he's managed to break out of Bougainville's hidden laboratory.'

Sudden anger flushed Polevoi's face. 'Damn . . . not now!'

'He called our New York covert action centre from a public telephone in Charleston, South Carolina, and asked for instructions.'

Polevoi rose and furiously paced the carpet. 'Why didn't he call the FBI and ask them for instructions too? Better yet, he could have taken out an advertisement in USA Today.'

'Fortunately his superior immediately sent a coded message to us reporting the incident.'

'At least someone is thinking.'

'There's more,' said Iranov. 'Suvorov took two of Dr Lugovoy's subjects with him.'

Polevoi halted and spun around. 'I'll have that son of a bitch shot. Who did he get?'

'Moran and Larimer.'

'The halfwit. Why couldn't he simply have made contact and given us the location of the laboratory? Then we could have moved in and removed the Huckleberry Finn operation from Bougainville's control.'

'As it is, Madame Bougainville may be angry enough to cancel the experiment.'

'And lose a billion dollars in gold? I doubt that very much. She still has the President and Vice President in her greedy hands. Moran and Larimer are no great loss to her.'

'Nor to us,' Iranov stated. 'The Bougainvilles were our smokescreen in case the American intelligence agencies scuttled Huckleberry Finn. Now, with two abducted Congressmen in our hands, it might be considered an act of war, or at the very least a grave crisis. It would be best if we simply eliminated Moran and Larimer.'

Polevoi shook his head. 'Not yet. Their knowledge of the inner workings of the United States' military establishment can be of incalculable benefit to us.'

'A hazardous game.'

'Not if we're careful and quickly dispose of them when and if the net tightens.'

'Then our first priority is to keep them from discovery by the FBI.'

'Has Suvorov found a safe place to hide?'

'Not known,' Iranov answered. 'He was only told by New York to report every hour until they reviewed the situation and received orders from us in Moscow.'

'Who heads our undercover operations in New York?'

'His name is Basil Kobylin.'

'Advise him of Suvorov's predicament,' said Polevoi, 'omitting, of course, any reference pertaining to Huckleberry Finn. His orders are to hide Suvorov and his captives in a secure place until we can plan their escape from US soil.'

'Not an easy matter to arrange.' Iranov helped himself to a chair and sat down. 'The Americans are searching under every rock for their missing heads of state. All air fields are closely watched, and our submarines can't come within five hundred miles of their coastline without detection by their underwater warning line.'

'There is always Cuba.'

Iranov looked doubtful. 'The waters are too closely guarded by the US Navy and Coast Guard against drug traffic. I advise against any escape by boat in that direction.'

Polevoi gazed out of the windows of his office overlooking Dzerzhinsky Square. The late morning sun was fighting a losing battle to brighten the drab buildings of the city. A tight smile slowly crossed his lips.

'Can we get them safely to Miami?'

'Florida?'

'Yes.'

Iranov stared into space. 'There is the danger of roadblocks, but I think that could be overcome.'

'Good,' said Polevoi, suddenly relaxing. 'See to it.'

Less than three hours after the escape, Lee Tong Bougainville stepped out of the laboratory's lift and faced Lugovoy. It was a few minutes before three in the morning, but he looked as if he never needed sleep.

'My men are dead,' Lee Tong said without a trace of emotion. 'I hold you responsible.'

'I didn't know it would happen,' Lugovoy spoke in a quiet but steady voice.

'How could you not know?'

'You assured me this facility was escape proof. I didn't think he would actually make an attempt.'

'Who is he?'

'Paul Suvorov, a KGB agent, whom your men picked off the Staten Island ferry by mistake.'

'But you knew.'

'He didn't make his presence known until after we arrived.'

179

'And yet you said nothing.'

'That's true,' Lugovoy admitted. 'I was afraid. When this experiment is finished I must return to Russia. Believe me, it doesn't pay to antagonise our state security people.'

The built-in fear of the man behind you. Bougainville could see it in the eyes of every Russian he met. They feared foreigners, their neighbours, any man in uniform. They'd lived with it for so long it became an emotion as common as anger or happiness. He did not find it in himself to pity Lugovoy. Instead he despised him for willingly living under such a depressing system.

'Did this Suvorov cause any damage to the experiment?'

'No,' Lugovoy answered. 'The Vice President has a slight concussion, but he is back under sedation. The President was untouched.'

'Nothing delayed?'

'Everything is proceeding on schedule.'

'And you expect to finish in three more days?'

Lugovoy nodded.

'You have two. I'm moving your deadline up.'

Lugovoy acted as though he hadn't heard correctly. Then the truth broke through to him. 'Oh God no!' he gasped. 'I need every minute. As it is, my staff and I are cramming into ten days what should take thirty. You're eliminating all our safeguards. We must have more time for the President's brain to stabilise.'

'That is President Antonov's concern, not mine or my mother's. We fulfilled our part of the bargain. By allowing a KGB man in here, you jeopardised yours.'

'I swear I had nothing to do with Suvorov's breakout.'

'Your story,' Bougainville said coldly. 'I choose to believe his presence was planned, most likely on President Antonov's orders. Certainly by now Suvorov has informed his superiors and every Soviet agent in the States is converging on us. We will have to move the facility.'

That was the final shattering blow. Lugovoy looked as if he was about to gag. 'Impossible!' he howled like an injured dog. 'Absolutely no way can we move the President and all this equipment to another site and still meet your ridiculous deadline.'

Bougainville glared at Lugovoy through narrowed slits of eyes. When he spoke again, his voice was rock calm.

'Not to worry, doctor. No upheaval is necessary.'

42

When Pitt walked into his office, he found Hiram Yaeger asleep on the couch. With his sloppy clothes, long knotted hair and beard, he looked like a derelict wino. Pitt reached down and gently shook him by the shoulder. An eyelid was slowly raised, then Yaeger stirred, grunted, and pushed himself to a sitting position.

'Hard night?' Pitt inquired.

Yaeger scratched his head with both hands and yawned. 'You have any Celestial Seasonings Red Zinger Tea?'

'Only yesterday's warmed over coffee.'

Yaeger clicked his lips sourly. 'The caffeine will kill you.'

'Caffeine, pollution, booze, women; what's the difference?'

'By the way, I got it.'

'Got what?'

'I nailed it; your cagey shipping company.'

'Jesus!' Pitt said, coming alive. 'Where?'

'Right in our own backyard,' Yaeger said with a great grin. 'New York.'

'How did you do it?'

'Your hunch about Korean involvement was the key, but not the answer. I attacked it from that angle, probing all the shipping and export lines that were based in Korea or sailed under their registry. There were over fifty of them, but none led to the trail of banks we checked earlier. With nowhere else to go, I let the computer fly on its own. My ego is shattered. It proved a better sleuth than I am. The kicker was in the name. Not Korean, but French.'

'French?'

'Based in the World Trade Centre in Lower Manhattan, their fleet of legitimate ships fly the flag of the Somali Republic. How does that grab you?'

'Go on.'

'A first rate company, no rust bucket operation, rated lily white by Fortune, Forbes and Dun & Bradstreet. So damned pure that their annual report comes accompanied with harp music. Scratch the surface deep enough though, and you find more phoney frontmen and dummy subsidiary companies than gays in San Francisco. Documentary ship fraud, bogus insurance claims, chartering phantom ships with nonexistent cargoes, substitution of worthless cargoes for ones of great value. And always beyond the jurisdiction of the private outfits and governments they screw.'

'What's their name?'

'Bougainville Shipping,' answered Yaeger. 'Ever heard of it?'

'Min Koryo Bougainville, the steel lotus,' said Pitt impressed. 'Who hasn't? She's right up there with the celebrity British and Greek shipping tycoons.'

'She was your Korean connection.'

'Your data is conclusive. No chance of error?'

'Solid stuff,' Yaeger replied adamantly. 'Take my word for it. Everything triple checks. Once I tuned in on Bougainville as the source, it became a simple chore of working backwards. It all came together; bank accounts, letters of credit – you wouldn't believe how the banks turn their backs on these frauds. The old broad reminds me of one of those East Indian statues with twenty arms, sitting there with a holy look on its face while the hands are making obscene gestures.'

'You did it,' Pitt said enthusiastically, 'you actually pinned Sosan Trading, the *San Marino* and the *Pilottown* on the Bougainville shipping empire.'

'Like a stake through the heart.'

'How far back did you go?'

'I can give you the old girl's biography almost to when she spit out the tit. A tough old bird. Started from scratch and a lot of guts after World War Two. Slowly added old tramp ships to her fleet, crewed by Koreans who were glad to work for a bowl of rice and pennies a day. With practically no overheads, she cut-rate her freight costs and built a thriving business. About twenty-five years ago, when her grandson joined the company, things really took off. A slippery customer, that one. Keeps in the background. Except for school records, his data file is almost blank. Min Koryo Bougainville built the foundations for maritime crime that spanned thirty nations. When her grandson, Lee Tong is his name, came along, he honed and smoothed the piracy and fraud part of the organisation to a fine art. I had the whole mess printed out. There's a hard copy on your desk.'

Pitt turned and for the first time noticed a five inch thick sheath of computer printout paper on his desk. He sat down and briefly scanned the notched pages. The incredible reach of the Bougainvilles was mind boggling. The only criminal activity they appeared to shy away from was prostitution. After several minutes he looked up and nodded at Yaeger.

'A super job, Hiram,' he said sincerely. 'Thank you.'

Yaeger nodded towards the printouts. 'I wouldn't let that out of my sight if I were you.'

'Any chance of us getting caught?'

'A foregone conclusion. Our illegal taps have been recorded on the bank's computer log and printed out on a daily form. If a smart supervisor scans the list, he'll wonder why an American oceanographic agency is snooping his biggest depositor's records. His next step would be to rig the computer's communications line with a tracing device.'

'The bank would most certainly notify old Min Koryo,' said Pitt thoughtfully. Then he looked up. 'Once they identify NUMA as the tap, can Bougainville's own computer network probe ours to see what we've gleaned from their data banks?'

'Our network is as vulnerable as any other. They won't learn much though. Not since I removed the magnetic storage discs.'

'When do you think they'll smoke us out?'

'I'd be surprised if they haven't pegged us already.'

'Can you stay one jump ahead of them?'

Yaeger gave Pitt an inquiring stare. 'What sneaky plan are you about to uncork?'

'Go back to your keyboard and screw them up but good. Re-enter the network and alter the data, foul up the Bougainville day-to-day operations, erase legitimate bank records, programme absurd instructions into their programmes. Let them feel the heat from somebody else for a change.'

'But we'll lose vital evidence for a Federal investigation.'

'So what?' Pitt declared. 'It was obtained illegally and can't be used anyway.'

'Now wait a minute. We can be stepping into big trouble.'

'Worse than that, we might get killed,' Pitt said with a faint smile.

An expression blossomed on Yaeger's face; one that wasn't there before. It was sudden misgiving. The game had ceased to be fun and was taking on darker dimensions. It never dawned on him that the search might turn ugly and he might be murdered.

Pitt read the apprehension in Yaeger's eyes. 'You can quit now and take a holiday,' he said. 'I wouldn't blame you.'

Yaeger seemed to waver for a moment, then he shook his head. 'No, I'll stick with it. These people should be put away.'

'Come down hard on them. Jam the works in all aspects of their shipping company, outside investments, subsidiary businesses, property dealings, everything they touch.'

'Okay, it's my ass, but I'll do it. Just keep the Admiral out of my hair for a few more nights. Now that I've broken through Bougainville's safeguard programmes I'm in a position to raise more hell than a turd in a wedding punchbowl.'

'You have a delicate way of expressing yourself.'

'I figure that mass of data in your hands is only chapter one of an epic scandal. The deeper we pry, the curiouser and curiouser I get.'

'Keep a lookout for any information relating to a ship called the *Eagle*.'

'The presidential yacht?'

'Just a ship called the *Eagle*.'

'Anything else?'

Pitt nodded grimly. 'I'll see that security is increased around your computer processing centre.'

'Mind if I stay here and use your couch? I've developed this sudden aversion to sleeping alone in my flat.'

'My office is yours.'

Yaeger stood up and stretched. Then he nodded at the data sheets again. 'What are you going to do with that?'

Pitt stared down at the first breach ever in the Bougainville criminal structure. The pace of his personal investigation was gaining momentum, pieces falling into his hands to be fitted in the overall picture, jagged edges meshing together. The scope was far beyond anything he'd imagined in the beginning.

'You know,' he said pensively, 'I don't have the vaguest idea.'

43

When Senator Larimer awoke in the rear seat of the limousine, the eastern sky was beginning to turn orange. He slapped at the mosquito whose buzzing had interrupted his sleep. Moran stirred in his corner of the seat, his squinting eyes unfocused, his mind still unaware of his surroundings. Suddenly a door was opened and a bundle of clothes was thrown in Larimer's lap.

'Put these on,' Suvorov ordered brusquely.

'You never told me who you are,' Larimer said, his tongue moving in slow motion.

'My name is Paul.'

'No surname?'

'Just Paul.'

'You FBI?'

'No.'

'CIA?'

'It doesn't matter,' Suvorov said. 'Get dressed.'

'When will we arrive in Washington?'

'Soon,' Suvorov lied.

'Where did you get these clothes? How do you know they'll fit?'

Suvorov was losing his patience with the inquisitive American. He shrugged off an impulse to crack the Senator in the jaw with the gun.

'I stole them off a clothesline,' he said. 'Beggars can't be particular. At least they're washed.'

'I can't wear a stranger's shirt and pants,' Larimer protested indignantly.

'If you wish to return to Washington in the nude, it is no concern of mine.'

Suvorov slammed the door, moved to the driver's side of the car and edged behind the wheel. He drove out of a picturesque residential community called Plantation Estates and cut onto Highway Number 7. The early morning traffic was starting to thicken when they crossed over the Ashley River bridge to Highway 26, where he turned north.

He was grateful that Larimer went quiet. Moran was climbing from his semiconscious state and mumbling incoherently. The headlights reflected off a green sign with white letters: AIRPORT – NEXT RIGHT. He took the off ramp and came to the gate of the Charleston Municipal Airport. Across the main landing strip the brightening sky revealed a row of jet fighters belonging to the Air National Guard.

Following the directions given over the phone, he skirted the airport, searching for a narrow cutoff. He found it and drove over a dirt road until he came to a pole holding a windsock that hung limp in the dank atmosphere.

He stopped and got out, checked his watch and waited. Less than two minutes later, the steady beat of a helicopter's rotor blades could be heard approaching from behind a row of trees. The blinking navigation lights popped into view and a teardrop, a blue and white shape, hovered for a few moments and then settled down beside the limousine.

The door behind the pilot's seat pivoted outward and a man in white overalls stepped to the ground and walked up to the limousine.

'You Suvorov?' he asked.

'I'm Paul Suvorov.'

'Okay, let's get the baggage inside before we attract unwanted attention.'

Together they led Larimer and Moran into the passenger compartment of the 'copter and belted them in. Suvorov noted that the letters on the side of the fuselage read, SUMPTER AIRBORNE AMBULANCE.

'This thing going to the capital?' asked Larimer with a spark of his old haughtiness.

'Sir, it'll take you any place you want,' said the pilot agreeably.

Suvorov eased into the empty copilot's seat and buckled the harness. 'I wasn't told our destination,' he said.

185

'Russia, eventually,' the pilot said with a smile that was anything but humorous. 'First thing is to find where you came from.'

'Came from?'

'My orders are to fly you around the back country until you identify the facility in which you and those two windbags in the back have spent the last eight days. When we accomplish that mission, I'm to fly you to another departure area.'

'All right,' said Suvorov. 'I'll do my best.'

The pilot didn't offer his name and Suvorov knew better than to ask. The man was undoubtedly one of the estimated five thousand.

Soviet paid 'charges' stationed around the United States, experts in specialised occupations, all waiting for a call instructing them to surface, a call that might never come.

The helicopter rose fifty feet in the air and then banked off towards Charleston Bay. 'Okay, which way?' asked the pilot.

'I can't be sure. It was dark and I was lost.'

'Can you give me a landmark?'

'About five miles from Charleston: I crossed a river.'

'From what direction?'

'West, yes, the dawn was breaking ahead of me.'

'Must be Stono River.'

'Stono, that's it.'

'Then you were travelling on State Highway 7.'

'I turned onto it about half an hour before the bridge.'

The sun had heaved itself above the horizon and was filtering through the blue summer haze that hung over Charleston. The helicopter climbed to nine hundred feet and flew south-westward until the highway unreeled beyond the cockpit windows. The pilot pointed downward and Suvorov nodded. They followed the out-bound traffic as the South Carolina coastal plain spread beneath them. Here and there a few cultivated fields lay enclosed on all sides by forests of long-leafed pines. They passed over a farmer standing in a tobacco field who waved his hat at them.

'See anything familiar?' the pilot asked.

Suvorov shook his head helplessly. 'The road I turned off might be anywhere.'

'What direction were you facing when you met the highway?'

'I made a left turn so I must have been heading south.'

'This area is called Wadmalaw Island. I'll start a circular search pattern. Let me know if you spot something.'

An hour slipped by, and then two. The scene below transformed into a maze of creeks and small rivers snaking through bottom land and swamps. One road looked the same as another from the air. Thin ribbons of reddish-brown dirt or pot-holed asphalt slicing through dense overgrowth like lines on the palm of a hand. Suvorov became more confused as time wore on, and the pilot lost his patience.

'We'll have to knock off the search,' he said, 'or I won't have enough fuel to make Savannah.'

'Savannah is in the state of Georgia,' Suvorov said as though reciting in a school class.

The pilot smiled. 'Yeah, you got it.'

'Our departure point for the Soviet Union?'

'Only a fuel stop.' Then the pilot clammed up.

Suvorov saw it was impossible to draw any information out of the man so he turned his attention back to the ground.

Suddenly he pointed excitedly over the instrument panel. 'There!' he shouted above the engine's roar. 'The small intersection to the left.'

'Recognise it?'

'I think so. Drop lower. I want to read the sign on that shabby building sitting on the corner.'

The pilot obliged and lowered the helicopter until it hovered thirty feet over the bisecting roadways. 'Is that what you want?' he asked, 'Glover Culpepper – gas and groceries?'

'We're close,' said Suvorov. 'Fly up the road that leads towards that river to the north.'

'The Intracoastal Waterway.'

'A canal?'

'A shallow channel that provides an almost continuous inshore water passage from the North Atlantic states to Florida and the Gulf of Mexico. Used mostly by small pleasure boats and tugs.'

The helicopter beat over the tops of the trees, whipping leaves and bending branches with the wash from its rotor blades. Suddenly, at the edge of a wide, marshy creek, the road ended. Suvorov stared through the windscreen.

'The laboratory, it must be around here.'

'I don't see anything,' the pilot said, banking the craft and studying the ground.

'Set us down!' Suvorov demanded nervously. 'Over there, a hundred metres from the road in that glade.'

The pilot nodded and gently eased the helicopter's landing skids into the soft grassy earth, sending up a swirl of dead and mouldy leaves. He set the engine in idle with the blades slowly turning and opened the door. Suvorov leaped out and ran, stumbling through the underbrush back to the road. After a few minutes of frantic searching he stopped at the bank of the creek and looked around in exasperation.

'What's the problem?' asked the pilot as he approached.

187

'Not here,' Suvorov said dazedly. 'A warehouse with a lift that dropped down to a laboratory. It's gone.'

'Buildings can't vanish in six hours,' said the pilot. He was beginning to look bored. 'You must be on the wrong road.'

'No, no, this has to be the right one.'

'I only see trees and swamp,' he hesitated and pointed, 'and that decrepit old houseboat on the other side of the creek.'

'A boat!' Suvorov said as though having a revelation. 'It must have been a boat.'

The pilot gazed down into the muddy water of the creek. 'The bottom here is only three or four feet deep. Impossible to bring a vessel the size of a warehouse, requiring a lift, in here from the waterway.'

Suvorov threw up his hands in bewilderment. 'We must keep searching.'

'Sorry,' the pilot said firmly. 'We haven't the time or the fuel to continue. To keep our appointment we've got to leave now.'

He turned without waiting for a reply and walked back to the helicopter. Slowly, Suvorov followed him, looking all the world like a man deep in a trance.

As the helicopter lifted above the trees and swung towards Savannah, a gunnysack curtain in the window of the houseboat was pulled aside to reveal an old Chinaman peering through an expensive pair of Celestron 11 × 80 binoculars.

Satisfied he had read the aircraft's identification number on the fuselage correctly, he laid down the glasses and dialled a number on a portable telephone scrambling unit and spoke in rapid Chinese.

44

'Got a minute, Dan?' Curtis Mayo asked as Dan Fawcett exited his car in the private street beside the White House.

'You'll have to catch me on the run,' Fawcett replied without looking in Mayo's direction. 'I'm late for a meeting.'

'Another heavy session in the situation room?'

Fawcett sucked in his breath. Then, as calmly as his trembling fingers would permit he locked the car door and picked up his attaché case.

'Care to comment?' Mayo asked.

Fawcett marched off towards the security gate. 'I shot an arrow in the air . . .'

'It fell to earth, I know not where,' finished Mayo, keeping step. 'Longfellow. Want to see my arrow?'

'Not particularly.'

'This one is going to land on the six o'clock news.'

Fawcett slowed his pace. 'Just what are you after?'

Mayo took a large tape cassette from his pocket and handed it to Fawcett. 'You might like to view this before air time.'

'Why are you doing this?'

'Call it professional courtesy.'

'Now *that's* news.'

Mayo smiled. 'Like I said, view the tape.'

'Save me the trouble. What's on it?'

'A folksy scene of the President playing farmer, only it isn't the President.'

Fawcett drew up and stared at Mayo. 'You're full of crap.'

'Can I quote you?'

'Don't get cute,' snapped Fawcett. 'I'm in no mood for a slanted interview.'

'Okay, straight question,' said Mayo. 'Who is impersonating the President and Vice President in New Mexico?'

'Nobody.'

'I've got proof that says otherwise. Enough to use as a news item. I release this and every muckraker between here and Portland will crawl over the White House like an army of killer ants.'

'Do that and you'll have a dozen eggs on your face when the President stands as close to you as I am and denies it.'

'Not if I find out what sort of mischief he's been up to while a double played hide and seek down on the farm.'

'I won't wish you luck because the whole idea is outlandish.'

'Level with me, Dan. Something big is going down.'

'Trust me, Curt. Nothing off limits is happening. The President will be back in a couple of days. You can ask him yourself.'

'What about the sudden burst of secret cabinet meetings at all hours?'

'No comment.'

'It's true, isn't it?'

'Who's your source for that little gem?'

'Someone who's seen a lot of unmarked cars entering the sub-basement of the Treasury Department at the dead of night.'

'So the Treasury people are burning the midnight oil.'

'No lights go on in the building. My guess is they're sneaking into the White House through the utility tunnel and congregating in the situation room.'

189

'Think what you like, but you're dead wrong. That's all I have to say on the subject.'

'I'm not going to drop it,' said Mayo defiantly.

'Suit yourself,' Fawcett replied indifferently. 'It's your funeral.'

Mayo dropped back and watched as Fawcett walked through the security gate. The Presidential Adviser had put up a good front, he thought, but that's all it was, a front. Any doubts Mayo might have entertained about sinister manouevres emanating behind the walls of the nation's executive branch were swept away.

He was more determined than ever to damn well find out what was going on.

Fawcett slid the cassette in a video tape recorder and sat down in front of the TV screen. He ran the tape three times, examining every detail until he knew what Mayo had caught.

Wearily he picked up a phone and asked for a secure line to the State Department. After a few moments the voice of Doug Oates answered through the ear piece.

'Yes, Dan, what is it?'

'We have a new development.'

'News of the President?'

'No sir. I've just had a talk with Curtis Mayo of ABC News. He's on to us.'

There was a taut pause. 'What can we do?'

'Nothing,' said Fawcett sombrely, 'absolutely nothing.'

Sam Emmett left the FBI building in downtown Washington and drove over to CIA headquarters in Langley, Virginia. A summer shower passed overhead, moistening the forested grounds of the intelligence complex and leaving behind the sweet smell of dampened greenery.

Martin Brogan stood outside his office when Emmett walked through the anteroom door. The tall ex-college professor offered an outstretched hand. 'Thank you for taking time from your busy schedule to drive over. It was most generous of you.'

Emmett smiled as he took his hand. Brogan was one of the few men around the President he genuinely admired. 'Not at all. I'm not a desk man. I jump at any excuse to get off my butt and move around.'

They entered Brogan's office and sat down. 'Coffee or a drink?' Brogan asked.

'No thanks.' Emmett opened his briefcase and laid a bound report on the CIA Director's desk. 'This spells out the Bureau's findings until an hour ago on the President's disappearance.'

Brogan handed him a similarly bound report. 'Likewise from

190

Central Intelligence. Damned little to add since our last meeting, I'm sorry to say.'

'You're not alone. We're miles from a breakthrough too.'

Brogan paused to light a ropelike Toscanini cigar. It seemed oddly out of place with his Brooks Brothers pinstripe suit and shirt. Together, the men began reading. After nearly ten minutes of quiet, Brogan's expression softened from deep concentration to curious interest, and he tapped a page of Emmett's report.

'This section about a missing Soviet psychologist?'

'I thought that would interest you.'

'He and his entire United Nations staff vanished the same night of the *Eagle*'s hijacking?'

'Yes, to date none of them have turned up. Could be merely an intriguing coincidence, but I felt it shouldn't be ignored.'

'The first thought that crossed my mind is that this . . .' Brogan glanced at the report again. '. . . Lugovoy, Dr Aleksei Lugovoy, may have been assigned by the KGB to use his psychological wiles to pry national secrets from the abducted men.'

'A theory we can't afford to dismiss.'

'The name,' Brogan said vacantly, 'it strikes a chord.'

'You've heard it before?'

Suddenly, Brogan's brows rose and his eyes widened ever so slightly and he reached for his intercom. 'Send up the latest file from the Interpol and the French Internal Security Agency.'

'You think you've got something?'

'A recorded conversation between President Antonov and his KGB chief Vladimir Polevoi. I believe Lugovoy was mentioned.'

'From French intelligence?' Emmett asked.

'Antonov was on a state visit. Our friendly rivals in Paris are quietly cooperative about passing along information they don't consider sensitive to their national interests.'

In less than a minute, Brogan's private secretary knocked on the door and gave him a transcription of the secret tape recording. He quickly consumed its contents.

'This is most encouraging,' he said. 'Read between the lines and you can invent all sorts of Machiavellian schemes. According to Polevoi, the UN psychologist disappeared off the Staten Island ferry in New York and all contact was severed.'

'The KGB lost several members of their family at one time?' Emmett asked in mild astonishment. 'That's a new twist, they must be getting sloppy.'

'Polevoi's own statement.' Brogan held out the transcript papers. 'See for yourself.'

Emmett read the typed print and reread it a second time. When he looked up, a trace of triumph brightened his eyes. 'So the Russians *are* behind the abduction.'

Brogan nodded in agreement. 'From all appearances, but they can't be in it alone. Not if they're ignorant of Lugovoy's whereabouts. Another source is working with them, someone here in the United States with the power to dictate the operation.'

'You?' Emmett asked wolfishly.

Brogan laughed. 'No, and you?'

Emmett shook his head. 'If the KGB, the CIA and the FBI are all kept in the dark, then who's dealing the cards?'

'The person they refer to as the "old bitch" and "Chinese whore".'

'No gentlemen these Communists.'

'The code word for their operation must be Huckleberry Finn.'

Emmett stretched out his legs, crossing them at the ankles, and sagged comfortably in his chair. 'Huckleberry Finn,' he repeated, enunciating every syllable of the name made famous by Mark Twain. 'Our counterpart in Moscow has a dark sense of humour. But what's important, he's unwittingly given us an eye to shove a sharp stick into.'

No one paid any attention to the two men seated silently in a pickup truck parked in a loading zone by the NUMA building. A cheap, plastic movable sign adhered to the passenger's door advertised "Gus Moore's Plumbing". Behind the cab in the truck's bed, several lengths of copper pipe and an assortment of tools lay in casual disorder. The men's overalls were stained with dirt and grease, and neither had shaved in three or four days. The only odd thing about their appearance was their eyes, they never shifted from the entrance to NUMA's headquarters.

The driver tensed and made a directional movement with a nod of his head. 'I think this is him coming.'

The other man raised a pair of binoculars wrapped in a brown paper bag with the bottom torn out and gazed at a figure exiting through the revolving glass doors. Then he laid the glasses in his lap and examined a face in a large eleven by fourteen inch glossy photograph.

'Confirmed.'

The driver checked a small row of numbers on a small black transmitter. 'Counting one hundred and forty seconds from . . . now.' He punctuated his words by pushing a toggle switch to the 'on' position.

'Okay,' said his partner. 'Let's get the hell away.'

Pitt reached the bottom of the broad stone steps as the plumber's truck drove past in front of him. He stood a moment to let another car by, and began walking through the car park. He was seventy yards from the Talbot-Lago when he turned at the honking of a horn.

Al Giordino drew up alongside in a Ford Bronco four-wheel drive. His curly black hair was shaggy and uncombed and a heavy growth covered his chin. He looked as if he hadn't slept in a week.

'Sneaking home early?' he said.

'I was until you caught me,' Pitt replied grinning.

'Lucky you, sitting around on your ass with nothing to do.'

'You wrap up the *Eagle* salvage?' Pitt asked.

Giordino gave a tired nod. 'Towed her up the river and pushed her into drydock about three hours ago. You can smell her death stink a mile away.'

'At least you didn't have to remove the bodies.'

'No, a navy diving team was stuck with that ugly chore.'

'Take a week off. You've earned it.'

Giordino spread his Roman smile. 'Thanks boss. I needed that.' Then his expression turned solemn. 'Anything new on the *Pilot-town*?'

'We're zeroing in – '

Pitt never finished the sentence. A thunderous explosion tore the air. A ball of flame erupted between the densely packed cars and jagged metal debris burst in all directions. A tyre and wheel, the chrome spokes flashing in the sun, flew in a high arc and landed with a loud crunch in the middle of Giordino's hood. Bounding inches over Pitt's head, it then rolled through a landscaped parkway before coming to rest in a cluster of rose bushes. The rumble from the blast echoed across the city for several seconds before it finally faded and died.

'God!' Giordino rasped in bewildered awe. 'What was that?'

Pitt took off running, dodging between the tightly parked cars, until he slowed and halted in front of a scrambled mess of metal that smouldered and coughed up a cloud of dense, black smoke. The asphalt underneath was gouged and melting from the heat, turning into a heavy sludge. The tangled wreck was nearly unrecognisable as a car.

Giordino ran up behind him. 'Jesus, whose was it?'

'Mine,' said Pitt, his features twisted in bitterness as he stared at the once beautiful remains of the Talbot-Lago.

PART III

THE LEONID ANDREYEV

45

Loren was greeted by Captain Yakov Pokofsky when she boarded the *Leonid Andreyev*. A charming man with thick silver hair and eyes as round and black as caviar. Though he acted politely and diplomatically, Loren sensed he wasn't exactly thrilled with having an American politician snooping about his ship, asking questions about its management. After the usual niceties, the first officer led her to a celebrity suite filled with enough flowers for a state funeral. The Russians, she mused, knew how to accommodate a visiting VIP.

In the evening, when the last of the passengers had boarded and settled down in their staterooms, the crew cast off the mooring lines and the cruise ship steamed out of Biscayne Bay through the channel into the Atlantic. The lights of the hotels on Miami Beach glittered under a tropical breeze and slowly closed together in a thin glowing line as the *Leonid Andreyev*'s twin screws thrust her further from shore.

Loren stripped off her clothes and took a shower. When she stepped out and towelled, she struck an exaggerated model's pose in front of a full length mirror. The body was holding up quite well, considering thirty-seven years of use. Jogging and ballet class four hours a week kept most of the flab away. She pinched her tummy and sadly noted that slightly more than an inch of flesh protruded between her thumb and forefinger. The lavish food on the cruise ship wasn't going to do her weight any good, she commiserated. She steeled her mind to lay off the alcohol and desserts. If her discipline held firm, that would slow the fat, she consoled herself.

She slipped on a thirties' style mauve silk damask jacket over a black lace and taffeta skirt. Loosening the business-like knot on top of her head, she let her hair down so that it spilled over her shoulders. Satisfied with the effect, she felt in the mood for a stroll around the deck before dinner at the captain's table.

The air was so warm she dispensed with a sweater. On the aft end of the sun deck she found a vacant deckchair, and relaxed, raising her knees and clasping her hands around the calves. For the next half hour she let her mind wander as she watched the half moon's reflection dash across the dark swells. Then the exterior deck lights abruptly went out from bow to stern.

Loren didn't notice the helicopter until it was almost over the fantail of the ship. It had arrived at wave top level, flying without navigation lights. Several crew members appeared from the shadows and quickly laid a roof over the boat deck swimming pool. Then a ship's officer signalled with a flashlight and the helicopter descended lightly onto the pool roof.

Loren rose to her feet and stared over the railing. Her vantage position was one deck above and forty feet distant from the closed in swimming pool. The area was dimly illuminated by the partial moon, enabling her to observe most of the action. She glanced around, looking for other passengers but saw only five or six who were standing fifty feet further away.

Three men exited from the craft. Two of them, it appeared to Loren, were treated roughly. The ship's officer placed the flashlight under his arm so he could have both hands free to brusquely shove one of the men into an open hatchway. For a brief instant the unaimed beam caught and held on a paper-white face, eyes bulging in fear. Loren saw the facial details clearly. Her hands gripped the deck rail and her heart felt locked in ice.

Then the 'copter rose into the night and turned sharply back towards shore. The cover over the pool was quickly removed and the crew melted away. In a few seconds the ship's lights came back on. Everything had happened so fast, Loren wondered for a moment if she had actually witnessed the landing and takeoff.

But there was no mistaking the frightened creature she saw on the pool deck below. She was positive it was Speaker of the House, Congressman Alan Moran.

On the bridge Captain Pokofsky peered at the radar scope. He was of medium height and portly. A cigarette dangled from one corner of his lips. He straightened and smoothed the jacket of his white dress uniform.

'At least they waited until we were beyond the twelve mile limit,' he said in a guttural voice.

'Any sign they were followed?' asked the officer of the watch.

'No aerial contacts and no craft approaching by sea,' answered Pokofsky. 'A smooth operation.'

'Like the others,' the watch officer said with a cocky smile.

Pokofsky did not return the smile. 'I'm not fond of taking deliveries on short notice under moonlit skies.'

'This one must be a high priority.'

'Aren't they all?' Pokofsky said caustically.

The watch officer decided to remain quiet. He'd served with Pokofsky long enough to recognise when the captain was in one of his sour moods.

Pokofsky checked the radar again and swept his eyes across the black sea ahead. 'See that our guests are escorted to my cabin,' he ordered, before turning and leaving the bridge.

Five minutes later, the ship's second officer knocked on the captain's door, opened it and ushered in a man wearing a rumpled business suit.

'I'm Captain Pokofsky,' he said, rising from a leather reading chair.

'Paul Suvorov.'

'KGB or GRU*?'

'KGB.'

Pokofsky gestured towards a sofa. 'Do you mind informing me of the purpose behind your unscheduled arrival?'

Suvorov gratefully sat down and took the measure of Pokofsky. He was uncomfortable with what he read. The captain was clearly a hardened seaman and not the type to be intimidated by state security credentials. Suvorov wisely chose to tread lightly.

'Not at all. I was instructed to smuggle two men out of the country.'

'Where are they now?'

'I took the liberty of having your first officer lock them in the brig.'

'Are they Soviet defectors?'

'No, they're American.'

Pokofsky's brows rose. 'Are you saying you've kidnapped American citizens.'

'Yes,' said Suvorov with an icy calm. 'Two of the most important leaders in the United States government.'

'I'm not sure I heard you correctly.'

'Their names do not matter. One is a Congressman, the other a Senator.'

Pokofsky's eyes burned with sudden belligerence. 'Do you have any idea of the jeopardy you've placed my ship in?'

'We're in international waters,' Suvorov said placidly. 'What can happen?'

'Wars have been started for less,' Pokofsky said sharply. 'If the Americans are alerted, international waters or not, they wouldn't hesitate for one instant to send their navy and coast guard to stop and board this vessel.'

Suvorov came to his feet and stared directly ino Pokofsky's eyes. 'Your precious ship is in no danger, Captain.'

* Soviet Military Intelligence.

199

Pokofsky stared back. 'What are you saying?'

'The ocean is a big dumping ground,' Suvorov said steadily. 'If the situation requires, my friends in your brig will simply be committed to the deep.'

46

Talk around the captain's table was dull and inane as could be expected. Loren's dining companions bored her with long, drawn out descriptions of their previous travels. Pokofsky had heard such travelogues a thousand times before. He smiled politely and listened with feigned courtesy. When asked, he told how he had joined the Russian Navy at seventeen, worked up through the officer's ranks until he commanded a troop transport, and after twenty years' service transferred to the Soviet subsidised passenger line.

He described the *Leonid Andreyev* as a 14,000-ton vessel, built in Finland for a capacity of 478 passengers with two crew members for every three of them. The modern, white-hulled liner had indoor and outdoor swimming pools, five cocktail bars, two nightclubs, ten shops featuring Russian merchandise and liquor, a movie and stage theatre, and a well stocked library. She cruised from Miami on ten-day sailings during the summer months to several resort islands in the West Indies.

During a lull in the conversation, Loren casually mentioned the helicopter landing. Captain Pokofsky lit a cigarette with a wooden match and waved out the flame.

'You Americans and your affluence,' he said easily. 'Two wealthy Texans missed the boat in Miami and hired a helicopter to fly them to the *Andreyev*. Very few of my countrymen can afford such luxury.'

'Not many of mine can either,' Loren assured him. The captain was not only congenial and charming, she thought, he was an accomplished liar as well. She dropped the subject and nibbled on her salad.

Before dessert, Loren excused himself and went to her suite on the sun deck. She kicked off her shoes, removed and hung up her skirt and jacket, and sprawled on the soft king size bed. She ran the picture of Alan Moran's terrified face through her mind, telling herself it must have been someone who resembled the 'Congressman, and perhaps the beam of the flashlight outlined similar features. Reasoning dictated that it was merely a trick of imagination.

Then the memory of Pitt's inquiry at the restuarant returned to her. He's asked if she'd heard any rumours of a missing party high in government. Now her gut instinct said she was right.

She laid out a ship's directory and deck diagram on the bed and flattened out the creases. To look for Moran in a floating city with 230 staterooms, quarters for a crew of over 300, cargo holds and engine room, all spread over eleven decks nearly 500 feet in length was a lost cause. She also had to consider that she was a representative of the American government on Russian property. Obtain permission from Captain Pokofsky to search every nook and cranny of his ship? She'd stand a better chance of persuading him to give up vodka for Kentucky bourbon.

Before she flew off like a decapitated turkey, the logical move would be to establish Alan Moran's presumed whereabouts. If he was at home in Washington watching TV, she could forget the whole madness and get a good night's sleep. She put her dress back on and went to the communications room. Thankfully it wasn't crowded and she didn't have to wait in line.

A pretty Russian girl in a trim uniform asked Loren where she wished to call.

'Washington DC,' she replied. 'Person to person to a Ms Sally Lindemann. I'll write out the number.'

'If you will please wait in stall five, I'll arrange your satellite transmission,' the communications girl said in near flawless English.

Loren sat patiently, hoping her secretary was at home. She was: a sleepy voice answered the operator and acknowledged her name was Sally Lindemann.

'That you boss?' asked Sally when Loren was put through. 'I bet you're dancing up a storm under Caribbean stars with some handsome playboy. Am I right?'

'You're not even close.'

'I should have known this was a business call.'

'Sally, I need you to contact someone.'

'One sec.' There was a pause. When Sally's voice came on again, it glowed with efficiency. 'I've got a pad and pencil. Who do I contact and what do I say?'

'The Congressman who opposed and shot down my Rocky Mountain water project.'

'You mean old prune face Mo – '

'He's the one,' Loren cut her off. 'I want you to talk to him, face to face if possible. Start with his home. If he's out, ask his wife where he can be reached. If she balks, tell her it's a matter of Congressional urgency. Say whatever it takes but get to him.'

'When I find him, then what?'

201

'Nothing,' said Loren. 'Say it was a mistake.'

There were a few seconds of silence. Then Sally said carefully, 'You drunk, boss?'

Loren laughed, knowing the puzzlement that must be running through Sally's mind.

'Dead sober.'

'Can this wait until morning?'

'I have to know his location as quickly as possible.'

'My alarm clock reads after midnight,' Sally protested.

'Now!' Loren said sharply. 'Call me the second you see his face and hear his voice.'

She hung up and walked back towards her suite. The moon was directly overhead and she lingered a few minutes on deck, wishing Pitt was standing there beside her.

Loren had just finished putting on her morning face when she heard a knock on the door.

'Who's there?'

'Steward.'

She went to the door and opened it. Her cabin steward raised his hand in a casual salute. He peered selfconsciously at the cleavage revealed by her loosely knotted dressing gown.

'An emergency call for you from the mainland, Congresswoman Smith,' he said in a heavy Slavic accent. 'They're holding it for you in the communications room.'

She thanked him and hurriedly dressed. A new girl directed her to a booth and the waiting call. Sally's voice came through the earpiece as clear as if she was in the next booth.

'Good morning, boss,' she said tiredly.

'Any luck?'

'Moran's wife said he went fishing with Senator Marcus Larimer,' Sally snapped out before Loren thought to stop her. 'She claimed they went to a place called Goose Lake, a private reserve for the good ole boys a few miles below the Quantico Marine Corp Reservation. So I hopped in my car and drove down. After bluffing my way past an outdoorsy type guarding the gate, I checked every cottage, boathouse and dock. No Congressman, no Senator. Then back to the Capitol. I called and woke up three of Moran's aides. Don't ever look for favours from his office. They backed up the fishing story. Same bull. In fact, nobody has seen either of them in over a week. Sorry I failed you, boss, but it looks like a smokescreen to me.'

Loren felt a cold chill run through her. The second man she saw manhandled from the helicopter, could he have been Marcus Larimer?

202

'Shall I stay on the hunt?' asked Sally.

'Yes, please,' Loren answered.

'Do my best,' Sally declared. 'Oh, I almost forgot. Have you heard the latest news?'

'How could I at ten in the morning on a boat in the middle of the ocean?'

'Concerns your friend Dirk Pitt.'

'Something happen to Dirk?' Loren asked anxiously.

'Persons unknown blew up his car. Lucky for him he wasn't inside at the time. Close though. Walking towards it when he stopped to talk to a friend. According to District police, another couple of minutes and they'd have swept him up with a broom.'

Everything caught up and jammed behind Loren's eyes. It was all happening too fast for her to accept. The mad events splashed behind her eyes in a complexity of colour, like scraps making up a bed quilt. The seams were pulling apart in all directions. She grasped the only thread that seemed to hold.

'Sal, listen carefully. Call Dirk and tell him I need – ' Suddenly a shrill buzzing sound flooded her eardrum. 'Can you hear me, Sal?'

Loren's only reply was the interference. She swung around to complain to the communications girl, but she was gone. Instead, there were two stewards, or rather two wrestlers in steward's uniforms, and the first officer. He opened the door to her booth and bowed curtly.

'Will you please come with me, Congresswoman Smith. The Captain would like to talk to you.'

47

The pilot set the helicopter on the ground at a small airport on the Isle of Palms near Charleston. He went through the standard shut down procedure, running the engine at low RPMs until it cooled down. Then he climbed out, lined up one of the rotor blades and tied it to the tail boom.

His back and arms ached from the long hours in the air, and he did stretching exercises as he walked to a small office next to the landing pad. He unlocked the door and stepped inside.

A stranger sat in the tiny lobby area, casually reading a newspaper. To the pilot he looked to be either Chinese or Japanese. The newspaper was lowered, revealing a shotgun with a pistol grip and twin sawn off barrels that ended barely four inches in front of the shells.

'What do you want?' asked the pilot stupidly.

'Information?'

'You're in the wrong place,' said the pilot, instinctively raising his hands. 'We're a helicopter ambulance service, not a library.'

'Very witty,' said the Oriental. 'You also carry passengers.'

'Who told you that?'

'Paul Suvorov. One of your Russian friends.'

'Never heard of the guy.'

'How odd. He sat next to you in the copilot's seat for most of yesterday.'

'What do you want?' the pilot repeated, the fear beginning to crawl up his spine.

The Oriental smiled wickedly. 'You have ten seconds to tell me the precise destination you flew Suvorov and two other men. If at the end of that time you feel stubborn, I shall blow away one of your knees. Ten seconds later you can bid goodbye to your sex life.' He enforced his request by releasing the safety on the shotgun. 'Countdown begins . . . now.'

Three minutes later the Oriental stepped from the building and locked the door. Then he walked to a car parked nearby, climbed behind the wheel and drove towards a sandy road leading to Charleston.

The car was barely out of sight when a torrent of orange flame gushed through the thin roof of the pilot's office and spiralled into the white, overcast sky.

Pitt spent the day dodging reporters and police detectives. He hid in a quiet pub called the Devil's Fork on Rhode Island Avenue and sat in a cushiony leather seat in a quiet corner, staring pensively at a half-eaten monte cristo sandwich and a third manhattan, a drink he seldom ordered.

A pert blonde waitress in a micro skirt and mesh stockings stopped by his table. 'You're the most pitiful person in the place,' she said with a motherly smile. 'Lose your best girl or your wife?'

'Worse,' said Pitt sadly. 'My car.'

She laid a look on him reserved for Martians and weirdos, shrugged and continued her rounds of the other tables.

Pitt sat there, idly stirring the manhattan with a cherry, scowling at nothing. Somewhere along the line he had lost his grip of things. Events were controlling him. Knowing who tried to kill him provided little satisfaction. Only the Bougainville hierarchy had the motive. He was getting too close. No brilliance required in solving that mystery.

He was angry at himself for playing adolescent computer games with their financial operation while they ran in a tougher league. Pitt felt like a prospector who discovered a safe full of currency in the middle of the Antarctic and no place to spend it. His only leverage was that he knew more than they thought he knew.

The enigma that nagged him was Bougainville's unlikely involvement with the *Eagle*. He knew of no motive for the sinking and murders. The only tie, and a slim one at that, was the over-abundance of Korean bodies.

No matter; that was the FBI's problem, and he was glad to be rid of it.

The time had come, he decided, to get rolling, and the first step was to marshal his forces. No brilliance required in that decision either.

He rose and walked over to the bar. 'Can I borrow your phone, Cabot?'

The bartender, a pixie face Irishman, name of Sean Cabot, who looked like a first cousin of every other Irish bartender, gave Pitt a doleful glare. 'Local or long distance?'

'Long distance, but don't cry in your cash register. I'll use a credit card.'

Cabot nodded indifferently and set a telephone on the end of the bar away from the other customers. 'Too bad about your car, Dirk. I saw her once. She was a pretty one.'

'Thanks. Buy yourself a drink and put it on my tab.'

Cabot filled a glass with ginger ale from the dispenser and held it aloft. 'To a good samaritan and a *bon vivant*.'

Pitt didn't feel like a good samaritan and even less like a *bon vivant* as he punched out the numbers on the phone. He gave his credit card number to the operator and waited for a voice to answer.

'Casio and Associates Investigatahs.'

'This is Dirk Pitt. Is Sal in?'

'One moment, sah.'

Things were looking up. He'd been accepted into the receptionist's club.

'Dirk?' came Casio's voice. 'I've been calling your office all morning. I think I've got something.'

'Yes?'

'A hunt through maritime union files paid dividends. Six of the Korean seamen who signed on the *San Marino* had prior crew tickets. Mostly with foreign shipping lines. But all six had one thing in common. At one time or another they sailed for Bougainville Maritime. Ever hear of it?'

'It figures,' said Pitt. Then he proceeded to tell Casio what he had found during the computer search.

'Damn!' Casio explained incredulously. 'Everything fits.'

'The maritime union, what did their records show on the Korean crew after the *San Marino* hijacking?'

'Nothing, they dropped from sight.'

'If Bougainville history ran true to form, they were murdered.'

Casio went silent, and Pitt guessed what was running through the investigator's mind.

'I owe you,' Casio said finally. 'You've helped me in on Arta's killer. But it's my show. I'll take it alone from here.'

'Don't dish me the eye-for-an-eye martyr routine,' Pitt said cuttingly. 'Besides, you still don't know who was directly responsible.'

'Min Koryo Bougainville,' said Casio, spitting out the name. 'Who else could it be?'

'The old girl might have given the orders,' said Pitt, 'but she didn't dirty her hands. It's no secret she's been in a wheelchair for ten years. No interviews or pictures of her have been published since Nixon was President. For all we know, Min Koryo Bougainville is a senile, bedridden vegetable. Hell, she may even be dead. No way she scattered bodies over the seascape alone.'

'You're talking of a corporate hit squad.'

'Can you think of a more efficient way to eliminate the competition?'

'Now you're insinuating she's a member of the Mafia,' grunted Casio.

'The Mafia only kills informers and each other. The evil beauty of Min Koryo's set-up is that by murdering crews in wholesale lots and stealing vessels from other shipping lines she built her assets with almost no overheads. And to do it she has to have someone organise and orchestrate the crimes. Don't let your hate blind you to hardcore reality, Sal. You haven't got the resources to take on Bougainville alone.'

'And you do?'

'Takes two to start an army.'

There was another silence, and Pitt thought the connection might have been broken.

'You still there, Sal?'

'I'm here,' Casio finally said in a thoughtful voice. 'What do you want me to do?'

'Fly to New York and pay a visit to Bougainville Maritime.'

'You mean toss their office?'

'I thought the term was "breaking and entering".'

'A cop and a judge use different dictionaries.'

'Just employ your talents to see what you can find of interest that doesn't show up in the computers.'

'I'll bug the place while I'm at it.'

'You're the expert,' said Pitt. 'Our advantage is that you'll be

206

coming from a direction they won't suspect. Me, I've already been marked.'

'Marked?' asked Casio. 'How?'

'They tried to kill me.'

'Christ!' muttered Casio. 'What method?'

'Car bomb.'

'The bastards!' he rasped. 'I'll leave for New York this afternoon.'

Pitt pushed the telephone across the bar and returned to his booth. He felt better after talking to Casio, and he finished the sandwich. He was contemplating his fourth manhattan when Giordino walked up to the table.

'A private party?' he asked.

'No,' Pitt said. 'A hate-the-world, feel-sorry-for-yourself, down-in-the-dumps party.'

'I'll join it anyway,' said Giordino sliding into the booth. 'The Admiral's concerned about you.'

'Tell him I'll pay for any damage to the car park.'

'Be serious. The old guy is madder than a stepped on rattler. Raised hell with the Justice Department all morning, demanding they launch an all-out investigation to find out who was behind the bombing. To him an attack on you is an attack on NUMA.'

'The FBI nosing around my flat and office?'

Giordino nodded. 'No less than six of them.'

'And reporters?'

'I lost count. What did you expect? The blast that disintegrated your car thrust your name in the limelight. Instant celebrity. First bomb explosion the city's had in seven years. Somebody broke the unwritten law. You don't assassinate a respected government employee in a high level position on their home turf. Like it or not, old friend, you've become the eye of the storm.'

Pitt sensed a mild elation at having scared the Bougainville interests enough for them to attempt his removal. They must have somehow learned he was nipping at their flanks, digging deeper into their secrets with each bite. But why the over reaction, the hunter becoming the hunted?

The fake announcement of his discovery of both the *San Marino* and the *Pilottown* no doubt alerted them. Yet it shouldn't have thrown them in a panic. Min Koryo wasn't the panicky type. A point demonstrated by the fact she did not respond to the doctored story.

How then did they realise he was so close?

Bougainville couldn't have tied him to the computer penetration and planned his death in such short time. Then the revelation struck

207

him. The notion had been there all the time, but he had pushed it aside, failing to pursue because it did not fit a pattern. Now it burst like a flare.

Bougainville had linked him to the *Eagle*.

Pitt was so engrossed in thought he didn't hear Giordino telling him he had a phone call.

'Your mind must be a million miles away,' said Giordino, pointing towards Cabot, the bartender, who was holding up the bar phone.

Pitt walked over to the bar and spoke in the mouthpiece.

'Hello.'

Sally Lindemann's voice bubbled excitedly over the wire. 'Oh thank heavens I've finally tracked you down. I've been trying to reach you all day.'

'What's wrong?' Pitt demanded. 'Is Loren all right?'

'I think so, and then maybe not,' said Sally, becoming flustered. 'I just don't know.'

'Take your time and spell it out,' Pitt said gently.

'Congresswoman Smith called me in the middle of the night from the *Leonid Andreyev* and told me to find the whereabouts of Speaker of the House, Alan Moran. She never gave me a reason. When I asked her what to say when I contacted him, she said to tell him it was a mistake. Make sense to you?'

'Did you find Moran?'

'Not exactly. He and Senator Marcus Larimer were supposed to be fishing together at a place called Goose Lake. I went there but nobody knew anything about them.'

'What else did Loren say?'

'Her last words to me were, "Call Dirk and tell him I need – ". Then we were cut off. I tried several times to reach her again, but there was no response.'

'Did you tell the ship's operator it was an emergency?'

'Of course, they claimed my messages were passed on to her stateroom, but she made no attempt to reply. This is the damnedest thing. Not like Congresswoman Smith at all. Sound crazy?'

Pitt was silent, thinking it out. 'Yes,' he said at last, 'just crazy enough to make sense. Do you have the *Leonid Andreyev*'s schedule?'

'One moment.' Sally went off the line for nearly a minute. 'Okay, what do you want to know?'

'When does it make the next port?'

'Let's see, it arrives in San Salvador at ten a.m. tomorrow and departs the same evening at eight p.m., for Kingston, Jamaica.'

'Thank you, Sally.'

'What's all this about?' Sally asked. 'I wish you'd tell me.'

'Keep trying to reach Loren. Contact the ship every two hours.'

'You'll call if you find out anything?' Sally said suspiciously.

'I'll call,' Pitt promised.

He returned to the table and sat down.

'What was that all about?' Giordino inquired.

'My travel agent,' Pitt answered, pretending to be nonchalant. 'I've booked us for a cruise in the Caribbean.'

48

Curtis Mayo sat at a desk amid the studio mock-up of a newsroom and peered at the television monitor slightly to his right and below camera number two. He was ten minutes into the evening news and waited for his cue after a commercial advertising a bathroom disinfectant. The thirty second spot wound down on a New York fashion model, who probably never cleaned a toilet bowl in her life, smiling demurely with the product caressing her cheek.

The floor director moved into Mayo's eye range, counted down the last three seconds and waved. The red light on the camera blinked on and Mayo stared into the lens, beginning the B segment of his news programme.

'At the President's farm in New Mexico there have been rumours that the nation's chief executive and the Vice President are using look-a-like stand-ins.'

As Mayo continued his storyline the engineer in the control booth cut to the tape of the President driving the tractor.

'These scenes of the President cutting alfalfa on his farm, when viewed close up, suggest to some that it is not him. Certain famous mannerisms seem exaggerated, different rings are seen on the fingers, the wristwatch is not the one he usually wears, and there appears to be a casual habit of scratching the chin that has not been noted before.

'John Sutton, the actor who bears a striking resemblance and who often imitates the President on TV shows and commercials, could not be found by reporters in Hollywood for comment. Which raises the question, why would our nation's leaders require doubles? Is it a secret security procedure, or a deception for darker motives? Could it be the pressures of the job are such that they have to be in two places at the same time? We can only speculate.'

Mayo let the story dangle on a thread of suspicion. The engineer in the booth switched back to the studio camera, and Mayo went into the next story.

'In Miami today police claimed a breakthrough in a string of drug related murders . . .'

After the programme, Mayo smiled in grim delight when informed of the hundreds of calls flooding the network news offices, asking for more information on the President's double story. The same reaction, if not far heavier, had to be pouring into White House phone lines. In a spiteful sort of glee, he wondered how the Presidential Press Secretary was taking it.

In New Mexico, Sonny Thompson stared blankly at a TV set long after Mayo left the air. He sat collapsed in his chair with the consistency of blubber. He envisioned his carefully nurtured world slamming to a rapid end. His peers in the news media were about to crucify him on a cross of sensationalism. When proven an accomplice to a conspiracy to deceive the American public, no newspaper or TV network would ever hire him after his looming White House departure.

John Sutton stood behind him with a drink in one hand. 'The vultures are circling,' he said.

'In giant flocks,' Thompson muttered.

'What happens now?'

'That's for others to decide.'

'I'm not going to jail like Liddy, Colson and those other guys,' Sutton said nastily.

'Nobody's going to jail,' said Thompson wearily. 'This isn't Watergate. The Justice Department is working with us.'

'No way I'm going to take a fall for a bunch of politicians.' Sutton's eyes began to take on a greedy gleam. 'A guy could make thousands, maybe a few million out of this.'

Thompson looked at him. 'How?'

'Interviews, articles, and there's book rights, royalties; the possibilities for making a bundle are endless.'

'And you think you're going to walk out of here and tell all.'

'Why not?' said Sutton. 'Who's going to stop me?'

It was Thompson's turn to smile. 'You haven't been told the reasons behind your employment. You have no idea how vital your little act is to our country's interests.'

'So who cares?' Sutton said indifferently.

'You may not believe it, Mr Sutton, but there are many decent people in our government who are genuinely concerned about its welfare. They will never allow you to endanger it by speaking your piece for profit.'

'How can those ego maniacs who run the fun house in Washington hurt me? Slap my hand? Draft me into a volunteer army at the age of sixty-two? Turn me over to the Internal Revenue Service? No sweat on that score. I get audited every year anyway.'

'Nothing so mundane,' said Thompson. 'You will simply be taken out.'

'What do you mean, taken out?' demanded Sutton.

'Perhaps I should have said, "disappear",' Thompson replied, delighting in the realisation that grew in Sutton's eyes. 'It goes without saying your body will never be recovered.'

49

Fawcett felt no enthusiasm for the day ahead. As he scraped the beard from his chin, he occasionally glanced at the stack of newspapers spilling off the bathroom sink. Mayo's story made front page news across every morning edition in the nation. Suddenly the press began to ask why the President hadn't been reachable for ten days. Half the editorial columns demanded he step forward and make a statement. The other half asked the question, "Where is the real President?"

Wiping the remaining lather away with a towel and slapping his face with a mild after-shave lotion, Fawcett decided his best approach was to play the Washington enigma game and remain silent. He would cover his personal territory, slide artfully into the background and gracefully permit Secretary of State Oates to carry the brunt of the media onslaught.

Time had slipped from days to a few hours. Soon only minutes would be left. The inner sanctum could stall no longer.

Fawcett couldn't begin to predict the complications that would arise with the announcement of the abduction. No crime against the government had ever approached this magnitude.

His only conviction was that the great perpetuating bureaucracy would continue to somehow function. The power élite were the ones who were swept in and swept out by the whim of the voters. But the institution endured.

He was determined to do everything within his shrinking realm of influence to make the next President's transition as painless as possible. With luck, he might even save his job.

Putting on a dark suit, he left the house and drove to his office, dreading every mile. Oscar Lucas and Alan Mercier were waiting for him as he entered the West Wing.

'Looks grim,' was all Lucas said.

211

'Someone has to make a statement,' said Mercier, whose face looked as if it belonged in a coffin.

'Anybody I know draw the short straw?' asked Fawcett.

'Doug Oates thought you'd be the best man to hold a press conference and announce the kidnapping.'

'What about the rest of the cabinet?' asked Fawcett incredulously.

'They concurred.'

'Screw Oates!' Fawcett said coarsely. 'The whole idea is stupid. He's only trying to save his own ass. I don't have the credentials to drop the bombshell. As far as the grassroots voters are concerned, I'm a nonentity. Not one out of a thousand can recite my name or give my position in the administration. You know exactly what would happen. The public would immediately sense their nation's leaders are floundering in a sinking boat, shrinking behind closed doors to save their political hides, and when it was over, any respect the United States ever had would be wiped out. No, I'm sorry. Oates is the logical choice to make the announcement.'

'But you see,' Mercier said patiently. 'If Oates is forced to take the heat and plead ignorance to a lot of embarrassing questions, it might seem he had something to do with the abduction. As next in line for the presidency he has the most to gain. Every muckraker in the country will scream "conspiracy".' Remember the public backlash when former Secretary of State, Alexander Haig, said he had everything under control right after Reagan was shot by Hinckley? His image, unwarranted or not, of a powerseeker mushroomed. The public didn't like the idea of him running the country. His base of influence eroded until he finally resigned.'

'You're comparing ketchup to mustard,' Fawcett said. 'I'm telling you, the people will be incensed if I stand up and state the President, Vice President and the two majority leaders in Congress have mysteriously vanished and are presumed dead. Hell, no one would believe me.'

'We can't sidestep the main issue,' Mercier said firmly. 'Douglas Oates has to go into the White House as pure as the driven snow. He can't do a decent job of picking up the pieces if he's surrounded by doubt and malicious rumour.'

'Oates is not a politician. He's never expressed the slightest wish of attaining the presidency.'

'He has no choice,' Mercier said. 'He must serve in the interim until the next elections.'

'Can I have the cabinet standing behind me for support during the press conference?'

'No, they won't agree to that.'

'So I'm to be run out of town on a rail,' said Fawcett bitterly. 'Is that the mutual decision?'

'You're overstating your case,' said Mercier mildly. 'You won't be tarred and feathered. Your job is secure. Doug Oates wants you to remain on as White House Chief of Staff.'

'And ask me to resign six months later.'

'We can't guarantee the future.'

'All right,' Fawcett said, his voice trembling in anger. He pushed past Mercier and Lucas. 'Go back and tell Oates he's got his human sacrifice.'

He never turned back but strode down the hallway and went directly to his office where he paced the floor, fuming in rage. The bureaucracy, he thought, its wheels were about to inexorably rumble over him. His priorities no longer mattered. He cursed the whole mess out loud, lost in self pity, and did not notice the President's secretary, Megan Blair, enter the room.

'Mercy, I've never seen you so agitated,' she said.

Fawcett turned and managed a smile. 'Just complaining to the walls.'

'I do that too, especially when my visiting niece drives me mad with her disco recordings. Blasts that awful music all over the house.'

'Can I help you with anything?' he asked impatiently.

'Speaking of complaining,' she said testily, 'why wasn't I told the President had returned from his farm?'

'Must have slipped my mind . . .' He stopped and gazed at her queerly. 'What did you say?'

'The President's back and no one on your staff warned me.'

Fawcett's expression turned to abject disbelief. 'He's in New Mexico.'

'Certainly not,' Megan Blair said adamantly. 'He's sitting at his desk this very moment. He chewed me out for coming in late.'

Megan was not a woman who could lie easily. Fawcett looked deeply into her eyes and saw she was telling the truth. She stared back at him, her head tilted questioningly.

'Are you all right?' she asked.

Fawcett didn't answer. He ran from his office and down the hallway, meeting Lucas and Mercier who were still conferring in hushed tones. They looked up startled as Fawcett frantically pounded around them.

'Follow me!' he shouted over one shoulder, arms flinging.

They stood stock-still for a moment, blinking in utter confusion. Then Lucas reacted and dashed after Fawcett with a huffing Mercier bringing up the rear.

213

Fawcett burst into the Oval Office and stopped dead, his face going dead white.

The President of the United States looked up and smiled. 'Good morning Dan. Ready to go over my appointment schedule?'

Less than a mile away, in a secure room on the top floor of the Russian Embassy, Aleksei Lugovoy sat in front of a large monitor and read the deciphered brainwaves of the President. The display screen showed the thoughts in English while a nearby printer produced paper copies translated into Russian.

He sipped a cup of thick black coffee, standing up, keeping his eyes on the green letters, the heavy bunched eyebrows raised in controlled conceit.

From a distance, the President's brain transmitted its every thought, speech pattern, and even the words spoken by others nearby as they were received and committed to memory.

The second stage of the Huckleberry Finn Project was a success.

Lugovoy decided to wait a few more days before he entered the final and most critical stage, the issuing of commands. If all went well, he knew with a sinking certainty, his revered project would be taken over by the men in the Kremlin. And then Chairman of the Party Antonov and not the President would direct policy for the United States.

50

The molten sun slipped below the western edge of the Aegean Sea as the ship cleared the Dardanelles and headed through the maze of Greek Islands. The surface rolled under gentle two foot swells and a hot breeze set in from the African coast to the south. Soon the orange faded from the sky and the sea lost its blue and they melted together into a solid curtain of black. There was no moon; the only light came from the stars and the sweeping beam of the navigation beacon on the island of Lesbos.

Captain James Mangyai, master of the 540 foot bulk freighter, *Venice*, stood on the bridge and kept a close watch over the bow. He took a cursory glance at the radar display and stared out of the window again, relieved that the sea was empty of other shipping.

Since departing the Russian port of Odessa in the Black Sea, six hundred nautical miles behind, he had been extremely restless. Now he began to breath easier. There were few tricks the Russians would dare attempt in Greek waters.

The *Venice* was in ballast, her only cargo was the gold shipment transferred from the Soviet Government to Madame Bougainville, and her hull rode high in the water. Her destination was Genoa, where the gold was to be secretly unloaded and shipped to Lucerne, Switzerland for storage.

Captain Mangyai heard footsteps behind him on the teak deck and recognised his first officer, Kim Chao, in the reflection on the window.

'How does it look to you, Mr Chao?' he said without turning.

Chao read over the hour-by-hour meteorological report from the automated data system. 'Calm sailing for the next twelve hours,' he said in an unhurried voice. 'Extended forecast looks good too. We're fortunate. The southerly winds are usually much stronger this time of year.'

'We'll need a smooth sea if we're to dock in Genoa under Madame Bougainville's schedule.'

'Why the hurry?' asked Chao. 'Another twelve hours of sailing won't matter.'

'It matters to our employer,' said Mangyai drily. 'She doesn't wish our cargo in transit any longer than necessary.'

'The chief engineer is making more wind than a typhoon. He claims he can't keep up this speed for the whole voyage without burning up the engines.'

'He always sees black clouds.'

'You haven't left the bridge since Odessa, Captain. Let me spell you.'

Mangyai nodded gratefully. 'I could use a short rest. But first, I should look in on our passenger.'

He turned over the bridge watch to Chao and walked down three decks to a heavy steel door at the end of an alleyway amidships. He pressed a transmit button on a speaker bolted to the bulkhead.

'Mr Hong, this is Captain Mangyai.'

He was answered by the gentle creak of the massive door as it was pulled open. A small, moon-faced man with thick-lensed spectacles peered cautiously around the edge.

'Ah yes, Captain. Please come in.'

'Can I get you anything, Mr Hong?'

'No, I'm quite comfortable, thank you.'

Hong's idea of comfort was considerably different from Mangyai's. The only suggestion of human habitation was a suitcase neatly stowed under a canvas folding cot, one blanket, a small electric burner with a pot of tea, and a desk hanging from a bulkhead whose surface was hidden under a pile of chemical analysis equipment. The rest of the compartment was packed with wooden crates

215

and gold bars. The gold was stacked thirty high and ten deep in several rows. Some were scattered on the deck next to the open crates, the unsanded sides stencilled with the disclosure:

HANDLE WITH CARE
MERCURY IN GLASS
SUZAKA CHEMICAL COMPANY, LIMITED
KYOTO, JAPAN

'How are you coming?' Mangyai asked.

'I should have it all examined and crated by the time we reach port.'

'How many gilded lead bars did the Russians slip in?'

'None,' said Hong, shaking his head. 'The count tallies, and every bar I've checksd so far is pure.'

'Strange they were so accommodating. The shipment arrived at the preset hour. Their dockworkers loaded it on board without incident. And we were cleared to depart without the usual administrative hassle. I've never experienced such efficiency in any of my previous dealings with Soviet port authorities.'

'Perhaps Madame Bougainville has great influence in the Kremlin!'

'Perhaps,' said Mangyai sceptically. He looked curiously at the piles of gleaming yellow metal. 'I wonder what was behind the transaction?'

'I'm not about to ask,' said Hong, carefully wrapping a bar in wadding and placing it in a crate.

Before Mangyai could answer, a voice came over the speaker. 'Captain, are you in there?'

He walked over and cracked the heavy door. The ship's communication officer was standing outside in the alleyway.

'Yes, what is it?'

'I thought you should know, Captain, someone is jamming our communications.'

'You know this for a fact?'

'Yes, sir,' said the young officer. 'I managed to get a fix on it. The source is less than three miles off our port bow.'

Mangyai excused himself to Hong and hurried to the bridge. First Officer Chao was calmly sitting in a high swivel chair, studying the instruments on the ship's computerised control panel.

'Do you have any ship contacts, Mr Chao?' asked Mangyai.

If Chao was surprised at the Captain's sudden reappearence, he didn't show it. 'Nothing visual, nothing on radar, sir.'

'What is our depth?'

Chao checked the reading on the depth sounder. 'Fifty metres, or about a hundred and sixty feet.'

The awful truth struck Mangyai's mind like a hammer. He leaned over the chart table and plotted their course. The keel of the *Venice* was passing over the Tzonston Bank, one of many areas in the middle of the Aegean where the seabed rose to within a hundred feet of the surface. Deep enough for a ship's safe passage, but shallow enough for a routine salvage operation.

'Steer for deep water!' he shouted.

Chao stared at the Captain, hesitating in bewilderment. 'Sir?'

Mangyai opened his mouth to repeat the order but the words froze in his throat. At that instant in time, two sound tracking torpedoes homed in on the freighter's engine room and exploded with devastating effect. Her bottom torn in gaping holes, the sea rushed into her innards. The *Venice* shuddered and entered her death throes.

She took only eight minutes to die, going down by the stern, and disappearing beneath the indifferent swells forever.

The *Venice* was hardly gone when a submarine surfaced nearby and began playing her searchlight on the fragmented, floating wreckage. The pitifully few survivors, clinging to the flotsam, were coldly machine-gunned until their shredded bodies sank out of sight. Boats were sent out, guided by the darting shaft of light. After searching for several hours until all the debris was pulled aboard, they returned to their ship.

Then the light was killed and the sub returned to the darkness.

51

The President sat at the centre of the oval mahogany conference table in the White House cabinet room. There were eleven men seated there besides himself. A bemused expression shone in his eyes as he surveyed the sombre faces around the table.

'I know you gentlemen are curious where I've been for the last ten days, and about the status of Vince Margolin, Al Moran and Marcus Larimer. Let me put any fear to rest. Our temporary disappearance was an event planned by me.'

'You alone?' Douglas Oates put to him.

'Not entirely. President Antonov of the Soviet Union was also involved.'

For several moments, stunned and disbelieving, the President's top advisers stared at him.

'You held a secret meeting with Antonov without the knowledge of anyone in this room?' Oates said, his face paled in dismay.

217

'Yes,' the President admitted. 'A face-to-face talk minus outside interference and preconceived notions, without the international news media second guessing every word and unbound by policy. Just our top four people against his.' He paused and his eyes swept the men before him. 'An unorthodox way of negotiating, but one I believe the electorate will accept when they come to accept the results.'

'Would you mind telling us how and where this talk was held, Mr President?' asked Dan Fawcett.

'After the exchange of yachts, we transferred to a civilian helicopter and flew to a small airport outside of Baltimore. From there we took a private airliner belonging to an old friend of mine and crossed the Atlantic to an abandoned airstrip deep in the desert east of Atar, Mauritania. Antonov and his people were waiting when we arrived.'

'I thought . . . rather it was reported,' Jesse Simmons said hesitantly, 'that Antonov was in Paris last week.'

'Georgi stopped over in Paris for a brief conference with President L'Estrange before continuing to Atar.' He turned and looked at Fawcett. 'By the way, Dan, that was a brilliant masquerade.'

'We came within a hair of getting caught.'

'For the time being, I'll deny the rumours of a double as too absurd to comment on. All will be explained to the press, but not before I'm ready.'

Sam Emmett placed his elbows on the table and leaned towards the President. 'Were you informed, sir, that the *Eagle* was sunk and its crew drowned?'

The President stared quizzically for a few moments. Then his eyes sharpened and he shook his head. 'No, I wasn't aware of it. I'd appreciate a full report, Sam, as soon as possible.'

Emmett nodded. 'It will be on your desk when we adjourn.'

Oates struggled to keep his emotions in rein. That a high level meeting of such enormous consequence to world foreign policy had taken place behind the back of the State Department was unthinkable. It was without precedent in anyone's memory.

'I think we'd all be interested in knowing what you and Georgi Antonov discussed,' he said stiffly.

'A very productive give and take,' answered the President. 'The most pressing item on the agenda was disarmament. Antonov and I hammered out an agreement to halt all missile production and start up a dismantling programme. We arrived at a complicated formula that in simple terms means they break down a nuclear missile and we match them on a one-for-one basis with on-site inspection teams overseeing the operation.'

'France and England will never buy such a proposal,' said Oates. 'Their nuclear arsenals are independent of ours.'

'We will begin with the long range warheads and work down,' said the President undaunted. 'Europe will eventually follow.'

General Clayton Metcalf shook his head. 'On the face of it, I'd have to say the proposal sounds incredibly naïve.'

'It's a beginning,' said the President adamantly. 'I believe Antonov is sincere in his offer, and I intend to show good faith by pursuing the dismantling programme.'

'I'll reserve judgement until I've had a chance to study the formula,' said Simmons.

'Fair enough.'

'What else did you discuss?' asked Fawcett.

'A trade agreement,' answered the President. 'Briefly explained, if we allow the Russians to transport their agricultural purchases in their own merchant ships, Antonov promised to pay our farmers top world prices, and most important, not to buy from any other nation unless we fail to provide the goods as ordered. In other words, American farmers are now the exclusive supplier of Soviet imported farm products.'

'Antonov bought your package?' Oates asked incredulously. 'I can't believe the old bear capable of giving away an exclusive licence to any nation.'

'I have his assurance in writing.'

'Sounds very idyllic,' said Martin Brogan. 'But I'd like someone to explain how Russia can afford to make wholesale agricultural purchases. Their East Bloc satellites have defaulted on massive loans to the West. The Soviet economy is in disastrous shape. They can't even pay their armed forces and government workers in anything but script good only for food and clothing. What are they going to use for money? Our farmers aren't about to go in hock for Communists. They need immediate payment to clear their own yearly debts.'

'There is a way out,' said the President.

'Your East Bloc bail-out theory?' said Fawcett, anticipating him.

The President nodded. 'Antonov agreed in principle to accept my economic assistance plan.'

'If you'll excuse me, Mr President,' said Oates, his hands clutched to keep them from visibly trembling, 'but your plan solves nothing. What you're proposing is that we give billions of dollars in financial aid to the Communist nations so they can turn around and buy from our own farming community. I see that as a rob Peter to pay Paul sucker game with our taxpayers footing the bill.'

'I'm with Doug,' said Brogan. 'What's in it for us?'

The President looked around the table, his face set in determination. 'I made up my mind that this is the only way to show the world

219

once and for all that in spite of her monstrous military machine, Russia's system of government is a failure not to be envied or copied. If we do this thing, no country in the world can ever again accuse us of imperialist aggression, and no Soviet propaganda or disinformation campaigns against us will be taken seriously. Think of it, the United States helped our enemies back on their feet after World War Two. And now we can do the same for a nation that has made a crusade out of condemning our democratic principles. I devoutly believe no greater opportunity will be laid on our doorstep to set humanity on a straight course into the future.'

'Frankly speaking, Mr President,' said General Metcalf in a stern voice, 'your grand design will change nothing. As soon as their economy has recovered, the Kremlin leaders will return to their old belligerent ways. They're not about to give up the military expansion and political strategies of seventy years out of gratitude for American generosity.'

'The General is right,' said Brogan. 'Our latest satellite surveillance photos show that even as we sit here, the Russians are installing a string of their latest SS-30 multiple warhead missiles along the north-east coast of Siberia, and each is targeted at a city in the US.'

'They will be dismantled,' the President said, his tone set in concrete. 'As long as we are aware of their existence, Antonov cannot sidestep his commitment.'

Oates was mad and he didn't care who knew it. 'All this talk is a waste of time.' He almost spat the words at the President. 'None of your giveaway schemes can be put into motion without Congressional approval. And that, sir, isn't damned likely.'

'The Secretary is quite correct,' said Fawcett. 'Congress still has to appropriate the money, and considering their present mood against Soviet troop incursions along the Iranian and Turkish borders, passage of your programme will most certainly die and be buried in committee.'

The men around the table felt uneasy, all of them realising that the President's administration would never function from a granite base of cohesion again. Differences would arise that were held in check before. From now on, reverence for teamwork was gone and the line holding personal likes and dislikes broken. Respect for the President and his office melted away. They saw only a man like themselves with more faults than they cared to acknowledge. The realisation laid a cloud upon the room and they looked to see if the President recognised it too.

He sat there, a strange expression of wickedness spreading across his face, the lips drawn back in cold anticipation of a triumph yet to come.

'I do not need Congress,' he said cryptically. 'They will have no voice in my policies.'

During the short walk from the cabinet room to the south portico, Douglas Oates made up his mind to submit his resignation as Secretary of State. The President's rude act of freezing him out of the negotiations with Antonov was an insult he refused to forgive. There was no turning back as the decision was reached and cemented. He smelled catastrophe in the political air, and he wanted no part of it.

He was standing on the steps awaiting his official car when Brogan and Emmett approached.

'Can we have a word with you, Doug?' asked Emmett.

'I'm not in a good mood for conversation,' Oates grumbled.

'This is critical,' said Brogan. 'Please hear us out.'

His car was not yet in sight on the drive so Oates shrugged wearily. 'I'm listening.'

Brogan looked around him and then said softly, 'Sam and I think the President is being manipulated.'

Oates shot him a sarcastic stare. 'Manipulated hell, he's fallen off his track, and I for one refuse to be a party to his madness. There's more to the sinking of the *Eagle* than he let on, and he never did explain the whereabouts of Margolin, Latimer and Moran. I'm sorry, gentlemen, you two can be the first to know. As soon as I get back to the State Department, I'm cleaning out my desk and calling a press conference to announce my resignation. Then I'm taking the next plane out of Washington.'

'We knew what was on your mind,' Emmett said. 'That's why we wanted to catch you before you went off the deep end.'

'What exactly are you trying to tell me?'

Emmett looked at Brogan for help and then shrugged. 'The idea is difficult to put across, but Martin and I suspect the President is under some sort of . . . well . . . mind control.'

Oates wasn't sure he heard right. But logic told him the Directors of the CIA and FBI were not men to make light of a serious allegation.

'Controlled by whom?'

'We think the Russians,' answered Brogan. 'But we haven't accumulated all the evidence yet.'

'We realise this sounds like science fiction,' explained Emmett, 'but it appears very real.'

'My God, was the President under this influence, as you suggest, when he flew to Mauritania for his talks with Antonov?'

Brogan and Emmett exchanged knowing looks. Then Brogan said, 'There isn't a plane in flight anywhere in the world the Agency doesn't know about. I'll stake my job that our data will show no trace of an aircraft flying on a course from Maryland to Mauritania and return.'

Oates' eyes widened. 'The meeting with Antonov . . .'

Emmett shook his head slowly. 'It never happened.'

'Then everything, the disarmament, the agricultural trade agreements, was a lie,' said Oates, his voice cracking slightly.

'A fact which is heightened by his vague denial of the *Eagle* murders,' added Brogan.

'Why did he conceive such a crazy nightmare?' Oates asked dazedly.

'It really doesn't matter why he came up with it,' said Emmett. 'The programmes probably were not even his idea. What matters is how his behaviour is guided; who is motivating his thought patterns and from where?'

'Can we find out?'

'Yes,' said Emmett. 'That's why we wanted to catch you before you cut bait.'

'What can I do?'

'Stay,' Brogan replied. 'The President is not fit for office. With Margolin, Moran and Larimer still missing, you remain the next man in line.'

'The President must be held in check until we can finish our investigation,' said Emmett. 'With you at the helm, we keep a measure of control in the event he must be removed from office.'

Oates straightened and took a deep breath. 'Lord, this is beginning to sound like a conspiracy to assassinate the President.'

'In the end,' Brogan said grimly, 'it may well come to that.'

52

Lugovoy turned from his notes and stared at his staff neurologist who sat at the console, monitoring the telemetric signals.

'Condition?'

'Subject has entered a relaxed state. Brain rhythms indicate normal sleep patterns.' The neurologist looked up and smiled. 'He doesn't know it, but he's snoring.'

'I imagine his wife knows it.'

'My guess is she sleeps in another bedroom. They haven't had sex since he returned.'

'Body functions?'

'All readings normal.'

Lugovoy yawned and read the time. 'Twelve minutes after one a.m.'

'You should get some sleep, Doctor. The President's internal clock wakes him between six and six-fifteen every morning.'

'This is not an easy project,' Lugovoy groused. 'The President requires two hours less sleep than I do. I detest early risers.' He paused and scanned the polysomnography screen that monitored the President's physiological parameters accompanying his sleep. 'It appears as though he's dreaming.'

'Be interesting to see what the President of the United States dreams about.'

'We'll get a rough idea as soon as his brain cell activity goes from coordinated thought patterns to disjointed abstractions.'

'Are you into dream interpretations, Doctor?'

'I leave that to the Freudians,' Lugovoy replied. 'I am one of the few who believe dreams are meaningless. It's merely a situation where the brain, freed from the discipline of daytime thinking, goes on holiday. Like a city dog who lives in a flat and is unleashed in the country, running in no particular direction, enjoying the new and different smells.'

'There are many who would disagree.'

'Dreams are not my speciality so I cannot argue from a purely scientific base. However, it seems odd that if they do have a message, why are most of the senses usually missing?'

'You're referring to the absence of smell and taste?'

Lugovoy nodded. 'Sounds are also seldom recorded. The same with touch and pain. Dreams are primarily only visual sensations. So my own opinion, backed up by a little personal research, is a dream about a one-eyed goat that spits fire, is simply that; a dream about a one-eyed goat that spits fire.'

'Dream theory is the cornerstone of all psychoanalytic behaviour. With your esteemed reputation, you'd shatter quite a few established icons with your goat opinion. Think how many of our psychiatrist comrades would be out of a job if it became known dreams are meaningless.'

'Uncontrolled dreams are quickly forgotten,' Lugovoy continued. 'But the demands and instructions we transmit to the President's brain cells while he is asleep will not be received as dreams. They are injected thoughts that can be recalled and acted upon by outside stimuli.'

'When should I begin programming his implant unit?'

'Transmit the instructions shortly before he wakes up, and repeat them when he sits down at his desk.' Lugovoy yawned again. 'I'm going to bed. Ring my room if there is a sudden change.'

The neurologist nodded. 'Rest well.'

223

Lugovoy stared briefly at the monitoring systems before he left the room. 'I wonder what his mind is envisioning?'

The neurologist waved casually at the data printer. 'It should be there.'

'No matter,' said Lugovoy. 'It can wait till morning.' Then he turned and walked to his room.

His curiosity needled, the neurologist picked up the top printout sheet containing the President's interpreted brain waves and glanced at the wording.

'*Green hills of summer,*' he muttered to himself as he read. '*A city between two rivers with many Byzantine style churches, topped by hundreds of cupolas. One called St Sophia. A river barge filled with sugar beets. The Catacombs of St Anthony.*' If I didn't know better, I'd say he was dreaming about the city of Kiev.

He stood beside a pathway on a hill overlooking a wide river, gazing at the ship traffic and holding an artist's brush. On the tree-covered slope below him he could see a large stone pedestal beneath a figure draped in robes and holding a tall cross as though it was a staff. An easel with a canvas stood slightly off to his right. The painting was nearly finished. The landscape before his eyes was perfectly mirrored in the exacting brush strokes, down to the stippled leaves in the trees. The only difference, if one looked close enough, was the stone monument.

Instead of a long flowing beard of some forgotten saint, the head was an exact likeness of Soviet President, Georgi Antonov.

Suddenly the scene changed. Now he found himself being dragged out of a small cottage by four men. The cottage walls were carved with Gothic designs and it was painted a garish shade of blue. The faces of his abductors were indistinct, yet he could smell their unwashed sweat. They were pulling him towards a car. He experienced no fear but rather blind rage and lashed out with his feet. His assailants began beating him, but the pain felt distant as though the agony belonged to someone else.

In the doorway of the cottage he could see the figure of a young woman. Her blonde hair was wrapped in a knot atop her head and she wore a full blouse and a peasant skirt. Her arms were upraised and she seemed to be pleading, but he could not make out the words.

Then he was thrown on the rear floor of the car and the door slammed shut.

224

53

The purser looked at the two tourists weaving up the boarding ramp in frank amusement. They presented an outlandish pair. The female was dressed in a loose fitting, ankle-length sundress, and to the Russian purser's creative eye, she could have passed for a rainbowed sack of Ukrainian potatoes. He couldn't quite make out her face because it was partially obscured by a wide brimmed straw hat, tied around the chin by a silk scarf, but he imagined if it was fully revealed, it would break his watch crystal.

The man who appeared to be her husband was drunk. He reeled onto the deck, smelling of cheap bourbon, and laughed constantly. Dressed in a loud flowered shirt and white duck trousers, he leered at his ugly wife and whispered gibberish in her ear. He noticed the purser and raised his arm in a comical salute.

'Hi-ho Captain,' he said with a slack grin.

'I am not the Captain. My name is Peter Kolodno. I am the purser. How can I help you?'

'I'm Charlie Gruber and this is my wife Zelda. We bought tickets here in San Salvador.'

He handed a packet to the purser who studied them carefully for a few moments.

'Welcome aboard the *Leonid Andreyev*,' said the purser officially. 'I regret we do not have our usual hospitality festivities to greet new passengers, but you've joined us rather late in the cruise.'

'We were sailing on a windjammer when the dumb helmsman ran us onto a reef,' the man called Gruber babbled. 'My little woman and I damn near drowned. Couldn't see going back home to Sioux Falls early. So we're finishing our holiday on your boat. Besides, my wife turns on to Greeks.'

'This is a Russian ship,' the purser explained patiently.

'No kidding?'

'Yes sir, the *Leonid Andreyev*'s home port is Sevastopol.'

'You don't say. Where is that?'

'The Black Sea,' the purser said, maintaining an air of politeness.

'Sounds polluted.'

The purser was at a loss as to how America ever became a super power with citizens such as these. He checked his passenger list and then nodded. 'Your cabin is number 34 on the Gorki deck. I'll have a steward show you the way.'

'You're all right pal,' said Gruber, shaking his hand.

As a steward led the Grubers to their cabin, the purser looked down at his palm. Charlie Gruber had tipped him a twenty-five cent piece.

As soon as the steward deposited their luggage and closed the door, Giordino threw off his wig and rubbed the lip gloss from his mouth. 'God, Zelda Gruber, how am I ever going to live this one down?'

'I still say you should have taped a couple of grapefruit to your chest,' Pitt said laughing.

'I prefer the flat look. That way I don't stand out.'

'Probably a good thing. There's not enough room in here for the four of us.'

Giordino waved his arms around the small confines of the windowless cabin. 'Talk about a discount excursion. I've been in bigger phone booths. Feel the vibration? We must be next to the engines.'

'I requested cheap accommodations so we could be on a lower deck,' Pitt explained. 'We're less visible down here, and closer to the working areas of the ship.'

'You think Loren might be locked up somewhere below?'

'If she saw something or someone she wasn't supposed to; the Russians won't let her mingle with the other passengers.'

'On the other hand, this could be a false alarm.'

'We'll soon know,' said Pitt.

'How shall we work it?' Giordino asked.

'I'll wander the crew's quarters. You check the passenger list in the purser's office for Loren's cabin. Then see if she's in it.'

Giordino grinned impishly. 'What shall I wear?'

'Go as yourself. Zelda, we'll keep in reserve.'

A minute after eight p.m., the *Leonid Andreyev* eased away from the dock. The engines beat softly as the bow came around. The sandy arms of San Salvador's harbour slid past as the ship entered the sea and sailed into a fiery sunset.

The lights flashed on and sparkled across the water like fireworks as the ship came alive with laughter and the music of two different orchestras. Passengers changed from shorts and slacks to suits and gowns, and lingered in the main dining-room or perched in one of the several cocktail lounges.

Al Giordino, dressed in a formal tux, strutted along the corridor outside the penthouse suites as though he owned them. Stopping at a door he looked around. A steward was approaching behind him with a tray.

Giordino stepped across to an opposite door marked 'Massage Room' and knocked.

'The masseuse goes off duty at six o'clock, sir,' said the steward.

Giordino smiled. 'I thought I'd make an appointment for tomorrow.'

'I'll be glad to take care of that for you, sir. What time would be convenient?'

'How about noon?'

'I'll see to it,' said the steward, his arm beginning to sag under the weight of the tray. 'Your name and cabin?'

'O'Callaghan, cabin 22, the Tolstoy Deck,' Giordino said. 'Thank you. I appreciate it.'

Then he turned and walked back to the passenger lift. He pushed the 'down' button so it would ring and then glanced along the corridor. The steward balanced the tray and knocked lightly on a door two suites beyond Loren's. Giordino couldn't see who responded, but he heard a woman's voice invite the steward inside.

Without wasting a second, Giordino rushed to Loren's suite, crudely forced in the door with a well aimed kick near the lock and entered. The rooms were dark and he switched on the lights. Everything was pin neat and luxurious with no hint of an occupant.

He didn't find Loren's clothes in the closet. He didn't find any luggage or evidence that she had ever been there. He combed every square foot carefully and slowly, room by room. He peered under the furniture and behind the curtains. He ran his hands over the carpets and under chair cushions. He even checked the bathtub and shower for pubic hairs.

Nothing.

But not quite nothing. A woman's presence lingers in a room after she leaves it. Giordino sniffed the air. A very slight whiff of perfume caught his nostrils. He couldn't have recognised Chanel No. 5 from bath cologne, but this aroma had the delicate fragrance of a flower. He tried to identify it, yet it hung just beyond his reach.

He rubbed soap on the wooden splinter that broke off when he kicked in the door and pressed it into place. A poor glue job, he thought, but enough to hold for a few openings in case the suite was checked again by the crew before the ship docked back in Miami.

Then he snapped the lock, turned off the light and left.

Pitt suffered hunger pangs as he dropped down a tunnel ladder towards the engine room. He hadn't eaten since Washington and the growls from his stomach seemed to echo inside the narrow steel access tube. He wished he was seated in the dining-room putting away the delicacies from the gourmet menu. Suddenly he brushed

227

away all thoughts of food as he detected voices rising from the compartment below.

He crouched against the ladder and gazed past his feet. A man's shoulder showed no more than four feet below him. Then the top of a head with stringy, unkept blonde hair moved into view. The crewman said a few words in Russian to someone else. There was a muffled reply followed by the sounds of footsteps on a metal grating. After three minutes, the head moved away and Pitt heard the thin clap of a locker door closing. Then footsteps again and silence.

Pitt swung around the ladder, inserted his feet and calves through a rung and hung upside down, his eyes peering under the lip of the tunnel.

He found himself with an inverted view of the engine room crew's locker room. It was temporarily vacant. Quickly he climbed down and went through the lockers until he found a pair of grease stained overalls that were a reasonable fit. He also took a cap that was two sizes too large and pulled it over his forehead. Now he was ready to wander the working areas. His next problem was that he only knew a few words of Russian.

Nearly half an hour passed before Pitt meandered into the main crew's quarters in the bow section of the ship. He had passed a cook from one of the kitchens, a quartermaster pushing a cart loaded with liquor for the cocktail bars, and a cabin maid coming off duty. None gave him a second glance except an officer who threw a distasteful eye at his grimy attire.

By a fortunate accident, he stumbled upon the crew's laundry room. A round faced girl looked up at him across a counter and asked him something in Russian.

He shrugged and mumbled, '*Nyet.*'

Bundles of washed uniforms lay neatly stacked on a long table. It dawned on him that the laundry room girl had asked him which bundle was his. He studied them for a few moments and finally pointed to one containing three neatly folded white overalls like the dirty pair he wore. By changing into clean ones he could have the run of the entire ship, pretending to be a crewman from the engine room on a maintenance assignment.

He nodded and said, '*Ya goloden.*'

The girl gave him an odd look indeed and handed him the bundle, making him sign for it which he did in a illegible scrawl. It was only after he found an empty cabin and switched overalls did he realise he'd actually said, 'I'm hungry.'

After pausing at a bulletin board to remove a diagram showing the compartments on the decks of the *Leonid Andreyev*, he calmly spent the next five hours browsing the lower hull of the ship. Detecting no

228

clue to Loren's presence, he returned to his cabin and found Giordino had thoughtfully ordered him a meal.

'Anything?' Giordino asked, pouring two glasses from a bottle of Russian champagne.

'Not a trace,' said Pitt wearily. 'We celebrating?'

'Allow me a little class in this dungeon.'

'You search her suite?'

Giordino nodded. 'What kind of perfume does Loren wear?'

Pitt stared at the bubbles rising from the glass for a moment. 'A French name; I can't recall it. Why do you ask?'

'Have an aroma like a flower?'

'Lilac . . . no, honeysuckle. Yes, honeysuckle.'

'Her suite was wiped clean. The Russians made it look like she'd never been there, but I could still smell her scent.'

Pitt drained the champagne glass and poured another without speaking.

'We have to face the possibility they killed her,' Giordino said matter-of-factly.

'Then why hide her clothes and luggage? They can't claim she fell overboard with all her belongings.'

'The crew could have stored them below and are waiting for an opportune moment, like rough weather, to announce the tragic news.'

'I love a cheery travelling companion.'

'Sorry, Dirk,' said Giordino, no apology in his voice. 'We've got to look at every aspect, good or bad.'

'Loren is alive and on board this ship somewhere,' Pitt said steadfastly. 'And maybe Moran and Larimer.'

'You're taking a lot for granted.'

'Loren is a smart girl. She didn't ask Sally Lindemann to locate Speaker of the House Moran unless she had a damn good reason. Sally claimes Moran and Senator Marcus Larimer have both mysteriously dropped from sight. Now Loren is missing too. What impression do you get?'

'You make a good sales pitch, but what's behind it.'

Pitt shrugged negatively. 'I just don't know. Only a crazy idea that this might somehow mix with Bougainville Maritime and the loss of the *Eagle*.'

Giordino was silent, thinking it over. 'Yes,' he said slowly, 'a crazy idea, but one that makes a lot of circumstantial sense. Where do you want me to start?'

'Put on your Zelda get-up and walk past every cabin on the ship. If Loren or the others are held prisoner inside, there will be a security guard posted outside the door.'

'And that's the giveaway,' said Giordino. 'Where will you be?'

Pitt laid out the diagram of the ship on his bunk. 'Some of the crew are quartered in the stern. I'll scrounge there.' He folded up the paper and shoved it in the pocket of the overalls. 'We'd best get started. There isn't much time.'

'At least we have until the day after tomorrow when the *Leonid Andreyev* docks in Jamaica.'

'No such luxury,' said Pitt. 'Study a nautical chart of the Caribbean and you'll see that about this time tomorrow night we'll be cruising within sight of the Cuban coast.'

Giordino nodded in understanding. 'A golden opportunity to transfer Loren and others off the ship where they can't be touched.'

'The nasty part is they may not stay on Cuban soil any longer than it takes to put them on a plane for Moscow.'

Giordino considered that for a moment and then went over to his suitcase, removed the mangy wig and slipped it over his curly head. Then he peered in a mirror and made a hideous face.

'Well, Zelda,' he said in a sour tone, 'let's go and walk the decks and see who we can pick up.'

54

The President went on national television that same evening to reveal his meeting and accord with President Antonov of the Soviet Union. In his short twenty-three minute address, he briefly outlined his programmes to aid the Communist countries. He also dropped a new blockbuster when he stated his intent to abolish the barriers and restrictions on purchases of American high technology by the Russians. Never once was Congress mentioned. He spoke of the Eastern Bloc trade agreements as though they were already budgeted and set in motion. He closed by promising his next task was to throw his energies behind a war to reduce the national crime rate.

The following uproar in government circles swept all other news before it. Curtis Mayo and other network commentators broadcast scathing attacks on the President for overstepping the limits of his authority. Spectres of an imperial presidency were raised.

Congressional leaders who remained in Washington during the recess launched a telephone campaign encouraging their fellow lawmakers, who were on holiday or campaigning in their home states, to return to the capital to meet in emergency session. House and Senate members, acting without the council of their majority leaders, Moran and Larimer, who could not be reached, solidly closed ranks against the President in a bipartisan flood.

Dan Fawcett burst into the oval office the next morning, anguish written on his face. 'Good God, Mr President, you can't do this thing!'

The President looked up calmly. 'You're referring to my talk last night?'

'Yes, sir, I am,' said Fawcett emotionally. 'You as good as went on record as saying you were proceeding with your aid programmes without Congressional approval.'

'Is that what it sounded like?'

'It did.'

'Good,' said the President, thumping his hand on the desk. 'Because that's exactly what I intend to do.'

Fawcett was astonished. 'Not under the Constitution. Executive privilege does not extend that far – .'

'Goddamn it, don't try and tell me how to run the Presidency,' shouted the President, suddenly furious. 'I'm through begging and compromising with those conceited hypocrites on the hill. No more bickering with the good old boys of the Senate and House. No more wrangling along party lines. The only way I'm going to get anything done, by God, is to put on the gloves and start swinging.'

'You're setting out on a dangerous course. They'll band together to freeze out every issue you put before them.'

'No they won't!' the President shouted, coming to his feet and coming around the desk to face Fawcett. 'Congress will not have a chance to upset my plans.'

Fawcett could only look at him in shock and horror. 'You can't stop them. They're gathering now, flying in from every state to hold an emergency session to block you.'

'If they think that,' the President said in a morbid voice Fawcett scarcely recognised, 'they're in for a big surprise.'

The early morning traffic was spreading thin when three military convoys flowed into the city from different directions. One Army Special Counter Terrorist Detachment from Fort Belvoir moved north along Anacostia Freeway while another from Fort Meade dropped down the Baltimore & Washington Parkway to the south. At the same moment, a Critical Operation Force attached to the Marine base at Quantico travelled over the Rochambeau Bridge from the west.

As the long lines of five-ton personnel carriers converged on the Federal Centre, a flight of Tilt-Rotored assault transports settled onto the grass of the mall in front of the Capitol reflecting pool, and disgorged their cargo of crack Marine field troops from Camp Lejeune, North Carolina. The two thousand man task force was made up of United Emergency Response Teams that were on twenty-four hour alert.

As they deployed around the Federal buildings, they quickly cleared everyone out of the Capitol chambers, the House and Senate offices. Then they took up their positions and sealed off all entrances.

Official Washington was taken completely by surprise.

At first the bewildered lawmakers and their aides thought it was a building evacuation due to a terrorist bomb threat. The only other explanation was an unannounced military exercise. When they learned the entire seat of American Government was shut down by order of the President, they stood shocked and outraged, conferring in heated indignation in small groups on the grounds east of the Capitol building. Lyndon Johnson had once threatened to lock out Congress, but no one could believe it was actually happening.

Arguments and demands went unheard by the purposeful looking men dressed in field camouflage and holding M-20 automatic rifles and riot guns. One Senator, nationally recognised for his liberal stands, tried to break through the cordon and was dragged back to the street by two grim-faced Marines who appeared little impressed with his vocal bluster.

The troops did not surround or close the executive departments or independent agencies. For most of the Federal offices it was business as usual. The streets were kept open and traffic directed in an efficient manner local citizens found downright enjoyable.

The press and television media poured onto the Capitol grounds. The grass was nearly buried under a blanket of cables and electronic equipment. Interviews before cameras became so hectic and crowded that Senators and Congressmen had to stand in line to voice their objections to the President's unprecedented action.

Surprisingly, reaction from most Americans across the country was one of amusement rather than distaste. They sat in front of their television screens and viewed the event as if it was a circus. The general consensus was that the President was throwing a temporary scare into Congress and would order the troops removed in a day or two.

At the State Department, Oates huddled with Emmett, Brogan and Mercier. The atmosphere was heavy with a sense of indecision and suspense.

'The President's a damned fool if he thinks he's more important than the Constitutional Government,' said Oates.

Emmett stared steadily at Mercier. 'I can't see why you didn't suspect what was going down.'

'He shut me out completely,' said Mercier, his face sheepish. 'He never offered the slightest clue of what was on his mind.'

'Surely Jesse Simmons and General Metcalf weren't a party to it,' Oates wondered aloud.

Brogan shook his head. 'My Pentagon sources say Jesse Simmons flatly refused.'

'Why didn't he warn us?' asked Emmett.

'After Simmons told the President in no uncertain terms he was off base, the roof fell in. A military security guard detail escorted him home where he was placed under house arrest.'

'Jesus,' muttered Oates in exasperation. 'It gets worse by the minute.'

'What about General Metcalf?' asked Mercier.

'I'm sure he voiced his objections,' answered Brogan. 'But Clayton Metcalf is a spit and polish soldier who's duty bound to carry out the orders of his Commander and Chief. He and the President are old, close friends. Metcalf obviously feels his loyalty is to the man who appointed him to be Chief of Staff, and not Congress.'

Oates' fingers swept an imaginary dust speck off the desk top. 'The President disappears for ten days, and after his return, falls off the deep end.'

'Huckleberry Finn,' Brogan said slowly.

'Judging from the President's behavioural patterns over the past twenty-four hours,' Mercier said thoughtfully, 'the evidence looks pretty conclusive.'

'Has Dr Lugovoy surfaced yet?' asked Oates.

Emmett shook his head. 'He's still missing.'

'We've obtained reports from our people inside Russia on the doctor,' Brogan elucidated. 'His speciality for the last fifteen years has been mind transfer. Soviet intelligence ministries have provided enormous funding for his research. Hundreds of Jews and other dissidents who vanished inside KGB operated mental institutions were his guinea pigs. And he claims to have made a breakthrough in thought interpretation and control.'

'Do we have such a project in progress?' Oates inquired.

Brogan nodded. 'Ours is code named "Fathom", which is working along the same lines.'

Oates held his head in his hands for a moment, then turned to Emmett. 'You still haven't a lead on Vince Margolin, Larimer and Moran?'

Emmett looked embarrassed. 'I regret to say their whereabouts is still unknown.'

'Do you think Lugovoy has performed the mind transfer experiment on them too?'

233

'I don't believe so,' Emmett answered. 'If I were in the Russian's shoes, I'd keep them in reserve in the event the President doesn't respond to instructions as programmed.'

'His mind could slip out of their grasp and react unpredictably,' Brogan added. 'Fooling around with the brain is not an absolute science. There's no way of telling what he'll do next.'

'Congress isn't waiting to find out,' said Mercier. 'They're out hustling for a place to convene so they can start impeachment proceedings.'

'The President knows that, and he isn't stupid,' Oates came back. 'Every time the House and Senate members gather for a session, he'll send in troops to break it up. With the armed forces behind him, it's a no win situation.'

'Considering the President is literally being told what to do by an unfriendly foreign power, Metcalf and the other Joint Chiefs can't continue giving him their support,' said Mercier.

'He refuses to act until we produce absolute proof of mind control,' added Emmett. 'But I suspect he's only waiting for a ripe excuse to throw his lot in with Congress.'

Brogan looked concerned. 'Let's hope he doesn't make his move too late.'

'So the situation boils down to the four of us devising a way to neutralise the President,' mused Oates.

'Have you driven past the White House today?' asked Mercier.

Oates shook his head. 'No. Why?'

'Looks like an armed camp. The military is crawling over every inch of the grounds. Word has it the President can't be reached by anybody. I doubt even you, Mr Secretary, could walk past the front door.'

Brogan thought a moment. 'Dan Fawcett is still on the inside.'

'I talked to him over the phone,' Mercier said. 'He presented his opposition to the President's actions a bit too strongly. I gather he's now persona non grata in the oval office.'

'We need someone who has the President's trust.'

'Oscar Lucas,' said Emmett.

'Good thinking,' snapped Oates, looking up. 'As head of the Secret Service, he's got the run of the place.'

'Someone will have to brief Dan and Oscar face to face,' Emmett advised.

'I'll handle it,' Brogan volunteered.

'You have a plan?' asked Oates.

'Not off the top of my head, but my people will come up with something.'

'Better be good,' said Emmett seriously, 'if we're too avoid the worst fear of our founding fathers.'

234

'And what was that?' asked Oates.

'The unthinkable,' replied Emmett. 'A dictator in the White House.'

55

Loren was sweating. She had never sweated so much in her life. Her evening gown was damp and plastered against her body like a second skin. The little windowless cell felt like a sauna and it was an effort just to breathe. A toilet and a bunk were her only creature comforts, and a dim bulb attached to the ceiling in a small cage glowed with continuous light. The ventilators, she was certain, were turned off to increase her discomfort.

When she was brought to the ship's brig, she saw no sign of the man she thought might be Alan Moran. She'd been given no food or water since the crew locked her up, and hunger pangs were gnawing at her stomach. No one had even visited her, and she began to wonder if Captain Pokofsky meant to keep her in solitary confinement until she wasted away.

In the end she decided to abandon her attempt at vanity and removed her clinging dress. She began to do stretching exercises to pass the time.

Suddenly she heard the muted sound of footsteps outside in the passageway. Muffled voices spoke in a brief conversation, and then the door was unlatched and swung open.

Loren snatched her dress off the bunk and held it in front of her, shrinking back into a corner of the cell.

A man ducked his head as he passed through the small doorway. He was fitted in a cheap business suit that looked to her as if it was used only for nineteen-forties costume parties.

'Congresswoman Smith, please forgive the condition I was forced to put you in.'

'No, I don't think I will,' she said defiantly. 'Who are you?'

'My name is Paul Suvorov. I represent the Soviet Government.'

Contempt flooded into Loren's voice. 'Is this an example of the way Communists treat visiting American VIP's?'

'Not under ordinary circumstances, but you gave us no choice.'

'Please explain,' she demanded, glaring at him.

He gave her an uncertain look. 'I believe you know.'

'Why don't you refresh my memory?'

He paused to light a cigarette, carelessly tossing the match on the deck. 'The other evening when the helicopter arrived, Captain Pokofsky's first officer observed you standing very close to the landing area.'

'So were several other passengers,' Loren snapped icily.

'Yes, but they were too far away to see a familiar face.'

'And you think I wasn't.'

'Why can't you be reasonable, Congresswoman? Surely you can't deny you recognised your own colleagues.'

'I don't know what you mean.'

'Congressman Alan Moran and Senator Marcus Larimer,' he said, closely watching her reaction.

Loren's eyes widened and suddenly she began to shiver in spite of the stifling heat. For the first time since she was made a prisoner, indignation was replaced by despair.

'Moran and Larimer, they're both here too?'

He nodded. 'In the next cell.'

'This must be an insane joke,' she said, stunned.

'No joke,' Suvorov said smiling. 'They are guests of the KGB, same as you.'

Loren shook her head, unbelieving. Life didn't happen this way, she told herself, except in nightmares. She felt reality drifting slowly from her grasp.

'I have diplomatic immunity,' she said. 'I demand to be released.'

'You carry no influence, not here on board the *Leonid Andreyev*,' said Suvorov in a cold, uninterested voice.

'When my government hears of this . . .'

'They won't,' he cut her off. 'When the ship leaves Jamaica on its return voyage to Miami, Captain Pokofsky will announce with deep regret and sympathy that Congresswoman Loren Smith was lost overboard and presumed drowned.'

A numbing hopelessness seized Loren. 'What will happen to Moran and Larimer?'

'I'm taking them to Russia.'

'But you're going to kill me,' she said, more as a statement than a question.

'They represent senior members of your government. Their knowledge will prove quite useful once they're persuaded to provide it. You, I'm sorry to say, are not worth the risk.'

Loren almost said, "As a member of the House Armed Forces Committee, I know as much as they do," but she recognised the trap in time and remained silent.

Suvorov's eyes narrowed. He reached over and tore the dress from in front of her and casually tossed it outside the doorway. 'Very nice,' he said. 'Perhaps if we were to negotiate, I might find a reason to take you with me to Moscow.'

'The most pathetic trick in the world,' Loren spat contemptuously. 'You're not even original.'

He took a step forward, his hand lashing out and slapping her on the face. She staggered back against the steel bulkhead and sagged to her knees, staring up at him, her eyes blazing with fear and loathing.

He grasped her by the hair and tilted her head back. The conversational politeness disappeared from his voice. 'I always wondered what it would be like to screw a high ranking capitalist bitch.'

Loren's answer was to swiftly reach out and grab him in the groin, squeezing with all her might.

Suvorov gasped in agony and swung his fist, connecting with her left cheekbone just below the eye. Loren fell sideways into the corner while Suvorov clutched himself and paced the tiny cubicle like a mad animal until the stabbing ache subsided. Then he brutally picked her up and threw her onto the bunk.

He leaned over and ripped off her remaining underclothes. 'You rotten bitch!' he snarled. 'I'm going to make you wish for a quick death.'

Tears of agony coursed from Loren's eyes as she teetered on the verge of unconsciousness. Vaguely, through the mist of pain, she could see Suvorov slowly take off his belt and wrap it around his hand, leaving the buckle free and swinging. She tried to tense her body for the coming blow as his arm lifted upward, but she was too weak.

Suddenly, as though she was seeing an astral scene through a distorted crystal, Suvorov seemed to grow a third arm. It snaked over his right shoulder and then locked around his neck. The belt dropped to the deck and his body stiffened.

Shock swept across Suvorov's face, the shock of disbelief, then horror at the full realisation of what was happening, and the torment as his windpipe was slowly and mercilessly crushed and his breathing choked off. He struggled against the relentless pressure, throwing himself around the cell, but the arm remained. In a sudden flash of certainty, he knew he would never live to feel the pressure ease. The terror and the lack of oxygen contorted his face and turned it reddish-blue. His starving lungs struggled for air and his arms flailed in frantic madness.

Loren tried to raise her hands over her face to shut out the horrible sight, but they refused to respond. She could only sit frozen and watch in morbid fascination as the life seeped out of Suvorov; watch his violent thrashings fade until finally the eyes bulged from their

237

sockets and he went limp. He hung there several seconds, supported by the ghostly arm until it pulled away from his neck and he fell on the deck on a crumpled heap.

Another figure loomed in Suvorov's place, standing inside the cell's doorway, and Loren found herself staring into a friendly face with deep green eyes and a faint, crooked grin.

'Just between you and me,' said Pitt, 'I've never believed that rot about getting there is half the fun.'

56

Noon, a brilliant azure sky with small cottonball clouds nudged by a gentle westerly breeze, found the *Leonid Andreyev* passing within eighteen miles of Cabo Maisi, the easternmost tip of Cuba. Many of the passengers, sunbathing around the swimming pools, took no notice of the palm-lined coastline on the horizon. To them it was just another one of the hundred islands they had passed since leaving Florida.

On the bridge, Captain Pokofsky stood with binoculars to his eyes. He was observing a small power boat that was circling from the land on his starboard quarter. She was old, her bow nearly straight up and down, and her hull painted black. The topsides were varnished mahogany, and the name 'Pilar' was lettered in gold across her transom. She looked an immaculately kept museum piece. On the ensign staff at her stern she flew the American stars and stripes in the inverted position of distress.

Pokofsky walked over to the automated ship's control console and pressed the 'SLOW SPEED' switch. Almost immediately he could feel the engines reduce revolutions. Then waiting a few minutes until the ship had slowed to a crawl, he leaned over and pressed the lever for 'ALL STOP'.

He was about to walk out on the bridge when his first officer came hurrying up the companionway from the deck below.

'Captain,' he said, catching his breath. 'I've just come from the brig area. The prisoners are gone.'

Pokofsky straightened. 'Gone, you mean escaped?'

'Yes sir, I was on a routine inspection when I found the two security guards unconscious and locked up in one of the cells. The KGB agent was dead.'

'Paul Suvorov killed?'

The first officer nodded. 'From all appearances, he was strangled.'

238

'Why didn't you call me immediately over the ship's phone?'

'I thought it best to tell you in person.'

'You're right, of course,' Pokofsky admitted. 'This couldn't have come at a worse time. Our Cuban security people are arriving to transport the prisoners to shore.'

'If you can stall them, I'm confident a search effort will quickly turn up the Americans.'

Pokofsky stared through the doorway at the closing boat. 'They'll wait,' he said confidently. 'Our captives are too important to leave on board.'

'There is one other thing, sir,' said the first officer. 'The Americans must have received help.'

'They didn't break out by themselves?' Pokofsky asked in surprise.

'Not possible. Two old men in a weakened condition and one woman could never have overpowered two security people and murdered a professional KGB man.'

'Damn!' Pokofsky cursed. He rammed a fist into a palm in exasperation, compounded equally by anxiety and anger. 'This complicates matters.'

'Could the CIA have sneaked on board?'

'I hardly think so. If the United States Government remotely suspected their government leaders were held on the *Leonid Andreyev*, their navy would be converging on us like mad bears. See for yourself; no ships, no aircraft, and their Guantanamo Bay naval station is only forty miles away.'

'Then who?' asked the first officer. 'Certainly none of our crew.'

'Can only be a passenger,' Pokofsky surmised. He fell silent, thinking. Utter stillness fell on the bridge. At last he looked up and began issuing orders. 'Collect every available officer and form five man search parties. Divide up the ship and hunt every deck from keel to sundeck. Alert the security guards and enlist the stewards. If questioned by the passengers, make up a believable pretext for entering their cabins. Changing the bed linen, repairing plumbing, inspecting fire equipment, any story that fits the situation. Say or do nothing that will cause suspicion among the passengers or set them to asking embarrassing questions. Be as subtle as possible and refrain from violence, but recapture the Smith woman and the two men quickly.'

'What about Suvorov's body?'

Pokofsky didn't hesitate. 'Arrange a fitting tribute to our comrade from the KGB,' he said sarcastically. 'As soon as it's dark, throw him overboard with the garbage.'

'Yes sir,' the first officer acknowledged with a smile and hurried away.

Pokofsky picked up a bullhorn from a bulkhead rack and stepped out on the bridge wing. The small pleasure boat was drifting about fifty yards away.

'Are you in distress?' he asked, his voice booming over the water.

A man with a squat body and the skin tone of an old wallet, cupped his hands to his mouth and shouted back. 'We have people who are quite ill. I suspect ptomaine poisoning. May we come aboard and use your medical facilities?'

'By all means,' Pokofsky replied. 'Come alongside. I'll drop the gangway.'

Pitt watched the mini-drama with interest, seeing through the sham. Two men and a woman struggled up the metal stairway, clutching their midriffs and pretending they were in the throes of abdominal agony. He rated them two stars for their performance.

After a suitable length of time for pseudo doctoring, he reasoned, Loren, Moran and Larimer would have taken their places in the pleasure boat. He also knew full well the captain would not resume the cruise until the ship was scoured and the Congressmen apprehended.

He left the railing and mingled with the other passengers, who soon returned to their deckchairs and tables around the swimming pools and cocktail bars. He took the lift down to his deck. As the doors opened and he stepped out into the passageway, he rubbed shoulders with a steward who was entering.

Pitt idly noticed the steward was Asian, probably Mongolian if he was serving on a Russian ship. He brushed past and continued to his cabin.

The steward stared at Pitt curiously. Then his expression turned to blank astonishment as he watched Pitt walk away. He was still standing there gawking when the door closed and the lift rose without him.

Pitt rounded the corner of the passageway and spied a ship's officer with several crewmen waiting outside a cabin three down across from his. None of them displayed their usual shipboard conviviality. Their expressions looked deadly earnest. He fished in his pocket for the cabin key while watching out of the corner of one eye. In a few moments, a female steward came out and said a few words in Russian to the officer and shook her head. Then they moved towards the next cabin and knocked.

Pitt quickly entered and closed the door. The tiny enclosure looked like a scene out of a Marx Brothers movie. Loren was perched on the upper pullman bunk while Moran and Larimer shared the lower. All three were ravenously attacking a tray of hors d'oeuvres that Giordino had smuggled from the dining-room buffet table.

240

Giordino, seated on a small chair, half in the bathroom, threw an offhand wave. 'See anything interesting?'

'The Cuban connection arrived,' Pitt answered. 'They're drifting alongside, standing by to exchange passengers.'

'The bastards will have a long wait,' said Giordino.

'Try four minutes. That's how long before we'll all be chained and tossed on a boat bound for Havana.'

'They can't help but find us,' Larimer uttered in a hollow voice. Pitt had seen many washed out men, the waxen skin, the eyes that once blazed with authority now empty, the vagrant thoughts. Despite his age and long years of over indulgent living amid the political arena, Larimer was still a powerfully built man. But the heart and circulation were no longer up to the stress and dangers of staying alive in a hostile situation. Pitt didn't require an internship to recognise a man who was in dire need of medical treatment.

'A Russian search party is just across the hall,' Pitt explained.

'We can't let them imprison us again,' Moran shouted, springing to his feet and looking around wildly. 'We must run!'

'You wouldn't make the lift,' snapped Pitt, grabbing him by the arm as he would a child throwing a tantrum. He didn't much care for Moran. The Speaker of the House struck him as an oily weasel.

'There's no place to hide,' said Loren, her voice not quite steady.

Pitt didn't answer her but brushed past Giordino and went into the bathroom. He pulled back the shower curtain and turned on the hot water. Less than a minute later clouds of steam billowed into the cramped quarters.

'Okay,' Pitt directed, 'everybody in the shower.'

Nobody moved. They all stared at him, standing wraithlike in the mist filled doorway, as though he was from another earth.

'Move!' he said sharply. 'They'll be here any second.'

Giordino shook his head in bewilderment. 'How are you going to get three people in that stall shower? It's hardly big enough for one.'

'Get your wig on. You're going in too.'

'The four of us?' Loren muttered incredulously.

'Either that or a free trip to Moscow. Besides, college kids cram entire fraternities in phone booths all the time.'

Giordino slipped the wig over his head as Pitt re-entered the bathroom and turned the water to lukewarm. He placed a trembling Moran in a squatting position between Giordino's legs. Larimer pressed his heavy body against the far corner of the stall as Loren climbed on Giordino's back. At last they were jammed awkwardly into the stall, drenched by the flow from the showerhead. Pitt was in the act of turning on the hot water in the sink to increase the steam cloud when he heard a knock on the door.

241

He hurried over and opened it so there was no suspicious hesitation. The ship's officer bowed slightly and smiled.

'Mr Gruber, is it? Very sorry to bother you, but we're making a routine inspection of the fire sprinklers. Do you mind if we enter?'

'Why sure,' Pitt said obligingly. 'No problem with me, but my wife's in the shower.'

The officer nodded to the female steward who eased past Pitt and made a show of checking the overhead sprinkler heads. Then she pointed to the bathroom door. 'May I?'

'Go on in,' said Pitt good-naturedly. 'She won't mind.'

The steward opened the door and was enveloped in a cloud of steam. Pitt went over and leaned in the bathroom. 'Hey luv, our steward lady wants to check the first sprinkler. All right with you?'

As the cloud began dissipating through the door, the steward saw a huge stringy mop of hair and a pair of heavy browed eyes peeking around the shower curtain.

'All right by me,' came Loren's voice. 'And could you bring us a couple of extra towels when you think of it?'

The steward simply nodded and said, 'I'll be back with the towels shortly.'

Pitt casually munched on a canape and offered one to the first officer, who gave a polite 'no thank you' shake of his head.

'Does my heart good to see you people so interested in the safety of the passengers,' said Pitt.

'Merely doing our duty,' said the first officer, looking curiously at the half-eaten stack of hors d'oeuvres. 'I see you also enjoy our shipboard cuisine.'

'My wife and I love appetisers,' said Pitt. 'We'd rather eat these than a main course.'

The steward came out of the bathroom and said something to the first officer. The only word Pitt made out was '*nyet*'.

'Sorry to have troubled you,' said the first officer courteously.

'Any time,' replied Pitt.

As soon as the doorlock clicked, Pitt rushed to the bathroom. 'Everybody stay just as you are,' he ordered. 'Don't move.' Then he reclined on a bunk and stuffed his mouth with caviar on thin toast.

Two minutes later the door suddenly popped open and the female steward sprang through like a jack-in-the-box, her eyes darting around the cabin.

'Can I help you?' Pitt mumbled with a full mouth.

'I brought the towels,' said the steward.

'Just throw them on the bathroom sink,' Pitt said indifferently.

She did precisely that and left the cabin, throwing Pitt a smile that was genuine and devoid of any suspicion.

242

He waited another two minutes, then cracked the door and peered into the hallway. The search crew was entering a cabin near the end of the passageway. He returned to the bathroom, reached in and turned off the water.

Whoever coined the phrase, 'they looked like drowned rats' must have had the poor souls huddled together in that pocket-sized shower in mind. Their fingertips were beginning to shrivel and all clothing was soaked through. Giordino came out first and hurled his sopping wig in the sink. Loren climbed off his back and immediately began drying her hair. Pitt helped Moran to his feet and half carried Larimer to a bunk.

'A wise move,' said Pitt to Loren, kissing her on the nape of the neck. 'Asking for more towels.'

'It struck me as the thing to do.'

'Are we safe now?' asked Moran. 'Will they be back?'

'We won't be in the clear till we're off the ship,' said Pitt. 'And we can count on their paying an encore visit. When they come up dry on this search, they'll redouble their efforts for a second.'

'Got any more brilliant escape tricks up your sleeve, Houdini?' asked Giordino.

'Yes,' Pitt replied, sure as the devil. 'As a matter of fact, I do.'

57

The second engineer moved along a catwalk between the massive fuel tanks that towered two decks above him. He was running a routine maintenance check for any trace of leakage in the pipes that transferred the oil to the boilers that fired the *Leonid Andreyev*'s 27,000-horsepower turbines.

He whistled an old Urals folktune to himself, his only accompaniment coming from the hum of the turbo-generators beyond the forward bulkhead. Every so often he wiped a rag around a pipe fitting or valve, nodding in satisfaction when it came away clean.

Suddenly he stopped and cocked an ear. The sound of metal striking against metal came from a narrow walkway leading off to his right. Curious, he walked slowly, quietly, along the dimly lit access. At the end, where the walkway turned and passed between the fuel tanks and the inner plates of the hull, he paused and peered into the gloom.

A figure in a steward's uniform appeared to be attaching something to the side of the fuel tank. The second engineer approached, stepping softly, until he was only ten feet away.

'What are you doing there?' he demanded.

243

The steward slowly turned and straightened. The engineer could see he was Oriental. The white uniform was soiled with grime and a seaman's duffel bag lay open behind him on the walkway. The steward flashed a wide smile and made no effort to reply.

The engineer moved a few steps closer. 'You're not supposed to be here. This area is off limits to the passenger service crew.'

Still no answer.

Then the engineer noticed a strange, misshapen lump pressed against the side of the fuel tank. Two strands of copper wire ran from it to a clock mechanism beside the duffel bag.

'A bomb!' he blurted in shock. 'You're planting a damn bomb!'

He swung around and began running wildly down the walkway shouting. He took no more than five steps when the narrow steel confines echoed with a noise like twin handclaps in quick succession, and the hollow point bullets from a silenced automatic tore into the back of his head.

The obligatory toasts were voiced and the glasses of iced vodka downed and quickly refilled. Pokofsky did the honours from the liquor cabinet in his cabin, avoiding the cold, piercing gaze of the man seated on a leather sofa.

Geidar Ombrikov, Chief of the KGB residency in Havana, Cuba, was not in a congenial mood. 'Your report won't sit well with my superiors,' he said. 'An agent lost under your command will be considered a clear case of negligence.'

'This is a cruise ship,' Pokofsy said, his face reddening in resentment. 'She was designed and placed in service for the purpose of bringing in hard western currency for the Soviet treasury. We are not a floating headquarters for the Committee for State Security.'

'Then how do you explain the ten agents our foreign directorate assigned on board your vessel to monitor the conversations of the passengers?'

'I try not to think about it.'

'You should,' Ombrikov said in a threatening tone.

'I have enough to keep me busy running this ship,' Pokofsky said quickly. 'There aren't enough hours in my day to include intelligence gathering too.'

'Still, you should have increased precautions. If the American politicians escape and tell their story, the horrendous repercussions will have a disastrous effect on our foreign relations.'

'I won't argue the point,' Pokofsky muttered. 'The sooner they're off a Soviet flag vessel, the better.' He set his vodka on the liquor cabinet without touching it. 'There is no place they can hide for long. They will be back in our hands inside the hour.'

244

'I do hope so,' said Ombrikov acidly. 'Their Navy will begin to wonder why a Soviet cruiser liner is drifting around off their precious Cuban base and send out a patrol.'

'They won't board the *Leonid Andreyev* on a mere whim.'

'No, but my small pleasure boat is flying the United States flag. They won't hesitate to come aboard for an inspection.'

'She's an interesting old boat,' Pokofsky said, trying to change the subject. 'Where did you find her?'

'A personal loan from our friend, Castro,' Ombrikov replied. 'She used to belong to the author, Ernest Hemingway.'

'Yes, I've read four of his books – '

Pokofsky was interrupted by the sudden appearance of his first officer who entered without knocking.

'My apologies for breaking in, Captain, but may I have a word in private with you?'

Pokofsky excused himself to Ombrikov and stepped outside his cabin.

'What is it?'

'We failed to find them,' the officer announced uneasily.

Pokofsky paused for some moments, lit a cigarette in defiance of his own regulations, and gave his first officer a look of disapproval. 'Then I suggest you search the ship again, more carefully this time. And take a closer look at the passengers wandering the decks. They may be hiding in the crowd.'

His first officer nodded and hurried off. Pokofsky returned to his cabin.

'Problems?' asked Ombrikov.

Before Pokofsky could answer he felt a slight shudder run through the ship. He stood there curious for perhaps half a minute, tensed and alert, but nothing more seemed to happen.

Then suddenly the *Leonid Andreyev* was rocked by a violent explosion that heeled her far over to starboard, flinging people off their feet and sending a convulsive shockwave throughout the ship. A great sheet of fire erupted from the port side of the hull, raining fiery steel debris and oil over the exposed decks. The blast reverberated over the water until it finally died away, leaving an unearthly silence in its wake and a solid column of black smoke that mushroomed into the sky.

What none of the seven hundred passengers and crew knew, what many of them would never come to learn, was that deep amidships the fuel tanks had detonated, blowing a gaping hole half above and half below the waterline, spraying a torrent of burning oil over the superstructure in blue and green flames, scarring the victims and blazing across the teak decks with speed of a brush fire.

Almost instantly, the *Leonid Andreyev* was transformed from a luxurious cruise liner into a sinking, fiery pyre.

Pitt stirred and wondered dully what had happened. For a full minute as the shock wore off, he remained prone on the deck where he'd been thrown by the force of the concussion, trying to orientate himself. Slowly he rose to his hands and knees, then hoisted his aching body erect by grabbing the inner door knob. Bruised but still functioning, nothing broken or out of kilter, he turned to examine the others.

Giordino was partly crouched, partly lying across the threshold of the shower stall. The last thing he remembered was standing in the cabin. He wore a surprised look in his eyes, but he appeared unhurt. Moran and Loren had fallen out of the bunks and were lying in the middle of the deck. They were both dazed and would carry a gang of black and blue marks for a week or two, but were otherwise uninjured.

Larimer was huddled in the far corner of the cabin. Pitt went over and gently lifted his head. There was an ugle welt rising above the Senator's left temple and a trickle of blood dripped from a cut lip. He was unconscious but breathing evenly. Pitt eased a pillow from the lower bunk under his head.

Giordino was the first to speak. 'How is he?'

'Just knocked out,' Pitt replied.

'What happened?' Loren murmured dazedly.

'An explosion,' said Pitt. 'Somewhere forward, probably in the engine room.'

'The boilers?' Giordino speculated.

'Modern boilers are safety-designed not to blow.'

'God,' said Loren, 'my ears are still ringing.'

A strange expression came over Giordino's face. He took a coin out of his pocket and rolled it across the hard carpeted deck. Instead of losing its momentum and circling until falling on one side, it maintained its speed across the cabin as though propelled by an unseen hand and clinked into the far bulkhead.

'The ship's listing,' Giordino announced flatly.

Pitt went over and cracked the door. Already the passageway was filling up with passengers who were stumbling out of their cabins and wandering aimlessly in bewilderment. 'So much for plan B.'

Loren gave him an inquisitive look. 'Plan B?'

'My idea to steal the boat from Cuba. I don't think we're going to find seats.'

'What are you talking about?' demanded Moran. He rose unsteadily to his feet, holding onto a bunk chain for support. 'A trick, it's a cheap trick to flush us out.'

'Damned expensive trick if you ask me,' Giordino said nastily. 'The

246

explosion must have seriously damaged the ship. She's obviously taking in water.'

'Will we sink?' Moran asked with the growing fright of a small child.

Pitt ignored him and peered around the edge of the door again. Most of the passengers acted calmly, but a few were beginning to shout and cry. As he watched, the passageway became clogged with people stupidly carrying armfuls of personal belongings and hastily packed suitcases. Then Pitt caught the smell of burning paint, quickly followed by the sight of a smoky wisp. He slammed the door and began tearing the blankets off the bunks and throwing them to Giordino.

'Hurry, soak these and any towel you can find in the shower!'

Giordino took one look at Pitt's dead-serious expression and did as he was told without comment. Loren knelt and tried to lift Larimer's head and shoulders from the deck. The Senator moaned and opened his eyes, looking up at Loren as if trying to recognise her. Moran cringed against the bulkhead, muttering to himself.

Pitt rudely pushed Loren aside and lifted Larimer to his feet, slinging one arm around his shoulder. Giordino came out of the bathroom and distributed the wet blankets and towels.

'All right, Al, you help me with the Senator. Loren, you hold onto Congressman Moran and stick close behind me.' He broke off and looked at everyone. 'Okay, here we go.'

He yanked open the door and was engulfed by a rolling wall of smoke that came out of nowhere.

Almost before the rumble of the explosion faded, Captain Pokofsky shook off stunned disbelief and rushed to the bridge. The young watch officer was pounding desperately on the automated ship console in agonised frustration.

'Close all watertight doors and actuate the fire control system!' Pokofsky shouted.

'I can't!' the watch officer cried helplessly. 'We've lost all power!'

'What about the auxiliary generators?'

'They're out too.' The watch officer's face was wrapped in undisguised shock. 'The ship's phones are dead. The damage control computer is down. Nothing responds. We can't give a general alarm.'

Pokofsky ran out on the bridge wing and stared aft. His once beautiful ship was vomiting fire and smoke from her entire midsection. A few moments before there was music and relaxed gaiety. Now the entire scene was one of horror. The open swimming pool and lounge decks had been turned into a crematorium. The two hundred people stretched under the sun were almost instantly

247

incinerated by the tidal fall of fiery oil. Some had saved themselves by leaping into the pools, only to die after surfacing for air when the heat seared their lungs, and many had climbed the railings and thrown themselves overboard, their skin and brief clothing ablaze.

Pokofsky stood sick and stunned at the sight of the carnage. It was a moment in time borrowed from hell. He knew in his heart that his ship was lost. There was no stopping the holocaust, and the list was increasing as the sea poured into the *Leonid Andreyev*'s bowels. He returned to the bridge.

'Pass the word to abandon ship,' he said to the watch officer. 'The port boats are burning. Load what women and children you can into the starboard boats still intact.'

As the watch officer hurried off, the chief engineer, Erik Kazinkin, appeared out of breath from his climb from below. His eyebrows and half his hair were singed away. The soles of his shoes were smouldering but he appeared not to notice. His mind was numb to the pain.

'Give me a report,' Pokofsy ordered in a quiet tone. 'What caused the explosion?'

'The port fuel tank blew,' answered Kazinkin. 'God knows why. Took out the power generating room and the auxiliary generator compartment as well. Boiler rooms two and three are flooded. We managed to manually close the watertight doors to the engine rooms, but she's taking on water at an alarming rate. And without power to operate the pumps . . .' He shrugged defeatedly without continuing.

All options to save the *Leonid Andreyev* had evaporated. The only morbid question was whether she would become a burned out derelict or sink first? Few would survive the next hour, Pokofsky accepted with dread certainty. Many would burn and many would drown, unable to enter the pitifully few lifeboats that were still able to be launched.

'Bring your men up from below,' said Pokofsky. 'We're abandoning the ship.'

'Thank you, Captain,' said the chief engineer. He held out his hand. 'Good luck to you.'

They parted and Pokofsky headed for the communications room one deck below. The officer-in-charge looked up from the radio as the Captain suddenly strode through the doorway.

'Send out the distress call,' Pokofsky ordered.

'I took the responsibility, sir, of sending out "MAYDAY" signals immediately after the explosion.'

Pokofsky placed a hand on the officer's shoulder. 'I commend your initiative.' Then he asked calmly, 'Have you managed to transmit without problem?'

'Yes, sir, when the power supply went off, I switched to the emergency batteries. The first response came from a Korean container ship only ten miles to the south-west.'

'Thank God someone is close. Any other replies?'

'The United States Navy at Guantanamo Bay is responding with rescue ships and helicopters. The only other vessel within fifty miles is a Norwegian cruise ship.'

'Too late for her,' said Pokofsky thoughtfully. 'We'll have to pin our hopes on the Koreans and American Navy.'

With the soaked blanket over his head, Pitt had to feel his way along the passageway and up the smoke filled staircase. Three, four times, he and Giordino tripped over the bodies of passengers who had succumbed to asphyxiation.

Larimer made a game effort of trying to keep in step, while Loren and Moran stumbled along behind, their hands clutching the belted trousers of Pitt and Giordino.

'How far?' Loren gasped.

'We have to climb four decks before we rise above the hull line and break out on the open promenade area,' Pitt panted in reply.

At the second landing they ran into a solid wall of people. The staircase became so packed with passengers struggling to escape the smoke it became impossible to take another step. The crew acted with coolness, attempting to direct the human flow to the boat deck, but calm gave way to the inevitable contagion of panic and they were trampled under the screaming, terror driven mass of thrashing bodies.

'To the left!' Giordino shouted in Pitt's ear. 'The passageway leads to another staircase towards the stern.'

Relying on a deep trust in his little friend, Pitt veered down the passageway, pulling Larimer along. The Senator finally managed to get his footing on the smooth surface and began carrying his own weight. To their vast relief the smoke decreased and the frightened tidal wave of people thinned. When at last they reached the aft staircase they found it practically empty. By not following the herd instinct, Giordino had led them to temporary safety.

They emerged into the clear on the deck aft of the observation lounge. After a few moments to ease their coughing spasms and cleanse their aching lungs with clean air, they looked in awe over the doomed ship.

The *Leonid Andreyev* was listing twenty degrees to port. Thousands of gallons of oil had spilled out into the sea and ignited. The water around the jagged opening caused by the blast was a mass of fire which spread around the bow. The entire midsection of the ship was a blazing torch. The tremendous heat was turning steel plates red hot and warping them into twisted, grotesque shapes. White paint was blistering black, teak decks were nearly burned through and the glass in the ports popped like gunshots.

The flames spread with incredible speed as the ocean breeze fanned them towards the bridge. Already the communications room was consumed and the officer-in-charge burned to death at his radio. Fire and swirling smoke shot upward through the companionways and ventilating ducts. The *Leonid Andreyev*, like all modern cruise liners was designed and constructed to be fireproof, but no precise planning or visionary foresight could have predicted the devastating results of a fuel tank explosion that showered the ship like a flamethrower.

An immense billowing cloud of oily smoke reached hundreds of feet above, flattening in the upper air currents, stretching over the ship like a pall. The base of the cloud was a solid torrent of flame that twisted and surged in a violent storm of orange and yellow. While below, in the deeper reaches of the hull, the flames were an acetylene blue-white, fed into molten temperatures by the intake of air through the shattered plates, creating the effect of a blast furnace.

Though many of the passengers were able to fight their way up the stairways, over a hundred lay dead below, some trapped and burned in their cabins, others overtaken by smoke inhalation during their attempt to escape topside. The ones who made it were being driven by the flames towards the stern and away from the lifeboats.

All efforts by the crew to maintain order were swept away by the chaos. The passengers were finally left to fend for themselves and no one knew which way to turn. All port lifeboats were ablaze and only three were lowered on the starboard side before the fire drove the crew back. As it was, one boat was beginning to burn by the time it hit the sea.

Now people began jumping into the water like migrating lemmings. The drop was nearly fifty feet, and a number of those who had lifejackets made the mistake of inflating them before plummeting over the side and broke their necks upon impact. Women stood spellbound with terror, too frightened to leap. Men cursed in desperation. In the water the swimmers struck out for the few lifeboats, but the crews who manned them started up the engines and sailed beyond reach for fear of being swamped by overloading.

In the middle of the frenzied drama, the container ship arrived. The captain eased his vessel within a hundred yards of the *Leonid Andreyev* and put his boats over as fast as they could be lowered. A few minutes later, US Navy sea rescue helicopters appeared and began plucking survivors from the sea.

58

Loren gazed in abstract fascination at the sheet of advancing fire. 'Shouldn't we jump or something?' she asked in a vague tone.

Pitt didn't answer immediately. He was studying the slanting deck and judged the list to be about forty degrees. 'No call to rush things,' he said with expressionless calm. 'The flames won't reach us for another ten minutes. The further the ship heels to port, the shorter the distance to jump. In the meantime, I suggest we start heaving deckchairs overboard so those poor souls in the water have something to hang onto until they're picked up.'

Surprisingly, Larimer was the first to react. He began sweeping up the wooden deckchairs in his massive arms and dropping them over the railings. He actually had the look on his face of a man who was enjoying himself. Moran stood huddled against a bulwark, silent, non-committal, frozen in fear.

'Take care you don't hit a swimmer on the head,' Pitt said to Larimer.

'I wouldn't dare,' the Senator replied with an exhausted smile. 'They might be a constituent and I'd lose their vote.'

After all the chairs in sight were deposited over the side, Pitt stood there for two or three seconds and took stock. The blast from the heat was not yet unbearable. The fire wouldn't kill those packed on the stern deck, at least not for a few more minutes. He shouldered his way through the dense throng to the port railing again. The waves rolled only twenty feet below.

He shouted to Giordino, 'Let's help these people over the side.' Then he turned and cupped his hands to his mouth. 'There's no more time to lose!' he yelled at the top of his lungs to make himself heard above the din of the frightened crowd and the roar of the holocaust. 'Swim for it or die!'

Several men took the hint and, clutching the hands of their protesting wives, straddled the railing and slipped out of sight below. Next came three teenage girls who showed no hesitation but dived cleanly into the blue-green swells.

'Swim to a deckchair and use it for a float,' Giordino instructed everyone repeatedly.

Pitt separated families into a group and while Loren cheered the children, he directed their parents to jump and latch onto a floating deckchair. Then he held the children over the side by the hands as far as he could reach and let them drop, holding his breath until the mother and father had them safely in tow.

The great curtain of flame crept closer and breathing became more difficult. The heat felt as though they were standing in front of an open furnace. A rough head count told Pitt only thirty people were left, but it would be a close race.

A great hulking fat man stopped and refused to move. 'The water's full of sharks!' he screamed hysterically. 'We're better off here, waiting for the helicopters.'

'They can't hover over the ship because of air turbulence from the heat,' Pitt explained patiently. 'You can burn to a cinder or take your chances in the water. Which is it? Be quick, you're holding up the others.'

Giordino took two paces, tensed his powerful muscles and lifted the fat procrastinator off his feet. There was no animosity, no expression of meanness in Giordino's unblinking eyes as he carried the man to the side and unceremoniously dumped him overboard.

'Send me a postcard,' Giordino shouted after him.

The diverting action seemed to motivate the few passengers who hung back. One after the other, with Pitt assisting the elderly couples to take the plunge, they departed the burning ship. When the last of them was finally gone, Pitt looked around to Loren.

'Your turn,' he said.

'Not without my colleagues,' she said with a feminine resolve.

Pitt stared below to make certain the water was clear. Larimer was so weak he could barely lift his legs over the rail. Giordino gave him a hand as Loren jumped arm in arm with Moran. Pitt watched anxiously until they all cleared the side and swam away, admiring Loren's endurance as she shouted words of encouragement to Larimer while towing Moran by the collar.

'Better give her a hand,' Pitt said to Giordino.

His friend didn't have to be urged. He was gone before another word passed between them.

Pitt took one last look at the *Leonid Andreyev*. The air around shimmered from the blasting heat waves as flames shot from her every opening. The list was passing fifty degrees and her end was only minutes away. Already her starboard propeller was clear of the water and steam was hissing in white tortured clouds around her waterline.

As he was poised to leap, Pitt abruptly went rigid in astonishment. At the outer edge of his peripheral vision he caught an arm snaking out of a cabin port forty feet away. Without hesitation, he picked up one of the still soggy blankets from the deck, threw it over his head and covered the distance in seven strides. A voice

252

inside the cabin was screaming for help. He peered in and saw a woman's face, eyes wide in terror.

'Oh my God, please help us?'

'How many are you?'

'Myself and two children.'

'Pass out your kids.'

The face disappeared and quickly a boy about six years of age was thrust through the narrow port. Pitt set him between his legs, keeping the blanket suspended above the two of them like a tent. Next came a little girl no more than three. Incredibly she was sound asleep.

'Give me your hand,' Pitt ordered, knowing in his heart it was hopeless.

'I can't get through!' the woman cried. 'The opening is too small.'

'Do you have water in the bathroom?'

'There's no pressure.'

'Strip naked!' Pitt shouted in desperation. 'Use your cosmetics. Smear your body with facial creams.'

The woman nodded in understanding and disappeared inside. Pitt turned and clutching a child under each arm rushed to the rail. With great relief he spied Giordino treading water, looking up.

'Al,' Pitt called. 'Catch.'

If Giordino was surprised to see Pitt collar two more children he didn't show it. He reached up and gathered them in as effortlessly as if they were footballs.

'Jump!' he yelled to Pitt. 'She's going over.'

Without lingering to answer, Pitt raced back to the cabin port. He realised with only a small corner of his mind that saving the mother was a sheer act of desperation. He passed beyond conscious thought, his movements seemed those of another man, a total stranger.

The air was so hot and dry his perspiration evaporated before it seeped from his pores. The heat rose from the deck and penetrated the soles of his shoes. He stumbled and nearly fell as a heavy shudder ran through the doomed ship, and she gave a sudden lurch as the deck dropped on an increasing angle to port. She was in her final death agony before capsizing and sinking to the seabottom.

Pitt found himself kneeling on the cabin wall reaching into the cabin. A pair of hands clasped his wrists and he pulled. The woman's shoulders and breasts squeezed into the open. He gave another heave and then her hips scraped through.

The flames were running up and licking at his back. The deck was dropping away beneath his feet. He held the woman around the waist and leaped off the edge of the cabin as the *Leonid Andreyev* rolled over, her propellers twisting out of the water and arching towards the sun.

They were sucked under by the fierce rush of water, swirled around like dolls in a maelstrom. Pitt lashed out with his free hand and feet and struggled upward, seeing the glimmering surface turn from green to blue with agonising slowness.

The blood pounded in his ears and his lungs felt as though they were filled with angry wasps. The thin veil of blackness began to tint his vision. He felt the woman go limp under his arm, her body creating an unwelcome drag against his progress. He used up the last particles of oxygen, and a pyrotechnic display flared inside his head. One burst became a bright orange ball that expanded until it exploded in a wavering flash.

He broke through the surface, his upturned face directed at the afternoon sun. Thankfully he inhaled deep waves of air, enough to ease the blackness, the pounding and the sting in his lungs. Then he quickly circled the woman's abdomen and squeezed hard, several times, forcing the saltwater from her throat. She convulsed and began retching, followed by a coughing spell. Only when her breathing returned to near normal and she groaned did he look around for the others.

Giordino was swimming in Pitt's direction. pushing one of the deckchairs in front of him. The two children were sitting on top, immune to the tragedy around them, gaily laughing at Giordino's repertory of funny faces.

'I was beginning to wonder if you were going to turn up,' he said.

'Bad pennies usually do,' said Pitt, keeping the children's mother afloat until she recovered enough to hang onto the deckchair.

'I'll take care of them,' said Giordino. 'You better help Loren. I think the Senator's bought it.'

His arms felt as if they were encased in lead and he was numb with exhaustion, but Pitt carved the water with swift even strokes until he reached the floating jetsam that supported Loren and Larimer.

Grey-faced, her eyes filled with sadness, Loren grimly held the Senator's head above water. Pitt saw with sinking heart she needn't have bothered; Larimer would never sit in the Senate again. His skin was mottled and turning a dusky purple. He was game to the end, but the half century of living in the fast lane had called in the inevitable IOUs. His heart went far beyond its limits and finally quit in protest.

Gently, Pitt prised Loren's hands from the Senator's body, and pushed him away. She looked at him blankly as if to object, then turned away, unable to watch as Larimer slowly drifted off, gently pushed by the rolling sea.

'He deserves a state funeral,' she said, her voice a husky whisper.

254

'No matter,' said Pitt, 'as long as they know he went out like a man.'

Loren seemed to accept that. She leaned her head on Pitt's shoulder, the tears intermingling with the saltwater on her cheeks.

Pitt twisted and looked around. 'Where's Moran?'

'He was picked up by a Navy helicopter.'

'He deserted you?' Pitt asked incredulously.

'The crewman shouted that he only had room for one more.'

'So the illustrious Speaker of the House left a woman to support a dying man while he saved himself.'

Pitt's dislike for Moran burned with a cold flame. He became obsessed with the idea of ramming his fist into the little ferret's face.

Captain Pokofsky sat in the cabin of the powerboat, his hands clasped over his ears to shut out the terrible cries of the people drowning in the water and the screams from those suffering the agony of their burns. He could not bring himself to look upon the indescribable horror or watch the *Leonid Andreyev* plunge out of sight to the seabed two thousand fathoms below. He was a living dead man.

He looked up at Geidar Ombrikov through glazed and listless eyes. 'Why did you save me?' Why didn't you let me die with my ship?'

Ombrikov could plainly see Pokofsky was suffering from severe shock, but he felt no pity for the man. Death was an element the KGB agent was trained to accept. His duty came before all consideration of compassion.

'I've no time for rituals of the sea,' he said coldly. 'The noble captain standing on the bridge saluting the flag as his ship sinks under him is so much rot. State Security needs you, Pokofsky, and I need you to identify the American legislators.'

'They're probably dead,' Pokofsky muttered distantly.

'Then we'll have to prove it,' Ombrikov snapped ruthlessly. 'My superiors won't accept less than positive identification of their bodies. Nor can we overlook the possibility they may still be alive out there in the water.'

Pokofsky placed his hands over his face and shuddered. 'I can't – '

Before the words were out of his mouth, Ombrikov roughly dragged him to his feet and shoved him out on the open deck. 'Damn you!' he shouted. 'Look for them!'

Pokofsky clenched his jaws and stared at the appalling reality of the floating wreckage and hundreds of struggling men, women and children. He choked off a sound deep inside him, his face blanched.

'No!' he shouted.

He leaped over the side so quickly, suddenly, neither Ombrikov nor his crew could stop him. He hit the water swimming and dived deep into the liquid void, deep until the white of his uniform was lost to view on the surface.

The boats from the container ship hauled in the survivors as fast as they could reach them, quickly filling to capacity and unloading their human cargo before returning to the centre of the flotsam to continue the rescue. The sea was filled with debris of all kinds, dead bodies of all ages, and those still fighting to live. Fortunately the water was warm and none suffered from exposure, nor did the threat of sharks ever materialise.

One boat jockeyed close to Giordino who helped lift the mother and her two children on board. Then he scrambled over the freeboard and motioned for the helmsman to steer towards Pitt and Loren. They were among the last few to be fished out.

As the boat slipped alongside Pitt raised his hand in greeting to the short, stocky figure that leaned over the side.

'Hello,' said Pitt grinning widely. 'Are we ever glad to see you.'

'Happy to be of service,' replied the steward whom Pitt had passed earlier at the lift. He was also grinning, baring a set of large upper teeth parted by a wide gap.

He reached down, grasped Loren by the wrists, and pulled her effortlessly out of the water and into the boat. Pitt stretched out his hand, but the steward ignored it.

'Sorry,' he said, 'we have no more room.'

'What – what are you talking about?' Pitt demanded. 'The boat is half empty.'

'You are not welcome aboard my vessel.'

'You damned well don't own it.'

'Oh but I do.'

Pitt stared at the steward in sheer incredulity, then slowly turned and took one long comprehensive look across the water at the container ship. The name of the starboard bow was *Chalmette*, but the lettering on the sides of the containers stacked on the main deck read "Bougainville". Pitt felt as though he'd been kicked in the stomach.

'Our confrontation is a lucky circumstance for me, Mr Pitt, but I fear a misfortune for yourself.'

Pitt turned back to the steward. 'You know me?'

The grin turned into an expression of hate and contempt. 'Only too well. Your meddling has cost Bougainville Maritime dearly.'

'Tell me who you are,' said Pitt, stalling for time and desperately glancing in the sky for a Navy recovery helicopter.

'I don't think I'll give you the satisfaction,' the steward said with all the warmth of an ice-box.

Unable to hear the conversation, Loren pulled at the steward's arm. 'Why don't you bring him on board? What are you waiting for?'

He turned and savagely backhanded her across the cheek, sending her stumbling backward, falling across two survivors who sat stunned in surprise.

Giordino, who was standing in the stern of the boat, started forward. A seaman produced an automatic shotgun from under a seat and rammed the wooden shoulder into his stomach. Giordino's jaw dropped open, he gasped for breath and lost his footing, dropping partially over the side of the boat, arms trailing in the water.

The steward's lips tightened and the smooth yellow features bore no readable expression. Only his eyes shone with evil. 'Thank you for being so cooperative, Mr Pitt. Thank you for so thoughtfully coming to me.'

'Get screwed!' Pitt snapped in defiance.

The steward raised an oar over his head. 'Bon voyage, Dirk Pitt.'

The oar swung downward and clipped Pitt on the right side of his chest, driving him under the water. The wind was crushed from his lungs and a stabbing pain swept over his ribcage. He resurfaced and lifted his left arm above his head to ward off the next inevitable blow. His move came too late. The oar in the hands of the steward mashed Pitt's extended arm down and struck the top of his head.

The blue sky turned to black as consciousness left him, and slowly Pitt drifted under the lifeboat and sank out of sight.

59

The President's wife entered his second floor study, kissed him goodnight, and went off to bed. He sat in a soft, highback embroidered chair and studied a pile of statistics on the latest economic forecasts. Using a large yellow legal pad, he scribbled a prodigious amount of notes. Some he saved, some he tore up and discarded before they were completed. After nearly three hours, he removed his glasses and closed his tired eyes for a few moments.

When he opened them again, he was no longer in his White House study, but in a small grey room with a high ceiling and no windows.

He rubbed his eyes and looked once more, blinking in the monotone light.

He was still in the grey room, only now he found himself seated in a hard wooden chair, his ankles strapped to square, carved legs and his hands to the armrests.

A violent fear coursed through him, and he cried for his wife and the secret service guards, but the voice was not his. It had a different tonal quality, deeper, more coarse.

Soon a door that was recessed into one wall swung inward and a small man with a thin, intelligent face entered. His eyes had a dark, bemused look, and he carried a syringe in one hand.

'How are we today, Mr President?' he asked politely.

Strangely, the words were foreign, but the President understood them perfectly. Then he heard himself shouting repeatedly, 'I am Yuri Belkaya, I am not the President of the United States, I am Yuri — ' he broke off as the intruder plunged the needle into his arm.

The bemused expression never left the little man's face; it might have been glued there. He nodded towards the doorway and another man wearing a drab prison uniform came in and set a cassette recorder on a spartan metal table that was bolted to the floor. He wired the recorder to four small eyelets on the table's surface and left.

'So you won't knock your new lesson on the floor, Mr President,' said the thin man. 'I hope you find it interesting.' Then he switched on the recorder and exited from the room.

The President struggled to shake off the bewildering terror of the nightmare. Yet it all seemed too real to be a dream fantasy. He could smell his own sweat, feel the hurt as the straps chafed his skin, hear the walls echo with his cries of frustration. His head sagged to his chest and he began to sob uncontrollably as the recorded message droned over and over. When at last he sufficiently recovered, he raised his head as if lifting a ponderous weight and looked around.

He was seated in his White House study.

Secretary Oates took Dan Fawcett's call on his private line. 'What's the situation over there?' he asked without wasting words.

'Critical,' Fawcett replied. 'Armed guards everywhere. I haven't seen this many troops since I was with the Fifth Marine Regiment in Korea.'

'And the President?'

'Spitting out directives like a gatling gun. He won't listen to advice from his aides any longer, myself included. He's getting increasingly harder to reach. Two weeks ago, he'd give full attention to opposing viewpoints or objective comments. No more. You agree with him or you're out of the door. Megan Blair and I are the only ones still with access to his office, and my days are numbered. I'm bailing out before the roof caves in.'

'Stay put,' said Oates. 'It's best for all concerned if you and Oscar

258

Lucas remain close to the President. You're the only open line of communications any of us have into the White House.'

'Won't work.'

'Why?'

'I told you, even if I stick around, I'll be closed out. My name is rapidly climbing to the top of the President's shit list.'

'Then get back in his good graces,' ordered Oates. 'Crawl up his butt and support whatever he says. Play yes-man and relay up-to-the-minute reports on every course of action he takes.'

There was a long pause. 'Okay, I'll do my best to keep you informed.'

'And alert Oscar Lucas to stand by; we're going to need him.'

'Can I ask what's going down?'

'Not yet,' Oates replied tersely.

Fawcett didn't press him. He switched tack. 'You want to hear the President's latest brainstorm?'

'Bad?'

'Very bad,' admitted Fawcett. 'He intends to withdraw our military forces from the NATO alliance.'

'Good lord!' Oates gasped. 'Is he set on this?'

'As dead set as a freight train hurtling down the Rockies with no brakes. He's already ordered the Pentagon to draw up plans for a slow withdrawal under the guise of troop rotation and replacement of worn and obsolete hardware.'

'Who's he trying to fool?' Oates demanded angrily. 'The leaders of our European Allies will be onto him before the first plane load of soldiers takes off for the States.'

'I tried to act as your devil's advocate, Mr Secretary,' said Fawcett, 'pleading your case and strongly advising him to consult with you and the State Department, but he brushed me off and said he'd handle it in his own way. I'm afraid this latest act will shake whatever confidence the people have in him.'

Oates clutched the phone until his knuckles turned ivory. 'He's got to be stopped,' he said grimly.

Fawcett's voice sounded far away. 'The President and I go back a long way together, but in the best interests of the country, I must agree.'

'Stay in touch.'

Oates put down the phone, turned in his desk chair and gazed out the window lost in thought. The afternoon sky had turned an ominous grey and a light rain began to fall on Washington's streets, their slickened surface reflecting the Federal buildings in eerie distortions.

In the end he would have to take over the reins of government,

Oates thought bitterly. He was well aware that every President in the last thirty years had been vilified and debased by events beyond their control. Eisenhower was the last Chief Executive who left the White House as venerated as when he entered. No matter how saintly or intellectually brilliant the next President, he would be stoned by an immovable bureaucracy and an increasingly hostile news media, and Oates held no desire to be a target of the rock throwers.

He was pulled out of his reverie by the muted buzz of his intercom. 'Mr Brogan and another gentlemen to see you.'

'Send them in,' Oates directed. He rose and came around his desk as Brogan entered. They shook hands briefly and Brogan introduced the man standing beside him as Dr Raymond Edgely.

Oates correctly pegged Edgely as an academic. The old fashioned crew-cut and bow tie suggested someone who seldom strayed from a university campus. Edgely was slender, wore a scraggly, barbed wire beard and bristly dark eyebrows that were untrimmed and brushed upwards in a Mephistopheles set and blow.

'Dr Edgely is the Director of "*Fathom*",' Brogan explained, 'the agency's special study into mind control techniques at Raton University in Colorado.'

Oates gestured for them to sit on a sofa and took a chair across a marble coffee table. 'I've just received a call from Dan Fawcett. The President intends to withdraw our troops from NATO.'

'Another piece of evidence to bolster our case,' said Brogan. 'Only the Russians would benefit from such a move.'

Oates turned to Edgely. 'Has Martin explained our suspicions regarding the President's behaviour to you?'

'Yes, Mr Brogan has filled me in.'

'And how does the situation strike you? Has the President been mentally forced to become an involuntary traitor?'

'I grant the President's actions demonstrate a dramatic personality change, but unless we can put him through a series of tests, there is no way of being certain of brain alteration or exterior domination.'

'He will never consent to an examination,' said Brogan.

'That presents a problem,' said Edgely.

'Suppose you tell us, Doctor,' asked Oates, 'how the President's mind transfer was performed?'

'If that is indeed what we are faced with,' replied Edgely, 'the first step is to isolate the subject in a womb-like chamber for a given length of time, removed from all sensory influences. During this sequence his brain patterns are studied, analysed and deciphered into a language that can be programmed and translated by computer. The next step is to design an implant, in this instance a microchip, with the desired data and then insert it by psychosurgery into the subject's brain.'

260

'You make it sound as elementary as a tonsillectomy,' said Oates.

Edgely laughed. 'I've condensed and oversimplified, of course, but in reality the procedures are incredibly delicate and involved.'

'After the microchip is embedded into the brain, what then?'

'I should have mentioned that a section of the implant is a tiny transmitter/receiver which operates off the electrical impulses of the brain and is capable of sending thought patterns and other bodily functions to a central computer and monitoring post located as far away as Hong Kong.'

'Or Moscow,' added Brogan.

'And not the Soviet embassy here in Washington, as you suggested earlier?' Oates asked, looking at Brogan.

'I think I can answer that,' offered Edgely. 'The communication technology is certainly available to relay data from a subject via satellite to Russia, but if I were in Dr Lugovoy's shoes, I'd set up my monitoring station nearby so I could observe the results of the President's actions at first hand. This would also allow me a faster response time to redirect my command signals to his mind during unexpected political events.'

'Can Lugovoy lose control over the President?' asked Brogan.

'If the President ceases to think and act for himself, he breaks the ties to his normal world. Then he may tend to stray from Lugovoy's instructions and carry them to extremes.'

'Is this why he's instigated so many radical programmes in such haste?'

'I can't say,' answered Edgely. 'For all I know he is responding precisely to Lugovoy's commands. I do suspect, however, that it goes far deeper.'

'In what manner?'

'The reports supplied by Mr Brogan's operatives in Russia show that Lugovoy has attempted experiments with political prisoners, transferring the fluid from their hippocampus – a structure in the brain's limbic system that holds our memories – to those of other subjects.'

'A memory injection,' Oates murmured wonderingly. 'So there really is a Dr Frankenstein.'

'Memory transfer is a tricky business,' Edgely continued. 'There is no predicting with any certainty the end results.'

'Do you think Lugovoy performed this experiment on the President?'

'I hate to say yes, but if he runs true to form, he might very well have programmed some poor Russian prisoner for months, even years, with thoughts promoting Soviet policy, and then transplanted the hippocampal fluid into the President's brain as a back up to the implant.'

261

'Under the proper care,' asked Oates, 'could the President return to normal?'

'You mean put his mind back as it was before?'

'Something like that.'

Edgely shook his head. 'Any known treatment will not reverse the damage. The President will always be haunted by the memory of someone else.'

'Couldn't you extract his hippocampal fluid as well?'

'I catch your meaning, but by removing the foreign thought patterns, we'd be erasing the President's own memories.' Edgely paused. 'No, I'm sorry to say, the President's behaviour patterns have been irrevocably altered.'

'Then he should be removed from office . . . permanently.'

'That would be my recommendation,' answered Edgely without hesitation.

Oates sat back in his chair and clasped his hands behind his head. 'Thank you, Doctor, you've reinforced our resolve.'

'From what I've heard, no one gets through the White House gates.'

'If the Russians could abduct him,' said Brogan, 'I see no reason why we can't do the same. But first we have to disconnect him from Lugovoy.'

'May I make a suggestion?'

'Please,' Oates replied.

'There is an excellent opportunity to turn this situation around to our advantage.'

'How?'

'Rather than cut off his brain signals, why not tune in on the frequency?'

'For what purpose?'

'So my staff and I can feed the transmissions into our own monitoring equipment. If our computers can receive enough data, say within a forty-eight hour period, we can take the place of the President's brain.'

'A substitution to feed the Russians false information,' said Brogan rising to Edgely's inspiration.

'Exactly!' Edgely exclaimed. 'Because they have every reason to believe the validity of the data they receive from the President, Soviet intelligence can be led down whichever garden path you choose.'

'I like the idea,' said Oates. 'But the stickler is whether we can afford the forty-eight hours. There's no telling what the President might attempt within that time frame.'

'The risk is worth it,' Brogan stated flatly.

There was a knock on the door and Oates' secretary leaned her head into the room. 'Sorry to interrupt, Mr Secretary, but Mr Brogan has an urgent call.'

Brogan got up quickly, lifted the phone on Oates' desk and pressed the winking button. 'Brogan.'

He stood there listening for close to a full minute without speaking. Then he hung up and faced Oates.

'Speaker of the House, Alan Moran just turned up alive at our Guantanamo Bay Naval Base in Cuba,' he said slowly.

'Margolin?'

'No report.'

'Larimer?'

'Senator Larimer is dead.'

'Oh good God!' Oates moaned. 'That means Moran could be our next President. I can't think of a more unscrupulous or ill-equipped individual to man the helm of government.'

'A Fagan poised at the White House gate,' commented Brogan. 'Not a pleasant thought.'

60

Pitt was certain he was dead. There was no reason why he shouldn't be dead. And yet, he saw no blinding light at the end of a tunnel, no faces of friends and relatives who had died before him. He felt as though he was dozing in his own bed at home. And Loren was there, her hair cascading on the pillow, her body pressed against his, her arms encircling his neck, holding tightly, refusing to let him drift away. Her face seemed to glow, and her violet eyes looked straight into his. He wondered if she was dead too.

Suddenly she released her hold, and began to blur, moving away, diminishing ever smaller until she vanished altogether. A dim light filtered through his closed eyelids and he heard voices in the distance. Slowly, with an effort as great as lifting a pair of hundred pound weights, he opened his eyes. At first he thought he was gazing at a flat white surface. Then as his mind crept past the veil of unconsciousness he realised he really was gazing at a flat white surface.

It was a ceiling.

A strange voice said, 'He's coming around.'

'Takes more than three cracked ribs, a skull concussion and a gallon of seawater to do this character in.' There was no mistaking this laconic voice.

'My worst fears,' Pitt managed to mutter. 'I've gone to hell and met the devil.'

'See how he talks about his best and only friend,' said Al Giordino to a doctor in naval uniform.

'He's in good physical shape,' said the doctor. 'He should mend pretty quickly.'

'Pardon the mundane question,' said Pitt, 'but where am I?'

'Welcome to the US Naval Hospital at Guantanamo Bay, Cuba,' the doctor answered. 'You and Mr Giordino were fished out of the water by one of our recovery craft.'

Pitt focused his eyes on Giordino. 'Are you all right?'

'He has a bruise the size of a cantaloupe on his abdomen, but he'll survive,' the doctor said smiling. 'By the way, I understand he saved your life.'

Pitt cleared the mist from his mind and tried to recall. 'The steward from the *Leonid Andreyev* was playing baseball with my head . . .'

'Pounded you under the boat with an oar,' Giordino explained. 'I slipped over the side, swam underwater until I grabbed your arm, and dragged you to the surface. The steward would have pounded me too except for the timely arrival of a navy helicopter whose paramedics jumped into the water and helped sling us on board.'

'And Loren?'

Giordino averted his gaze. 'She's listed as missing.'

'Missing, hell!' Pitt snarled. He grimaced from the sudden pain in his chest as he rose to his elbows. 'We both know she was alive and sitting in the lifeboat.'

A solemn look clouded Giordino's face. 'Her name didn't appear on a list of survivors given out by the container ship's captain.'

'A Bougainville ship!' Pitt blurted as his memory came flooding back. 'The Oriental steward who tried to brain us pointed towards the . . .'

'*Chalmette*,' Giordino prompted.

'Yes, the *Chalmette*, and said it belonged to him. He also spoke my name.'

'Stewards are supposed to remember passengers' names. He knew you as Charlie Gruber in cabin 34.'

'No, he rightly accused me of meddling in Bougainville affairs, and his last words were, "Bon voyage, Dirk Pitt".'

Giordino gave a puzzled shrug. 'Beats hell out of me how he knew you. But why would a Bougainville man work as a steward on a Russian cruise ship?'

'I can't begin to guess.'

'And lie about Loren's rescue?'

Pitt merely gave an imperceptible shake of his head.

264

'Then she's being held prisoner by the Bougainvilles,' said Giordino as if suddenly enlightened. 'But for what motive?'

'You keep asking questions I can't answer,' Pitt said irritably. 'Where is the *Chalmette* now?'

'Headed towards Miami to land the survivors.'

'How long have I been unconscious?'

'About thirty-two hours,' replied the doctor.

'Still time,' said Pitt. 'The *Chalmette* won't reach the Florida coast for several hours yet.'

He raised himself to a sitting position and swung his legs over the side of the bed. The room began to seesaw back and forth, and his chest and head felt as if they had a contest going to see which could provide the most torment.

The doctor moved forward and steadied him by both arms. 'I hope you don't think you're rushing off somewhere.'

'I intend to be standing on the dock when the *Chalmette* arrives in Miami,' Pitt said implacably.

A stern medical profession look grew on the doctor's face. 'You're staying in this bed for the next four days. You can't travel around with those fractured ribs, and we don't know how serious your concussion is.'

'Sorry Doc,' said Giordino, 'but you've both been overruled.'

Pitt stared at him stonily. 'Who's to stop me?'

'Admiral Sandecker, for one, Secretary of State Doug Oates for another,' answered Giordino as detachedly as though he was reading aloud the stock market quotes for the day. 'Orders came down for you to fly to Washington the minute you came out of your coma. We may be in big trouble. I have a hunch we dipped into the wrong cookie jar when we discovered Congressman Moran and Senator Larimer imprisoned on a Soviet vessel.'

'They can wait until I search the *Chalmette* for Loren.'

'My job. You go to the Capitol while I go to Miami and play customs inspector. It's all been arranged.'

Pacified to a small degree, Pitt relaxed on the bed. 'What about Moran? I recall seeing him rescued.'

'He couldn't wait to cut out,' Giordino said angrily. 'He arrogantly demanded the Navy drop everything and fly him home the minute he was brought ashore. I had a minor confrontation with him in the hospital corridor after his routine examination. Came within a millimetre of cramming his hook nose down his gullet. The bastard didn't demonstrate the slightest concern about Loren, and he seemed downright delighted when I told him of Larimer's death.'

'He has a talent for deserting those who help him,' Pitt said disgustedly.

265

An orderly rolled in a wheelchair and together with Giordino eased Pitt into it. A small groan escaped his lips as a piercing pain ripped through his chest.

'You're leaving against my express wishes,' said the doctor. 'I want that understood. There is no guarantee you won't have complications if you overtax yourself.'

'I release you from all indemnity, Doc,' Pitt said smiling. 'I won't tell a soul I was your patient. Your medical reputation is secure.'

Giordino laid a pile of Navy issue clothing and a small paper sack in Pitt's lap. 'Here's some presentable clothes and the stuff from your pockets. You can dress on the plane to save time.'

Pitt opened the sack and fingered a vinyl pouch inside. Satisfied the contents were secure and dry, he looked up at Giordino and shook hands. 'Good hunting, friend.'

Giordino patted him on the shoulder. 'Don't worry, I'll find her. You go on to Washington and give 'em hell.'

No one could have suffered from a Rip Van Winkle syndrome and awakened more surprised than Alan Moran. He remembered going to sleep on the presidential yacht almost two weeks earlier, and his next conscious sensation was being dragged into a limousine somewhere in the river country of South Carolina. The imprisonment and escape from the burning Russian cruise ship seemed a distorted blur. Only when he returned to Washington and found both Congress and the Supreme Court evicted from their hallowed halls did he come back on track and retrieve his mantle of political power.

With the government in emotional and political turmoil, he saw his chance to fulfill the deep, unfathomable ambition to become president. Not having the popular support to take the office by election, he was determined now to grab it by default. With Margolin missing, Larimer out of the way, and the President laid open for impeachment there was little to stop him.

Moran held court in the middle of Jackson Square across Pennsylvania Avenue from the White House and answered questions fired by a battery of correspondents. He was the man of the hour and was enjoying every second of the attention.

'Can you tell us where you've been the last two weeks?' asked Ray Marsh of the *New York Times*.

'Be glad to,' Moran replied gracefully. 'Senate Majority Leader, Marcus Larimer and I went on a fishing holiday in the Caribbean, partly to try our luck at snagging a record marlin, mostly to discuss the issues facing our great nation.'

'Initial reports state that Senator Larimer died during the *Leonid Andreyev* tragedy.'

'I'm deeply saddened to say that is true,' said Moran, abruptly becoming solemn. 'The Senator and I were trolling only five or six miles away from the Russian cruise ship when we heard and observed an explosion that covered her in fire and smoke. We immediately ordered our skipper to change course for the disaster area. When we arrived, the *Leonid Andreyev* was ablaze from stem to stern. Hundreds of frightened passengers were tumbling into the sea, many with their clothes in flames.' Moran paused for effect, and then enunciated in a vivid, descriptive tone. 'I leaped into the water, followed by the Senator, to help those who were badly injured or unable to swim. We struggled for what seemed like hours, keeping women and children afloat until we could lift them into our fishing boat. I lost track of Senator Larimer. When I looked for him, he was floating face down, an apparent victim of a heart attack due to over-exertion. You can quote me as saying he died a real hero.'

'How many people do you reckon you saved?' This from Joe Stark of the United Press.

'I lost count,' answered Moran, serenely pitching out the lies. 'Our small vessel became dangerously overloaded with burned and half drowned victims. So rather than become the straw that might capsize it, so to speak, I remained in the water so one more pitiful creature could cheat death. Luckily for me, I was picked up by the Navy, who performed magnificently.'

'Were you aware that Congresswoman Loren Smith was travelling on the *Leonid Andreyev*?' asked Marion Tournier of the Associated Press Radio Network.

'Not at the time,' replied Moran changing back to his solemn demeanour again. 'Regretfully, I've only just been informed that she's reported as missing.'

Curtis Mayo signalled his cameraman and edged closer to Moran. 'Congressman, what is your feeling regarding the President's unprecedented closing of Congress?'

'Deeply mortified that such an arrogant deed could take place in our government. It's obvious the President has taken leave of his senses. With one terrible blow, he has swept our nation from a democracy into a fascist state. I fully intend to see that he is removed from office, the sooner, the better.'

'How do you propose to do it?' Mayo pushed him. 'Every time the House and Senate members congregate to launch impeachment proceedings, the President sends in troops to disband them.'

'The story will be different this time,' Moran said confidently. 'Tomorrow morning at ten o'clock, members of Congress will hold a joint session in Lisner Auditorium at George Washington University. And in order to meet without interference or disruption by the

President's unauthorised and immoral use of the military, we intend to confront force with force. I have conferred with my House and Senate colleagues from the neighbouring states of Maryland and Virginia who have prevailed upon their governors to protect our constitutional right to assemble by providing troops from their National Guard units.'

'Will they have orders to shoot?' asked Mayo, smelling newsworthy blood.

'If attacked,' Moran replied coldly, 'the answer is an absolute yes.'

'And so Civil War Two erupts,' said Oates wearily as he switched off the TV set and turned to face Emmett, Mercier and Brogan.

'Moran is as daft as the President,' Emmett said, shaking his head in disgust.

'I pity the American public for being forced to accept such miserable leadership material,' Mercier grumbled.

'How do you read the upcoming confrontation at Lisner Auditorium?' Oates asked Emmett.

'The special forces of Army and Marines patrolling Capitol Hill are highly trained professionals. They can be counted on to stand firm and not attempt anything stupid. The National Guard is the real danger. All it takes is one weekend warrior to panic and fire off a round. Then we'll witness another Kent State University bloodbath, except much worse. This time the Guard will have their fire returned by deadly marksmen.'

'The situation won't be helped if a few Congressmen fall in the crossfire,' added Mercier.

'The President must be put on the shelf. The timetable must be moved up,' said Oates.

Mercier looked unsold. 'That means cutting back Dr Edgely's evaluation of the President's brain signals.'

'Preventing wholesale slaughter must take priority over a plan to mislead the Russians,' said Oates.

Brogan gazed at the ceiling thoughtfully. 'I think we might steal our chicken and pluck it too.'

Oates smiled. 'I hear the gears meshing in your head, Martin. What wild Machiavellian scheme has the CIA got up its sleeve now?'

'A way to give Edgely an advantage,' answered Brogan with a fox-like grin. 'A little something borrowed from the "Twilight Zone".'

268

61

A limousine was waiting at Andrews Air Force Base when Pitt slowly eased his way down the boarding stairs from a Navy passenger jet. Admiral Sandecker was sitting in the car, hidden by the tinted windows.

He opened the door and helped Pitt inside. 'How was the flight?'

'Thankfully, it was smooth.'

'Do you have any luggage?'

'I'm wearing it,' said Pitt. He winced and clenched his teeth as he slipped into the seat beside the Admiral.

'You in much pain?'

'A little stiff. They don't tape cracked ribs like they did in the old days. Just let them heal on their own.'

Sandecker knew Pitt could be suffering agonised torment but never admit it. 'Sorry I insisted on your return in mad haste, but things in Washington are boiling up a storm, and Doug Oates is hoping you possess information that might clear up a few entanglements.'

'I understand,' said Pitt. 'Has there been any news of Loren?'

'Nothing, I'm afraid.'

'She's alive,' said Pitt, staring out of the window.

'I don't doubt it,' Sandecker concurred. 'Probably an oversight her name isn't on the survivor list. Maybe she requested anonymity to avoid the press.'

'Loren had no reason to hide.'

'She'll turn up,' said Sandecker. 'Now, suppose you tell me how you managed to be present at the worst maritime tragedy in fifty years.'

Pitt marvelled at how the Admiral could twist a conversation in another direction with the abruptness of leaping from a sauna into the snow.

'In the brief time we had together on the *Leonid Andreyev*,' Pitt began, 'Loren told me she was strolling the deck on the first night of the cruise when the lights around the exterior of the ship went out, followed by the landing of a helicopter. Three passengers were taken off, two of them roughly handled. Loren thought she recognised one of them in the dim light as Alan Moran. Not certain whether her eyes were playing tricks, she called her aide, Sally Lindemann, over ship-to-shore phone and asked her to locate Moran's whereabouts. Sally turned up false trails covered over by vague reports and no Moran.

She also discovered he and Marcus Larimer were supposed to be together. She then related the negative results to Loren, who told her to contact me. But the call was cut off. The Russians, with their usual love for information gathering had monitored her calls and learned she'd accidentally stumbled into the middle of a delicate operation.'

'So they made her a prisoner along with her Congressional pals who were on a one way trip to Moscow.'

'Except that Loren was more risk than an asset. She was to be conveniently lost overboard.'

'And after Lindemann contacted you?' Sandecker probed.

'Al Giordino and I drew up a plan and flew south, catching up with the ship in San Salvador and boarding there.'

'Over two hundred people died on the *Leonid Andreyev*. You're lucky to be alive.'

'Yes,' Pitt said meditatively. 'It was a near thing.'

He went quiet, his mind's eye seeing only a face. The face of the steward who stood in the lifeboat, leering down at him with the look of a man who enjoyed his work; a murderer without a shred of remorse, the oar raised above his head.

'In case you're interested,' said Sandecker, breaking the spell, 'we're going to the State Department. Secretary Oates wants to know what happened down there in the Caribbean and what you think *you* know.'

'Make a detour by the *Washington Post*,' Pitt said abruptly.

Sandecker gave him a negative look. 'We can't spare the time to buy a newspaper.'

'If Oates wants to hear what I've got, he'll damn well have to wait.'

Sandecker made a sour expression and gave in. 'Ten minutes is all you get. I'll call Oates and say your plane was delayed.'

Pitt had met the Secretary of State previously, during the North American Treaty affair. The neatly trimmed hair was slate coloured, and the brown eyes moved with practised ease as they read Pitt. Oates wore a five hundred dollar grey tailored suit and highly polished black lace shoes. There was a no-nonsense aggressiveness about him, and he moved well, almost like a track and field athelete.

'Mr Pitt, how nice to see you again.'

'Good to see you, Mr Secretary.'

Oates wrung Pitt's hand, then turned to the other men in the conference room and went through the introductions. The inner sanctum had turned out. Brogan of the CIA, Emmett of the FBI, National Security's Alan Mercier, whom Pitt also knew, and Dan Fawcett representing the White House. Admiral Sandecker remained at Pitt's side, keeping a wary eye on his physical condition.

270

'Please sit down,' said Oates, waving them all to chairs.

Sam Emmett turned towards Pitt and regarded him with interest, noting the drawn lines in his face. 'I've taken the liberty of reading your file, Mr Pitt, and I must confess your service with the government reads like a novel.' He paused to scan the dossier. 'Directly responsible for saving innumerable lives during the Vixen operation. Instrumental in obtaining the Canadian merger treaty. Heading the project to raise the *Titanic* with subsequent discovery of a rare element for the Sicilian Project. You have an uncanny knack for getting around.'

'I believe the word is ubiquitous,' injected Oates.

'You were in the Air Force before joining NUMA,' Emmett continued. 'Rank of major. Excellent record in Vietnam.' He hesitated, a strange inquisitive look growing on his face. 'I see here you received a commendation for destroying one of our own aircraft.'

'Perhaps I should explain that,' said Sandecker, 'since I was on the aircraft Dirk shot down.'

'I realise we're pressed for time, but I'd be interested in hearing that tale,' said Oates.

Sandecker nodded agreeably. 'My staff and I were flying on a twin turbo prop transport from Saigon to a small coastal port north of Da Nang. Unknown to us, the field we were supposed to land on was overrun by North Vietnamese regulars. Our radio malfunctioned and my pilot was unable to receive the warning. Dirk was flying nearby, returning to his base from a bombing mission. The local commander directed him to intercept and alert us by whatever means available.' Sandecker looked over at Pitt and smiled. 'I have to say he tried everything short of holding up a neon sign. He played charades from his cockpit, fired several bursts from his guns across our nose, but nothing penetrated our thick skulls. When we were on our final landing approach, coming in from the sea towards the airstrip, in what has to be a rare exhibition of precision aerial marksmanship, he shot out both our engines, forcing my pilot to ditch our plane in the water only one mile from shore. Dirk then flew cover, strafing enemy boats putting out from the beach, until everyone was taken aboard a Navy patrol vessel. After learning that he saved me from certain imprisonment and possible death, we became good friends. Several years later, when President Ford asked me to launch NUMA, I persuaded Dirk to join me.'

Oates looked at Pitt through bemused eyes. 'You lead an interesting life. I envy you.'

Before Pitt could reply, Alan Mercier said, 'I'm sure Mr Pitt is curious why we asked him here.'

'I'm quite aware of the reason,' said Pitt.

271

He looked from man to man. None of them looked as if they'd slept in a month. There was a heavy trace of tenseness in their eyes. At last he addressed himself directly to Oates.

'I know who was responsible for the theft and subsequent spill of Nerve Agent S into the Gulf of Alaska which killed hundreds of unsuspecting people,' he said, speaking slowly and distinctly. 'I know who committed nearly thirty murders while hijacking the presidential yacht and its passengers. I know the identities of those passengers and why they were abducted. And lastly I know who sabotaged the *Leonid Andreyev*, killing two hundred men, women and children. There is no speculation or guesswork on my part. The facts and evidence are rock solid.'

The room took on an almost deathly stillness. No one made even the slightest attempt to speak. Pitt's statement had stunned them down to the soles of their feet. Emmett had a distraught expression on his face. Fawcett clasped his hands to conceal his nervousness. Oates appeared dazed.

Brogan was the first to question Pitt. 'I must assume, Mr Pitt, you're alluding to the Russians?'

'No, sir, I am not.'

'No chance you're mistaken?' asked Mercier.

'None.'

'If not the Russians,' asked Emmett in a cautious voice, 'then who?'

'The head of the Bougainville Shipping empire, Min Koryo and her grandson, Lee Tong.'

'I happen to know Lee Tong Bougainville personally,' said Emmett. 'He is a respected business executive who donates heavily to political campaigns.'

'So does the Mafia and every charlatan who's out to milk the government money machine,' said Pitt icily. He laid a photograph on the table. 'I borrowed this from the morgue file of the *Washington Post*. Do you recognise the man, Mr Emmett, who is coming through the door in the picture?'

Emmett picked up the photograph and examined it. 'Lee Tong Bougainville,' he said. 'Not a good likeness, but one of the few photos I've ever seen of him. He avoids publicity like herpes. You're making a grave error, Mr Pitt, of accusing him of any crime.'

'No error,' Pitt said firmly. 'This man tried to kill me. I have reason to believe he is accountable for the explosion that burned and sank the *Leonid Andreyev*, and the kidnapping of Congresswoman Loren Smith.'

'Congresswoman Smith's kidnapping is pure conjecture on your part.'

'Didn't Congressman Moran explain what occurred on board the ship?' Pitt asked.

'He refuses to be questioned by us,' answered Mercier. 'All we know is what he told the press.'

Emmett was becoming angry. He saw Pitt's revelations as an indictment against FBI fumbling. He leaned across the table with fire in his eyes.

'Do you honestly expect us to believe your ridiculous fairytales?' he demanded in a cracking voice.

'I don't much care what you believe,' Pitt replied, pinning the FBI Director with his stare.

'Can you say how you collared the Bougainvilles?' asked Oates.

'My involvement stems from the death of a friend by Nerve Agent S. I began a hunt for the responsible parties, I admit, purely for revenge. As my investigations gradually centred on Bougainville Maritime, other avenues of their illicit organisation suddenly unfolded.'

'And you can prove your accusations?'

'Of course,' answered Pitt. 'Computer data describing their hijacking activities, drug business and smuggling operations is in a safe at NUMA.'

Brogan held up a hand. 'Wait one moment. You stated the Bougainvilles were also behind the hijacking of the *Eagle*?'

'I did.'

'And you know who they abducted?'

'I do.'

'Not possible,' Brogan stated flatly.

'Shall I name names, gentlemen?' said Pitt. 'Let's begin with the President, then Vice President Margolin, Senator Larimer and House Speaker Moran. I was with Larimer when he died. Margolin is still alive and held somewhere by the Bougainvilles. Moran is now here in Washington, no doubt conspiring to become the next messiah. The President sits in the White House immune to the political disaster he's causing, while his brain is wired to the apron strings of a Soviet psychologist whose name is Dr Aleksei Lugovoy.'

If Oates and the others sat stunned before, they looked positively petrified now. Brogan appeared as though he'd just consumed a bottle of Tabasco sauce.

'You couldn't know all that!' he gasped.

'Quite obviously, I do,' said Pitt calmly.

'My God, how?' demanded Oates.

'A few hours prior to the holocaust on the *Leonid Andreyev*, I killed a KGB agent by the name of Paul Suvorov. He was carrying a notebook which I borrowed. The pages describe the events after the President was abducted from the *Eagle*.'

273

Pitt took the tobacco pouch from under his shirt, opened it, and casually tossed the notebook on the table.

It lay there for several moments until Oates finally reached over and pulled it toward him slowly, as if it might bite his hand. Then he thumbed through the pages.

'That's odd,' he said after a lapse. 'The writing is in English. I would have expected some sort of Russian worded code.'

'Not so strange,' said Brogan. 'A good operative will write in the language of the country he's assigned. What is unusual is that this Suvorov took notes at all. I can only assume he was keeping an eye on Lugovoy, and the mind control project was too technical for him to commit to memory so he recorded his observations.'

'Mr Pitt,' addressed Fawcett. 'Do you have enough evidence for the Justice Department to indict Min Koryo Bougainville?'

'Indict yes, convict no,' Pitt answered. 'The government will never put an eighty-six-year-old woman as rich and powerful as Min Koryo behind bars. And if she thought her chances were on the down side, she'd skip the country and move her operations elsewhere.'

'Considering her crimes,' mused Fawcett, 'extradition shouldn't be too tough to negotiate.'

'Min Koryo has strong ties with the North Koreans,' said Pitt. 'If she goes there, you'll never see her stand trial.'

Emmett considered that, and said stonily, 'I think we can take over at this point.' Then he turned to Sandecker as if dismissing Pitt. 'Admiral, can you arrange to have Mr Pitt available for further questioning, and supply us with the computer data he's accumulated on the Bougainvilles?'

'You can bank on full cooperation from NUMA,' Sandecker said. Then he added caustically. 'Always glad to help the FBI off a reef.'

'That's settled,' said Oates, stepping in as referee. 'Mr Pitt, do you have any idea where they might be holding Vice President Margolin?'

'No, sir. I don't think Suvorov did either. According to his notes, after he escaped from Lugovoy's laboratory, he flew over the area in a helicopter but failed to pinpoint the location or building. The only reference he mentions is a river south of Charleston, South Carolina.'

Oates looked from Emmett to Brogan to Mercier. 'Well, gentlemen, we have a starting point.'

'I think we owe a round of thanks to Mr Pitt,' said Fawcett.

'Yes, indeed,' said Mercier. 'You've been most helpful.'

Christ! Pitt thought to himself. They're beginning to sound like the Chamber of Commerce expressing their gratitude to a streetcleaner who followed a parade.

'That's all there is?' he asked.

'For the moment,' replied Oates.

'What about Loren Smith and Vince Margolin?'

'We'll see to their safety,' said Emmett coldly.

Pitt awkwardly struggled to his feet. Sandecker came over and took his arm. Then Pitt placed his hands on the table and leaned toward Emmett, his stare enough to wither cactus.

'You better,' he said with a voice like steel. 'You damned well better.'

62

As the *Chalmette* steamed towards Florida, communications became hectic. Frantic inquiries flooded the ship's radio room, and the Koreans found it impossible to comply. They finally gave up and supplied only the names of the survivors on board. All entreaties by the news media demanding detailed information on the *Leonid Andreyev's* sinking went unanswered.

Friends and relatives of the passengers, frantic with anxiety, began collecting at the Russian cruise line offices. Here and there around the country flags were flown at halfmast. The tragedy was a subject of conversation in every home as newspapers and television networks temporarily swept the President's closing of Congress out of the limelight and devoted special editions and newscasts covering the disaster.

The Navy began airlifting the people their rescue operation had pulled from the water, flying them to naval air stations and hospitals nearest their homes. These were the first to be interviewed, and their conflicting stories blamed the explosion on everything from a floating mine of World War Two, to a cargo of weapons and munitions being smuggled by the Russians into Central America.

The Soviet diplomatic missions across the United States reacted badly by accusing the US Navy of carelessly launching a missile at the *Leonid Andreyev*; a charge that had good play in the Eastern Bloc countries but was generally shrugged off elsewhere as a crude propaganda ploy.

The excitement rose to a crescendo over a human interest story not seen since the sinking of the *Andrea Doria* in 1956. The continued silence from the *Chalmette* infuriated the reporters and correspondents. There was a mad rush to charter boats, aeroplanes and helicopters to meet the ship as she neared the coastline. Fuelled by the Korean captain's silence, speculation ran rampant as the tension built. Investigations into the cause were being demanded by every politician who could contrive at an interview.

The *Chalmette* remained obstinate to the end. As she entered the main channel she was surrounded by a wolfpack of buzzing aircraft and circling pleasure yachts and fishing boats, crawling with reporters blasting questions through bullhorns. To their utter frustration, the Korean seamen simply waved and shouted back in their native tongue.

Slowly approaching the docking terminal at Dodge Island in the Port of Miami, the *Chalmette* was greeted by a massive crowd of over a hundred thousand people, surging against a police cordon blocking the entrance to the pier. A hundred video and film cameras recorded the scene as the giant container ship's mooring lines were dropped over rusting bollards, gangways were rolled against the hull, and the survivors stood at the railings, astounded at the turn-out.

Some appeared joyous to see dry land once again, others displayed solemn grief for husbands or wives, sons or daughters, they would never see again. A great hush suddenly fell over the mass of spectators. It was later described by an anchorman on the evening TV news as, 'the silence one experiences at the lowering of a coffin into the ground'.

Unnoticed in the drama, a host of FBI agents dressed in the uniforms of immigration officials and customs inspectors swarmed aboard the ship, confirming the identities of the surviving passengers and crewmen of the *Leonid Andreyev*, interrogating each on the whereabouts of Congresswoman Smith, and searching every foot of the ship for any sign of her.

Al Giordino questioned the people whose faces he recalled seeing in the lifeboat. None of them could remember what happened to Loren or the Oriental steward after climbing aboard the *Chalmette*. One woman thought she saw them led away by the ship's captain, but she couldn't be sure. To many of those who narrowly escaped death, their minds conveniently blanked out much of the catastrophe.

The captain and his crew claimed to know nothing. Photos of Loren provoked no recognition. Interpreters interrogated them in Korean, but their stories were the same. They never saw her. Six hours of in depth search turned up nothing. At last the reporters were allowed to scramble on board. The crew were acknowledged heroes of the sea. The image harvested by Bougainville Maritime and their courageous employees, who braved a sea of blazing oil to save four hundred souls, was a public relations windfall, and Min Koryo made the most of it.

It was dark and raining when Giordino wearily made his way

276

across the now emptied dock and entered the customs office of the terminal. He sat at a desk for a long time staring out into the rain-soaked murk, his dark eyes mere shadows on his face.

He turned and looked at the telephone as though it were the enemy. Hyping his courage by a drink of brandy from a half-pint bottle in his coat pocket and lighting a cigar he stole from Admiral Sandecker, he dialled a number and let it ring, almost hoping no one would answer. Then a voice came on.

Giordino moistened his lips with his tongue and said, 'Forgive me, Dirk. We were too late. She was gone.'

The helicopter came in from the south and flashed on its landing lights. The pilot settled his craft into position, and then lowered it onto the roof of the World Trade Centre in Lower Manhattan. The side door dropped open and Lee Tong stepped out. He swiftly walked over to a privately guarded entrance and took a lift down to his grandmother's living quarters.

He bent down and kissed her lightly on the forehead. 'How was your day, *aumuni*?'

'Disastrous,' she said tiredly. 'Someone is sabotaging our bank records, shipping transactions, every piece of business that goes through a computer. What once was a study in efficient management procedures is now a mess.'

Lee Tong's eyes narrowed. 'Who can be doing it?'

'The trail leads to NUMA.'

'Dirk Pitt.'

'He's the prime suspect.'

'No more,' said Lee Tong reassuringly. 'Pitt is dead.'

She looked up, her aged eyes questioning. 'You know that for a fact?'

He nodded. 'Pitt was on board the *Leonid Andreyev*. An opportune stroke of luck. I watched him die.'

'Your Caribbean mission was only half favourable. Moran lives.'

'Yes, but Pitt is out of our hair and the *Leonid Andreyev* evens the score for the *Venice* and the gold.'

Min Koryo dismissed this with a gesture. 'Pitt was a nuisance, nothing more. Ships and their crews are expendable. The Christian eye-for-an-eye proverb may satisfy the vindictive soul, but never adds to a bank account. Antonov put the gold where his navy can salvage it, and he has the President while we have lost our bargaining power.'

'Vice President Margolin is still secure at the laboratory,' said Lee Tong. 'And we have an unexpected bonus in Congresswoman Loren Smith.'

'You abducted her?' she asked in surprise.

'She was also on board the cruise ship. After the sinking, I arranged to have her flown off the *Chalmette* to the laboratory.'

'She might prove useful,' Min Koryo conceded.

'Don't be disheartened, *aumuni*,' said Lee Tong. 'We are still in the game. Antonov and his KGB bedfellow, Polevoi, badly underestimated the American's pathological devotion to individual rights. Instructing the President to close Congress to increase his powers with a stupid blunder. He will be impeached and thrown out of Washington within the week.'

'Not so long as he has the backing of the Pentagon.'

Lee Tong inserted a cigarette in the long, silver holder. 'The Joint Chiefs are sitting on the fence. They can't keep the House and Senate from meeting forever.

'Once the impeachment legislation is passed, the generals and admirals won't waste any time in swinging their support to Congress and the new Chief Executive.'

'Which will be Alan Moran,' Min Koryo said as if she had a bad taste in her mouth.

'Unless we release Vincent Margolin.'

'And cut our own throat. We'd be better off making him disappear for good or arrange to have his body found floating in the Potomac River.'

'Listen, *aumuni*,' said Lee Tong, his black eyes glinting. 'We have two options. One, the laboratory, is in perfect working order. Lugovoy's data is still in the computer discs. His mind control techniques are ours for the taking. We can hire other scientists to programme Margolin's brain. This time it will not be the Russians who control the White House, but Bougainville Maritime.'

'But if Moran is sworn in as President before the brain control transfer is accomplished, Margolin will be of no use to us.'

'Option two,' said Lee Tong. 'Strike a deal with Moran to eliminate Margolin and pave his way to the White House.'

'Can he be bought?'

'Moran is a shrewd manipulator. His political power base is mortared with underhand financial dealings. Believe me, *aumuni*, Alan Moran will pay any price for the presidency.'

Min Koryo looked at her grandson with great respect. He possessed an almost mystical grasp of the abstract. She smiled faintly. Nothing excited her merchant blood more than reversing a failure into a success.

'Strike your bargain,' she said.

'I'm happy you agree.'

'You must move the laboratory facility to a safe place,' she said, her mind beginning to shift gears. 'At least until we know where we

278

stand. Government investigators will soon fit the pieces together and concentrate their search on the eastern seaboard.'

'My thoughts also,' said Lee Tong. 'I took the liberty of ordering one of our tugs to move it out of South Carolina waters to our private receiving dock.'

Min Koryo nodded. 'An excellent choice.'

'And a practical one,' he replied.

'How do we handle the Congresswoman?' Min Koryo asked.

'If she talks to the press she might bring up a number of embarrassing questions for Moran to answer about his presence on board the *Leonid Andreyev*. He'd be smart to pay for her silence also.'

'Yes, he lied himself into a hole on that incident.'

'Or, we can run her through the mind control experiment and send her back to Washington. A servant in Congress could prove a great asset.'

'But if Moran includes her in the deal?'

'Then we sink the laboratory along with Margolin and Loren Smith in a hundred fathoms of water.'

Unknown to Lee Tong and Min Koryo, their conversation was transmitted to the roof of a nearby building where a secondary reception dish relayed the radio frequency signals to a voice activated tape recorder in a dusty, vacant office several blocks away on Hudson Street.

The turn-of-the-century brick building was due to be demolished, and although most of the offices were empty, a few tenants took their sweet time about locating and moving to new quarters.

Sal Casio had the tenth floor all to himself. He squatted in this particular site because the janitorial crew never bothered to step off the lift and the window had a direct line of sight to the secondary receiver. A bed, a sleeping bag and a small electric burner was all he needed to get by, and except for the receiver/recorder, his only other piece of furniture was an old faded and torn lobby chair he'd salvaged out of a back alley rubbish bin.

He turned the lock with his master key and entered, carrying a paper sack containing the corned beef sandwich and three bottles of beer. The office was hot and stuffy, so he opened a window and stared at the lights across the river in New Jersey.

Casio performed the tedious job of surveillance automatically, welcoming the isolation that gave him a chance to let his mind run loose. He recalled the happy times of his marriage, the growing up years with his daughter, and he began to feel mellowed. His long quest for retribution had finally threaded the needle and was drawing

279

to a close. All that was left, he mused, was to write the Bougainvilles' epilogue.

He looked down at the recorder while taking a bite out of the sandwich and noted the tape had rolled during his trip to the delicatessen. Morning would be soon enough to rewind and listen to it, he decided. Also, if he was playing back the recording when voices activated the system again, the previous conversation would be erased.

Casio had no way of guessing the critical content on the tape. The decision to wait was dictated by routine procedure, but the delay was to prove terribly costly.

63

The President was sitting at a writing table in his pyjamas and bathrobe when Fawcett walked into the bedroom.

'Well, did you speak with Moran?'

Fawcett's face was grim. 'He refused to listen to any of your proposals.'

'Is that it?'

'He said you were finished as President, and nothing you could say was of any consequence. Then he threw in a few insults.'

'I want to hear them,' the President demanded sharply.

Fawcett sighed uncomfortably. 'He said your behaviour was that of a madman and that you belonged in the psycho ward. He compared you with Benedict Arnold and claimed he would see your administration wiped from the history books. After he ran through several more irrelevant slurs, he suggested you'd do the country a great service by committing suicide, thereby saving the taxpayers a long drawn out investigation and expensive trial.'

The President's face became a mask of rage. 'That snivelling little bastard thinks he's going to put me in a courtroom?'

'It's no secret, Moran is pulling out all the stops to take your place.'

'His feet are too small to fill my shoes,' the President said through tight lips, 'and his head too big to fit the job.'

'To hear him tell it, his right hand is already raised to take the oath of office,' said Fawcett. 'The proposed impeachment proceeding is only the first step in a blueprint for a transition from you to him.'

'Alan Moran will never sit in the White House,' the President said, his voice flat and hard.

'No Congressional session, no impeachment,' said Fawcett. 'But you can't keep them corralled indefinitely.'

'They can't meet until I give the word.'

'What about tomorrow morning at Lisner Auditorium?'

'The troops will break that up in short order.'

'Suppose the Virginia and Maryland National Guardsmen stand their ground?'

'For how long against veteran soldiers and marines?'

'Long enough for a great many to die,' said Fawcett.

'So what?' the President scoffed coldly. 'The longer I keep Congress in disarray, the more I can accomplish. A few deaths are a small price to pay.'

Fawcett looked at him uneasily. This was not the same man who solemnly swore during his campaign for the presidency that no American boy would be ordered to fight and die under his administration. It was all he could do to act out his role of friend and adviser. After a moment he shook his head. 'I hope you're not being overly destructive.'

'Getting cold feet, Dan?'

Fawcett felt trapped in a corner, but before he could reply, Lucas entered the room carrying a tray with cups and a teapot.

'Anyone care for some herbal tea?' he asked.

The President nodded. 'Thank you, Oscar. That was very thoughtful of you.'

'Dan?'

'Thank, I could use some.'

Lucas poured and passed out the cups, keeping one for himself. Fawcett drained his almost immediately.

'Could be warmer,' he complained.

'Sorry,' said Lucas. 'It cooled on the way up from the kitchen.'

'Tastes fine to me,' the President said, between sips. 'I don't care for liquid so hot it burns your tongue.' He paused and set the cup on the writing desk. 'Now then, where were we?'

'Discussing your new policies,' Fawcett said, deftly sidestepping out of the corner. 'Western Europe is in an uproar over your announcement to withdraw American support from the NATO alliance. The joke circulating around Embassy Row is that Antonov is planning a coming out party at the Savoy Hotel in London.'

'I don't appreciate the humour,' the President said coldly. 'President Antonov has given me his personal assurances that he will stay in his own yard.'

'I seem to remember Hitler telling Neville Chamberlain the same thing.'

The President looked as if he was going to make an angry retort, but suddenly he yawned and shook his head, fighting off a creeping drowsiness. 'No matter what anyone thinks,' he said slowly. 'I've defused the nuclear threat and that's all that matters.'

Fawcett took the cue and yawned contagiously. 'If you don't need me any more tonight, Mr President, I think I'll head for home and a soft bed.'

'Same here,' said Lucas. 'My wife and kids are beginning to wonder if I still exist.'

'Of course. I'm sorry for keeping you so late.' The President moved over to the bed, kicked off his slippers and removed his robe. 'Turn on the TV, will you, Oscar? I'd like to catch a few minutes of the twenty-four hour cable news.' Then he turned to Fawcett. 'Dan, first thing in the morning, schedule a meeting with General Metcalf. I want him to brief me on his troop movements.'

'I'll take care of it,' Fawcett assured him. 'Goodnight.'

In the lift going down to the first floor Fawcett looked at his watch. 'Two hours should do it.'

'He'll sleep like the dead and wake up sicker than a dog,' said Lucas.

'By the way, how did you manage it? I didn't see you slip anything into his tea, and yet you poured all three cups from the same pot.'

'An old magician's trick,' Lucas said laughing. 'The teapot had two interior compartments.'

The lift doors opened and they met Emmett who was standing to one side. 'Any problems?' he asked.

Fawcett shook his head. 'As smooth as glass. The President went down like a baby.'

Lucas looked at him, his eyes cautious. 'Now comes the grand finale . . . fooling the Russians.'

'He's sleeping unusually soundly tonight,' said Lugovoy.

The monitoring psychologist who drew the early morning shift nodded. 'A good sign. Less chance for Comrade Belkaya to penetrate the President's dreams.'

Lugovoy studied the display screen that recorded the President's body functions. 'Temperature up one degree. Congestion forming in the nasal passages. Appears as though our subject is coming down with either a summer cold or the flu.'

'Fascinating, we know he's been attacked by a virus before he feels it.'

'I don't think it's serious,' Lugovoy said. 'But you'd better keep a tight watch in case it develops into something that could jeopardise the project . . .'

Abruptly the green data filling the dozen screens encompassing the console faded into distorted lines and vanished into blackness.

The monitoring psychologist tensed. 'What in hell – '

Then, as quickly as the display data were wiped clean, they returned in bright, clear readings. Lugovoy quickly checked the circuit warning lights. They all read normal.

'What do you suppose that was?'

Lugovoy looked thoughtful. 'Possibly a temporary failure in the implant transmitter.'

'No indication of a malfunction.'

'An electrical interference, perhaps?'

'Of course. An atmospheric disturbance of some kind. That would explain it. The symptoms match. What else could it be?'

Lugovoy passed a weary hand across his face and stared at the monitors. 'Nothing,' he said sombrely, 'nothing of any concern.'

General Metcalf sat in his military residence and swirled the brandy around in his glass as he closed the cover of the report in his lap. He looked up sadly and stared at Emmett who was sitting across the room.

'A tragic crime,' he said slowly. 'The President had every chance of achieving greatness. No finer man ever sat in the White House.'

'The facts are all there,' said Emmett, gesturing at the report. 'He's mentally unfit to continue in office.'

'I must agree, but it's no easy thing. He and I have been friends for nearly forty years.'

'Will you call off the troops and allow Congress to meet at Lisner Auditorium tomorrow?' Emmett pressed.

Metcalf sipped the brandy and gave a weary nod to his head. 'I'll issue orders for their withdrawal first thing in the morning. You can inform the House and Senate leaders they can hold session in the Capitol building.'

'Can I ask a favour?'

'Of course.'

'Is it possible to remove the Marines from around the White House by midnight?'

'I don't see why not,' said Metcalf. 'Any particular reason?'

'A deception, General,' Emmett replied. 'One you will find most intriguing.'

64

Sandecker stood in the chart room of NUMA and peered through a magnification enhancer at an aerial photo of Johns Island, South Carolina. He straightened and looked at Giordino, then at Pitt, who were standing on the opposite side of the table. 'Beats me,' he said after a short silence. 'If Suvorov pinpointed his landmarks correctly, I can't understand why he didn't find Bougainville's lab facility from a helicopter.'

Pitt consulted the Soviet agent's notebook. 'He used an old abandoned garage for his base point,' he said, pointing to a tiny structure on the photograph, 'which can be distinguished here.'

'Emmett or Brogan know you made a copy?' asked Giordino, nodding towards the notebook.

Pitt smiled. 'What do you think?'

'I won't tell if you won't.'

'If Suvorov escaped the lab at night,' said Sandecker, 'it's conceivable he got his bearings crossed.'

'A good undercover operative is a trained observer,' Pitt explained. 'He was precise in his description of landmarks. I doubt he lost his sense of direction.'

'Emmett has two hundred agents crawling over the area,' Sandecker said. 'As of fifteen minutes ago, they came up empty handed.'

'Then where?' Giordino asked in a general sense. 'No structure the size Suvorov recorded shows on the aerial survey. A few old houseboats, some scattered small homes, a couple of decrepit sheds, nothing of the order of a warehouse.'

'An underground facility?' Sandecker speculated.

Giordino mused the point. 'Suvorov did say he took the lift up to break out.'

'On the other hand, he mentions walking down a ramp to a gravel road.'

'A ramp might suggest a boat,' Giordino ventured.

Sandecker looked doubtful. 'No good. The only water near the spot Suvorov puts the lab is a creek with a depth no more than two or three feet at most. Far too shallow to float a vessel large enough to require a lift.'

'There is another possibility,' said Pitt.

'Which is?'

'A barge.'

Giordino looked across the table at Sandecker. 'I think Dirk may have something.'

Pitt stepped over to a telephone, dialled a number and switched the call to a speaker.

'Data Department,' came a groggy voice.

'Yaeger, you awake?'

'Oh God, it's you Pitt. Why do you always have to call after midnight?'

'Listen, I need information on a particular type of vessel. Can your computers come up with a projection on its class if I supply on the dimensions?'

'Is this a game?'

'Believe you me this is no game,' Sandecker growled.

'Admiral!' Yaeger muttered, coming alert. 'I'll get right on to it. What are your dimensions?'

Pitt thumbed to the correct page in the notebook and read them off into the speaker phone. 'A hundred and sixty-eight feet in length at inside perpendiculars by thirty-three feet in the beam. The approximate height is ten feet.'

'Not much to go on,' Yaeger grumbled.

'Try,' Sandecker replied sternly.

'Hold on. I'm moving to the keyboard.'

Giordino smiled at the Admiral. 'Care to make a wager?'

'Name it.'

'A bottle of Chivas Regal against a box of your cigars Dirk's right.'

'No bet,' said Sandecker. 'My specially rolled cigars cost far more than a bottle of scotch.'

Yaeger could be heard clearing his throat. 'Here it is.' There was a slight pause. 'Sorry, not enough data. Those figures are a rough match for any one of a hundred different craft.'

Pitt thought a moment. 'Suppose the height was the same from bow to stern.'

'You talking about a flat superstructure?'

'Yes.'

'Hold on,' said Yaeger. 'Okay, you've lowered the numbers. Your mystery vessel looks like a barge.'

'Eureka,' exclaimed Giordino.

'Don't cash in your coupons yet,' Yaeger dampened him. 'The dimensions don't fit any known barge in existence.'

'Damn!' blurted Sandecker. 'So near, yet . . .'

'Wait,' Pitt cut in. 'Suvorov gave us interior measurements.' He leaned over the speaker phone. 'Yaeger, add two feet all around and run it through again.'

'You're getting warmer,' Yaeger's voice rasped over the speaker.

'Try this on for size – no pun intended – one hundred and ninety-five by thirty-five by twelve feet.'

'Beam and height correspond,' said Pitt, 'but your length is way off.'

'You gave me interior length between perpendicular bulkheads. I'm giving you overall length including a raked bow of twenty-five feet.'

'He's right,' said Sandecker. 'We didn't allow for the scoop of the forward end.'

Yaeger continued. 'What we've got is a dry cargo barge, steel construction, two hundred and eighty to three hundred tons. Self enclosed compartments for carrying grain, lumber and so forth. Probably manufactured by the Nashville Bridge Company, Nashville, Tennessee.'

'The draft?' Pitt pushed.

'Empty or loaded?'

'Empty.'

'Eighteen inches.'

'Thanks, pal, you've done it again.'

'Done what?'

'Go back to sleep.'

Pitt switched off the speaker and turned to Sandecker. 'The smoke clears.'

Sandecker fairly beamed. 'Clever, clever people, the Bougainvilles.'

Pitt nodded. 'I have to agree. The last place anyone would look for an expensively equipped laboratory is inside a rusty old river barge moored in a swamp.'

'She also has the advantage of being moveable,' said Sandecker. The Admiral referred to any vessel, scow or aircraft carrier in the feminine gender. 'A tug can transport and dock her anywhere the water depth is over a foot and a half.'

Pitt stared at the aerial photo pensively. 'The next test is to determine where the Bougainvilles hid it again.'

'The creek where she was tied leads into the Stono River,' Sandecker noted.

'And the Stono River is part of the Intracoastal Waterway,' Pitt added. 'They can slip it into any one of ten thousand rivers, streams, bays and sounds from Boston to Key West.'

'No way of second guessing the destination,' Giordino murmured dejectedly.

'They won't keep it in South Carolina waters,' said Pitt. 'Too obvious. The catch as I see it boils down to north or south, and a distance of six or maybe eight hundred miles.'

'A staggering job,' Sandecker said in a soft voice, 'untangling her

286

from the other barges plying the eastern waterways. They're thicker than leaves during a New England October.'

'Still, it's more than we had to go on before,' Pitt said hopefully.

Sandecker turned from the photo. 'Better give Emmett a call and steer him onto our discovery. Someone in his army of investigators may get lucky and stumble on the right barge.' The Admiral's words were empty of feeling. He didn't want to say what was on his mind.

If Lee Tong Bougainville suspected government investigators were breathing down his neck, his only option would be to kill the Vice President and Loren, and dispose of their bodies to cover his tracks.

65

'The patient will live to fight another day,' said Dr Harold Gwynne, the President's physician, cheerfully. He was a cherubic little man with a balding head and friendly blue eyes. 'A common case of the flu bug. Stay in bed for a couple of days until the fever subsides. I'll give you an antibiotic and something to relieve the nausea.'

'I can't stay on my back,' the President protested weakly. 'Too much work to do.'

There was little fight in his words. The chills from a 103° fever sandbagged him, and he was constantly on the verge of vomiting. His throat was sore, his nose stuffed up, and he felt rotten from scalp to toenails.

'Relax and take it easy,' ordered Gwynne. 'The world can turn without you for a few hours.' He jabbed a needle into the President's arm and then held a glass of water for him to wash down a pill.

Dan Fawcett entered the bedroom. 'About through, Doc?' he inquired.

Gwynne nodded. 'Keep him off his feet. I'll check back around two o'clock this afternoon.' He smiled warmly, closed his black bag and stepped through the door.

'General Metcalf is waiting,' said Fawcett.

The President pushed a third pillow behind his back and struggled to a sitting position, massaging his temples as the room began to spin.

Metcalf was ushered in, resplendent in a uniform decorated by eight rows of vividly hued ribbons. There was a briskness about the General that was not present at their last meeting.

The President looked at him, his face pallid, his eyes drooping and watery. He began to hack uncontrollably.

Metcalf came over to the bed. 'Is there anything I can get you, sir?' he asked solicitously.

The President shook his head and waved him away. 'I'll survive,' he said at last. 'What's the situation, Clayton?'

The President never called his Joint Chiefs by rank, preferring to lower them a couple of notches down their pedestal by addressing them by their Christian names.

Metcalf shifted in his chair uncomfortably. 'The streets are quiet at the moment, but there were one or two isolated incidents of sniping. One soldier was killed and two marines wounded.'

'Were the guilty parties apprehended?'

'Yes, sir,' answered Metcalf.

'A couple of criminal radicals, no doubt.'

Metcalf stared at his feet. 'Not exactly. One was the son of Congressman Jacob Whitman of South Dakota and the other the son of Postmaster General Kenneth Potter. Both were under seventeen years of age.'

The President's face looked stricken for an instant and then it quickly hardened. 'Are your troops deployed at Lisner Auditorium?'

'One company of Marines is stationed on the grounds around the building.'

'Hardly seems enough manpower,' said the President. 'The Maryland and Virginia guard units combined will outnumber them five to one.'

'The Guard will never come within rifle shot of the auditorium,' said Metcalf knowingly. 'Our plan is to defuse their effectiveness by stopping them before they arrive in the city.'

'A sound strategy,' the President said, his eyes gleaming briefly.

'I have a special news report,' said Fawcett, who was kneeling in front of the television set. He turned up the volume and stood aside so the picture could be seen from the bed.

Curtis Mayo was standing beside a highway blocked by gun toting soldiers. In the background a line of heavy tanks stretched across the road, the muzzles of their cannon pointing ominously at a convoy of personnel carriers.

'The Virginia National Guard troops that Speaker of the House, Alan Moran, was relying on to protect a meeting of Congress on the George Washington University campus this morning have been turned back outside the nation's capital by armoured units of the Army special forces. I understand the same situation exists with the Maryland guard north-east of the city. So far there has been no threat of fighting. Both state guardsmen units appeared subdued, if not in numbers, by superior equipment. Outside Lisner Auditorium, a company of Marines, under the command of Colonel Ward Clarke, a

288

Vietnam medal of honour holder, is turning away members of Congress, refusing them entrance to hold session. And so once again, the President has thwarted House and Senate members while he continues his controversial foreign affairs programmes without their approval. This is Curtis Mayo, ABC news, on a highway thirty miles south of Washington.'

'Seen enough?' asked Fawcett, turning off the set.

'Yes, yes,' the President rasped happily. 'That ought to keep that egomaniac Moran floundering without a rudder for a while.'

Metcalf rose to his feet. 'If you won't need me any further, Mr President, I should be getting back to the Pentagon. Conditions are pretty unsettled with our division commanders in Europe. They don't exactly share your views on pulling back their forces to the States.'

'In the long haul they'll come to accept the risks of a temporary military unbalance in order to dilute the dreaded spectre of nuclear conflict,' the President said confidently. Then he shook Metcalf's hand. 'Nice piece of work, Clayton. Thank you for keeping Congress paralysed.'

Metcalf walked along the corridor for fifty feet until it emptied into the vast interior of a barren warehouse-like structure.

The stage set that contained an exact replica of the President's White House bedroom sat in the middle of the Washington Navy Yard's old brick ordnance building, which had gone virtually unused since World War Two.

Every detail of the description was carefully planned and executed. A sound technician operated a stereo recorder whose tape played the muted sounds of street traffic at a precise volume. The lighting outside the bedroom windows matched the sky exactly, with an occasional shadowed effect to simulate a passing cloud. The filters over the lamps were set to emit changing yellow-orange rays to duplicate the day's movement of the sun. Even the plumbing in the adjacent bathroom worked with the familiar sounds of the original, but emptying its contents into a septic tank rather than the Washington city sewer system. The huge concrete floor was heavily populated with Marine guards and Secret Service agents while overhead, amid great wooden rafters, men stood on catwalks, manning the overhead lighting system.

Metcalf stepped across a network of electrical cables and entered a large mobile trailer parked against the far wall. Oates and Brogan were waiting and invited him into a walnut panelled office.

'Coffee?' Brogan asked, holding up a glass urn.

Metcalf nodded thankfully, reached for a steaming cup and sank into a chair. 'My God, for a minute there I swore I was in the White House.'

'Martin's people did an amazing job,' said Oates. 'He flew in a crew from a Hollywood studio and constructed the entire set in nine hours.'

'Did you have a problem moving the President?'

'The easy part,' replied Brogan. 'We transferred him in the same moving van as the furniture. Strange as it might sound, the toughest hurdle was the paint.'

'How so?'

'We had to cover the walls with a material that didn't have the smell of new paint. Fortunately, our chemists at the agency lab came up with a chalky substance they could tint that left no aroma.'

'The news programme was an ingenious touch,' commented Metcalf.

'It cost us,' Oates explained. 'We had to make a deal with Curtis Mayo to give him the exclusive story in return for his cooperation in broadcasting the phoney news report. He also agreed to hold off a network investigation until the situation cools.'

'How long can you continue to deceive the President?'

'For as long as it takes,' answered Brogan.

'For what purpose?'

'To study the President's brain patterns.'

Metcalf threw Brogan a very dubious look indeed. 'You haven't convinced me. Stealing back the President's mind from the Russians who stole it in the first place is stretching my gullibility past breaking point.'

Brogan and Oates exchanged looks and smiled. 'Would you like to see for yourself?' asked Oates.

Metcalf put down the coffee. 'I wouldn't miss it for a fifth star.'

'Through here,' said Oates, opening a door and gesturing Metcalf to enter.

The entire midsection and one end of the mobile trailer was filled with exotic electronic and computer hardware. The monitoring data centre was a generation ahead of Lugovoy's equipment on board the Bougainville laboratory.

Dr Raymond Edgely noticed their appearance and came over. Oates introduced him to General Metcalf.

'So you're the mysterious genius who heads up "Fathom",' said Metcalf. 'I'm honoured to meet you.'

'Thank you, General,' said Edgely. 'Secretary Oates tells me you have some suspicions about the project.'

Metcalf looked around the busy complex, studying the scientists who were engrossed in the digital readings on the monitors. 'I admit I'm puzzled by all this.'

'Basically, it's quite simple,' said Edgely. 'My staff and I are intercepting and accumulating data on the President's brain rhythms in preparation for switching control from his cerebral implant to our own unit which you see before you.'

Metcalf's scepticism melted away. 'Then this is all true; the Russians really are dominating his thoughts?'

'Of course. It was their instructions to close down Congress and the Supreme Court so he could instigate projects beneficial to the Communist bloc without legislative roadblocks. The order to withdraw our troops from NATO is a perfect example. Exactly what the Soviet military wants for Christmas.'

'And you people can actually take the place of the President's mind?'

Edgely nodded. 'Do you have any messages you wish sent to the Kremlin? Some misleading information perhaps?'

Metcalf brightened like a searchlight. 'I think my intelligence people can write some interesting science fiction that should spur them to draw all the wrong conclusions.'

'When do you expect to release the President from Lugovoy's command?' asked Brogan.

'I think we can make the transfer in another eight hours,' answered Edgely.

'Then we'll get out of the way and leave you to your work,' said Oates.

They left the data acquisition room and returned to the outer office where they found Sam Emmett waiting. Oates could see that the expression on his face spelled trouble.

'I've just come from Capitol Hill,' said Emmett. 'They're acting like animals in a zoo who haven't been fed. Debate over impeachment is raging on both floors of Congress. The President's party is making a show of loyalty, but that's all it is, a show. There is no support on a broad front. Desertions come in wholesale lots.'

'What about committee?' asked Oates.

'The opposition party rammed through a floor vote to bypass a committee investigation to save time.'

'A guess as to when they'll decide?'

'The House may vote on impeachment this afternoon.'

'The odds?'

'Five to one in favour.'

'The Senate?'

'They're moving slower. Probably take a vote the day after.'

'Any hope for a stand-off?'

'Not on the cards. A straw-vote indicates the Senate will pass the measure with considerably more than the necessary two-thirds majority.'

'They're not wasting any time.'

'Considering the President's recent actions, the impeachment proceedings are looked upon as a national emergency.'

'Any show of support for Vince Margolin?'

'Of course, but no one can stand behind him if he doesn't put in an appearance. Sixty seconds after the President is swept from office, someone has to take the oath as successor. The rumour mills have him hiding out until the last minute so he won't be associated with the President's crazy policies.'

'What about Moran?'

'This is where it gets sticky. He's claiming he has proof that Margolin committed suicide and that I am covering up the act.'

'Anybody believe him?'

'Doesn't matter if he's believed. The news media are jumping on his statements like ants on honey. His news conferences are getting massive attention, and he's demanding Secret Service protection. His aides have already drafted a transition plan and named his inner circle of advisers. Shall I go on?'

'The picture is clear,' Oates said resignedly. 'Alan Moran will be the next President of the United States.'

'We can't allow it,' Emmett said coldly.

The others stared at him. 'Unless we can produce Vince Margolin by tomorrow,' said Brogan, 'how can we prevent it?'

'Any way possible,' said Emmett. He produced a folder from an attaché case. 'I'd like you gentlemen to take a look at this.'

Oates opened the folder and studied the contents without comment, and then passed it on to Brogan who in turn handed it to Metcalf. When they had finished they gazed at Emmett as if silently nominating him to speak first.

'What you gentlemen read in the report is true,' he said simply.

'Why hasn't this come out before?' Oates demanded.

'Because there was never a reason to order an in depth investigation into the man before,' answered Emmett. 'The FBI is not in the habit of revealing skeletons in our legislators' closets unless there is solid evidence of criminal activity in their backgrounds. Dirt on divorces, petty misdemeanours, sexual perversions, or traffic violations, we file in a vault and look the other way. Moran's file showed him to be clean, too clean for someone who clawed his way to the top without benefit of education, average intelligence, a penchant for hard work, wealth or important contacts. Nothing about his character indicated aggressiveness or talent. So I decided to clear a bigger hole into his past. As you can see the results aren't exactly a recommendation for Pope.'

Metcalf scanned the report again. 'This stock brokerage firm in Chicago, what is it called? Ah yes, Shaw, Hampshire and Farquher.'

'A front to launder Moran's bribery and pay-off operation. The three names came off tombstones in a Fargo, North Dakota cemetery. Bogus stock transactions are conducted to hide bribe money from shady special interest groups. Defence contractors, state and city officials seeking Federal funding and not caring how they get it, underworld payments for favours. Speaker of the House, Moran, makes the Bougainvilles look like Boy Scouts.'

'We've got to go public with this,' Brogan said adamantly.

'I wouldn't push it,' cautioned Oates. 'Moran would go to any length to deny it, claiming it was a second-rate frame-up to keep him from leading the country to reconciliation and unity. I can see him pleading for the American tradition of fair play while he's hanging from the cross. And by the time the Justice Department can make things tough for him, he will have sworn in as president. Let's face it, you can't put the country through two impeachment proceedings in the same year.'

Metcalf nodded his head in agreement. 'Coming on the heels of the President's insane policies and Moran's ravings about the Vice President's presumed death, the upheaval may prove more than the public can accept. A complete loss in Federal confidence could ignite a voter's revolt during the next election, and wreck the two-party political system.'

'Or worse,' added Emmett. 'More and more people are refusing to pay taxes under the rationale they don't like where their tax dollars are spent. And you can't blame them for not wanting to support a government managed by inept leaders and rip-off artists. You get five million people out there who tear up their tax forms come next April fifteenth, and the Federal machinery as we know it will cease to function.'

The four men sat in the trailer office like frozen figures in a painting. The fantasy of their conjecture was not implausible. Nothing like this had ever happened before. The prospects of surviving the storm unscathed seemed remote.

At last Brogan said, 'We're lost without Vince Margolin.'

'That fellow Pitt over at NUMA gave us our first tangible lead,' said Brogan.

'So what have you got?' asked Metcalf.

'Pitt deduced that the mind control laboratory where Margolin is held is inside a river barge.'

'A what?' Metcalf asked as if he hadn't heard right.

'River barge,' explained Emmett. 'Moored God knows where along the inland water route.'

'Are you searching?'

'With every available agent Martin and I can spare from both our agencies.'

'If you give me a few more details and come up with a quick plan to coordinate our efforts, I'll throw in whatever forces the Defence department can muster in the search areas.'

'That would certainly help, General,' said Oates. 'Thank you.'

The phone rang and Oates picked it up. After listening silently for a moment, he set it down. 'Crap!'

Emmett had never heard Oates use such an expletive before. 'Who was that?'

'One of my aides reporting from the House of Representatives.'

'What did he say?'

'Moran just railroaded through passage of the impeachment vote.'

Brogan said, 'Then nothing stands between him and the presidency except the Senate.'

'He's moved up the timetable by a good ten hours,' said Metcalf.

'If we can't produce the Vice President by this time tomorrow,' said Emmett, 'we can kiss honest government goodbye.'

66

Giordino found Pitt in his hangar, sitting comfortably in the back seat of an immense open touring car, his feet propped sideways on a rear door. Giordino couldn't help admiring the classic lines of the tourer. Italian built in 1925, with coachwork by Cesare Sala, the red torpedo bodied Isotta-Fraschini sported long, flared fenders, a disappearing top and a coiled cobra on the radiator cap.

Pitt was contemplating a blackboard mounted on a tripod about ten feet from the car. A large nautical chart depicting the entire inland water route was tacked to the outer frame. Across the board he had written several notations and what appeared to Giordino as a list of ships.

'I've just come from the Admiral's office,' said Giordino.

'What's the latest?' Pitt asked, his eyes never leaving the blackboard.

'The Joint Chiefs of Staff have thrown the armed forces into the hunt. Combined with agents from the FBI and CIA, they should be able to cover every inch of shoreline by tomorrow evening.'

'On the ground, by the sea and in the air,' Pitt murmured uninterestedly. 'From Maine to Florida.'

'Why the sour grapes?'

'A damned waste of time. The barge isn't there,' Pitt said, flipping a piece of chalk in the air.

Giordino shot him a quizzical look. 'What are you babbling about? The barge has to be in there somewhere.'

'Not necessarily.'

'You saying they're searching in the wrong place?'

'If you were the Bougainvilles, you'd expect an exhaustive, whole-hog hunt, right?'

'Elementary reasoning,' Giordino said loftily. 'Me, I'd be more inclined to camouflage the barge under a grove of trees, hide it inside an enclosed waterfront warehouse, or alter the exterior to look like a giant chicken coop or whatever. Seems to me concealment is the logical way to go.'

Pitt laughed. 'Your chicken coop brainstorm, now that's class.'

'You got a better idea?'

Pitt stepped out of the Isotta, went to the blackboard and folded over the inland waterway chart, revealing another chart showing the coastline along the Gulf of Mexico. 'As it happens, yes I do.' He tapped his finger on a spot circled in red ink. 'The barge holding Margolin and Loren captive is somewhere around here.'

Giordino moved closer and examined the marked area. Then he looked at Pitt with an expression usually reserved for people who held signs announcing the end of the world.

'New Orleans?'

'Below New Orleans,' Pitt corrected. 'I judge it to be moored there now.'

Giordino shook his head. 'I think your brakes went out. You're telling me Bougainville towed a barge from Charleston, around the tip of Florida and across the Gulf to the Mississippi River, almost seventeen hundred miles in less than four days? Sorry, pal, the tug isn't built that can push a barge that fast.'

'Granted,' Pitt allowed. 'But suppose they cut off seven hundred miles?'

'How?' inquired Giordino, his voice a combination of doubt and sarcasm. 'By installing wheels and driving it cross country?'

'No joke,' Pitt said seriously. 'By towing it through the recently opened Florida Cross State Canal from Jacksonville on the Atlantic to Crystal River in the Gulf, short-cutting the entire southern half of the state.'

The revelation sparked Giordino. He peered at the chart again, studying the scale. Then using his thumb and forefinger as a pair of dividers, he roughly measured the reduced distance between Charleston and New Orleans. When he finally turned and refaced Pitt, he wore a sheepish smile.

'It works.' Then the smile quickly faded. 'So what does it prove?'

'The Bougainvilles must have a heavily guarded dock facility and terminal where they unload their illegal cargoes. I judge it to sit on the banks of the river somewhere between New Orleans and the entrance to the Gulf.'

'The Mississippi Delta?' Giordino showed his puzzlement. 'How'd you pull that little number out of the hat?'

'Take a look,' Pitt said, pointing to the list of ships on the blackboard and then reading them off. 'The *Pilottown, Belle Chasse, Buras, Venice, Boothville, Chalmette*, all ships under foreign registry but at one time owned by Bougainville Maritime.'

'I fail to make the connection.'

'Take another look at the chart. Every one of those ships is named after a town along the river delta.'

'A symbolic cipher?'

'The only mistake the Bougainvilles ever let slip, using a code to designate their area of covert operations.'

Giordino peered closer. 'By God, it fits like a girl in tight shorts.'

Pitt rapped the chart with his knuckles. 'I'll bet my Isotta-Fraschini against your Bronco that's where we'll find Loren.'

'You're on.'

'Run over to the NUMA air terminal and sign out a Lear jet. I'll contact the Admiral and explain why we're flying to New Orleans.'

Giordino was already heading towards the door. 'I'll have the plane checked out and ready for take-off when you get there,' he called over his shoulder.

Pitt hurried up the stairs to his flat and threw some clothes in an overnight bag. He opened a gun cabinet and took out an old Colt Thompson submachine-gun, serial number 8545, and two loaded drums of 45-calibre cartridges and laid them in a violin case. Then he picked up the phone and called Sandecker's office. He identified himself to Sandecker's private secretary and was put through.

'Admiral?'

'Dirk?'

'I think I've got the barge area fixed.'

'Where?'

'The Mississippi River Delta. Al and I are leaving for there now.'

'What makes you think it's in the Delta?'

'Half guess, half deduction, but it's the best lead we've got going for us.'

Sandecker hesitated before replying. 'You'd better hold up.' he said quietly.

'Hold up? What are you talking about?'

'Alan Moran is demanding the search be called off.'

Pitt was stunned. 'What in hell for?'

'He says it's a waste of time and taxpayer's money to continue because Vince Margolin is dead.'

'Moran is full of crap.'

'He has the clothes Margolin was wearing the night they all disappeared to back up his claim.'

'We still have Loren to think about.'

'Moran says she's dead too.'

Pitt felt he was sinking in quicksand. 'He's a damned liar!'

'Maybe so, but if he's right about Margolin, you're defaming the next President of the United States.'

'The day that little creep takes the oath is the day I turn in my citizenship.'

'You probably won't be alone,' Sandecker said sourly. 'But your personal feelings don't alter the situation.'

Pitt stood unbudging. 'I'll call you from Louisiana.'

'I was hoping you'd say that. Stay in close contact. I'll do everything I can to help from this end.'

'Thanks, you old fraud.'

'Get your ass in gear and tell Giordino to stop swiping my cigars.'

Pitt grinned and hung up. He finished packing and hurried from the hangar. Three minutes after he drove off, his phone began to ring.

Two hundred miles away an ashen faced Sal Casio despairingly waited in vain for an answer.

67

Ten minutes after twelve noon, Alan Moran walked through the main corridor of the Capitol, down a narrow staircase and opened the door to an out of the way office kept for privacy. Most men in his position were constantly surrounded by a hive of aides, but Moran preferred to travel a solitary trail, unhindered by inane conversation.

He always wore the wary look of an antelope scanning the African plain for predators. He had the expressionless eyes of a man whose only love was power, power attained by whatever means, at whatever cost. To achieve his prestigious position in Congress, Moran had carefully nurtured a billboard image. In his public life he oozed a religious fervour, the personification of the friendly shy man with a warm sense of humour, the appeal of the neighbour next door ever ready to lend his lawnmower, and the past of a man born under-privileged but self made.

His private life couldn't have been more at odds. He was a closet atheist who looked upon his constituents and the general public as ignorant rabble whose chronic complaints were an open licence to twist and control for his own advantage. Never married, with no close friends, he lived frugally like a penitent monk in a small, rented flat. Every dollar up and above subsistence level went into his secret corporation in Chicago where it was added to funds obtained through illegal contributions, bribes, and other corrupt investments. Then it was spread and sown to increase his power base until there were few men and women with top positions in business and government who weren't tied to his coat tails by political favours and influence.

Douglas Oates, Sam Emmett, Martin Brogan, Alan Mercier and Jesse Simmons, who was recently released from house arrest, were seated in Moran's office as he entered. They all rose as he took his place behind a desk. There was an air of smugness about him that was obvious to his visitors. He had summoned them to his private territory and they had no choice but to respond.

'Thank you for meeting with me, gentlemen,' he said with a false smile. 'I assume you know the purpose.'

'To discuss your possible transition to the Presidency,' replied Oates.

'There is no *possible* about it,' Moran came back waspishly. 'The Senate is scheduled to end debate and take a vote for impeachment at seven o'clock this evening. As next in line to the Executive Office, I feel it is my sworn duty to take the oath immediately afterwards and assume the responsibility for healing the wounds caused by the President's harmful delusions.'

'Aren't you jumping the gun?' asked Simmons.

'Not if it means stopping the President from any more outrageous actions.'

Oates looked dubious. 'Some people might interpret your undue reaction, at least until Vince Margolin is proven dead, as an improper attempt to usurp power, especially when considering your part in motivating the President's ouster.'

Moran glared at Oates and shifted his stare to Emmett. 'You have the Vice President's clothing that was found in the river.'

'My FBI lab has identified the clothing as belonging to Margolin,' acknowledged Emmett, 'but it shows no indication of being immersed in water for two weeks.'

'Most likely it washed onshore and dried out.'

'You say the fisherman who came to your office with the evidence stated he snagged it in the middle of the river.'

'You're the Director of the FBI,' snapped Moran angrily, 'you figure it out. I'm not on trial here.'

'Perhaps it would be in the best interests of everyone present,' said Oates quietly, 'to continue the search for Margolin.'

'I'm in total agreement,' said Brogan. 'We can't write him off until we find his body.'

'Questions will most certainly arise,' added Mercier. 'For example, how did he die?'

'Obviously he drowned,' answered Moran. 'Probably when the *Eagle* sank.'

'Also,' Mercier continued, 'you never satisfactorily explained when and how you and Marcus Larimer disembarked the *Eagle* and travelled to an as yet undisclosed resort for your Caribbean fishing trip.'

'I'll be happy to answer any questions before a Congressional investigating committee,' said Moran. 'Certainly not here and now in front of people who are in opposition to me.'

'You must understand, in spite of his mistakes, our loyalties lie with the President,' said Oates.

'I don't doubt it for a minute,' said Moran. 'That's why I summoned you here this morning. Ten minutes after the impeachment vote clears the Senate, I will be sworn in as President. My first official act will be to announce either your resignations or firings; you have your choice. As of midnight tonight, none of you will be working for the United States Government.'

The narrow paved road snaked through the high hills that dropped steeply into the Black Sea. In the rear seat of a Cadillac Seville stretch limousine, Vladmir Polevoi sat reading the latest report from Aleksei Lugovoy. Every once in a while he looked up and gazed at the dawn sun creeping past the horizon.

The limousine turned heads wherever it rolled. Custom built with inlaid wood cabinets, colour TV, electric divider, spirits bar and overhead stereo console, Polevoi had ordered it purchased and transported to Moscow under the guise of studying its mechanical technology. But shortly after its arrival, he commanded it as his own.

The long car climbed round the forested edge of a craggy cliff until the road ended at a huge wooden door hinged to a high brick wall. A uniformed officer saluted the KGB chief and pressed a switch. The door swung silently open to a vast garden that blazed with flowers, and the car drove in and parked beside a spreading one-storey house, constructed in a western contemporary design.

Polevoi walked up circular stone steps and entered a foyer, where he was greeted by President Antonov's secretary and escorted to a table and chairs on a terrace overlooking the sea.

After a few moments Antonov appeared, followed by a pretty servant girl carrying a huge plate of smoked salmon, caviar and iced vodka. Antonov seemed in a happy mood and casually sat on the iron railing around the terrace.

'You have a beautiful new dacha,' said Polevoi.

'Thank you. I had it designed by a firm of French architects. Didn't charge me a ruble. Won't pass critical inspection by a state building committee, of course. Too bourgeois. But what the hell. Times are changing.' Then he switched the subject abruptly. 'What news of events in Washington?'

'The President will be removed from office,' answered Polevoi.

'When?'

'By this time tomorrow.'

'No doubt of this?'

'None.'

Antonov picked up his vodka glass and emptied it, and the girl immediately refilled it. Polevoi suspected the girl did more than simply pour vodka for the head of the Soviet Union.

'Did we miscalculate, Vladimir?' asked Antonov. 'Did we expect to accomplish too much too quickly?'

'Nobody can second guess the Americans. They don't behave in traditional ways.'

'Who will be the new President?'

'Alan Moran, Speaker of the House of Representatives.'

'Can we work with him?'

'My sources say he has a devious mind, but can be swayed.'

Antonov stared at a tiny fishing boat far below on the water. 'If given the choice, I'd prefer Moran over Vice President Margolin.'

'Most definitely,' agreed Polevoi. 'Margolin is a dedicated enemy of our Communist society, and an adamant believer in expanding the American military machine beyond our own.'

'Anything our people can do, discreetly of course, to assist Moran into the White House?'

Polevoi shook his head. 'Very little worth the risk of exposure and adverse propaganda.'

'Where is Margolin?'

'Still in the hands of the Bougainvilles.'

300

'Any chance that old Oriental bitch will release him in time to cut out Moran?'

Polevoi shrugged helplessly. 'Who can predict her schemes with any accuracy?'

'If you were her, Vladimir, what would you do?'

Polevoi paused thoughtfully, then said: 'I'd strike a deal with Moran to dispose of Margolin.'

'Has Moran the guts to accept?'

'If one man who was held prisoner in an extremely vulnerable situation stood between you and leadership of a super power, how would you play it?'

Antonov broke into a loud laugh that frightened a nearby bird into flight. 'You read me like glass, old friend. I see your point. I wouldn't hesitate to remove him.'

'The American news media report that Moran is claiming Margolin committed suicide by drowning.'

'So your theory is on firm ground,' said Antonov. 'Maybe the old iron lotus will end up doing us a favour after all.'

'At least our deal with her didn't cost us anything.'

'Speaking of cost, what is the status of the gold?'

'Admiral Borchavski has begun salvage operations. He expects to raise all the bars within three weeks.'

'That's good news,' said Antonov. 'And what of Dr Lugovoy? Can he continue his project after the President is cast from office?'

'He can,' Polevoi replied. 'Locked inside the President's head is a vast treasure store of United States secrets. Lugovoy has yet to tap it.'

'Then keep the project going. Provide Lugovoy with an extensive list of delicate political and military subjects we wish explored. All American leaders who leave office are consulted for their experience, regardless of the inept handling of their administrations. The capitalist masses have short memories. The knowledge the President now possesses and has yet to learn from briefings by his successors can be of great benefit to us in the future. This time we shall practise patience and probe slowly. The President's brain may turn out to be a goose that lays golden intelligence eggs for decades to come.'

Polevoi raised his glass. 'A toast to the best secret agent we ever recruited.'

Antonov smiled. 'Long may he produce.'

Across half a world, Raymond Edgely sat at a console and read the data that unrolled from a paper recorder. He raised his glasses and rubbed his reddened eyes. Despite the seeming tiredness, there was a tightly contained nervous energy about him. His competitive juices were stirred. The opportunity to beat his most esteemed colleague in

301

a game of psychological intrigue drove him beyond any thought of sleep.

Dr Harry Greenberg, a respected psychiatric researcher in his own right, lit a curved stem clay pipe. After stoking the yellow stained bowl to life, he pointed the mouthpiece at the recorder.

'No sense in waiting any longer, Ray. I'm satisfied we have the necessary data to make the switch.'

'I hate to rush in before I'm certain we can fool Aleksei.'

'Do it,' Greenberg urged. 'Stop screwing around and go for it.'

Edgely looked around at his ten-member team of psychologists. They stared back at him expectantly. Then he nodded. 'Okay, everybody stand by to transfer thought communication from the President's implant to our central computer.'

Greenberg walked around the room, briefly talking to everyone, double checking the procedures. Three sat at the computer console, their hands poised over the buttons. The rest studied the display screens and monitored the data.

Edgely nervously wiped his palms on a handkerchief. Greenberg stood slightly off to one side and behind him.

'We don't want to break in during a thought pattern or in the middle of Lugovoy's instructions,' Greenberg cautioned.

'I'm aware of that,' Edgely said without taking his eyes from the brainwave translater display. 'Our computer transmission also has to match his heart rate and other life functions exactly.'

The programmer punched in the command and waited. They all waited, watching the empty screen that would reveal success or failure. The minutes ticked by, nobody speaking; the only sounds coming from the soft hum of the electronic hardware as the computer poised for the precise millisecond to take command. Then suddenly the display screen read: 'COMMUNICATIONS TRANSFER ACCOMPLISHED'.

They all expelled collective sighs of relief and began talking again, and shaking hands with the enthusiasm of a NASA flight control centre after a successful rocket launch.

'Think Aleksei will fall for it?' asked Edgely.

'Don't worry. No suspicion will ever cross his mind. Aleksei Lugovoy's ego will never allow him to believe somebody pulled the wool over his eyes.' Greenberg paused to puff a smoke ring. 'He'll swallow everything we hand him and send it off to Moscow as if he was God's gift to espionage.'

'I hope so,' said Edgely dabbing at his sweating forehead. 'The next step is to get the President over to Walter Reed Hospital and remove the implant.'

'First things first,' said Greenberg, producing a bottle of champagne as a staff member passed out glasses. The cork was popped and the bubbly poured. Greenberg held up his glass.

'To Doc Edgely,' he said grinning, 'who just set the KGB back by ten years.'

PART IV

THE STONEWALL JACKSON

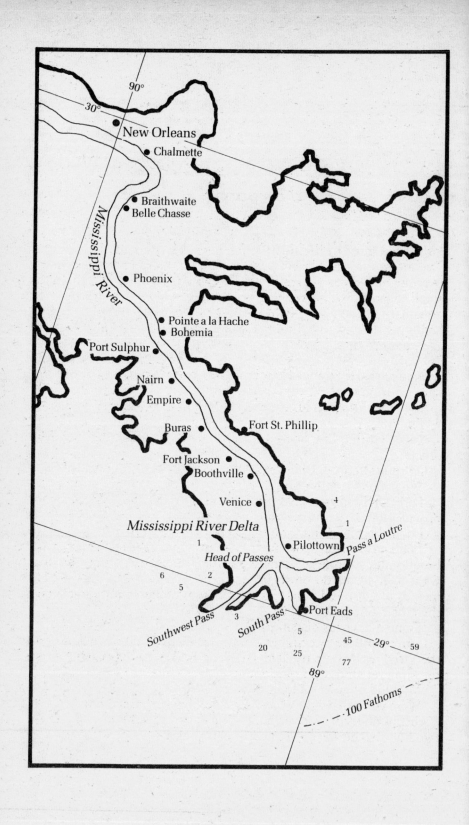

68

Pitt dozed most of the flight while Giordino manned the controls. The afternoon sun blazed from a clear sky as they dropped down over the blue-green waters of Lake Ponchartrain and lined up on the small airport that poked out from the New Orleans shore. The aquamarine coloured NUMA jet touched down on the asphalt landing strip and rolled to a stop near a helicopter with 'Delta Oil Ltd', painted on the side.

Nearby, a man in a seersucker suit stepped from a parked car and walked over. He removed his sunglasses and held out his hand as Pitt climbed from the Lear Jet's cabin.

'Mr Pitt?' he inquired, white teeth gleaming in a tanned face.

'I'm Pitt.'

'Clyde Griffin, FBI, Special Agent in Charge of the Louisiana field office.'

Giordino stepped to the ground and Pitt made the introductions.

'What can we do for you, Mr Griffin?'

'Director Emmett asked me to state officially the Bureau cannot provide official assistance on your hunt.'

'I don't recall asking for any,' said Pitt.

'I said no "official assistance", Mr Pitt.' The white teeth locked in a broad smile. 'Unofficially, this is Sunday. The Director suggested that what field agents do on their day off is their business. I have eight men at my disposal who feel what you're doing is more important then their golf game.'

'Emmett gave his blessing?'

'Strictly off the record, he strongly insinuated that if we don't find the Vice President pretty damned quick, he'll put a boot up my ass so far I'll never sit down at the piano again.'

'My kind of guy,' said Giordino.

'Were you briefed on what we're looking for?' asked Pitt.

Griffin nodded. 'A river barge. We've already checked out about two hundred between here and Baton Rouge.'

'You searched north. I figure it to be south.'

Griffin stared down at the ground doubtfully. 'Nearly all the incoming frieghters and tankers unload at the city docks. Then the cargo is transferred north by towboat. Few barges ply the delta waters south except those carrying trash and garbage to be dumped in the ocean.'

'All the more reason to look in that direction.'

Griffin made an inviting gesture towards the helicopter. 'My men are waiting in cars along the river front. We can direct them from the air.'

'Delta Oil make a good cover?' Pitt asked.

'Oil company whirleybirds are a common sight around these parts,' answered Griffin. 'They're heavily used to carry men and supplies to offshore rigs in the Gulf and pipe construction throughout the bayous. Nobody gives them a second glance.'

Pitt excused himself and returned to the NUMA plane, reappearing a minute later with the violin case. Then he entered the helicopter and was introduced to the pilot, a thin blonde, dreamy-eyed woman who spoke in a slow, deep drawl. Pitt wouldn't have taken her for an FBI agent, which she was, nor did she fit her name, 'Slats' Hogan.

'Ya'all play the violin when ya fly?' Hogan asked curiously.

'Soothes my fear of heights,' Pitt replied smiling.

'We get all kinds,' Hogan muttered incredulously.

They fastened their seatbelts and Hogan lifted the craft into the air and made a pass over the heart of the city before turning south.

A tiny green streetcar crept along St Charles Avenue, the tracks glinting as they reflected the sun through the trees. Pitt could easily make out the massive white roof of the Superdome, the largest sports structure of its kind in the world. The tightly packed houses and narrow streets of the French Quarter, the green grass of Jackson Square and the spires of the St Louis Cathedral slipped past off to their right. And then they broke over the muddy brown-green waters of the Mississippi River.

'There it is,' announced Hogan. 'Old Man River, too thick to drink and too thin to plough.'

'Spend any time on it?' Griffin asked Pitt.

'I conducted a historical survey a few years ago on a pair of Confederate Civil War wrecks about sixty miles further down river in Plaquemines Parish.'

'I know this great little restaurant in the parish – '

'So do I. The name is *Tom's*. Excellent Gulf oysters on the half-shell. Be sure and ask for Tom's mama's special chili pepper juice. Fantastic on the oysters.'

'You get around.'

'I try.'

'Got any ideas where the barge might be hidden?'

'Keep an eye open for a dock and warehouse that appears run down and little used, but well protected with heavy security – excessive number of guards, high fencing, perhaps dogs. The barge, rusted and in disrepair, will be stashed nearby. My guess is somewhere between Chalmette and Pilottown.'

'You can only reach Pilottown by boat,' said Griffin. 'The Delta highway ends ten miles above at a town called Venice.'

'I stand corrected.'

They went silent for a minute while the river below flowed along at almost four knots between the great levees that shielded the land from flood. Small farms with cows grazed in pastures and orange groves spread across the narrow strips of solid ground bordering the levees, before sliding away into marshland. They flew over Port Sulphur with its great piers entrenched along the west bank. Small mountains of yellow sulphur rose fifty feet over the flat, poisoned ground.

The next half hour produced the first of three false alarms. A few miles below Port Sulphur they spotted an abandoned cannery with two barges tied up beside it. Griffin radioed his team of agents who were chasing the helicopter from the road on the west bank. A quick search proved the building to be empty and the barges contained only bilge water and silt.

They continued south, flying over the vast marshes and meandering bayous towards the Gulf, spotting several grazing deer, a number of alligators sunning themselves in the mud, and a small herd of goats who looked up at their passing with indifferent curiosity.

A huge freighter churned upriver, thrusting its blunt bow against the current. The flag of registry on its stern flapped red with a gold star and hammer and sickle.

'Russian,' Pitt observed.

'The Soviets own a fair percentage of the five thousand ships that steam into New Orleans every year,' said Griffin.

'Want to see what's on that barge?' Hogan asked pointing. 'There, tied up behind that dredge on the east bank.'

Griffin nodded. 'We'll check this one out ourselves.'

Hogan nodded her blonde mane. 'I'll set you down on the levee.'

She expertly dropped the wheels of the helicopter onto the crushed shell road that ran along the top of the levee. Three minutes later Griffin ran across a creaking ramp to the barge. Another three minutes and he was back strapping himself in his seat.

'No luck?' asked Pitt.

'A bummer. The old tub is half filled with oil. Must be used as a refuelling station for the dredge.'

Pitt looked at his watch. Two-thirty. Time was sifting away. A few more hours and Moran would be sworn in as President. He said, 'Let's keep the show moving.'

'Ah hear ya'll talkin',' Hogan said as she brought the craft up and over the river in one quick bank that had Giordino feeling his stomach to see if it was still in place.

Eight more miles and they drew another blank after spying a barge moored suspiciously under a marine maintenance repair shed. A quick search by the ground team showed it as an abandoned derelict.

They pushed on past the fishing towns of Empire and Buras. Then suddenly, after dipping around a bend, they saw a sight straight out of the golden years of the river, a spectacular and picturesque vision almost forgotten. A long white hull, wide beam with a plume of steam drifting over her decks, a sidewheel paddle steamer sat with her flat nose nudged into the west embankment.

'Shades of Mark Twain,' said Giordino.

'She's a beauty,' Pitt said as he admired the gingerbread carvings on the many-storeyed superstructure.

'The *Stonewall Jackson*,' Griffin explained. 'She's been an attraction on the river for seventy years.'

The steamer's landing stages were lowered on the bank in front of an old brick fortress constructed in the shape of a pentagon. A sea of parked cars and a crowd of people wandered the parade ground and brick ramparts. In the centre of a nearby field a cloud of blue smoke billowed above two opposing lines of men who seemingly stood shooting at each other.

'What's the celebration?' asked Giordino.

'A war of the rebellion re-enactment,' Hogan replied.

'Run that by me again.'

'A staging of an historic battle,' Pitt explained. 'As a hobby men form brigades and regiments based on actual fighting units from the Civil War. They dress in authentic woven uniforms and shoot blanks out of exact replica or original guns. I witnessed a re-enactment at Gettysburg. They're quite spectacular, almost like the real thing.'

'Too bad we can't stop and watch the action,' said Griffin.

'Plaquemines Parish is a storehouse of history,' said Hogan. 'The star-shaped structure where they're staging the mock battle is called Fort Jackson. Fort St Philip, what little is left of it, is directly across the river. This is the area where Admiral Farragut ran the forts and captured New Orleans for the Yankees in 1862.'

It required no imagination at all to see and hear in their minds the thundering clashes of cannon fire between Union gunboats and Confederate batteries. But the curve in the river where Admiral Farragut and his fleet forced their passage over a century past was

310

now quiet. The water rolled silently between the scrub lined shores, having long ago covered over the bones of the ships that sank during the battle with a shroud of silt.

Hogan suddenly stiffened in her seat and peered over the instrument panel through the cockpit window. Not more than two miles away, a ship with her bows aimed down river was tied alongside an old wooden dock whose pilings ran under a large metal warehouse. Behind the stern of the ship, lay a barge and a towboat.

'This could be it,' she said.

'Can you read the name on the ship?' Pitt asked from the rear passenger's seat.

Hogan momentarily took her left hand off the collective pitch control lever to shield her eyes. 'Looks like . . . no, that's a town we just passed.'

'Which town?'

'Buras.'

'Could be it hell,' Pitt said with triumph in his voice. 'This *is* it.'

'No crew members about on the ship,' observed Griffin. 'You've got your high fence about the place, but I don't see any sign of guards or dogs. Looks pretty quiet to me.'

'Don't bet on it,' Pitt said. 'Keep flying downriver, Slats, until we're out of sight. Then swing back below the west levee and rendezvous with your people in the chase cars.'

Hogan continued her course for five minutes and then came around in a great half circle to the north and landed on a high school football field. Two cars crammed with FBI agents were waiting when the helicopter touched down.

Griffin twisted in his seat to face Pitt. 'I'll take my team and enter through the front gate that opens onto the loading dock. You and Giordino remain with Hogan and act as aerial observers. Should be a routine operation.'

'Routine operation,' Pitt repeated acidly. 'Walk up to the gate, flash your shiny FBI badge and watch everybody cringe. Never happen. These people kill like you and me swat mosquitos. Driving up in the open is an invitation to get your head blown off. You'd be smart to wait and call up reinforcements.'

Griffin's face showed he was not one to be told how to run his business. He ignored Pitt and gave instructions to Hogan.

'Give us two minutes to reach the gate before you take off and circle the warehouse. Open a frequency with our field communications office and inform them of the situation. And tell them to relay our reports to bureau headquarters in Washington.'

He stepped to the ground and got in the lead car. They drove around the high school gymnasium onto the almost invisible road

311

that led to the Bougainville docking facility and disappeared over the levee.

Hogan raised the helicopter into the air and went on the radio. Pitt moved to the copilot's seat and watched as Griffin and his men approached a high chain link fence enclosing the pier and warehouse. With a mounting uneasiness he observed Griffin exit the car and stand at the gate, but no one appeared to confront him.

'Something's happening,' said Hogan. 'The towboat and barge are moving.'

She was right. The towboat began to slip away from the pier, pushing the barge with its blunt snout. The helmsman expertly manoeuvred the two craft into the main stream and turned towards the gulf.

Pitt grabbed a spare microphone/headset. 'Griffin!' he snapped, 'the barge is being moved from the area. Forget the ship and warehouse. Return to the road and take up the chase.'

'I read you,' Griffin's voice acknowledged.

Abruptly, doors flew open on the ship and the crew scrambled across the decks, tearing canvas covers off two hidden gun emplacements on the foredeck and stern. The trap was sprung.

'Griffin!' Pitt shouted into the microphone. 'Get out. For God's sake, get out . . .'

The warning came too late. Griffin leaped into the lead car which roared off towards the safety of the levee as twenty millimetre Oerlikon machine-guns began rapping out a deadly hail. Bullets tore into the wildly careening cars, shattering windows, shredding the thin metal like cardboard, and ripping through the flesh and bone of those inside. The rear car coasted to a stop, bodies spilling out onto the ground, some lying still, some trying to crawl for cover. Griffin and his men made it over the top of the levee, but all of them were badly wounded.

Pitt had whipped open the violin case, stuck the barrel of the Thompson out the side window and sprayed the bow gun of the *Buras*. Hogan instantly realised what he was up to and banked the helicopter to give him a better angle of fire. Men fell around the deck, never knowing where the deadly barrage came from. The gunners on the stern were more alert. They swung their Oerlikon from Griffin and his agents and began spewing its shells into the sky. Hogan made a game effort to dodge the fire that missed by not feet, but inches. She kicked the helicopter around the ship as though it had a charmed life as the one-sided gun duel clattered over the river.

Then the trajectory from the *Buras* swayed through the air and hammered into the helicopter. Pitt threw up an arm to protect his eyes as the windscreen disintegrated and blew into the cockpit.

Steel-nosed bullets punctured the thin aluminium fuselage and wreaked havoc with the engine.

'Ah can't see,' Hogan announced in a surprisingly calm voice. Her face ran crimson from several cuts, the majority of the blood streaming from a scalp wound into her eyes, blinding her.

Except for a few deep scratches on his arm, Pitt was untouched. He passed the machine-gun to Giordino, who was wrapping a sleeve torn from his shirt around a shell gash on his right calf. The helicopter was losing power and dipping sharply towards the middle of the river. Pitt reached out and took the controls from Hogan and banked away from a sudden murderous fire that erupted from the towboat. A dozen men appeared from the pilot house and a hatch on top of the barge and wildly threw automatic weapons' fire at the battered helicopter.

Oil was streaming out of the engine and the rotor blades were madly vibrating. Pitt reduced the collective pitch to keep the rotor speed from falling too quickly. He saw the instrument panel break into fragments from a storm of bullets. He was fighting a hopeless battle; he couldn't hold on to the sky much longer. The forward motion dropped off and he was losing lateral control.

On the ground behind the levee, Griffin sat on his knees in helpless rage, holding a shattered wrist, watching the helicopter struggle like a great mortally wounded bird. The fuselage was so riddled by holes he couldn't believe anybody on board was still alive. He watched the craft slowly die, dragging a long trail of smoke as it faltered and limped upriver, barely clearing a grove of trees along the bank and disappearing from sight.

69

Sandecker sat in Emmett's private office at FBI headquarters and chewed idly on a cigar stub, his thoughts depleted. Brogan nervously juggled a half empty cup of coffee that had long since turned cold.

General Metcalf walked in and sat down. 'You all look like pallbearers,' he said with forced cheerfulness.

'Isn't that what we are?' said Brogan sourly. 'As soon as the Senate takes a vote, all that's left is to hold a wake.'

'I've just come from the Senate reception room,' said Metcalf. 'Secretary Oates is buttonholing members of the President's party, trying to persuade them to hold off the vote.'

'What are his chances?' asked Sandecker.

'Nil. The Senate is only going through the formality of a debate. Four hours from now, it will all be over.'

Brogan shook his head disgustedly. 'I hear Moran has Chief Justice O'Brien standing by to administer the oath.'

'The oily bastard won't waste a second,' muttered Emmett.

'Any word from Louisiana?' asked Metcalf.

Emmett gave the General a negative stare. 'Not for an hour. The last report from my agent in charge of the field office said he was making a sweep of a promising dock site.'

'Any concrete reason to believe Margolin is hidden in the Delta?'

'Only a stab in the dark notion by my Special Projects Director,' replied Sandecker.

Metcalf looked at Emmett. 'What are you doing about the Bougainvilles?'

'I've assigned nearly fifty agents to the case.'

'Can you make an arrest?'

'A waste of time. Min Koryo and Lee Tong would be back on the streets in an hour.'

'Surely there must be enough evidence.'

'Nothing the Attorney General can sink his teeth into. Most of their illegal operations are managed outside our borders in third world nations who aren't overly friendly towards the United States — '

The phone buzzed.

'Emmett.'

'Agent Goodman in communications, sir.'

'What is it Goodman?'

'I have contact with agent Griffin in Louisiana.'

'About time,' Emmett snapped impatiently. 'Put me through.'

'Hold on.' There was a pause broken by an audible click, and then Emmett heard the sound of laboured breathing. He switched on the speaker amplifier so the others could hear.

'Griffin, this is Sam Emmett, can you hear me?'

'Yes sir . . . very clearly.' The words seemed uttered in pain. 'We ran . . . ran into trouble.'

'What happened?'

'We spotted a Bougainville cargo ship tied to a pier beside a barge and towboat about seventy miles below New Orleans. Before my team and I could gain entry for a search, we were fired upon by heavy weapons mounted on the ship. Everyone was hit . . . I have two killed and seven wounded including myself. It was a massacre . . .' The voice choked and went quiet for a few moments. When it came back on the line the tone was noticeably weaker. 'Sorry for not making contact sooner, but our communications gear was shot out and I had to walk two miles before I could find a telephone.'

Emmett's face took on a compassionate look. The thought of a badly wounded man trailing blood for two miles in the scorching heat of summer stirred his normally rock-hard emotions.

Sandecker moved close to the speaker. 'What of Pitt and Giordino?'

'The NUMA people and one of my agents were flying surveillance in our helicopter,' Griffin answered. 'They got the hell shot out of them and crashed somewhere upriver. I doubt there were any survivors.'

Sandecker stepped back, his expression gone lifeless. He turned away and clenched his fists in fury.

Emmett leaned over the speaker. 'Griffin?'

His only reply was a vague muttering.

'Griffin, listen to me. Can you go on?'

'Yes sir . . . I'll try.'

'The barge, what is the situation with the barge?'

'Tug . . . tug pushed it away . . .'

'Pushed it where?'

'Downriver . . . last seen going towards Head of Passes.'

'Head of Passes?'

'The bottom end of the Mississippi where the river splits into three main channels to the sea,' answered Sandecker. 'South Pass, South-west Pass, and Pass à Lourtre. Most major shipping uses the first two.'

'Griffin, how long since the barge left your area?'

There was no answer, no buzzing of a broken connection, no sound at all.

'I think he's passed out,' said Metcalf.

'Help is on the way. Do you understand, Griffin?'

Still no reply.

'Why move the barge out to sea?' Brogan wondered aloud.

'No reason I can think of,' said Sandecker.

Emmett's phone buzzed on his inter-office line.

'There's an urgent call for Admiral Sandecker,' said Don Miller, his Deputy Director.

Emmett looked up. 'A call for you, Admiral. If you wish, you can take it in the outer office.'

Sandecker thanked him and stepped into the anteroom where Emmett's private secretary showed him to a telephone at an empty desk.

He punched the blinking white button. 'This is Admiral Sandecker.'

'One moment, sir,' came the familiar voice of the NUMA headquarters' chief operator.

315

'Hello?'

'Sandecker here. Who's this?'

'You're a tough nut to crack, Admiral. If I hadn't said my call concerned Dirk Pitt, your secretary would never have arranged our connection.'

'Who is this?' Sandecker demanded again.

'My name is Sal Casio. I'm working on the Bougainville case with Dirk.'

Ten minutes later, when Sandecker walked back into Emmett's office, he appeared stunned and shaken. Brogan instantly sensed something was wrong.

'What is it?' he asked. 'You look like you've rubbed shoulders with a banshee.'

'The barge,' Sandecker murmured quietly. 'The Bougainvilles have struck a deal with Moran. They're taking it out into the open sea to be scuttled.'

'What are you saying?'

'Loren Smith and Vince Margolin are sentenced to die so Alan Moran can be president. The barge is to be their tomb in a hundred fathoms of water.'

70

'Any sign of pursuit?' the river pilot asked, synchronising the control levers of the helm console with the finesse of a conductor leading an orchestra.

Lee Tong stepped back from the large open window at the rear of the pilothouse and lowered the binoculars. 'Nothing except a strange cloud of black smoke about two or three miles astern.'

'Probably an oil fire.'

'Seems to be following.'

'An illusion. The river has a habit of doing weird things to the eyes. What looks to be a mile away is four. Lights where no lights are supposed to be. Ships approaching in a channel that fade away as you get closer. Yes, the river can fool you when she gets playful.'

Lee Tong gazed up the channel again. He had learned to tune out the pilot's never ending commentary on the Mississippi, but he admired his skill and experience.

Captain Kim Pujon was a long time professional river pilot for Bougainville Maritime Inc, but he still retained his Asian superstitious nature. He seldom took his eyes off the channel and the barge ahead as he expertly balanced the speeds of the four engines generating 12,000 horsepower and delicately guided the towboat's four forward rudders and six backing rudders. Under his feet the huge diesels pounded over at full power, driving the barge through the water at nearly sixteen miles an hour, straining the cables that held the two vessels together.

They hurtled past an inbound Swedish oil tanker, and Lee Tong braced himself as the barge and towboat swept up and over the wash. 'How much further to deep water?'

'Our hull passed from fresh to salt about ten miles back. We should cross the coastal shallows in another fifty minutes.'

'Keep your eyes open for a research ship with a red hull and flying the British blue ensign.'

'We're boarding a Royal Navy ship after we scuttle?' Pujon asked in surprise.

'A former Norwegian merchantman,' explained Lee Tong. 'I purchased her seven years ago and refitted her out as a research and survey vessel – a handy disguise to fool custom authorities and the Coastguard.'

'Let us hope it fools whoever chases after us.'

Lee Tong grunted. 'Why not? Any American search force will be told we were picked up and are under lock and key by the finest English accent money can buy. Before the research ship docks in New Orleans, you, I, and our crew will be long gone.'

Pujon pointed. 'The Port Eads light coming up. We'll be in open water soon.'

Lee Tong nodded in grim satisfaction. 'If they couldn't stop us by now, they're too late, far too late.'

General Metcalf, laying his long and distinguished career on the line, ignored Moran's threats and ordered a military alert throughout the Gulf Coast states. At Eglin Air Force Base and Hurlburt Field in Florida, tactical fighter wings and special operations gun ships scrambled and thundered west while attack squadrons rose from Corpus Christi Naval Air Station in Texas and swept towards the east.

He and Sandecker raced by car to the Pentagon to direct the rescue operation from the war room. Once the vast machine was set into motion, they could do little but listen to reports and stare at an enormous satellite photomap thrown on the screen by a rear projector.

Metcalf failed to conceal his apprehension. He stood uneasily rubbing his palms together, peering at the lights on the map indicating the progress of the air strike as the planes converged on a circle lit in red.

'How soon before the first planes arrive?' asked Sandecker.

317

'Ten, no more than twelve minutes.'

'Surface craft?'

'Not less than an hour,' replied Metcalf bitterly. 'We were caught short. No naval craft are in the immediate area except a nuclear sub sixty miles out in the Gulf.'

'Coastguard?'

'There's an armed rescue-response cutter off Grand Island. It might make it in time.'

Sandecker studied the photomap. 'Doubtful. It's thirty miles away.'

Metcalf wiped his hands with a handkerchief. 'The situation looks grim,' he said. 'Except for scare tactics the air mission is useless. We can't send in planes to strike the towboat without endangering the barge. One is practically on top of the other.'

'Bougainville would quickly scuttle the barge in any case.'

'If only we had a surface craft in the area. At least we might attempt a boarding.'

'And capture Smith and Margolin alive.'

Metcalf sank into a chair. 'We might pull it off yet. A Navy special warfare SEAL attachment is due to arrive by helicopter in a few minutes.'

'After what happened to those FBI agents, they could be going to a slaughter.'

'Our last hope,' Metcalf said helplessly. 'If they can't save them, nobody can.'

The first aircraft to arrive on the scene was not a screaming jet fighter, but a Navy four-engined reconnaissance plane that had been diverted from weather patrol. The pilot, a boyish-faced young man in his middle twenties tapped his copilot on the arm and pointed down to his left.

'A towboat pushing one barge. She must be what all the fuss is about.'

'What do we do now?' asked the copilot, a narrow jawed, slightly older man with bushy red hair.

'Notify base with the cheery news. Unless, of course, you want to keep it a secret.'

Less than a minute after the sighting report was given, a gruff voice came over the radio. 'Who is the aircraft commander?'

'I am.'

'I am, who?'

'You go first.'

'This is General Clayton Metcalf of the Joint Chiefs.'

The pilot smiled and made a circular motion around the side of his head with an index finger. 'Are you crazy or is this a gag?'

'My sanity is not at issue here, and no, this is not a gag. Your name and rank please.'

'You won't believe it.'

'I'll be the judge.'

'Lieutenant Ulysses S. Grant.'

'Why would I doubt you?' Metcalf laughed. 'There was a great third baseman by that name.'

'My father,' Grant said in awe. 'You remember him?'

'They don't hand out four stars for bad memories,' said Metcalf. 'Do you have television equipment on board, Lieutenant?'

'Yes . . . yes, sir,' Grant stammered as he realised whom he was really talking to. 'We tape storms close-on for the meteorologists.'

'I'll have my communications officer give your video operator the frequency for satellite transmission to the Pentagon. Keep your camera trained on the towboat.'

Grant turned to his copilot. 'My God, what do you make of that?'

71

The towboat surged past the lookout at the South Pass pilot station, the last outpost of the muddy Mississippi, and swept into the open sea.

Captain Pujon said: 'Thirty minutes to deep water.'

Lee Tong nodded as his eyes studied the circling weather plane. Then he picked up the binoculars and scanned the sea. The only ship in sight was his counterfeit research vessel approaching from the east about eight miles off the port bow.

'We've beaten them,' he said confidently.

'They can still blow us out of the water from the air.'

'And risk sinking the barge? I don't think so. They want the Vice President alive.'

'How can they know he's on board?'

'They don't, at least not for certain. One more reason they won't attack what might be an innocent towboat unloading a trash barge at sea.'

A crewman scrambled up the steps to the pilot house and stepped through the door. 'Sir,' he said, pointing. 'An aircraft coming up astern.'

Lee Tong swung the binoculars in the direction of the crewman's outstretched arm. A US Navy helicopter was beating its way towards the towboat only fifty feet above the waves.

He frowned and said: 'Alert the men.'

The crewman threw a salute and hurried off.

'A gun ship?' Pujon asked uneasily. 'It could hover fifty feet off, blast us to bits without scratching the barge.'

'Fortunately no. She's an assault transport. Probably carrying a team of Navy SEALS. They mean to assault the towboat.'

Lieutenant Homer Dodds stuck his head out the side jump door of the chopper and peered down. The two vessels looked peaceful enough, he thought, as a crewman stepped from the pilothouse and waved a greeting. Nothing unusual or suspicious. The armament he had been warned about was not visible.

He spoke into a microphone. 'Have you established radio contact?'

'We've hailed on every marine frequency in the book and they don't answer,' replied the pilot from the cockpit.

'Okay, drop us over the barge.'

'Roger.'

Dodds picked up a bullhorn and spoke into the mouthpiece. 'Ahoy, the towboat. This is the US Navy. Reduce speed and slow to a stop. We are coming aboard.'

Below, the crewman cupped hands to his ears and shook his head, signalling he couldn't hear above the exhaust whine of the helicopter's turbines. Dodds repeated the message and the crewman made an inviting wave of his arm. By now Dodds was close enough to see he was an Oriental.

The speed of the towboat and barge dropped off, and they began to roll in the swells. The pilot of the helicopter played the wind and hovered over the flat deck of the barge in preparation for Dodds' assault team to jump the final three or four feet.

Dodds turned and took a final look at his men. They were lean and hard, and probably the toughest, raunchiest, meanest bunch of multi-purpose killers in the Navy. They were the only group of men Dodds ever commanded who genuinely liked combat. They were eager, their weapons at the ready and prepared for anything. Except, perhaps, for total surprise.

The 'copter was only ten feet above the barge when trapdoors were sprung, hatch covers thrown back, and twenty crewmen opened up with Steyr-Mannlicher AUG assault carbines.

.223 calibre shells flew into the SEALS from all directions, smoke and the grunts of men being hit erupted simultaneously. Dodds and his men reacted savagely, cutting down any towboat crewman who exposed himself, but bullets sprayed into their compartment as if propelled out of a firehose and turned it into a slaughter den. There was no escape. It was as if their backs were against the wall of a dead-end alley.

The noise of the concentrated firepower drowned out the sound of the helicopter's exhaust. The pilot was hit in the first burst which exploded the canopy, hurling bits of metal and plexiglass throughout the cockpit. The chopper shuddered and veered sharply around on its axis. The copilot wrestled with the controls but they had lost all response.

The Air Force fighters arrived and instantly appraised the situation. Their squadron leader gave hurried instructions and dived, skimming low over the stern of the towboat in an attempt to draw fire away from the battered and smoking helicopter. But the ploy didn't work. They were ignored by Lee Tong's gunners. With growing frustration at the orders not to attack, their passes became ever lower until one pilot clipped off the towboat's radar antenna.

Too badly mauled to remain in the air any longer, the crippled chopper and its pitiful cargo of dead and wounded finally gave up the struggle to remain airborne and fell into the sea beside the barge.

Sandecker and Metcalf sat in shock as the video camera on board the weather plane recorded the drama. The war room became deadly quiet and nobody spoke as they watched and waited for the camera to reveal signs of survivors. Six heads were all they could count in the blue of the sea.

'The end of the game,' Metcalf said with chilly finality.

Sandecker didn't answer. He turned away from the screen and sat heavily in a chair beside the long conference table, the pepper and vinegar spirit gone out of him.

Metcalf listened without reaction to the voices of the pilots over the speakers. Their anger at not being able to pound the towboat turned vehement. Not told of the people held captive inside the barge, they voiced their anger at the high command, unaware their heated words were heard and recorded at the Pentagon a thousand miles away.

A shadow of a smile touched Sandecker's face. He could not help but sympathise with them.

Then a friendly voice cut in. 'Lieutenant Grant calling . . . is it okay to call you direct, General?'

'It's all right, son,' said Metcalf quietly. 'Go ahead.'

'I have two ships approaching the area, sir. Stand by for a picture of the first one.'

With a new shred of hope, their eyes looked on the screen. At first the image was small and indistinct. Then the weather plane's camera man zoomed in on a red-hulled vessel.

'From up here I'd judge her to be a survey ship,' reported Grant.

A gust of wind caught the flag on the ensign staff and stretched out its blue colours.

'British,' announced Metcalf dejectedly. 'We don't dare ask foreign nationals to die for our sake.'

'You're right, of course. I've never known an oceanographic scientist to carry an automatic rifle.'

Metcalf turned and said: 'Grant?'

'Sir?'

'Contact the British research vessel and request they pick up survivors from the helicopter.'

Before Grant could acknowledge the video image distorted and the screen went black.

'We've lost your picture, Grant.'

'One moment, General. My crewman manning the camera informs me the battery pack on the recorder went dead. He'll have it replaced in a minute.'

'What's the situation with the towboat?'

'She and the barge are underway again, only more slowly than before.'

Metcalf turned to Sandecker. 'Luck just isn't on our side, is it Jim?'

'No, Clayton. We've had none at all . . .' he hesitated. 'Unless, of course, the second ship is an armed Coastguard cutter.'

'Grant?' Metcalf boomed.

'Won't be long, sir.'

'Never mind that. What type of vessel is the second ship you reported? Coastguard or Navy?'

'Neither. Strictly civilian.'

Metcalf dissolved in defeat, but a spark stirred within Sandecker. He leaned over the microphone.

'Grant, this is Admiral James Sandecker. Can you describe her?'

'She's nothing like you'd expect to see on the ocean.'

'What's her nationality?'

'Nationality?'

'Her flag, man. What flag is she flying?'

'You won't believe me.'

'Spit it out.'

'Well, Admiral, I was born and raised in Montana, but I've read enough history books to recognise a Confederate flag when I see one.'

72

Out of a world all but vanished, her brass steam whistle splitting the air, the seawater frothing white beneath her churning paddle wheels, and spewing black smoke from her towering twin stacks, the *Stonewall Jackson* pitched towards the towboat with the awkward grace of a pregnant southern belle, hoisting her hooped skirts whilst crossing a mud puddle.

Shrieking gulls rode the wind above a giant stern flag displaying the crossed stars and bars of the Confederacy, while on the roof of the 'Texas' deck, a man furiously pounded out the old South's national hymn, 'Dixie', on the keyboard of an old-fashioned steam calliope. The sight of the old riverboat charging across the sea stirred the souls of the men flying above. They knew they were witnessing an adventure none would ever see again.

In the ornate pilothouse, Pitt and Giordino stared at the barge and towboat that loomed closer with every revolution of the thirty-foot paddle wheels.

'The man was right,' Giordino shouted above the steam whistle and calliope.

'What man?' Pitt asked loudly.

'The one who said, "save your Confederate money, the South will rise again".'

'Lucky for us it has,' Pitt said, smiling.

'We're gaining.' This from a wiry-built little man who twisted the six foot helm with both hands.

'They've lost speed,' Pitt concurred.

'If the boilers don't blow, and the sweet old darlin' holds together in these damned waves . . .' The man at the wheel paused in midsentence, made an imperceptible turn of his big, white bearded head and let fly a spurt of tobacco juice with deadly accuracy into a brass cuspidor before continuing. 'We ought to overhaul them in the next two miles.'

Captain Melvin Belcheron had skippered the *Stonewall Jackson* for thirty of his sixty-two years. He knew every buoy, bend, sandbar and riverbank light from St Louis to New Orleans by heart. But this was the first time he'd ever taken his boat into the open sea.

The *sweet old darlin'* was built in 1915 at Columbus, Kentucky, on the Ohio River. Her like was the last to stoke the fires of imagination during the golden years of steamboating, and her like would never be seen again. The smell of burning coal, the swish of the steam engine, and the rhythmic splash of the paddle wheels would soon belong only in history books.

Her shallow wooden hull was long and beamy, measuring two hundred and seventy feet by forty-four. Her horizontal non-condensing engines ran at about forty revolutions per minute. She was rated at slightly over one thousand tons, yet despite her bulk she walked the water with a draft of just thirty-two inches.

Down below on the main deck, four men, sweat-streaked and blackened with soot, furiously shovelled coal into the furnaces under four high-pressure boilers. When the pressure began to creep into the red, the chief engineer, a crusty old Scot by the name of McGeen, hung his hat over the steam gauge.

McGeen was the first man to vote for pursuit after Pitt crashlanded the helicopter in shallow water near Fort Jackson, waded ashore with Giordino and Hogan, and described the situation. At first there was undisguised disbelief, but after seeing their wounds, the bullet riddled aircraft, and then hearing a deputy sheriff describe the dead and injured FBI agents a few miles downriver, McGeen stoked up his boilers, Belcheron rounded up his deck crew and forty men from the 6th Louisiana Regiment tramped on board, hooting and hollering, and dragging along two ancient field cannon.

'Pour on the coal, boys,' McGeen pressed his black gang. He looked like the devil with his trimmed goatee and brushed up eyebrows in the flickering glare of the open furnace doors. 'If we mean to save the Vice President, we've got to have more steam.'

The *Stonewall Jackson* thrashed after the towboat and barge, almost as if sensing the urgency of her mission. When new, her top speed was rated at fifteen miles an hour, but in the past forty years she was never called upon to provide more than twelve.* She thrust downriver with the current at fourteen, then fifteen . . . sixteen . . . eighteen miles an hour. When she burst from the South Pass Channel, she was driving through the water at twenty, smoke and sparks exploding through the flared capitals atop her stacks.

The men of the 6th Louisiana Regiment – the dentists, plumbers, accountants, who marched and re-fought battles of the Civil War as a hobby – grunted and sweated in the nondescript woollen grey and butternut uniforms that once made up the army of the Confederate States of America. Under the command of a major, they heaved huge cotton bales into place as breastworks. The two Napoleon twelve-pounder cannon were wheeled into place on the bow, their smooth-

---

* Speed on inland waterways is rated in miles per hour, never in knots.

bore barrels loaded with ballbearings scrounged from McGeen's engine room supply locker.

Pitt stared down at the growing fortress of wired bales. Cotton against steel, he mused, single-shot muskets against automatic rifles.

It was going to be an interesting fight, if not a losing one.

Lieutenant Grant tore his eyes from the incredible sight under his wings and radioed the ship flying the British flag.

'This Air Force Weather Recon zero-four-zero calling oceanographic research vessel. Do you read?'

'Righto, yank, hear you clearly,' came back a cheery voice fresh off a cricket field. 'This is Her Majesty's Ship *Pathfinder*. What can we do for you, zero-four-zero?'

'A chopper went into the drink about three miles west of you. Can you effect a rescue of survivors, *Pathfinder*?'

'We bloody well better. Can't allow the poor chaps to drown, can we?'

'I'll circle the crash sector, *Pathfinder*. Home in on me.'

'Jolly good. We're on our way. Out.'

Grant took up position over the struggling men in the water. The Gulf current was warm so there was no fear of their succumbing to exposure, but any bleeding wounds were certain to attract sharks.

'You don't carry much influence,' said his copilot.

'What do you mean?' asked Grant.

'The limey ship isn't responding. She's turned away.'

Grant leaned forward and banked the plane to see out the opposite cockpit window. His copilot was right: the *Pathfinder*'s bow had come around on a course away from the helicopter's survivors and was aimed towards the *Stonewall Jackson*.

'*Pathfinder*, this is zero-four-zero,' Grant called. 'What is your problem? Repeat. What is your problem?'

There was no reply.

'Unless I'm suffering one hell of an hallucination,' said Metcalf, staring in wonder at the video transmission, 'that old relic from "Tom Sawyer" intends to attack the towboat.'

'She's giving every indication,' agreed Sandecker.

'Where do you suppose she came from?'

Sandecker stood with his arms crossed in front of him, his face radiating an elated expression. 'Pitt,' he muttered under his breath, 'you wily, irrepressible son of a bitch.'

'You say something?'

'Just speculating to myself.'

'What can they possibly hope to accomplish?'

'I think they mean to ram and board.'

'Insanity, sheer insanity,' snorted Metcalf gloomily. 'The gunners on the towboat will cut them to pieces.'

Suddenly, Sandecker tensed, seeing something in the background on the screen. Metcalf didn't catch it, no one else watching caught it either.

The admiral grasped Metcalf by the arm. 'The British vessel!'

Metcalf looked up, startled. 'What about it?'

'Good God, man, see for yourself. She's going to run down the steamboat.'

Metcalf saw the distance between the two ships rapidly narrowing, saw the wake of the *Pathfinder* turn to foam as she surged ahead at 'Full Speed'.

'Grant!' he bellowed.

'Here, sir.'

'The limey ship, why isn't she headed towards the men in the water?'

'I can't say, General. Her skipper acknowledged my request for rescue, but chased after the old paddleboat instead. I haven't been able to raise him again. He appears to be ignoring my transmissions.'

'Take them out!' Sandecker demanded. 'Call in an air strike and take the bastards out!'

Metcalf hesitated, torn by indecision. 'But she's flying the British flag, for Christ's sake.'

'I'll stake my rank she's a Bougainville ship, and the flag is a decoy.'

'You can't know that.'

'Maybe. But I do know that if she crushes the steamboat into firewood, our last chance to save Vince Margolin is gone.'

73

In the pilothouse of the towboat a burst of fire from the SEALS had shattered the inner workings of the command console, fouling the rudder controls. Captain Pujon had no option but to reduce speed and steer by jockeying the throttle levers.

Lee Tong did not spare him a glance. He was busy issuing orders over the radio to the commander of the *Pathfinder*, while keeping a wary eye on the wallowing steamboat.

Finally, he turned to Pujon. 'Can't you regain our top speed?'

'Eight miles is the best I can do if we want to maintain a straight course.'

'How far?' he asked for the tenth time that hour.

'According to the depth sounder the bottom's beginning to drop off. Another two miles should do it.'

'Two miles,' Lee Tong repeated thoughtfully. 'Time to set the detonators.'

'I'll alert you by blowing the airhorn when we come over a hundred fathoms,' said Pujon.

Lee Tong stared across the dark sea, stained by the run-off from the Mississippi River. The masquerading research ship was only a few hundred yards away from slicing through the brittle sides of the *Stonewall Jackson*. He could hear the haunting wail of the calliope drifting with the wind. He shook his head in disbelief, wondering who was responsible for the old riverboat's sudden appearance.

He was about to leave the pilothouse and cross over to the barge when he noticed one of the milling aircraft overhead abruptly slip out of formation and dive towards the sea.

A ghost white, F/A 21, Navy strike aircraft levelled off two hundred feet above the wave tops and unleashed two anti-ship missiles. Lee Tong watched in numbed horror as the laser controlled warheads skimmed across the water and slammed into the red-hulled decoy ship, stopping her dead in her tracks with a blast that turned the entire upper works into a grotesque tangle of shattered steel. Then came a second, even stronger explosion that enveloped the ship in a ball of flame. For an instant she seemed to hang suspended as if locked in time.

Lee Tung stood tensed in despair as the broken vessel slowly rolled over and died, falling to the floor of the Gulf and sealing all hope of his escape.

Fiery fragments of the *Pathfinder* rained down around the *Stonewall Jackson*, igniting several small fires that were quickly extinguished by the crew. The surface over the sunken ship turned black with oily bubbles as a hissing cloud of steam and smoke spiralled into the sky.

'Christ in heaven!' Captain Belcheron gasped in astonishment. 'Will you look at that. Those Navy boys mean business.'

'Somebody is watching over us,' Pitt commented thankfully. His eyes returned to the barge. His face was expressionless; but for the swaying of his body to compensate for the roll of the boat, he might have been sculpted from solid teak. The gap had closed to three-quarters of a mile, and he could make out the tiny figure of a man scrambling across the bow of the towboat onto the barge before disappearing down a deck hatch.

An enormous man with the stout build of an Oliver Hardy barrelled up the ladder from the 'Texas' deck and came through the door. He wore the grey uniform and gold braid of a Confederate

327

major. The shirt under the unbuttoned coat was damp with perspiration, and he was panting from exertion. He stood there a moment, wiping his forehead with a sleeve, catching his breath.

At last he said, 'Doggone, I don't know if I'd rather die by a bullet in the head, by drowning or a heart attack.'

Leroy Laroche operated a travel agency by day, functioned as a loving husband and father by night, and acted as commander of the 6th Louisiana Regiment of the Confederate States Army on weekends. He was popular among his men and was re-elected every year to lead the regiment in battlefield re-enactments around the country. The fact that he was about to engage in the real thing didn't seem to faze him.

'Lucky for us you had those cotton bales on board,' he said to the captain.

Belcheron smiled. 'We keep them on deck as historic examples of the sweet old darlin's maritime heritage.'

Pitt looked at Laroche. 'Your men in position, Major?'

'Loaded, prime full of Dixie beer and rarin' to fight,' Laroche replied.

'What sort of weapons do they own?'

'Fifty-eight calibre Springfield muskets, which most rebels carried late in the war. Shoots a Minie ball five hundred yards.'

'How fast can they fire?'

'Most of my boys can get off three rounds a minute, a few can do four. But I'm putting the best shots on the barricade while the others load.'

'And the cannon? Do they actually fire?'

'You bet. They can hit a tree with a can of cement at half a mile.'

'Can of cement?'

'Cheaper to make than real cannon shot.'

Pitt considered that and grinned. 'Good luck, Major. Tell your men to keep their heads down. Muzzle loaders take more time to aim than machine-guns.'

'I reckon they know how to duck,' said Laroche. 'When do you want us to open fire?'

'I leave that to you.'

'Excuse me, Major,' Giordino cut in. 'Do any of your men happen to carry a spare weapon?'

Larouche unsnapped the leather holster on his belt and passed Giordino a large pistol. 'A Le Mat revolver,' he said. 'Shoots nine forty-two calibre shells through a rifled barrel. But if you'll notice, there's a big smoothbore barrel underneath that holds a charge of buckshot. Take good care of it. My great granddaddy carried it from Bull Run to Appomatox.'

Giordino was genuinely impressed. 'I don't want to leave you unarmed.'

Laroche pulled his sabre from its scabbard. 'This will do me just fine. Well, I best get back to my men.'

After the big, jovial major left the pilothouse, Pitt bent down and opened the violin case, lifted out the Thompson and inserted a full drum. He held his side with one hand and cautiously straightened, his lips pressed tight from the pain that speared his chest.

'You be all right up here?' he asked Belcheron.

'Don't pay no mind to me,' the captain answered. He nodded at a cast iron potbellied stove. 'I'll have my own armour when the fireworks start.'

'Thank God for that,' exclaimed Metcalf.

'What is it?' Sandecker asked.

Metcalf held up a paper. 'A reply from the British Admiralty in London. The only *Pathfinder* on duty with the Royal Navy is a missile destroyer. They have no research ship by that name, nor is any in the Gulf area.' He gave Sandecker a thankful look. 'You called a good play, Jim.'

'We had a bit of luck after all.'

'The poor bastards on that steamboat are the ones who need it now.'

'Any more we can do? Anything we've overlooked?'

Metcalf shook his head. 'Not from this end. The Coastguard cutter is only fifteen minutes away and the nuclear sub is not far behind.'

'Neither will arrive in time.'

'Perhaps the people on the steamboat can somehow stall the towboat until . . .' Metcalf didn't finish.

'You don't really believe in miracles, do you, Clayton?'

'No, I guess I don't.'

74

A maelstrom of automatic weapons fire lashed into the *Stonewall Jackson* as Lee Tong's crew opened up at three hundred yards. Bullets hummed and whistled, splintering the gleaming white wood and gingerbread carvings on the rails and deck cabins, clanging and ricocheting off the ship's bronze bell. The huge, unglazed window in the pilothouse disintegrated into silvery fragments. Inside, Captain Belcheron was stunned by a shell that grazed the top of his head and turned his white hair red. His vision blurred and went double, but he hung onto the spokes of the great wheel with savage determination while harking tobacco juice out of the broken window.

The calliope player, protected by a forest of brass plumbing, began playing the 'Yellow Rose of Texas', which fell on several flat tones as holes suddenly appeared in his steam whistles.

On the main deck, Major Laroche and his regiment, along with Pitt and Giordino, crouched out of sight. The cotton bales made strong defensive works and no bullets penetrated. The open boiler area behind the main staircase caught the worst of it. Two of McGeen's stokers were hit and the overhead tubing was penetrated, allowing steam to escape in scalding streams. McGeen took his hat off the pressure gauge. It was pegged in the red. He expelled a long sigh. A miracle nothing had burst, he thought, the rivets were straining on the boilers. He quickly began spinning relief valves to let off the immense pressure in preparation for the coming collision.

The *Stonewall Jackson*'s paddle wheels were still driving her at twenty miles an hour. If she had to die, she was not going to end up like her former sisters, rotting away in some forgotten bayou or broken up for wharf wood. She was going out a legend and intended to end her time on the water in style.

Brushing aside the waves that pounded her bow, shrugging off the frightful torrent of lead that shredded her flimsy superstructure, she forged ahead.

Lee Tong watched in bitter fascination as the steamboat came on steadily. He stood in an open hatch on the barge and poured a stream of bullets at her, hoping to hit a vital part and slow her down. But he might as well have been shooting air pellets at a rampaging elephant.

He set aside his Steyr-Mannlicher carbine and raised the binoculars. None of the crew was visible behind the barricade of cotton bales. Even the sieved pilothouse looked deserted. The gold letters of the smashed nameplate were visible, but all he could make out was the 'JACKSON'.

The flat bow was pointed square for the towboat's port side. It was a stupid, futile gesture, he reasoned, a stalling tactic, nothing more. In spite of its superior size, the wooden paddle steamer could not expect to damage the towboat's steel hull.

He retrieved the Steyr-Mannlicher, inserted another ammo clip and concentrated his fire into the pilothouse in an attempt to damage the helm.

Sandecker and Metcalf watched too.

They sat captivated by the hopeless, irresistible magnificence of it

330

all. Radio contact was attempted with the steamboat, but there was no response. Captain Belcheron had been too busy to answer, and the old river rat didn't think he had anything worth saying anyway.

Metcalf called Lieutenant Grant. 'Spiral in closer,' he ordered.

Grant acknowledged and made a series of tight banks over the vessels below. The detail of the towboat was quite sharp. They could pick out nearly thirty men blasting away across the water. The steamboat, however, was obscured by the smoke shooting from her stacks and great clouds of exhaust steam spurting out of the 'scape pipes' aft of the pilothouse.

'She'll bash herself to bits when she strikes,' said Sandecker.

'Give them credit. They're doing more than we can.'

Metcalf nodded slowly. 'Yes, we can't take that away from them.'

Sandecker came out of his chair and pointed. 'Look, there, on the steamboat where the wind has blown the smoke off to the side.'

'What is it?'

'Isn't that a pair of cannon?'

Metcalf came alert. 'By God, you're right. They look like old relics from a town park.'

At two hundred yards Laroche raised his sword and yelled, 'Batteries one and two, train and prime your guns.'

'Battery one primed and aimed,' shouted back a man in antique wire spectacles.

'Battery two ready, Major.'

'Then fire!'

The lanyards were jerked and the two antique cannon belched their load of ballbearing grapeshot from their muzzles in earsplitting claps. The first shot actually penetrated the side of the towboat, crashing into the galley and mangling the ovens. The second soared into the pilothouse, taking off Captain Pujon's head and carrying away the wheel. Dazed by the unexpected barrage, Lee Tong's men slackened their fire for several seconds, recovered and opened up with renewed ferocity, concentrating on the narrow slits between the cotton bales where the cannon barrels protruded.

Now the smooth bores were run back while the artillery men quickly rammed home the sponges and began reloading. Bullets whined over their heads and shoulders, and one man was struck in the neck. But in less than a minute the old Napoleons were ready to blast again.

'Aim for the cables!' Pitt shouted. 'Cut the barge away!'

Laroche nodded and relayed Pitt's orders. The guns were run out and the next broadside swept the towboat's bow, causing an

331

explosion of coiled rope and cable, but the tenacious grip on the barge remained unbroken.

Coldly, almost contemptuous of the terrific blitz that swept the *Stonewall Jackson*, the make-believe soldiers lined up the sights on their single shot muskets and waited for the command to fire.

Only two hundred yards separated the vessels when Laroche raised his sword again. 'Firing rank, take aim. Okay boys, give 'em hell. Fire!'

The front of the steamboat exploded in a tremendous torrent of fire and smoke. The towboat was raked with a seemingly solid wall of Minie bullets. The effect was devastating. Glass dissolved in every port and window, paint chips flew off the bulkheads, and bodies began falling, deluging the decks with blood.

Before Lee Tong's gunners could recover, Pitt stitched the towboat from bow to stern with a steady stream of fire from the Thompson. Giordino hunched against the cotton barricade, waiting for the range to close to fire the revolver, watching in rapt interest as the second and third ranks ran through the dozen cumbersome procedures of re-arming a muzzle-loading musket.

The Confederates laid down a killing fire. Volley after volley followed in succession, almost every other shot striking flesh and bone. The smoke and shattering sounds were punctuated by the cries of the wounded. Laroche, swept away by the carnage and commotion, thundered and swore at the top of his voice, prodding his sharp shooters to aim true, exhorting the loaders to move more rapidly.

One minute passed, two, then three, as the fighting reached a savage pitch. Fire broke out on the *Jackson* and flames soared up her wooden sides. In the pilothouse, Captain Belcheron yanked on the steam whistle cord and shouted into the voice tube leading to McGeen in the engine area. The riflemen ceased their fire and everyone braced themselves for the approaching collision.

A strange, unearthly silence fell over the steamboat as the crack of the guns faded and the haunting wail of the calliope died away. She was like a boxer who had taken a fearful beating from a far stronger adversary and could take no more, but had somehow reached deep into her exhausted reserves for one last knockout punch.

She struck square amidships with a rumbling crunch that knocked over the cotton bale barricade, heeling the towboat over on its starboard beam, crushing back her bow by six feet as planks and beams gave way like lathes. Both stacks fell forward, throwing sparks and smoke over the battle that rapidly resumed its intensity. Guns fired at point blank range. The support ropes burned through and the landing stages dropped onto the towboat's decks like great fingers, gripping the two vessels fast together.

332

'Fix bayonets!' Laroche boomed.

Someone broke out the regiment's battle flag and began waving it wildly in the air. Muskets were reloaded and bayonets attached. The calliope player had returned to his post and was pounding out 'Dixie' once again. Pitt was amazed that no one showed any sign of fear. Instead, there was a general feeling of uncontrolled delirium. He couldn't help thinking he'd somehow crossed a time barrier into the past.

Laroche whipped off his officer's hat, hung it on the tip of his sword and raised it into the air. 'Sixth Louisiana!' he cried. 'Go git 'em!'

Screaming the rebel yell like demons emerging from the centre of the earth, the men in grey stormed on board the towboat. Laroche was struck in the chin and one knee, but hobbled and pressed on. Pitt laid down a covering fire until the last cartridge poured from the Thompson. Then he laid the gun on a cotton bale and charged after Giordino who hopped across a landing stage, favouring his injured leg and firing the revolver like a wild man. McGeen and his boiler crew followed, wielding their shovels like clubs.

Bougainville's men bore no resemblance to their attackers. They were hired killers, ruthless men who offered no mercy nor expected it, but they were not prepared for the incredible onslaught of the Southerners and made the mistake of leaping from the protected steel bulkheads and meeting the surge head on.

The *Stonewall Jackson* was wreathed in fire. The artillery men fired one last volley at the towboat, aiming forward of the men fighting amidships, their shot sweeping away the cables attached to the barge. Shoved sideways by the continued momentum of the steamboat, the two steel vessels jackknifed around her crushed bow.

The 6th Louisiana overran the decks, lunging with their bayonets, but keeping up a deadly rate of fire. There was a score of individual hand-to-hand struggles; the five-foot Springfield musket and two-foot bayonet combining into a nasty close-in weapon. None of the weekend soldiers paused: they fought with a strange kind of reckless-ness, too caught up in the unimaginable din and excitement to be afraid.

Giordino didn't feel the blow. He was steadily advancing into the crew's quarters, firing at any Oriental face that showed itself when suddenly he was flat on his face, a bullet breaking the calf bone of his good leg.

Pitt lifted Giordino under the arms and dragged him into an empty passageway. 'You're not armour plated, you know.'

'Where in the hell have you been?' Giordino's voice tensed as the pain increased.

333

'Staying out of the way,' Pitt replied. 'I'm not armed.'

Girodino handed him the Le Mat revolver. 'Take this. I'm through for the day anyway.'

Pitt gave his friend a half smile. 'Sorry to leave you, but I've got to get inside the barge.'

Giordino opened his mouth to make an offhand reply, but Pitt was already gone. Ten seconds and he was snaking through the debris on the towboat's bow. He was almost too late. Free of its hold, the barge had drifted twenty feet away. A head and pair of shoulders raised from a hatch and fired off a burst. Pitt felt the passing bullets fan his hair and cheek. He dropped to the railing and rolled over the side into the sea.

Further aft, the Bougainville crew grimly hung on, obstinately giving way until they were finally overwhelmed by grey uniforms. The shouting and the gunfire slackened and went silent. The Confederate battle flag was run up the towboat's radio mast and the fight was over.

The amateur soldiers of the 6th Louisiana Regiment had handled themselves well. Surprisingly, none had been killed in the mêlée. Eighteen were wounded, only two critically. Laroche staggered from the midst of his cheering men and sagged to the deck beside Giordino. He reached over and the two injured bleeding men solemnly shook hands.

'Congratulations, Major,' said Giordino. 'You just made the play-offs.'

A big grin spread across Laroche's face. 'By God, we whipped 'em good, didn't we?'

Lee Tong emptied his weapon at the figure on the bow of the towboat, observing it fall into the water. Then he slumped against the edge of the hatch and watched the Confederate battle flag flutter in the gulf breeze.

With a distant kind of detachment, he accepted the unexpected disaster which had overtaken his carefully conceived operation. His crew was either dead or prisoner, and his escape ship was destroyed. Yet he was not ready to oblige his unknown opponents by surrendering. He was determined to carry out his grandmother's bargain with Moran and take his chances on escaping later.

He dropped down the side ladder of the lift shaft into the laboratory quarters and ran along the main corridor until he came to the door of the chamber that held the isolation cocoons. He entered and peered through the insulated plastic lid at the body within the first one. Vince Margolin stared back, his body too numb to respond, his mind too drugged to comprehend.

334

Lee Tong moved to the next cocoon and looked down at the serene, sleeping face of Loren Smith. She was heavily sedated and in a deep state of unconsciousness. Her death would be a waste, he thought. But she could not be allowed to live and testify. He leaned over and opened the cover and stroked her hair, staring at her through half-open eyes.

He had killed countless men, their features forgotten in less than seconds of their death. But the faces of the women lingered. He remembered the first, so many years ago on a tramp steamer in the middle of the Pacific Ocean; her haunting expression of bewilderment as her chained, nude body was dropped over the side.

'Nice place you have here,' came a voice from the doorway, 'but your lift is out of order.'

Lee Tong spun around and gaped at the man who stood wet and dripping, pointing a strange antique revolver at his chest.

'You!' he gasped.

Pitt's face – tired, haggard, and dark with beard stubble – lit up in a smile. 'Lee Tong Bougainville. What a coincidence.'

'You're alive!'

'A trite observation.'

'And responsible for all this: those mad men in the old uniforms, the riverboat . . .'

'The best I could arrange on the spur of the moment,' Pitt said apologetically.

Lee Tong's moment of utter confusion passed and he slowly curled his finger around the trigger of the Steyr-Mannlicher that hung loosely in one hand, muzzle aimed at the carpeted deck.

'Why have you pursued my grandmother and me, Mr Pitt?' he demanded, stalling. 'Why have you set out to wreck Bougainville Maritime?'

'That's like Hitler asking why the allies invaded Europe. In my case, you were responsible for the death of a friend.'

'Who?'

'Doesn't matter,' said Pitt indifferently. 'You never met her . . .'

Lee Tong swung up the barrel of his carbine and pulled the trigger.

Pitt was faster, but Giordino had used up the last cartridge and the revolver's hammer fell on an empty cylinder. He stiffened, expecting the impact of a bullet.

It never came.

Lee Tong had forgotten to insert a new clip after firing his final round at Pitt on the towboat. He lowered the carbine, his lips stretched into an inscrutable smile. 'It seems we have a stand-off, Mr Pitt.'

'Only temporary,' said Pitt, re-cocking the hammer and keeping

335

the revolver raised and aimed. 'My people will be coming aboard any minute now.'

Lee Tong sighed and relaxed. 'Then I can do little else but surrender and wait for arrest.'

'You'll never stand trial.'

The smile turned into a sneer. 'That's not for you to decide. Besides, you're hardly in a position to . . .'

Suddenly he flipped the carbine around, gripping the barrel and raising it as a club. The rifle butt was on a vicious downswing when Pitt squeezed the trigger and blasted Lee Tong in the throat with the barrel loaded with buckshot. The carbine poised in mid air and then fell from his hand as he stumbled backwards until striking the wall and dropping heavily to the deck.

Pitt left him where he lay and threw off the cover over Loren's cocoon. He gently lifted her out and carried her to the open lift. He checked the circuit breakers and found them on, but there was still no response from the lift motors when he pressed the 'UP' button.

He had no way of knowing the generators that provided electricity to the barge had run out of fuel and shut down, leaving only the emergency battery power to illuminate the overhead lighting. Scrounging through a supply locker, he found a rope which he tied under Loren's arms. Then he pulled himself through the lift roof's trap door and scaled the shaft ladder to the top deck of the barge.

Slowly, gently, he eased Loren's limp body upwards until she lay on the rusting deck. Winded, he took a minute to catch his breath and look around. The *Stonewall Jackson* was still burning fiercely, but the flames were being fought with firehoses from the towboat. About two miles to the west a white Coastguard cutter was driving through the light swells towards their position while to the south he could just make out the sail tower of a nuclear submarine.

Taking a short length of the rope, Pitt tied Loren loosely to a cleat so she wouldn't roll into the sea and returned below. When he entered the isolation chamber again, Lee Tong was gone. A trail of blood led up the corridor and ended at an open hatch to a storage deck below. He saw no reason to waste time on a dying murderer and turned to rescue the Vice President.

Before he took two steps, a tremendous blast lifted him off his feet and hurled him face downward twenty feet away. The impact from the concussion drove the breath from his lungs and the ringing in his ears prevented him from hearing the sea rush in through a gaping hole torn in the hull of the barge.

Barely conscious, Pitt awkwardly rose to his hands and knees and tried to orient himself. Then slowly, as the haze before his eyes melted away, he realised what happened and what was coming. Lee

336

Tong had detonated an explosive charge before he died and already the water was flowing across the corridor deck.

Pitt pushed himself to his feet and reeled drunkenly into the isolation chamber again. The Vice President looked up at him and tried to say something, but before he could utter a sound, Pitt had hoisted him over a shoulder and was lurching towards the lift.

The water was surging around Pitt's knees now, splashing up the walls. He knew only seconds were left before the barge began its dive to the seabed. By the time he reached the open lift, the sea was up to his chest and he half walked, half swam inside. It was too late to repeat the rope lift procedure. Furiously he manhandled Margolin through the ceiling trapdoor, clasped him under the chest, and began climbing the iron ladder to the tiny square patch of blue sky that seemed miles away.

He remembered then that he had tied Loren to the upper deck to keep her unconscious body from rolling into the sea. The sickening thought coursed through him that she would be pulled to her death when the barge sank.

Beyond fear lies desperation, and beyond that a raging drive to survive that cuts across the boundaries of suffering and exhaustion. Some men yield to hopelessness, some try to sidestep its existence, while a very few accept and face it head on.

Watching the froth tenaciously dog his rise up the lift shaft, Pitt fought with every shred of his will to save the lives of Margolin and Loren. His arms felt as if they were tearing from their sockets. White spots burst before his eyes and the strain on his cracked ribs passed from mere pain to grinding agony.

His grip loosened on flakes of rust and he almost fell backward into the water boiling at his heels. It would have been so easy to surrender, to let go and drop into oblivion and release the torture that racked his worn body. But he did not let go. Rung by rung he struggled upward, Margolin's dead weight becoming heavier with each step.

His ears regained a partial sense of hearing and picked up a strange thumping sound which Pitt wrote off as blood pounding in his head. The sea rose above his feet now, and the barge shuddered; it was about to go under.

A nightmare world closed in on him. A black shape loomed above, and then his hand reached out and clasped another hand.

337

ACCOUNTING

THE LIFTONIC QW-607

75

House Speaker Alan Moran, his face wreathed in a confident smile, circulated around the East Room of the White House, conversing with his aides and inner circle of advisers while awaiting final word of the impeachment vote taking place on the floor of the Senate.

He greeted a small group of party leaders and then turned and excused himself as Secretary of State Douglas Oates and Defence Secretary Jesse Simmons entered the room. Moran came over and held out his hand which Oates ignored.

Moran shrugged off the snub. He could well afford to. 'Well it seems you're not of a mind to praise Caesar, but you haven't a prayer of burying him either.'

'You've just reminded me of an old gangster movie I saw when I was a boy,' Oates said icily. 'The title fits you perfectly.'

'Oh, really, what movie was that?'

'"*Little Caesar*".'

Moran's smile transformed into a sinister glare. 'Have you come with your resignation?'

Oates pulled an envelope part way out of his inside breast pocket. 'I have it right here.'

'Keep it!' Moran snarled. 'I won't give you the satisfaction of bowing out gracefully. Ten minutes after I take the oath I'm holding a press conference. Besides assuring the nation of a smooth succession I intend to announce that you and the rest of the President's cabinet planned a conspiracy to set up a dictatorship, and my first order as Chief Executive is to fire the whole rotten lot of you.'

'We expected no less. Integrity was never one of your character traits.'

'There was no conspiracy and you know it,' Simmons said angrily. 'The President was a victim of a Soviet plot to control the White House.'

'No matter,' Moran replied nastily. 'By the time the truth comes out, the damage to your precious reputations will have been done. You'll never work in Washington again.'

341

Before Oates and Simmons could retort, an aide rushed up and spoke softly into Moran's ear. He dismissed his enemies with a snide look and turned away. Then he stepped to the centre of the room and raised his hands for silence.

'Ladies and gentlemen,' he announced. 'I've just been informed that the Senate has passed the resolution for impeachment by the required majority. Our beleaguered President is no longer in office and the Vice Presidency is vacant. The time has come for us to put our house in order and begin anew.'

As if on cue, Chief Justice of the Supreme Court, Nelson O'Brien rose from a chair, smoothed his black robes and cleared his throat. Everyone crowded around Moran as his secretary held what was dubiously touted as his family bible.

Just then Sam Emmett and Dan Fawcett came through the doorway and paused. Then they spied Oates and Simmons and approached.

'Any word?' Oates asked anxiously.

Emmett shook his head. 'None. General Metcalf ordered a communications blackout. I haven't been able to reach him at the Pentagon to find out why.'

'Then it's all over.'

No one replied as they all turned in unison and stood in powerless frustration as Moran raised his right hand to take the oath of office as President, his left hand on the bible.

'Repeat after me,' Chief Justice O'Brien spoke like a drum roll. 'I, Alan Robert Moran, do solemnly swear . . .'

'I, Alan Robert Moran, do solemnly swear . . .'

Oates could feel the excitement mount in the East Room. He could not bear to watch the proceedings that he was certain would blacken the nation's future destiny. Instead, he looked out of the window at a group of tourists standing on the pavement, gawking through the iron fence that ran around the White House grounds.

'. . . that I will faithfully execute the office of the President of the United States . . .' O'Brien droned on.

Suddenly, the room behind Oates went quiet. The prompting of the oath by the Chief Justice went unanswered by Moran. Curious, Oates turned around and refaced the crowd. They were all staring in frozen astonishment at Vice President Vincent Margolin who walked through the doorway preceded by Oscar Lucas and flanked by General Metcalf and Admiral Sandecker.

Moran's upraised arm slowly fell and his face went ashen. The silence smothered the room like an insulating cloud as Margolin stepped up to the Chief Justice, the stunned audience parting for him. He gave Moran a frigid look and then smiled at the rest.

'Thank you for the rehearsal,' he said warmly. 'But I think I can take over from here.'

August 13, 1989
New York City

76

Sal Casio was waiting in the vast lobby of the World Trade Center when Pitt came slowly through the entrance. Casio looked at him in stark appraisal. He couldn't remember when he'd seen any man so mired in exhaustion, so near the edge of physical collapse.

Pitt moved with the tired shuffle of a man who had endured too much. He wore a borrowed foul-weather jacket two sizes too small. His right arm hung slack while his left was pressed against his chest as if holding it together, and his face was etched in a strange blending of suffering and triumph. The eyes burned with a sinister glow that Casio recognised as the fires of revenge.

'I'm glad you could make it,' Casio said without referring to Pitt's haggard appearance.

'It's your show,' said Pitt. 'I'm only along for the ride.'

'Only fitting and proper we be together at the finish.'

'I appreciate the courtesy, thank you.'

Casio turned and guided Pitt over to a private lift. Pulling a small push-button transmitter from his pocket, he pressed the correct code and the doors opened. Inside was an unconscious guard who was bound with laundry cord. Casio stepped over him and opened a polished brass door to the circuit panel with the words *Liftonic Elevator QW-607* engraved on it. He made an adjustment in the settings and then pushed the button that read '100'.

The lift rose like a rocket and Pitt's ears popped three times before it slowed and the doors finally opened onto the richly furnished anteroom of Bougainville Maritime Inc.

Before he stepped out, Casio paused and reprogrammed the lift circuitry with his transmitter. Then he turned and stepped out into the thick carpet.

'We're here to speak with Min Koryo,' Casio announced mundanely.

The woman eyed them suspiciously, particularly Pitt, and opened a

343

leather bound journal. 'I see nothing in Madame Bougainville's schedule that shows any appointments this evening.'

Casio's face furrowed into his best hurt look. 'Are you sure?' he asked, leaning over the desk and peering at the appointment book.

She pointed at the blank page. 'Nothing is written in – '

Casio chopped her across the nape of the neck with the edge of his palm, and she fell forward, head and shoulders striking the desk top. Then he reached inside her blouse and extracted a vest pocket twenty-five calibre automatic pistol.

'Never know it to look at her,' he explained, 'but she's a security guard.'

Casio tossed the gun to Pitt and took off down the corridor displaying paintings of the Bougainville shipping fleet. Pitt recognized the *Pilottown*, and his weary expression hardened. He followed the brawny private investigator up an intricately carved rosewood circular staircase to the living quarters above. At the top of the landing Casio met another ravishing Asian woman who was exiting from a bathroom. She was wearing silk lounging pants with a kimono top.

Her eyes widened and in a lightning reflex she lashed out with one foot at Casio's groan. He anticipated the thrust and shifted his weight ever so slightly, catching the blow on the side of his thigh. Then she flashed into the classic judo position and hurled several rapid cuts to his head.

She would have done more damage to an oak tree. Casio shook off her attack, crouched and sprung like an offensive back coming off the line. She spun to her left in an impressive display of feline grace but was knocked off balance by his shoulder. Then Casio straightened and smashed through her defence with a vicious left hook that nearly tore her head off. Her feet left the floor and she flew into a five-foot high Sung Dynasty vase, breaking it into dust.

'You certainly have a way with women,' Pitt remarked casually.

'Lucky for us there's still a few things we can do better than they can.'

Casio motioned towards a large double door carved with dragons and quietly opened it. Min Koryo was propped up in her spacious bed, browsing through a pile of audit reports. For a moment the two men stood mute and unmoving, waiting for her to look up and acknowledge their intrusion. She looked so pathetic, so fragile that any other trespassers might have wavered. But not Pitt and Casio.

Finally she lifted her reading glasses and gazed at them, showing no apprehension or fright. Her eyes were fixed in frank curiosity.

'Who are you?' she asked simply.

'My name is Sal Casio. I'm a private investigator.'

344

'And the other man?'

Pitt stepped from the shadows and stood under the glow from the spotlights above the bed. 'I believe you know me.'

There was a faint flicker of surprise in her eyes, but nothing else. 'Mr Dirk Pitt.'

'Yes.'

'Why have you come?'

'You are a slimy parasite who sucked the life out of untold innocent people to build your filthy empire. You're responsible for the death of a personal friend of mine and Sal's daughter. You tried to kill me, and you ask why I'm here?'

'You are mistaken, Mr Pitt. I am guilty of nothing so criminal. My hands are unstained.'

'A play on words. You live in your museum of Oriental artifacts, shielded from the outside world while your grandson did your dirty work for you.'

God she was cool. Pitt thought. She didn't bat an eye.

'You say I am the cause of your friend's death?'

'She was killed by the nerve agent you stole from the government and left on the *Pilottown*.'

'I'm sorry for your loss,' she said gently. Her politeness and sympathy were all but devastating. 'And you, Mr Casio. How am I to blame for your daughter?'

'She was murdered along with the crew of the same ship, only then it was called the *San Marino*.'

'Yes, I recall,' said Min Koryo, dropping all pretence of blindness. 'The girl with the stolen money.'

Pitt stared into the old woman's face, examining it. The blue eyes were bright and glistening, and the skin was smooth with only a bare hint of aging lines. She must have truly been a beautiful woman once. But beneath the veneer Pitt detected an ugliness, a cesspool locked in ice. There was a black malignity inside her that filled him with contempt.

'I suppose you've smashed so many lives,' he said, 'you've become immune to human suffering. The mystery is how you got away with it for so long.'

'You have come to arrest me?' she asked.

'No,' Casio answered stonily. 'To kill you.'

The piercing eyes blazed briefly. 'My security people will come through the door any second.'

'We've already eliminated the guard at the receptionist's desk and the one outside your door. As to others . . .' He paused and pointed a finger at a TV camera mounted above her bed. 'I've reprogrammed the tapes. Your guards at the monitors are watching whatever occurred in your bedroom a week ago last night.'

345

'My grandson will hunt you both down, and your punishment will not be quick.'

'Lee Tong is dead,' Pitt informed her, relishing every syllable.

The face altered. Now the blood flowed out of it and it became a pale yellow. But not with the emotions of shock and hurt, thought Pitt. She was waiting, waiting for something. Then the flicker of expectancy vanished as quickly as it had come.

'I do not believe you,' she said at last.

'He sank with the laboratory barge after I shot him.'

Casio moved around to the side of the bed. 'You must come with us now.'

'May I ask where you're taking me?' The voice was still soft and gracious. The blue eyes remained set. They didn't notice her right hand move beneath the covers.

Pitt never really accounted for the instinctive move that saved his life. Maybe it was the sudden realisation that the TV camera was not exactly shaped like a camera. Maybe it was the complete absence of dread in Min Koryo or the aura that she was in firm command, but as the beam of light stabbed out from above her bed, he pitched himself to the floor.

Pitt rolled to his side, tugging the automatic from his coat. Out of the corner of his eye he saw the laser beam sweep the room, cutting through furniture, scorching the curtains and wallpaper with a needle-thin spear of energy. The gun was in his hands, blasting away at the electron amplifier. At his fourth shot, the beam blinked out.

Casio was still standing. He reached out towards Pitt and then stumbled and fell. The laser had cut through his stomach as neatly as a surgeon's scalpel. He twisted over on his back and stared up. Casio was seconds away from death. Pitt wanted to say something, but he couldn't get the words out.

The case-hardened old investigator raised his head, his voice came in a rasping whisper. 'The lift . . . code four-one-one-six . . .' And then his eyes became sightless and his breathing ceased.

Pitt took the transmitter from Casio's pocket, rose and trained the automatic just ten inches from Min Koryo's heart. Her face was locked in a fearless smile. Then Pitt lowered the gun and reached under the covers and silently lifted her out of the bed into her wheelchair.

She made no move to resist, spoke no words of defiance. She sat wizened and mute as Pitt pushed her into the corridor and onto a small lift that lowered them to the office floor. When they reached the reception lobby, she noted the unconscious security guard and looked up at him.

'What now, Mr Pitt?'

'The final curtain for Bougainville Maritime,' he said. 'Tomorrow your rotten business will be no more. Your Oriental art objects will be given away to museums. A new tenant will come in and redecorate your offices and living quarters. In fact your entire fleet of ships will be sold off. From now on the name of Bougainville will be nothing but a distant memory in newspaper microfilm files. No friends or relatives will mourn you, and I'll personally see that you're buried in a potter's field with no marker.'

At last he had broken through and her face revealed a searing hate.

'And your future, Mr Pitt?'

He grinned. 'I'm going to rebuild the car you blew up.'

She weakly lifted herself from the wheelchair and spat at him. Pitt made no move to wipe away the spittle, simply stood there and grinned wickedly, looked down and saw the evil viciousness erupt as she cursed him in Korean.

Pitt pressed the code numbers Casio had given him into the transmitter and watched as the doors to *Liftonic QE-607* opened.

But there was no lift, only an empty shaft.

'Bon voyage, you diabolic old crone.'

Then he shoved the wheelchair into the vacant opening and stood there listening as it clattered like a pebble down a well, echoing off the sides of the shaft until there was only the faint sound of impact a hundred storeys below.

Loren was sitting on a bench in the concourse as he came through the main door of the Trade Centre. She came towards him and they met and embraced. They clung together without saying anything for a few moments.

She could feel the fatigue and the pain in him. And she sensed something more. A strange inner peace that she had never known was there. She kissed him lightly several times about the craggy, worn face. Then she took his arm and led him to a waiting taxi.

'Sal Casio?' she asked.

'With his daughter.'

'And Min Koryo Bougainville?'

'In hell.'

She caught the distant look in his eyes. 'You need rest. I better check you into a hospital.'

Suddenly the old devilish look flashed on his face. 'I had something else in mind.'

'What?'

'The next week in a suite in the best hotel in Manhattan. Champagne, gourmet dinners sent up by room service, you making love to me . . .'

A coquettish expression gleamed in her eyes. 'Why do I have to do all the work?'

'Obviously I'm in no condition to take command.'

She held onto him comfortingly. 'I suppose it's the least I can do after you saved my life.'

'*Semper paratus*,' he said.

'*Semper* what?'

'The Coastguard motto. Always Ready. If their rescue helicopter hadn't arrived over the barge when it did we'd both be lying on the bottom of the Gulf of Mexico.'

They reached the taxi and Loren held onto Pitt as he entered stiffly and sank into the seat. She eased in beside him and kissed his hand while the driver sat patiently looking out of his windscreen.

'Where to?' he asked.

'The Helmsley Palace Hotel,' Pitt answered.

Loren looked at him. 'You're getting a suite at the Helmsley?' she said.

'A penthouse suite,' he corrected her.

'And who's going to pay for this opulent interlude?'

Pitt looked down at her in mock astonishment. 'Why the Government, of course. Who else?'